Also by Meagan Brandy

MEAGAN BRANDY

Bloom *books*

Copyright © 2024 by Meagan Brandy
Cover and internal design © 2024 by Sourcebooks
Cover design by Antoaneta Georgieva/Sourcebooks
Cover images © Purbella / Imazins/GettyImages, Baac3nes/GettyImages

Sourcebooks, Bloom Books, and the colophon are registered trademarks of Sourcebooks.

Published by Bloom Books, an imprint of Sourcebooks
P.O. Box 4410, Naperville, Illinois 60567-4410
(630) 961-3900
sourcebooks.com

Cataloging-in-Publication data is on file with the Library of Congress.

Printed and bound in the United States of America.
PAH 10 9 8 7 6 5 4 3 2 1

CHAPTER 1
PAYTON

Now, July 2

Deaton cries, arching his back and kicking his feet all around, doing his absolute best to fight against the fresh onesie I'm sliding his arms into, his third outfit change of the day. And mine.

"Okay, okay, little man." I manage to get the two outside buttons done and decide the middle one isn't necessary. Tickling his tiny, sock-covered feet, I grab ahold, wiggling them back and forth with a big smile to pretend we're playing a game. It works like a charm, and he stops flailing for half a second, just long enough for me to quickly slide on his cotton shorts.

He screams then, his arms stretched out, fists opening and closing over and over, making grabby hands to let me know he wants me to pick him back up.

"One second, mister." I turn to my own mess of a wardrobe in search of another clean top, but my drawer is empty aside from the T-shirts I wear to bed, and when I look in my closet, bare hangers stare back. That is, on the side dedicated to the clothes that actually fit. My eyes fall to the clean basket of laundry at the foot of the bed, and I sigh, reaching in and digging around for the least wrinkled one. I still need to shower, so what's the point of worrying about ironing or, hell, matching.

Ironing. I scoff. Yeah right. The most I'll take the time to do is throw the entire load back in the dryer and hope it works out the mess I created by tossing them carelessly into the basket in the first place.

"Well, mister man, looks like we're officially adding laundry back to the never-ending to-do list."

Deaton cries harder, reminding me why it's so important to keep him to his normal routine no matter what's going on outside of it.

"I know, I know. It's my fault you missed your nap, and we're all going to pay for it." I yank the shirt over my head, my lack of finesse causing it to tug the bun I seem to be living in down with it, but I don't bother to pull the now loose strands out from under the thin cotton, let alone fix the damn thing.

I scoop up the little boy who suddenly hates being put down for any and every reason that doesn't include water. Foolishly, I thought he'd grow more independent with age, but it seems the opposite is true. Too bad I can only give him so many baths a day to free up my hands, and even then, it's not to get anything done. It's the ten-ish minutes of sitting on the tile floor with zero responsibilities that make the fight to dry him off and put on his diaper and clothes worth it.

Well, no responsibilities other than the ever-present fear I'll mistakenly look away for the split second it would take for him to twist and slip under the water.

Yeah, baths aren't all that relaxing, but the little smile when he splashes water all over the place is better than any restful moment could be.

I bounce around the room, walking back and forth from one corner to the next, but Deaton continues to fuss, rubbing his face in my chest and playing with the curls of his hair.

"Are you tired, sweet boy?" I kiss his head, cradling him against me, but my little man hates to miss a thing. The moment he recognizes the move for what it is—my attempt to sway him until he's sleeping—he lifts his little head, blowing air between his lips and sending drool sliding down his chin.

"Oh, we're blowing bubbles while we cry, huh?" I swiftly snag a bib and snap it into place, not once pausing the bouncing of my body. My eyes catch the clock and widen. "Shit."

My lips snap closed, and I sigh. I was supposed to be ready an hour ago. Knowing what's coming this evening, I suck it up and take a deep breath.

"It's now or never, mister man." Blanket flung over my shoulder and a toy in my hand, I slide into a pair of flip-flops, doing what I told myself I wouldn't do today.

I head over to Lolli and Nate's house next door.

Inside, I pause to listen, the bickering in the hall cluing me in on where to go, and I throw the door open to Lolli's office.

"Someone, for the love of hot coffee, help. *Please.*" The words leave me before I fully take in the sight, and sadly, I don't even have the energy to gape. Or laugh.

Lolli, the girl terrified of marriage and most anything that has to do with acknowledging feelings, though she is getting better at that, stands on a stool in the center of the room wearing a giant, white wedding gown. Her cousin and new roommate, Mia, kneels beside her with a needle and measuring tape in her hand. Mia is lucky Lolli loves her and wants her new business endeavor as a seamstress to work out, or Lolli would never be caught dead in that gown.

My shoulders fall instantly. So much for sneaking away for five minutes.

"Aw…" Lolli's attention locks on Deaton, and she attempts to step down, but Mia is quick to hold her still.

"Ha! Lolli, get real!" She shakes her head. "Baby puke is another big fat no to be spilled on this dress," she says, as if they've already had this argument.

"Again, Mia, *potentially*. And you're getting on my nerves now." She looks to me, an apology drawing lines to her forehead. "Sorry, she's being full drill sergeant."

"It's fine. I just…" I hesitate, deciding one truth is enough.

"Really wanted to shower before Nate's parents get here. I hate looking like I suck at life when they come." Again.

I look out the large back window, watching as a few people run by on their way to the ocean, and hope she doesn't call me out for any *other* potential reason my stress meter is clearly overflowing today. Thankfully, she doesn't.

"You don't suck at life and know that Sarah and Ian would never judge." Kalani, or Lolli as we call her, reminds me of what I already know.

If she ever decides to give in and let Nate marry her like he wants, she will officially have one of the best sets of in-laws on the planet. Though I have to say, they're tied with another certain set of parents I know. Not mine, of course. *His.*

I swallow, shaking away the thought.

"Bright side is they won't be getting into town until around five," Mia adds with a grin.

"True!" Lolli agrees.

My brows snap together, and I decide they're not joking. Seems I'm not the only one time got away from today. "It's five thirty." I break the bad news.

Lolli swings her glare to Mia, who laughs loudly, and I watch the two as I move Deaton from one arm to the other, swinging slightly as he grows more and more restless.

Fussy baby or not, I can't help but smile as I listen to the two bicker like sisters.

Lolli lets out a little growl. "I gotta get out of this before they get back and—"

"We're back!"

Lolli cuts off at the sudden intruding voice, the shouted words coming from the front of the house, and like being dipped in liquid nitrogen, we freeze instantly.

My stomach drops to my feet, a cool sweat breaking out over my palms.

Oh god. No, no, no…

My eyes snap up, locking with the girls'. The panic whirling its way through me is reflected on both their faces, none of our reactions related to the reasons of the others', but the reason for mine is secret. Not the best kept one, but a secret nonetheless.

A soft thunk snaps us out of our stupor, and at once, we start moving.

Mia hurries to unzip Lolli while Lolli reaches up, yanking clips from her long, dark hair.

I spin on my heels, doing everything I can to escape, my hand wrapping around the handle of the door, fully prepared to race through the back side of the house so no one sees me.

I'm not ready for this. I thought I could put on a brave face, but it turns out I'm not brave. I feel sick at the mere thought, and I just…cannot.

I need a little more—

The door is shoved open from the other side, and I yelp, nearly knocking myself off balance, but then my eyes snap up to the newcomer. I swallow my tongue.

It's as if cement is injected into my veins, every inch of me growing heavy before turning to stone. My pulse pounds, then plummets as my eyes lock on a pair of pensive brown ones so familiar, I could pick them out in a lineup of hundreds.

My fingers curl into Deaton's blanket, and I open my mouth, but nothing comes out.

Those dark eyes narrow, searching, seeing.

Softening.

My stomach flips and twists, and I can't tell if it's unease or elation. Or downright dread.

How can they still turn so tender when trained on me?

"What's wrong?" His words are a low demand, and I want to scream and cry at the same time.

"Nothing." *Everything.* "Everything's fine."

"She needs help with Deaton," Lolli says, calling me out.

"Lolli," I hiss, my head snapping her way briefly. I try to stay

5

focused on her, but it's too obvious, not to mention *hard*, so I slowly move them back to the man before me.

And he is a man. I swear, every time I see him, there's a little something about him that's changed. Sometimes it's subtle, a shorter haircut than the time before or a deeper tan than the one his olive skin keeps all year—a result of the endless hours he puts in on the football field or natural, I couldn't say. Other times it's more than that. His shoulders have grown wider in the year since I met him, his jaw sharper. His hands…

I swallow, unable to break away from the choke hold of his gaze.

If there is one thing that hasn't changed, it's his eyes. The honey-brown irises are as rich as ever, the perfect mix of dark and light, vivid yet grave. A flawless illustration of his character.

Mason Johnson is as fierce as he is tender. He's yin *and* yang.

And after nearly nine weeks of sudden silence, he's standing before me with an expression that threatens to break me down right here, right now.

He doesn't say a word, but he doesn't have to. The slight frown blanketing his features says enough—he's worried, frustrated.

Angry.

It's deeper than that, though. I can see it in his troubled gaze.

Did something happen? Did I do something wrong? Did you change your mind…

Those are just a few of the questions he's asking without opening his mouth, none of which I want to answer right now. To be honest, I'm not so sure I could.

Did something change? I ask myself, swallowing the needles that seem to have appeared in my throat.

Still, angry or not, he's as gentle as ever, shuffling closer, and I know before he so much as lifts his arms, he's going to reach for Deaton.

I hesitate, if only for a split second, but it's long enough for him to notice, and his lips press together more firmly than they already were. I look away as I pass him my little boy and all but run from the room. In the hall, I'm ready to go full sprint, but my feet don't seem to get the message, instead lingering in the hall, out of sight but not earshot.

Mason's voice reaches me instantly, and I know by the lulling in his tone, he's swaying my son just as I was. "What's wrong, little man, hmm?"

A sharp pain stings my chest, and I consider going in and taking him back, but not a second after he speaks, what I couldn't seem to do is done—Deaton stops crying.

I drop my chin to my chest and speedwalk out of there, softly closing the back door behind me so no one in the front of the house is alerted to my escape. It's bad enough I'm clearly going out of my way to avoid everyone who has just arrived, but I can't pause. Pausing will lead to too many thoughts, none of which I'm prepared for right now. At all. In any fashion.

I walk quickly down the deck, across the twenty feet of sand, and back up the deck of the house right next door. Yes, my older brother, Parker, owns the home right next door to his best friend. When Lolli told him she had purchased the home beside this one, it felt like a blessing I didn't deserve. It's how he was able to offer me my own room—and his nephew a nursery once he was born—after I ran away from our mother's place.

It's times like this, though, I wonder if I should have taken my dad's offer to move in with him, as out-of-left-field and awkward as the conversation was, considering we hardly know each other these days. But even as I think it, I know I made the right choice when I gave him the swift and instant answer of a hard no way in hell. My refusal had nothing to do with him on a personal level, though I'm not sure he believed me when I told him so, considering I didn't go into much more details outside of that. If he knew me better, he would have never asked. He would under-stand living with him would mean going back to Alrick, where my mother lives, where the family that shares my son's last name lives. The last thing I want is my Deaton anywhere near those vile people. They hated their son as much as much as my mother hates me.

Leaving that place was both the best and worst decision I have ever made.

On one hand, my son will never be exposed to the toxicity that is Ava Baylor. On the other, it is the very reason his daddy died.

I am the reason he's dead.

Swallowing, I swiftly lock my bedroom door, dropping my head against it. I no sooner close my eyes than hurried footsteps sound on the hardwood floors in the hall. I hold my breath, the sound of his heavy exhales causing my hand to clench the knob I've yet to let go of.

I know who's on the other side. Of course he followed.

"Where you are is where I want to be..."

I squeeze my lids closed tight.

There's the smallest of raps, as if he lifted his knuckles to knock, to demand an answer or beg for a reason, but changed his mind at the last second. My eyes open, pointed at the floor where the shadow of his shoes sits just inches from my own, watching as it fades into nothing as he walks away a moment later.

I grit my teeth, jump into the shower, and get myself together as quickly as possible, which I've found is a lot faster than I ever would have thought now that every minute is one I can no longer waste.

Smoothing my hair back, I take the front pieces and twist them slightly to allow a small center part before tying it up into a high ponytail. I swiftly braid the thick, wet strands, the long blond length still reaching to midback. Using some wax, I smooth my baby hairs down to my skull, opting for a quick bronzer, blush, mascara, and, at the last minute, a touch of lip gloss.

Nearly nothing I own fits, not that my mother sent all my belongings, but the things she did box up are three sizes too small,

8

even eight months after birth. When I was emancipated last year, I was able to drain my bank account before my mom got ahold of it, but she ignored the court's order to allow me to take my things. In the end, I found material items didn't mean enough anymore if it meant having to look her in the eye and ask for it. She wasn't worth the fight, and that is *all* she was after. A reaction. So I stopped giving her the chance to get one.

The money I had saved from winning pageants she forced me to enter and secret photography contests she knew nothing about was enough to get the things I needed, but only because my brother refuses to accept a penny for rent. Because of that, it should hold me over for another six months or so, longer if Lolli and Parker keep going out of their way to buy things for Deaton and me before I get the chance to do it myself. Not that I want them to, but chances are they won't.

My lack of clothing mixed with the added weight my body seems to want to keep means I've basically been living in stretchy bottoms, loner T-shirts, and lightweight hoodies for the better part of a year. Glancing at myself in the long mirror beside my closet, I sigh at my reflection.

It's a far cry from the girl I was when I first showed up on my brother's doorstep in two-hundred-dollar jeans and a purse that cost more than the down payment on his new truck. I was a certified rich girl, shiny and perfect on the outside, suffocating and starving on the inside—literally, thanks to my mother's need for her version of a trophy daughter. She would let me eat so long as she saw me throw it up after. The only thing I was allowed to keep down was whatever she handed me with the "vitamins" she gave me each morning.

Nothing like an appetite suppressant and a handful of whole natural almonds for breakfast, right, Mom?

Shaking off the thoughts that will do nothing but sour my mood further, I look over my outfit—a sage-green skort and a loose-fitting vanilla, neckless style sweater that hangs off the left shoulder, a matching tank underneath to hide the giant straps of my nursing bra. The built-in shorts suffocate my thighs, but the hem of the skirt mostly hides it, and the waist comes up high enough to smash some of the curves into a hint of a shape.

I couldn't fit into my old clothes if I starved myself for a year.

My hips are wider, my legs thicker, and every other part of me is right there with it. My ass, breasts, and belly. Even my feet are larger, unable to fit in several of the shoes gathering dust in my closet, or maybe they're just swollen from carrying around not only a twenty-three-pound baby boy but the extra forty or so I was left with after delivery.

Closing my eyes, I take a deep breath and force myself from the room before I lose my nerve and ask Parker to bring Deaton back over with the excuse of nap time. They're catching on to that, though, if the playpen that Lolli bought for her place, knowing the gang was planning to hang out over there for most of the week, is any indication.

My lips tip up at the thought.

There's one thing I can say about all the new people in my life—they make me feel like they want to be there, not because they're friends of my brother's or family to his girlfriend, and not because I'm always around but because they truly, genuinely care.

They like me, and more importantly, they love my son.

With my head held high and a practiced smile in place, I walk out the back door, waving as everyone on the deck next door shouts their excitement at seeing me.

The fake smile on my face shifts instantly, and a real one takes its place, growing more eager to join the party with each step toward it.

That is until I meet the small scowl of the man with his forearms perched over the edge of the railing as if he was waiting for me to appear.

I have no doubt he was. It's written in the sharp set of his jaw and tight smash of his full lips. He's upset with me, and rightfully so.

Everyone is here for the holiday, so he knows my weekend is booked, that there's nowhere to go aside from shuffling from my house to Lolli's, to the one he co-owns with his friends down the road, but that doesn't mean I won't do what I can to avoid... everything.

His eyes narrow as if reading my thoughts, and the look that takes over his face sends a chill down my spine, whispering words he doesn't have to speak aloud. The message is as clear as day in those expressive eyes: *I dare you to try.*

Sorry, Mase, but I will.

The sun set a few hours ago, and with it came a whole new sense of dread.

The afternoon was bustling, no less than five conversations happening all at once, making it easy to stay busy and keep my mind off things, but over the last half hour, couple after couple, group after group, has left, and when my brother and his girlfriend, Kenra, are the next to stand, a knot forms in my throat. Before I can follow and agree to calling it a night, the pair looks my way.

"Stay awhile," Parker suggests, as I knew he would. "We'll take Deaton with us and put him in his bed."

Anxiety spikes, sending a wave of nausea though me, and I look to the sleeping baby nestled beside me on the patio couch, his blankets tucked tight up to his chin, nothing but his little face to be seen and a hint of dark curls along his forehead.

"It's okay." I rush to stand, but my brother puts a hand on my shoulder, pressing me back into the seat.

His blue eyes, nearly the exact shade as mine, soften. "Stay, Peep. I'll turn on the monitors and watch him like a hawk. We're gonna finish that docuseries we started anyway, so we'll be up for a while. Relax, visit. Come home when you feel like it."

I want to argue what if he wakes ups and needs me, but we both know he won't.

Deaton, while attached to me at the hip and unable to fall asleep without being rocked or patted or hummed to, sleeps through the night, and it's exactly his bedtime. That, and he will take a bottle if it came to that.

When I hesitate, Kenra nudges my knee with hers, drawing my attention. "I could go get the monitor, and you could watch him from here?"

"No, it's fine." I shake my head, smiling from her to my brother. They know I trust them completely with his nephew. She's only offering because she wants to make sure I have no excuse to refuse the little bit of freedom they're gifting me.

"Thanks." It's all I can say, and I stare as Parker bends and picks up his nephew Deaton, my gaze trailing after them as he carries him to the house beside this one.

As my eyes cut back across the sand, I spot Mason, watching them as I was, and I know what's coming next. His head turns, attention latching on to me, and whatever he was saying to Brady, one-third of his best friend triangle, dies on his lips. He excuses himself immediately, climbing the stairs leading to the deck at what I would almost consider a run.

My nerve endings tingle, apprehension and more trickling over my limbs as he advances, no one close enough to inter-cept, though the look on his face tells me he wouldn't let that happen.

He's been waiting all day for this, an uninterrupted moment between him and me, just as much as I've dreaded it.

Rather than sinking into the vacant seat at my side, Mason loops his ankle around the leg of the small table across from where I'm sitting, tugs it closer, and drops down directly in front of me, accepting nothing less than my full, undivided attention.

He's quiet a moment, a frown he tries to fight but can't seem to erase pulling at the edges of his eyes. Several seconds pass, maybe a minute or two even before he opens his mouth, his voice a warm, wounded whisper.

"Hi, Pretty Little."

My lungs expand with a full breath hearing the nickname he gave me the day we met. It was born of innocence, a tease really from the fun and flirty man living it up on the beach, but it's become so much more than that, and the affectionate way in which he speaks it pulls me back from the panic threatening to take over. My lips curve into a soft smile, and his follow.

"Hi, Mase."

He stares, gaze traveling over my face before settling on my single braid. This time, when his eyes come back to mine, there's a spark there. It's fleeting, and if I had blinked, I'd have missed it. Something warms in my chest, and I wonder if, subconsciously, I decided on a braid for his benefit or if it really was for the time factor.

My cheeks heat at the thought, but thankfully it's dark out.

Mason looks to the sky, dewy with the July night air, and when he looks back to me, his entire demeanor softens.

It's too much, and I drop my gaze to my lap, picking at the little balls of lint on the blanket covering my thighs.

"Payton—"

"I think I'll go to bed after all." I push to my feet swiftly, my knees bumping his as I do.

When my feet won't move and Mason doesn't either, I chance a glance at him.

A crestfallen expression takes over his features, and slowly he stands. We're so close, both wedged between the seat and table.

My chest is pressed to his stomach, and if I were to tip my chin the slightest bit, my forehead would rest against his pecs. His hand raises, and I jolt when the heat of his knuckle grazes my cheek. He pulls back, and when I look up at him in question, his smile is forced.

"Just a little water," he whispers, and only then do I realize a tear slipped.

I didn't even feel it.

The sound of the sliding glass door opening reaches us, so Mason turns, heading straight to the ice chest. He grabs two beers, popping open a third and finishing it before his feet reach the sand. Walking in the opposite direction of his friends, he disappears under the dark night sky.

Dropping back in my seat, I close my eyes, hoping the deep breath will help hide the turmoil in my mind.

He walked away, knowing I needed him to. I fight the tears threatening to come back, guilt swimming through me for liking how he always knows what I'm feeling and hating that I do. He shouldn't be able to read me the way he does.

But he's always been that way, hasn't he?

The cushion beside me dips, and I drop my head back to the soft pillow behind me, glancing over at my friend.

Arianna Johnson stares in the direction her twin brother just headed before turning to me with a small smile. "Want to tell me what happened between you two?"

Tensing, I swallow the knot in my throat and look out over the moonlit water.

I force my lips to lift in the corners, accepting the can of cream soda she passes my way. "Nothing happened."

She tips her head a bit, and after a moment, she nods.

Ari doesn't call me out on my lie, but we both know it is one.

What happened between Mason and me?

God. Where would I even begin…

CHAPTER 2
PAYTON

Before, July

This was a huge mistake. I never should have come to California, and I have no idea what possessed me to do so. I mean, I haven't talked to my brother in who the hell knows how long, and I thought it would be a good idea to show up on his doorstep and drop bombs?

Hey, Parker, I ignored your attempts to talk to me for hella long because I was pissed you left me with that vile woman who gave birth to us, and by the way, I'm a junior in high school, pregnant, ran away from home, and oh! Who's the baby daddy, you ask? None other than the little brother to the asshole who stole and mistreats the girl you're in love with.

I scrub my hands down my face.

Jesus Christ, how did he not toss me out on my ass right there, or worse...call our mother to come pick me up? Even if I think it, I know he would never, and while I'm stressing over everything, he's doing the opposite.

Well, he's probably stressing just the same, but his big brother instincts are second to none. I've been a brat, and he's been nothing but supportive and encouraging.

What's crazy, his friends have been the same, including me in every little thing they do, and it doesn't seem forced or leave me feeling like the shadow they can't get rid of.

They're all pretty chill and easygoing. Way more tight-knit

and meddling in one another's business than I'm used to, but from what I can tell, there's nothing malicious about it. More like a little family of friends who actually give a shit.

Still, as I glance from where Parker's huddled beside a swing with Kenra to the others splashing around in the water not too far from where I stand, it's clear I don't belong here.

I'm not...like them.

They're in swimsuits with wind-dried hair, and the girls wear not a speck of makeup, the norm for a day at the beach I'd assume.

I'm standing at the water's edge in a designer jumper that hasn't even been released in stores yet, my face painted as flawlessly as my hair is curled.

They're laughing and joking and playing around.

I'm sixty seconds from a nervous breakdown and might vomit on my toes.

I'm not a high school graduate on the cusp of college.

I'm not easygoing and free, and I don't have my whole future ahead of me.

My life is over.

I close my eyes.

Girl, get a grip. You're pregnant, not dying.

Pregnant.

Holy shit.

There's a tiny little human growing inside my body.

What the fuck am I going to do?

My breathing picks up and my chest clenches, panic building in my gut. I can't do this. I can't handle it. It's not just my life, but Deaton's, too. He was offered a scholarship to wrestle at Penn State. He's so excited.

My lungs shrivel, and I gasp. A baby will ruin everything. I ruined everything and I can. Not. Do. This. I—

"You know, pretty clothes and prettier hair won't keep you safe out here."

My head snaps left, finding the source of the teasing voice.

16

I should have recognized whose it was instantly, as he's the one who's spoken to me the most since I crashed their summer with my drama. He's grinning playfully as he sweeps a hand through his hair, a darker shade of brown now that it's dripping wet…as is the rest of his body.

It takes me a moment to realize what he means, and he knows the second I catch on.

That grin on his lips turns wicked, and he circles me like he's found the perfect prey.

"Mason—"

"You say my name so pretty, Pretty Little," he chuckles, and then he's darting forward, his arms locking around my legs and hauling me into the air before I can even think.

A gasp escapes, and I wait for the annoyance and anger to hit, but it never comes.

A strange whirl of relief and excitement flits through me, and I laugh, closing my eyes and clutching on for dear life when suddenly both our bodies are dipping into the water.

I squeal, nearly giggling at the icy absurdity of the water temperature. "Oh my god!" My arms lock tighter. "Why is it so cold?"

Mason chuckles into my ear, spinning in circles and dunking me lower until I scream. "Hold your breath. One…"

"Don't you—"

"Two."

"Dare—"

My shoulders pop out of the water, and then we're lowering again, and I gasp, pulling in a long breath. He submerges us both, but only for a split second before we resurface.

I shake from the cold, but an unexpected laugh bubbles up my throat, and I groan, blinking through the water in my fake lashes as he moves us back until my feet can reach the ground.

My hands unwind themselves, and I slap water his way, but I'm unable to wipe the grin off my face.

"How's the hair now?" I mock myself.

"Still looks pretty perfect to me." His eyes meet mine, and he quickly looks away, clearing his throat. Then he looks back with a smirk. "I gotta admit, I was only eighty percent sure you wouldn't rage on me for tossing you in."

"Yet you still chose to do so."

"Hey, I can do about anything with an eighty percent chance. You should see my stats."

"That's right." I nod, dipping low into the water until the waves are softly splashing against my chin. "Big bad football star, huh?"

"Damn straight." His smile is as cocky as it is teasing. "You ever watch?"

"Not interested."

He gapes at me, literally gapes, his head whipping around to see if his friends heard. I imagine he was looking for some backup, but they're too far away, and now I'm laughing.

As my laughter settles, I begin to swim in place, and a long sigh leaves me.

My eyes find Mason's, and this time, his smile is soft.

"That's what I was waiting for," he whispers, but a moment later, he starts to shake his head. "Don't bring them back."

Confusion draws my brows in, and he wades closer.

Reaching up, he runs his knuckle down the creases the frown I didn't know I was wearing created on my forehead. "They only just disappeared." His gaze meets mine again, and while I can't quite read his expression, it has something in my chest tightening.

It's almost like...like he cares. Likes he's worried and he wants me to know everything I'm feeling is okay. That it will all *be* okay and my life isn't over.

That I didn't ruin everything by running away from home and that I'm not unjustified in hiding the pregnancy from the boy I love, if only for a little longer while I figure out what to do.

But that's crazy talk, right?

I hardly know Mason, literally met him days ago.

Yet there it is, in the golden hue of his eyes.

A promise from him to me.

My bottom lip trembles, and he extends his arm yet again, the roughness of his knuckle sweeping along my cheekbone.

"Just a little water," he whispers, erasing the stupid tear that slipped without permission.

We both know it's a lie, and because of it, my smile seems to slide right back into place.

"So." I turn away, peeking at him from the corner of my eye. "How boring *is* football?"

His glare is quick, but his laughter is quicker. "Well, Pretty Little." He leads me from the water. "Let me tell you all about it…"

And he does.

For hours, he tries all sorts of ways to explain the game. He scribbles lines in the sand, Xs and Os all over the place, and when he hands me the stick, telling me to show him where the ball is going, I slide it across his entire drawing and take off laughing when he gasps in horror.

We play catch, and he shows me how to grip the laces for the perfect throw. The others join, and suddenly there are teams. The competitive nature of each and every male, and Lolli of course, shines through.

By the end of the day, Ari, her best friend Cameron, and I are panting and dropping our asses into the sand, exhausted to the max, but not the boys.

"How are they still able to run? I can hardly talk."

The girls laugh, leaning back and pointing their faces to the sky, the sun directly above us now.

"Girl, those boys have stamina for days." Cameron pops an eye open, grinning. "Well, them and Lolli."

Grinning, I face the group, shaking my head when they go straight from the game to the ground, showing not a single sigh

19

of expelled energy outside the sheen of sweat gleaming across their skin.

Lolli bends, clapping her hands, and starts playing the role of the coach as the boys pair up and start to wrestle—a result of their inability to agree on who won.

Wrestling.

Boyfriend.

Baby.

My smile falls, and I jump to my feet, spinning and heading in the opposite direction of everyone else…but I don't make it far.

"Sneaking away, are we? You know the girls are about to walk down to the pier for lunch?"

I freeze, swallowing, and force my lips to curve up as I spin around.

Chase, Mason's best friend, is dusting sand from his knees as he jogs for me.

"Yeah, I'm not hungry. Just going to grab a drink off the deck and sit for a while."

He flashes me pearly whites and strides forward until he's ahead, whirling to walk backward so he can face me as he speaks. "Perfect. I'm parched."

A grin pulls at my mouth. "Parched?"

He chuckles, turning and taking the stairs up the deck two at a time. "Aren't you all sophisticated and shit."

"Oh yeah, I'm a real scholar." I wince at my own words.

Even if I were, which I'm not, it wouldn't matter now. You can't exactly go to college with a baby.

Deaton is though. He has a 4.2 GPA and a full-ride offer for athletics. He's a freaking genius, and I'm the dummy who's destroying everything.

Chase's features soften a moment, but he quickly replaces the expression with an easygoing grin. Digging into the ice chest, he comes back with two waters.

He settles in the space at my side, offering me one, and we sit in silence for a little while, doing nothing but watching his friends and the many other people randomly making their way down the sand.

After several minutes, Chase sits back with a sigh. "It's not usually this busy here."

I look his way, and he continues, his eyes staying on the passersby.

"Summer always gets a little crazy. Everyone wants to hit the beach at least once, and they drive in from all over to find a spot like this."

"Not a fan of big crowds?" I wonder.

He shrugs, taking a long drink. "I don't know, I guess I don't like…change." He trails off, like he's not so sure that's the right word.

I'm not so sure it makes sense in context, but I do sort of get what he's saying. If you're used to something being a certain way, a crowd of strangers will definitely throw that off.

"The best time to be here is, well, about when we have to leave." He chuckles. "August, September. You should stick around. I think you'll like it."

When I glance his way, I find he's already staring, and around us, the voices of the others grow louder, the boys headed this way.

"If the gang gets to be too much, let me know," he says before standing up and catching a ball no one warned him was coming. Mason appears then, throwing his arm around his best friend.

"We're playing heads-up, and you're on our team. Win and get whatever your little heart desires." Both boys smile down at me, and I can't help but smile back.

They step away, setting up to play on the picnic table, so I take a moment to myself, realizing the heaviness that is my life has been absent nearly all day, and in its place is an easy lightheartedness I'm not sure I've ever known.

As the day turns to night and I look out over the never-ending blue waters ahead, I can't help but wonder…

What if...what if coming here *wasn't* a mistake?

My gaze travels over the people I've met this week, my eyes catching on Mason's briefly before they continue across the horizon.

Tentatively, maybe even subconsciously, my hand falls to my belly.

What if I'm right where I'm meant to be?

CHAPTER 3
PAYTON

Now, July 3

"Knock, knock." The soft whisper has me looking toward the hall to find Mia sneaking in on her tiptoes.

Deaton whips his head around so fast he almost falls off my lap and instantly starts speaking baby talk as he clenches his hands together in excitement at a new face to play with.

I lift him, spinning him to face her on my lap, and take his hand, waving it at her. "Say hi, Mia."

"So he is awake," she singsongs, her feet carrying her faster across the room until she's stealing him from my arms and lifting him into the air. "And here I thought you didn't come to brunch because someone was napping." She points a raised, red brow my way.

"So what's up?" I ignore her comment, pushing to my feet and using the moment of free hands to pick up the mess of toys, socks, and more.

"Oh, you know, another day, another shitstorm." Mia follows me into the kitchen, Deaton in her arms.

I give her a questioning look and drop my head back dramatically, laughing when Deaton tries to stick his hand in her mouth.

"So I have a problem. Well, not me, and honestly, I don't even know why I'm trying to help at this point, but—"

"Mia, come on." I fight a smile. "Out with it."

"Fine." She rolls her eyes. "Ever wanted to photograph a wedding reception?"

My brows snap together. "I'm listening."

Mia nods and goes into explaining how her client, whose wedding dress Lolli was modeling yesterday for last-minute alterations, was cancelled on and is now in need of a new photographer. "So I thought of you…but I also sort of already told her you would do it…"

"Mia," I chuckle, shaking my head. "I've only been interning with Embers Elite for, what, six months or something. And that's sports photography."

"Same thing."

"Not even a little bit." I laugh lightly, fighting with the stupid bottle scrubber to work with me. "I take action shots…mostly."

"See!" She smiles. "Come on. It's no pressure. The ceremony is covered, so it's just the reception, and they only want candid shit, no posing. So snap a few pics, no contract, and get a fat paycheck from a spoiled-ass Southern chick. It's a win."

I chew my lip, ideas of what moments I would want to capture already flying through my mind at warp speed. My expression must show the internal excitement at the opportunity, because Mia squeals.

"Yes!" she shouts, dancing around with Deaton, making him grin like crazy. "And before you start worrying about not being able to go for this or that reason, Ari and Noah were *very* quick to offer to babysit."

Sadness blooms in my chest for the couple that's been through more than anyone should go through in a lifetime, but before I start comparing their rotten apples to my sour oranges, I shut that train of thought down.

"Yeah, okay. Deal." I agree before I think too hard about it. It's not like I'm in a position to turn down work anyway. But honestly… "I'd love to."

Mia makes a giant, overexaggerated happy face for Deaton's

24

benefit, and then without a word to me, she heads out the back door, taking my son right along with her.

I don't wait around to see when she'll pop back in but take advantage of the moment and run to the shower.

This is good, perfect even.

Today, I'll be out all afternoon with Mason's and Nate's parents. Tomorrow is the holiday, so everyone will be around, talking a mile a minute and taking up every moment I could possibly have. Later that night, when my subconscious fights against sleep, I'll spend the time getting my camera bag ready. Then the wedding will be here, and it will be the perfect distraction to make it through. I can do this.

I can.

―――――

"Isn't that just the sweetest thing you've ever even?" Vivian gushes, the gleam in her eyes one of happiness, but the way her hand raises to her chest at the same time tells me a little part of her is thinking of the loss her family faced not all that long ago.

Mason's mom, Vivian, is one of the kindest women I have ever met, along with Lolli's future mother-in-law, Sarah. From the moment we met last year, those two have become something I didn't know I needed—women to look up to.

I've always known my mother was a horrible woman, but I guess I never stopped to think of what it meant to be a good one. Not to your core anyway, and these two? Well, I'd say they were one of a kind, but there's two of them.

Gracious and forgiving, understanding and caring. Selfless and driven to give their love freely—an entirely new concept for me—and they have, to both Deaton *and* me.

No one calls me as much as Vivian, and no one sends care packages as much as Sarah, something I've asked her not to do because I don't want her to feel obligated, and the more she

25

does, the more likely she will. Of course, she waves me off every time, and a few days later, there's a new box on my front porch. I swear, the only time I buy baby clothes is when I see something I want him to have. Thanks to the two of them, Lolli, and Parker, Deaton's closet is fuller than mine.

I smile down at the little man when he starts making random sounds, his slobbery fingers reaching out to slap on the glass before us. The little bear cub on the other side comes closer and slaps his palm in the same spot.

Deaton jerks, his whole body flailing with one of those baby jump scares, and the three of us laugh as he looks up at us with big blue eyes, seeking confirmation he is, in fact, perfectly fine.

"Oh, sweet boy," Vivian coos, bending to have a full-on conversation with the infant.

Another cry catches my attention, and I look to the left to find a little boy with blond hair stretching his arms up into the air from where he's strapped into his stroller. He's reaching for the man with matching features who I can only assume is his dad. Instantly, the man drops down and frees the little guy from his seat, happily bouncing him around as he turns them back toward the zoo exhibit.

I watch as the little boy drops his head down on the man's shoulder, and it's like a boulder bears down on mine in the same second.

Deaton...

"Come, honey." Sarah's soft voice wraps around me, and she curls her arm through mine, leading us to where my smiling baby waits with Vivian.

I didn't even realize they'd continued forward.

Vivian's eyes find mine, a knowing look within them as she offers a small smile, one that quickly grows when she points at the curly-haired boy now in her arms. "I think it's time for lunch. What do you say, sweet pea?"

Together, we head for the food court, my phone ringing all

the way, but I don't answer, and I don't look at the screen. I don't need to know who's calling.

I know it's him.

It's *always* him.

MASON

My leg is bouncing so fast, the headboard of the bed hits against the wall in steady knocks. Later, I'll likely have Brady down my throat, demanding to know who I snuck in for a bit of afternoon fun. Little does he know I haven't touched another since—

Swallowing my frustration, I jump to my feet and tug a hoodie over my head.

I'm out the door and jogging down the beach in seconds, making this my third official run of the day.

I can't sit still, not knowing I'm literal feet from Payton, something I've wished for for months now, and I can't see or talk to her. To be fair, she's not home. I know because I've gone by there the last two times I tugged a hoodie on and went for the same damn run. The second spin around, Parker was home, but she still wasn't, so I can't exactly stop—again—and ask if she is back without looking like a possessive jackass.

Not that I care. I kind of am one, if I'm honest, but I've been holding in my inner need to flip the fuck out considering everyone is around. And god *damn*, everyone is *always* around. I can never get her alone, not during visits like this one.

If it were up to me I'd make a whole-ass scene, knock the doors down, and beat my chest like a caveman. I won't, though, for her sake and no one else's.

Still, as I approach Payton's house, my feet move a little slower, my eyes slicing across every inch of the place. Nothing I can see from here gives away if she's in there or not. I mean, I could knock, but Parker will just ask what he asked before.

Did I call her?

I scoff.

What kind of question is that?

Of course I fuckin' called her. Texted her, too.

Been calling and texting without a response for fifty-seven days. Yes, I counted, and you know what? It doesn't sound as bad as saying months does, but it's July, and that was May, and fuck me. It feels shitty. Worse than.

I'm caught in quicksand, and there's no one around to pull me out.

I jog past her house, then Nate's, and I keep going, running longer than my five a.m. cardio session and farther than round two when I thought I was being the right kind of sneaky and would catch her when I know Deaton would be awake. I didn't, and if the lack of her answering the knock I couldn't help but bring down on her window was any indication, she was already gone.

Why is she doing this?

What the fuck happened?

The questions are too daunting, so I block them out. I run until my lungs burn, and only when my legs are jelly do I turn around and drag my ass the five miles back, this time taking the street so I can get a view of the front of the house in case it reveals anything different.

It doesn't, and now I'm getting pissy.

Sweat pours from my temples as I pant my way up the drive of the beach house I co-own with my sister, her best friend Cameron, and my boys, Brady and Chase, so I tug my hoodie over my head and swipe at it, following the wraparound deck from front to back. I toss my top onto the picnic bench and snag a football from the bucket by the door.

I no sooner toss it in the air than the slider opens, and the man of all fucking men walks out.

28

His eyes meet mine a moment before dropping to my calves, both tight and twitching. "You're overdoing it."

"I'm good." I flex through it, nearly numb to the ache, and head down the stairs into the sand. Spinning so I'm walking backward, I point the ball his way.

Noah's hands go open instantly, and I toss him the ball.

"Run some routes for me?"

He hesitates, then nods, joining me on the beach and channeling his old receiver position, or new depending on how you look at it considering he was drafted as a wide receiver, officially retiring his quarterback arm and helping me perfect mine.

The first half hour, we're just warming up with short distance passes, but the minute we get into running routes, I'm all over the fucking place.

I'm overthrowing and underthrowing, and when a pass I rocket to him, one I could normally make with my eyes closed, lands ten feet to his left, his head whips in my direction.

The concern in his expression isn't ill placed as he walks back toward me. "Have you been working with your offseason coaches?"

I look off, spinning the ball in my hands. "Every day."

"Footwork? Mechanics? Hip rotation—"

"Yeah, Noah." I cut him off. "I'm doing the whole-ass Noah Riley thing. Working my way out of your shadow and all that bull."

Noah frowns but says nothing. He's great, but maybe I should have had Chase out here. At least he would let me pick a fight and fight back. Noah's just too...Noah for that.

I can tell he wants to say something that would be in line with what my dad would say, and it would sound something like I'm not filling a shadow but stepping into a role I was made for as the next starting quarterback of Avix University now that he's been drafted to the big boys' game. Of course, he wouldn't add that last little bit in—the man is far too humble for that.

It's wild to think my twin sister, baby sister if you ask me, is dating a man who was picked in the first round of the NFL draft. I like to think she has me to thank for that—all those after-school and weekend hours spent on the bleachers paid off in a big way for her, and I'm not talking money.

I'm talking that gravity-defying, soul-defining, epic love story shit.

She has that.

I want that.

Fuck.

Shoving my hand through my hair, I look his way. "I'm just off my game today, that's all. I've been slaying in practice. Doing two a day and ending in an ice bath, rotating to heat packs when called for. I've had no offseason and been in all summer so far. Coach says I'm solid."

Noah nods, eying me curiously. "You do know there is such a thing as overdoing it, right?"

"Yeah, man. I know."

"Then why are we out here when your calves are spasming? You could pull something if you don't rehab right."

"I said I'm doing ice baths."

"I'm talking about now. Not at school." He cocks his head a bit, and I know he's done pretending he isn't seeing more than an off day of practice. "You know you can talk to me, right?" he asks. "I mean, I'm not Chase or Brady or whatever, but we're friends, Mason."

"Come on, man." I wave that off. "You're fucking family, and you know it, so don't start with that shit again."

He smiles wide, and I can't help the chuckle that leaves me.

It's on the tip of my tongue to ask when he'll propose to my sister. After the year they had and the love they had to fight for, I almost wonder if he already did and they haven't told us yet. But when he looks back at me, an expectant look in his eye that says we're not changing the subject, I face away.

30

He won't pry. He's not the type.

Shit, he was in love with my sister for months, listened to her talk about another dude for most of that, and never so much as said a word. He's got the inner strength and willpower of a saint.

He's the picture of patience, and here I am with a bobby pin I stole from Ari's bathroom in my pocket, just waiting for night to fall so I can pick the lock on Payton's room tonight and force her to talk to me.

Why won't she talk to me?

A frustrated groan leaves me, and I glance toward Noah, but he isn't looking at me anymore. A slow smile is spreading across his face, a faraway look taking over, and I don't have to turn to know who stepped out onto the deck.

"Sister," I call out to test my theory.

"Brother."

Grinning, I peek over to find her leaning against the railing, chin pressed in her palm. Slowly, her eyes leave Noah's and meet mine for a brief smile before sliding back to the man beside me.

The warmth in her gaze fills me with happiness, but just as quickly, the sentiment switches into something else.

He has his girl.

I thought one day, I'd have mine.

Maybe I won't.

Maybe that's a pipe dream never to see the light of day.

Maybe I need to work a little harder.

"I'm gonna go see what Nate's up to."

"Uh-huh," Ari teases, like she knows what's up.

She couldn't possibly. No one does.

No one but me...and the girl I want to be mine.

"You do know she's at the zoo with Mom and Aunt Sarah today, right?"

Ari not only proves she's more in tune than I thought but shocks the shit out of me with her question. Or admission, because no, I did not know that. It should settle me knowing

31

Payton's spending time with my family, the people who love me most, but it doesn't.

I want to be the person she spends her time with. I want to be the one to show Little D the monkeys and the bears. Maybe this is good, though, a twisted sort of sign she's still in reach, if only through those closest to me.

She will be. She *has* to be.

What the fuck will I do if she won't be?

CHAPTER 4
PAYTON

Now, July 4

I never understood why people enjoyed trips to the beach. Who would *want* to swim in freezing cold water? Anyone who has so much as put their feet in the ocean off the coast of California knows the one thing this sunny state does not have…is warm ocean water. Sure, sometimes it's less than freezing, but it's never warm, and don't even get me started on the sand.

Dare to swim and you're gifted with a suit full of it, but not only that, you get ratted hair as a bonus, even if the tips never so much as graze the water's surface. Oh, and good luck vacuuming the bits that make it back to your car with you. No matter how many times you beat your sandals against the curb or shake your towel out, it's never enough. The sand demons win every time.

So yeah, who the hell would want to spend a single minute at the beach, right?

God, what a prissy brat my mother raised me to be.

Thankfully, my brother is the furthest thing from his mother's son and showed me what I wasn't seeing, encouraged me to open not only my eyes but my mind.

Now?

I don't understand how anyone could ever hate the beach.

To be honest, I have no idea where I would be right now without it.

The waves, while unforgiving, don't judge.

The sun doesn't sear you with worried eyes and taut expressions.

The wind doesn't push for words when you don't feel like talking.

The sand doesn't crunch beneath your feet like the eggshells everyone seems to walk on around me. Metaphorically speaking, of course.

Here, there's no pity for the *poor little thing*, and that's exactly what I have become. To everyone.

Poor Payton lost the boy she loved.

Poor Payton never got to finish her senior year of high school.

Poor Payton is a teenage mom.

Poor Payton is a *single* mom.

Poor poor pitiful me, right? That's how the song goes?

It's not as hard as you'd think to avoid your feelings, but how could it be when everyone around tells you how okay you're going to be? It's why I like it better when school is in session and everyone is back in their dorms at their respective colleges, leaving the house empty. There's no one to hover, no one to pretend to be fine in front of when all you want to do is freak the fuck out every now and then—because it's not like it's all the time. Or it was, but then it wasn't.

It is again, though, isn't it?

Groaning, I rub my hands down my face. God, maybe I am this little lost soul everyone sees me as.

Well, not *everyone*.

He doesn't. He sees so much more than the broken girl with a battered heart. He—no.

I squeeze my eyes closed, pushing away the thought. I can't think of him. It's...wrong.

Sighing, I force myself to sit up, glancing back at the swing that sways slightly under the giant pergola thanks to the morning draft Oceanside has to offer, even in July. It's an old, wooden two-seater with lights twining up the chain securing it to the thick beams above—a gift for Lolli from her man. It's deep and meaningful and theirs, a tangible item of love.

Jealousy whirls through me like a tidal wave, knocking me in the chest and thieving the air from my lungs. She gets to share the most meaningful thing in her life.

I don't.

I should be happy about that. I have one of the greatest gifts love could ever offer all to myself, a perfectly healthy baby boy, and in some twisted ways only a girl raised by a vicious mother could reason, I am. But that's the scared, selfish part of me. The part that doesn't want the cruel world to touch the innocence I can protect if it's me and me alone, but the reality of it all is I don't want to. My choice was taken from me in the blink of an eye, and I'm supposed to deal.

I have no choice but to deal.

My eyes fall to the screen of the monitor in my hand, and I smile at the little man who's sound asleep in his crib, the little plush football tucked under his arm like he was born to hold it.

He wasn't. His daddy was a wrestler, not a football player, but he'll never get to tell him about that or teach him his favorite moves.

Deaton will never even get to hear his daddy's voice.

Tears fill my eyes instantly, and I close them, letting the hot streaks warm my cheeks, the wind quickly turning the heat to a chill, but I don't swipe them away.

I welcome the guilt that flows through me, the pain and anger and longing. The regret.

The love for the boy who isn't here anymore is still there, heavy in my heart, as broken and bruised as it is.

A soft click sounds, and my eyes open, falling back on the monitor, and my pulse jumps into my throat in anticipation.

The door to my son's bedroom opens ever so slowly, and *he* slips right inside.

I stare with trembling lips as Mason steps up to the edge of the old crib, peeking in on Deaton with an expression so tender it can't be mistaken for anything but adoration, but when he reaches out, his hand so large it nearly hides all those dark curls as he gently glides his palm along them, his eyes close on a slow, painful blink. His head hangs the slightest bit, and a choked sob escapes me, the heaviness in my heart doubling in size, the weight of another hovering just above the gaping hole Deaton's death left behind. It presses there like a needle to the skin, eager to slip right through. To break the surface and burrow deeper than it already has.

I can't let it in.

I can't let *him* in.

As if you have a say.

As if it's not too late…

Eyes locked on the video monitor, I try not to cry as he reaches into the crib, gently taking Deaton's tiny hand in his large one. He stares down at my sleeping baby boy with the softest yet saddest of smiles written on his lips.

"Don't tell anyone, but I'm scared, little man," he whispers. "Your mama's avoiding me, and I have no idea what to do about it."

He goes quiet for a moment, and I struggle to breathe, staring at my son's hand as it opens, his tiny fingers wrapping around Mason's thumb.

Mason's lips spread into a wide grin, a soft, quiet chuckle slipping free. "This your way of telling me you won't let me go?"

A knot forms in my throat, and I lock my hand around my neck.

Suddenly, Mason's face falls, and he bends, his forehead now resting on the edge of the crib. "Please don't let me go."

Gasping, I cut the camera off. I can't listen anymore. Can't watch.

I sit there in the sand for a while longer before I dare to turn the monitor back on. My muscles ease when I find no one but my sleeping baby on the screen.

Closing my eyes, I push to my feet, pulling in a lungful of salty air.

I've worn many masks over the years, something my mother demanded in her pursuit for a perfect daughter. It will be no different from that...and no different from the one I've worn on and off for almost a year now.

But he saw through that mask.

I wince, glancing up over the small sand hill to the large bay window at the back of my brother's home. My home.

All our friends and their families will be in one spot today. It's a whole-ass affair that just a few days ago I was looking forward to. Now I wish I didn't have a part in the decision to make our house the main point instead of saying we should do it at Mason and the others' place down the beach. That way, I could make an excuse and stay behind. I can't do that now.

I wanted to visit with everyone. I need the distraction, now more than ever, but the mere thought of laughing and celebrating with everyone has me as nauseated as the morning sickness used to. That's the thing about grief and the million other emotions flickering through me, though, right? It messes with my mind in a single blink. It can be a memory or a feeling or a sight. A song, a single word, or even a damn snack. Everything is fine, sometimes better than fine...until it isn't.

Until guilt dirties it, or anger buries it, or fear wraps its vicious claws around and chokes it.

Get a grip, Payton. Everything is fine. You're fine.

A few more days.

I just have to fake it, stay busy, and then the day will pass, taking the rope around my lungs with it. They'll go back to college, and I'll find all that progress I made but seem to have misplaced.

I can do this.

Besides, not much can happen in a week, right?
If my memory were a person, she would laugh in my face.
If anyone knows how bullshit such a thought can be, it's me.

"What a royal dick move that would be." Mia grins.

"What dick move are we talking about?"

We squeal, surprised by the intruding voice, and look up as Mia's ex walks over, but that's not what has me swallowing. It's the person who trails right behind him, an easy, not completely genuine grin in place. Still, it adds to his undeniable appeal.

Mason is effortlessly attractive with messy, dark brown hair he keeps trimmed short, and he chooses this exact moment to run a hand through it, accentuating the tapered muscles of his torso that are in no way hidden by the shirt he's wearing, if you can even call it a shirt anymore. He has the arms completely cut off, the sides slit down to the waist, where his palm tree–covered board shorts lie low against his hips.

He is the perfect specimen with the mind and heart to match.

I look away.

"Your face, Austin. Forcing us to stare at it is a dick move," Lolli teases, and I know she's feeling a little buzz. She turns to Mason. "Where're your people?"

He sidesteps her, walking around the blanket until he's right beside me, and I fight the urge not to swallow.

"My sister and Cameron should be here any time." He makes a goofy face, reaching down and snagging Deaton from the saucer chair he was sitting in. He chuckles when Deaton blows little bubbles through his lips, and I can't help the smile that forms on mine. "But Chase and Brady won't be back until late tonight."

At that, I reach for my phone with a slight frown. "Are you sure, because Chase texted me and said he'd be here for lunch."

Mason freezes, Deaton halfway to his chest, his eyes snapping over to lock on mine. "Chase texts you?"

I don't know why, but my cheeks flame. Before I can respond, Mia starts talking, but I tune her out and stand, grabbing the baby seat and dusting off the Lamb Chop toy Deaton dropped onto the sandy blanket the second Mason smiled at him.

I turn to Mason again, an excuse of Deaton needing a change on the tip of my tongue, but Mason has already spun on his heels, headed for the water's edge. He drops onto his butt right there, shifting my son so he's standing between his bent legs, his little feet pressed into the wet sand.

Deaton's face is in my line of sight, and when he smiles wide, shoving his hands in his mouth because he's so excited he doesn't know what else to do, a low laugh leaves me. I suck in a deep breath, set the things back in the sand, and move to join them, because how could I not?

Nerves fire off in my stomach, but I count through it, doing all I can to keep myself from running with my tail between my legs.

Mason doesn't look up as I lower beside the pair, but when Deaton turns his smile on me, stomping his feet and sending little speckles of wet sand all around, he laughs and glances my way.

Our eyes meet, but he swiftly averts his gaze.

After a moment, he asks, "Think he'll be too cold if his feet touch the water?"

That's right. He hasn't gotten to see him enjoy the water yet this summer.

I shake my head. "No, he loves the water, even as chilly as it is."

"Yeah?" Mason grins but keeps his attention on Deaton as he spins him so he's facing the ocean. Mason shifts, walking on his knees the three feet forward to where the waves die out against the sand. "Okay, little man, here it comes."

I bite back a smile at the uncertainty in his tone. When

Deaton jolts, his eyes bugging wide as a small, surprised whine escapes, Mason panics, tugging him straight into his chest and looking to me in, well, panic.

A laugh leaves me instantly, and slowly Mason relaxes, a low chuckle pushing past his lips.

"Here." I reach out.

Mason holds on to Deaton a second longer, almost like if he hands him over, he has no idea how long it might be before he gets the chance to hold him again, and it's heartbreaking.

It's your fault, Payton.

Hesitantly, he passes him to me. I turn Deaton to face me, and when a wave comes, I make an excited little sound, widening my eyes and opening my mouth wide.

Deaton tenses from the cool water but just as quickly starts stomping his feet, fighting to bend at the waist so he can slap at it with his palms. I hold him back at first but end up setting him on his butt between my legs so he can play for a few minutes.

"He's a total water baby," I say, though I'm not sure why I'm whispering. "Bath times are his favorite times."

When I look at Mason, he's not looking at me. He's smiling softly at my son, and a heavy sense of longing washes over me.

"Look how strong he is now, sitting up all by himself," he notes, reaching out to splash at the water with him.

"Yeah."

He must hear the happiness in my voice, because he looks at me then, an agonizing tenderness in his gaze. "You've been avoiding me."

"No." My denial is too fast. Too rushed. Too loud.

"I've been here four times this summer." Mason's brown eyes hold mine. "You were gone every single one of those times."

"My internship at Embers Elite is demanding and—"

"And you wrapped that up in May, freeing up your schedule until it starts again at the end of summer." He studies me.

"We talked all about it…when you were still taking my calls and answering my messages."

My lips clamp closed, and I swallow. A gust of wind kicks, and a piece of hair falls into my face. Instantly, his hand lifts, but as if he didn't even know it was happening, he frowns and drops it back to his lap.

A heavy ache settles in my bones, and I don't know if it's because he was going to touch me or because he didn't.

Clearing my throat, I push to my feet, taking Deaton with me. "I should get him cleaned off and—"

"Payton."

"—inside so he can take a nap and—"

"Payton."

I all but run back toward the house, bypassing the others and happy to find the kitchen empty when I tear through the back patio door into the house, but before I can close it behind me, Mason's hand slips in, gently easing it back open. Leaving him there, I hurry toward the bathroom, looking for a place to set Deaton down.

Mason appears, pulling him from my hands, and I drop to my knees, turning on the bathtub and securing his bath seat in the center.

I don't look at him as I take Deaton from his hands and strip him down to nothing, sliding him into the plastic seat.

Mason doesn't leave. He bends, grips my chin, and turns my head toward his, frustration drawing creases to the edges of his depthless brown eyes.

Tears prick my own, and at the sight, whatever he wanted to say dies on his lips.

He stands and walks away, and it's not until I hear the soft click of the slider door that I fall to my ass, burying my face in my hands.

He's right. I am avoiding him, and he did come here three times this summer. According to the messages I left on read, the only reason he came…was for me.

41

My eyes fall to Deaton, who plays happily in the warm water, and I know that's not right.

Mason didn't come home for me.

He came for us.

CHAPTER 5
PAYTON

Before, July 5

The pounding on the door sounds again, and my heart leaps into my throat, suffocating me.

Oh god. This is it.

"Payton, open the door!" the boy I left behind when I ran hysterically shouts from outside. "Please open the door. Please." He bangs his fist again.

He's here. He found me.

He came for me...

"Peep"—Parker holds his hands out—"talk to me. What do we do?"

I don't respond. I *can't*. I'm frozen in place, staring at the white wood like it might crack and splinter into a million pieces, revealing a broken boy on the other side.

"Payton," Lolli whispers, and I jolt. I hadn't even noticed her walking closer. "He sounds worried. Maybe we should let him in, if only to show him you're okay."

Shit. shit, shit.

Another knock.

"Open it," I rasp, pressing my hand to my stomach, hoping to settle the sudden queasiness.

My brother opens the door, and there he is, sagging against the frame.

His hair is all over the place instead of in the neat styled curls he normally wears, and his collared shirt is wrinkled from every angle.

He hasn't spotted me yet, pleading for Parker to put him out of his misery. "Please tell me she's here. I've...I don't know where else to go. She just...she disappeared and—"

The worry in his tone does it, and I call out, "Deaton."

The broken laugh that leaves him makes my bones ache, and then his eyes find mine, his own squeezing closed in relief. With his next breath, he's rushing my way.

The minute his arms wrap around me, the tears fall, and I honestly don't know if they're from relief or fear. Relief that he's here and fear for the very same reason.

If my mother is vicious, his is the devil, but that's not really why I'm seconds from vomiting all over the both of us. I'm going to have to tell him, and I am not ready.

"Baby, I didn't know what had happened. Suddenly, you were gone and—" His voice cracks, and his hold on me tightens. "I thought your mom... Why did you leave me there? I would have come with you if you wanted to run away." He keeps talking, but I can't hear past the echo of my own pulse pounding hard against my temples.

"Deaton, please." I pull away, and his arms fall to his sides in defeat.

"Talk to me. Tell me what I did. I'll fix it. I promise you."

Shame and frustration in my own self boil over inside me, and I shake my head. "You can't fix it." My voice is but a whisper.

He steps closer, but I step back, wincing when his face pales at the movement.

"What's going on?" he pleads. "I don't understand."

"I..." Damn it. There is no soft way to say this, no easing him into our new reality, so I suck it up, forcing the words from my lips and hoping it's the right decision. "I'm pregnant."

Deaton's entire body locks in place as if my words have pressed

44

pause on the wheel of time. One second passes, and then another. Slowly, or so it feels, a whirl of emotion flashes across his features, and the next thing I know, he's bending in front of me. I'm lifted off the floor, and his feet carry us across the room, not stopping until we're out the sliding glass door. On the back deck, he eases me down until I'm sitting on the outdoor sofa.

He drops down before me, and I bury my face in my palms, unable to meet his gaze.

"You've been avoiding me," he finally says. "Ignoring all my calls and texts."

"I know. I'm sorry."

"It's been days, Payton." He sounds tired, but there's no anger in his tone. There's not even really hurt, just concern, and that makes me feel worse.

He's not overly emotional, having come from a cold family, but he also never really gets mad. Sometimes I wish he would so I would know he was as jacked up as I am.

"I know" is all I manage to say.

"Look at me. Please." He pauses, and I force myself to listen. A small smile forms on his lips. "Tell me everything about the baby."

I jump up so fast he tumbles back a bit as I make a mad dash past him, running right down the steps and out into the warm sand. I'm halfway to the water's edge when he gently catches me by the wrist, swinging himself around so he's in front of me.

With my free hand, I press against his chest, my head shaking feverishly, but he only pushes himself closer.

His mouth opens as tears roll down my cheeks, and then a body comes out of nowhere, slamming into Deaton's side so hard he's airborne for a solid second.

I nearly stumble onto my ass with a screech, but warm hands wrap around me, keeping me on my feet.

"I've got you" is whispered into my ear, but I'm too busy gaping at the sight before me.

45

Mason jumps to his feet, and I'm so shocked I don't realize he's moved to straddle Deaton until his arm tugs back, his fist flying forward in a swift swing.

My brain finally catches up to what's happening in front of me, and it's my sudden shriek that breaks through the fog of Mason's...whatever the hell this is, and his fist freezes in the air mere inches from Deaton's face.

His head snaps to me instantly, eyes narrowed and pinned on mine, heavy, bursting breaths heaving from his lungs as his gaze slices across my form as if searching for something. I think he's shaking.

I think *I'm* shaking.

Somehow, when his wild eyes slide back to mine, it must click. His arm lowers, and when Deaton shoves at him, Mason allows him to knock him onto his ass in the sand.

"What the hell, man?" Deaton frowns, climbing to his feet and dusting himself off.

Mason has already hopped up and moves to stand in front of me just as the arms that kept me from tumbling fall away, and then Chase is there, too, both guys looking from me to Deaton with hard expressions.

Mason wants to ask questions—what those would be, I don't know—but there must be something he sees in my gaze, as in the next moment, he steps back.

In the blink of an eye, the tension tightening his features falls away, and a wide smile spreads across his lips. "My bad. Thought you were some dick touching her, then I saw her crying and, you know. Game over."

"Thanks?" Deaton frowns but accepts Mason's hand when he offers up one of those bro handshakes. "I'm Deaton, but it seems you already know that." He looks to me expectantly.

I reach out, taking Deaton's hand and entwining our fingers as I move to his side.

"These are Mason and Chase, friends of my brother." I

46

pause, thinking better of it. "Actually, Mason is Kenra's cousin," I mention, because Kenra was seeing Deaton's asshole older brother, so he knows her.

"Hey, sorry, man," Chase apologizes, though he doesn't look all that sorry, not that he's the one who tackled Deaton to the ground. He does look annoyed, though. "We didn't know you were here."

"It's fine." Deaton looks to me and back. "Thanks for looking out for her."

I offer a small smile, my free hand pressing into his chest as I glance toward the others. "Can you guys leave us alone, please?"

The boys hesitate but then nod, heading up the deck we just came down.

Sighing, I step in to Deaton, resting my cheek against his chest. We're nearly the same height, so when his arms come around me, lifting me a tiny bit, my toes still dig into the sand.

"Well, this has been a lot more eventful of a reunion than I anticipated," he muses, rubbing my back.

I grin into his neck, a light chuckle escaping. "Yeah, they're kind of a lot. And there's more of them."

It's Deaton's turn to chuckle. "Well, I'm glad to know there are other people you can depend on."

I close my eyes. "I missed you, and I know I should have told you where I was going so you didn't worry, but I knew you'd ask questions, and I just...didn't want to answer them."

I pull back, looking at him.

"Why?" he asks softly.

"Because I know you, Deaton. I can see it in your eyes right now. You've already accepted this, and you're rearranging puzzle pieces in your mind, and I'm—" I swallow, biting on the inside of my cheek.

He clasps my shoulders with soft hands, and I force my eyes to stay on his when I want to look away. "It's okay to be afraid,

Payton. Or even a little sad. We have, what?" he smiles softly. "Eight months to figure it out, at least?"

Wrong. How do I tell him I've known for over a month now, having suspected even longer but was too afraid to find out for sure? Because of the extensive workout plan and stress of my day-to-day life, both thanks to my mother, it was normal for me to skip a month or two of my cycle. I thought nothing of it until that third month rolled around and the box of tampons I'd restocked still sat unopened under the sink. He couldn't have guessed any of this, though, as my body hasn't changed much, so it's been nothing a sweater or flowy sundress couldn't hide. And I did hide it.

Swallowing, I pull back, putting a little space between us but keeping our hands connected.

This is the hardest part.

The real part I was afraid of and the reason that I was avoiding him. That I ran.

I meet his gaze and speak the words I've been desperate to hide, maybe even from myself.

"That's the thing," I whisper shakily. "I don't know if I want to figure it out, Deaton. I...don't know if I'm keeping the baby."

CHAPTER 6
PAYTON

Now, July 4

It's late, the visitors have gone, and Deaton is fast asleep in his crib.

For the last couple of hours, the rest of us have shuffled between huddling around the firepit and squeezing in at the patio picnic table turned game table. Stacked quarters sit in front of us, a small cup full resting in the middle, as we close out our third round of left, right, center, and my right knee's bouncing spreads to my left.

Tension tugs at my chest, anxiety building at a slow yet steady place, only this time it doesn't break when I finally give in and tap the screen of my phone for the hundredth time. With the end of every game, the night closes in, the digital clock reading five after ten.

The day is almost over. Gone.

How are things here and then gone in the blink of an eye? In the pass of a single second? Poof. No more.

I swallow, trying not to draw attention to myself as I attempt to breath in through my nose and out through my mouth, but it doesn't help.

I'm suffocating.

Most of us stand, stretching or refilling cups, but I wait for their backs to turn, taking the opportunity to step away. Pushing onto shaky legs, I move toward my brother, take his hand, and gently set the baby monitor in his palm.

He looks at me with concern, but a quick squeeze of his fingers is all I can give.

Panicked and unable to catch a full breath, I clutch my phone in my fist, running down the deck stairs and onto the sand.

Ari and Noah are in their own little world, cuddled by the fire, but both jerk my way when I hurry past.

"Payton?" she calls, but I keep running, down the side of the house and toward the front, across the grass and onto the sidewalk.

I pause there in the shadows, gripping my head and squeezing my eyes closed as tears threaten to take me under, to drown me.

My jaw is clenched tight, and I tug on the strings of my hoodie, letting it bite into my neck as I drop my head back, welcoming the cold air against my clammy skin.

Headlights flick on, and I jolt, eyes narrowing when they flash a second time.

I sniffle, swiping my cheeks with my sleeves and run over to the old red truck sitting idling at the curb. Curling my fingers over the edge of the windowsill, eyes the color of emeralds meet mine.

"Where are you going?" I blurt out before he can ask me what's wrong.

Chase visibly winces, looking out the windshield at the road ahead. "Is it bad if I say anywhere but here?" Slowly, he faces my way.

I know that look. It mirrors one of mine.

My shoulders fall a little, and I offer a small smile. Chase is waiting for me to question him, to ask if the reason he would rather be *anywhere but here* has anything to do with a certain couple sitting by the fire that he may or may not be able to handle seeing together.

Not everyone knows how important it can be to dodge a question. Sometimes it's the only thing keeping that final string from snapping and leaving behind a welt you can't hide. So no, I don't ask him any of that, saying instead, "Is it bad if I want to go with you?"

Chase stares a moment, and then he reaches across the cab, pushing open the door in invitation.

I don't hesitate, not when I know Deaton is safe and sound, asleep in his crib with my brother watching over him. I climb in the cab, buckle my seat belt, and meet his gaze.

He tips his head. "Where do you want to go?"

A grin pulls at my lips, my limbs suddenly feeling ten pounds lighter with the promise of an escape. "Anywhere but here."

Chase chuckles, tosses me the blanket he pulls from behind his seat, and puts the truck in drive. He doesn't tell me where we're headed, and honestly, I'm not sure he even knows, but I don't care.

I'm along for the ride either way.

Just as we're pulling away, a flash of something catches my eye. I turn, glancing toward the house as we roll past, and there he is.

Mason stands at the edge of the house, a can of cream soda hanging from his fingertips…eyes on me.

My head snaps forward so fast, I know Chase notices.

Whether he sees Mason or not, he doesn't say.

He doesn't stop either. Instead, his foot hits the gas a little harder, leading farther down the road.

The streets are lively tonight, the usually dark sky lit by bonfires, string lights, and cell phone flashes. The people of Oceanside, both young and old, enjoying the last holiday of the summer before most go back to their normal, everyday lives. People run the roads barefoot, dragging wagons stuffed with ice chests, blankets, toddlers, and dogs. One guy is even rolling a keg around, his friends laughing and helping push it from behind but tripping over one another, liquid spilling from their plastic cups.

Chase and I both chuckle at the sight and end up sitting at the stop sign for almost three minutes, just waiting for a chance to turn among the crowd.

"Looks like the beach is clearing out," I comment, a strange mix of numbness and relief settling over my bones. "I wonder if we'll see a bunch of people packing up to go home tomorrow."

Chase glances over with a grin. "Aw, she's a real ocean girl now? Tired of sharing the beach with drunk college kids and screaming babies—" Chase clamps his mouth closed so fast I can't help but laugh. He looks away, rubbing the back of his head, short brown strands sliding along his fingers. At the light, he finally looks back. "I'm sorry. That was...shit."

"Don't worry about it." My lips turn up slightly, and I pull the blanket up to my neck, watching the small shops as we go by. "Because you're absolutely right. The lungs on some of those babies, I'd pull my hair out."

Chase and I share a smile, and then he reaches forward, turning up the music.

I sit back, humming along to the music that fills the cab. When we pick up a little speed and the wind hits my face a little harder, I don't roll the window up.

I close my eyes and breathe in deeply, and I don't open them until Chase kills the engine.

My eyes slide his way as he unbuckles and starts to climb out, so I do the same, following him around back.

He pulls the tailgate down as my eyes move across the giant field ahead, where some people are scattered across what looks to be several hundred yards or more of grass.

"This is where the fireworks show was tonight," he tells me as he sits. "I thought maybe we'd catch the grand finale at least, but I guess it's later than I realized."

Apparently, fireworks are illegal in Oceanside, and from what Ari said, there's usually a dedicated spot where the city will put on a safe showing for the townspeople. I guess this was it this year.

"Why didn't we come tonight to watch?" I glance back, and he pats the spot beside him, so I hop up, settling on the chilled metal.

"Probably because we're all grown now." He shrugs, then looks to me with a smile. "Next year, though, I'd bet money we're the first at the show if Sarah or Viv have any say."

Warmth blossoms in my chest. Not only at the thought of the love my friend's parents have for Deaton but the fact that he and I are so effortlessly included in plans that don't even exist yet.

Smiling to myself, I look out over the space. "I wonder if he'll like all the colors but hate the loud booms that come with them."

"If he does..." Chase reaches behind him, revealing a small plastic bag I didn't see him grab from the truck. "We go to plan B."

A small frown builds along my brow, and I watch, curious, as he pulls a long rectangular box out with one hand, revealing a lighter in the other.

A low laugh leaves me, and I hold my hand out, tearing into the thin cardboard after he slaps it into my palm.

I pull out two, holding them past my dangling legs, and he leans forward, lighting the paper ends. Once it catches and green and red sparks start to shoot from the end, I pass one his way.

Chase spins his in circles, making shapes with the smoke, and I do the same, my muscles relaxing even more. He must notice as he looks over then.

"See?" His grin is proud. "Everyone likes a sparkler."

"These were my favorite when I was little," I share. "My dad would always make a big deal of the holiday. He'd buy me one of those wire garland crowns, you know, the kind with ribbons that hung almost to the floor, and when he put it on my head, he'd bow like I was some kind of princess waving around a scepter of sorts. I'd pretend to cast spells and make Parker my minion." I smile at the memory, but a frown quickly washes it away. "That's probably why my mom refused to buy fireworks of any kind once they separated. She'd usually just...tell us to go down the road and watch the neighbors'." A second, more spiteful smile pulls at my lips as I reach into the box in my lap. "Serves her right. Deaton lived down the street then."

The moment the words leave my mouth, my muscles lock, and I try not to look at Chase but do it anyway. I wait for the hint of pity to draw his features in, but it never comes.

He just...smiles.

"Yeah?" he asks. "That how you two got close?"

Biting into my lower lip, I face forward. "That's sort of how it started, yeah." I spin the stick between my thumb and pointer finger, glancing his way. "So, you excited to get back to school soon?" I say to change the subject.

He shrugs at the same time as he nods, and when he looks over, I laugh.

"What?" he wonders.

I mimic his movement, down to the faint scowl he had on his face, and Chase bumps my shoulder playfully.

After a moment, he sighs loudly. "We've been in training camps with the team on and off all summer, and technically me and the guys have been back on campus for weeks now since coach talked us into summer classes." He shrugs again. "I just don't feel like I've had much of a break, you know? I can't say I'm not happy for the distraction." He tenses a moment, gaze flicking my way as if he said that by mistake.

When I don't react, he keeps going.

"The end of the school year was always when I felt like I could breathe a bit. Like whatever was going on was finally over and there was a fresh start. But this summer was...different." He looks away then, glaring at nothing ahead of us. "I knew last year would be my last real summer. We all talked about it enough, that's for sure, but man. It hits different when you realize it's even further from what you expected it to be. It kind of feels like the year that was supposed to fly by just won't end, you know?" He cuts a quick glance from the corner of his eye.

I swallow, my eyes moving between his, because, man, do I feel that deep in my bones.

Last summer, I was secretly four months pregnant, ran away

54

from home, and found a new one here. I was going to have a baby with my high school boyfriend. Now, that boyfriend is dead, and my son is nearly eight months old.

Chase looks away, and I wonder what caused the obvious ache in his eyes.

Is it just that he is in love with Ari, his best friend's twin sister who's now in love with someone else, or is there something more going on he hasn't shared?

I don't know, but what I do know is not to ask people questions they clearly don't want to answer, so I dig into the box once more and light two fresh sparklers, holding his out with a small bow.

"For you, prince of pigskin."

Chase grins, taking my offering. "Why, thank you, princess of—"

"Puke?"

Chase looks at me horrified, but when I smile wide, tugging out the bib I forgot I had stuffed in my hoodie pocket, we both end up laughing.

We light a few more, drawing our names in the road with the ends, knowing it will fade into nothing in no time. At some point, we move farther into the bed of the truck, our legs stretched out and heads resting against the window behind us.

The quiet is nice, something I've missed amid the crazy but at the same time do my best to avoid because quiet brings peace, peace brings thoughts, and all my thoughts roll together in one giant, spiky lump of regret that seems to live in my gut.

My phone alarm beeps, breaking the comfortable silence we fell into, and I wince as I blindly press the button to cut off the piercing sound.

Chase says nothing, letting me decide if I want to talk about why my alarm is set for twelve a.m. on the dot.

I don't. I haven't said a word to anyone about where my mind has been. In fact, I've gone to ridiculous lengths to avoid it, so I have no idea why my next words leave my lips. Maybe it's because he didn't pity me earlier. I don't know. Still, the truth tumbles out in a voice so low, I scowl.

"This was the last holiday he had. Which makes it my last first holiday without him." As my whispers settle between us, a huffed sigh slips past my lips. "That probably sounds so dumb. It's not like I'm an eighty-year-old woman who shared half her life with someone and then lost him."

"Forty years or four months, it makes no difference." Chase is frowning at the night when I turn. "It hurts either way."

"Yeah," I whisper, staring at his profile. "Love sucks."

His laughter is low, and slowly he looks over, his green gaze holding a moment before he reaches out, throwing his arm around my shoulder. "Yeah, princess. It does."

I lay my head on his shoulder and close my eyes.

We don't stay much longer, making it back to my house a lot faster now that the roads are clear and nothing but the crash of the waves can be heard in the distance.

I smile as I pull the handle and climb out, closing the door behind me.

"Hey, Payton?"

Glancing over my shoulder, I meet his gaze through the open window.

"Just so you know," he begins. "It's okay *not* to be okay...even if it's not for the reason everyone thinks."

I hold his gaze a moment and slowly nod. "You know, I think you might be the first person who has ever said that to me."

"It's true."

My mouth curves slightly, and Chase nods back, his truck sitting there idling as I turn and walk away.

I put the code in the door and tiptoe down the hall. My son's bedroom door is open, so I slip inside and gently lift him from his crib and into my arms, turning off the monitor.

He stretches a bit but doesn't wake, instead tucking his little hands between my chest and his as I carry him across the hall and into my room. I don't bother changing, just climb into bed, gently laying him beside me and sliding my finger between his. He squeezes slightly, his lips parted as he sleeps, and a small smile pulls at my lips as I stare at my dark curly-haired baby boy.

"Happy Fourth of July, Deaton," I whisper into the night, unsure if I'm speaking to him or to the boy who didn't get to live to today.

Maybe both.

CHAPTER 7
PAYTON

Now, July 5

Camera in my hands, I tentatively pull the memory card free, sliding it into the slot on my PC. The import screen pops up, and with it, my heart jolts in my rib cage.

During my internship, I was clearing and uploading every couple of days, but this particular memory card has remained inside its slot for several months now. Since May.

Since my little trip to a certain college a couple of hours away...

Distractions. Today is about distraction.

Swallowing, I click the large "yes" on the screen, swiftly turning away so I don't have to see the images as they flash there in rapid succession.

I focus on my bag of accessories, taking out my small traveling tripod and setting it up to make sure nothing's broken or missing. I clean my lenses and sensor, attaching each piece and then detaching before placing them back into their designated slots.

It's ten after twelve in the afternoon, and I know little mister will be waking up from his nap any moment, so I hurry and finish packing up my camera bag, adding in all the necessities that I've discovered I need along the way. My internship at Embers Elite this past year taught me a lot, one very important thing being I'm pretty worthless when I'm lacking in sugars. So on that note, I add a few small packs of chocolate-covered almonds to the side pouch, some tissues, ChapStick, and super-glue to the other.

It was my first assignment as the newest member of the sports photography team when I discovered superglue could be my best friend on the field. There's nothing worse than when you're awkwardly bent, lying against the grass, or raised in the air, however the heck you manage that, and you break something you can't piece back together. Sure, the superglue destroys it and you're still screwed later, forced to replace the part regardless, but at least at the end of the day, you got the shot you came for. And when you're hanging around, sometimes literally, a six-foot, three-hundred-pound lineman for that money shot, things are bound to break.

Today will be different, though. I'm not headed to a field where I'll be taking pictures of athletes but instead under what I imagine will be dainty string lights or glowing fluorescent ones to set the ambiance in a romantic glow.

I'll be following the happy couple with my lens from every corner of the room, catching what they believe to be private moments between the two. I'll freeze them in time, and down the road, when they look back at the images of them whispering to each other, they'll remember their little secret.

Mason was my little secret.

Okay. So not really a distraction for me but in fact a horrible idea.

A laugh escapes, and I run a hand over my long ponytail. "What the hell was I thinking?"

Deaton's soft, baby gibberish sounds at the perfect time, and when I look at the little screen, seeing he's awake, I practically run from the room, happy to lose myself in him for the next few hours.

As I enter, he looks up with blue eyes that mirror mine and shows off a mouth full of gums as he smiles.

"Well, hello, little man." I reach in, allowing him to latch his fists over my pointer fingers so he can use his own strength to pull himself into a standing position. I transfer his hands to the edge of the crib, bending down so we're face-to-face. "Did someone have a good nap?"

He presses his forehead to mine, making the sweetest little baby sounds as he starts to jump.

Smiling, I turn back to the changing table and pull out a fresh diaper and wipes. As I go to take him into my arms, he drops onto his butt, reaching for his plush toy. I tense, watching as he hugs the little football to his chest, pressing his cheek into the soft side of it. He looks up, his big blue eyes fully slanted at the side. His smile is so wide and sudden, a soft, sob-laced laugh leaves me.

He's just so happy all the time, completely oblivious to the battles that go on inside my head, just as I hoped he would be. When I'm with him, I block out everything else. It might not be the best coping mechanism, attaching his every waking moment I can to my hip, but it works. Sure, I've basically taken independent play off the table, but he is learning how to entertain himself, if only little by little. For now, I don't think it matters.

He's growing and curious about his little world, and in my arms is where he gets to explore. He can see all the things I see and touch all the things his little arm is long enough to reach. He loves being everywhere I am.

I must be doing something right, right?

Warmth blooms in my chest, and a bittersweet sigh slips. I take him and the football into my arms, my eyes instantly falling to the signatures on the side.

Lolli is the one who bought the plush, and as a joke, Nate signed it before giving it to him.

Lowering him onto the changing mat, I tickle his belly as I quickly unsnap his onesie, my eyes falling to the bright red ink, scribbled large and purposely swallowing the name beneath it.

Yes, the moment Mason spotted Deaton's new plush, he scowled and started digging through the kitchen drawers, coming back with a Sharpie in his hands. He signed right over the top of Nate's name, passing it back to Deaton with a satisfied smile.

He said not a word before or after, and neither did I, but I was laughing on the inside.

"Silly man, huh, baby boy?" I whisper, pretending I don't hear the ache in my own voice as I make quick work of getting him changed and into a pair of bottoms. "Okay. What do you say we go for a little walk and have lunch on the pier?"

Deaton squeaks as if he understands, and I lift him into the air, spinning as I carry him from the room.

Parker and Kenra are lounging on the couch when I walk out, both glancing back with a smile.

"You headed out?" my brother asks.

"Yeah, I'm going to take him on a walk and maybe down to the water before Ari comes for him later."

"Is she keeping him at their place?"

I nod. "Yeah, for the early part of the evening, but they're coming back here for bedtime."

"You know we can keep him, Peep." My brother looks to me.

"I know, but she's been asking, so I thought I'd give you guys a break."

Parker frowns, but not in an angry sort of way. "You never leave him with us, Payton. After bed, he's out like a light, so it's not even babysitting, and you've only done that twice in the past several months...and both were this week." He watches me closely, clearly detecting I'm off my game now that he's been home longer than his usual one- to two-day breaks. "You know we do want to hang out with him, right?"

I offer a small smile, nodding. "I know, and if she lets you, you can keep him up as long as his little eyes allow once she comes back with him."

Kenra scoffs, and I share a smile with her. Fat chance Ari will share once she has him.

Grabbing some squashable baby food, a snack pack, and a

water, I toss it all in the diaper bag. I fill Deaton's sippy cup with half water, half pear juice and cross my fingers today is the day he figures out how to drink out of it instead of just using it as a teething toy, so then I grab a bottle just in case.

Parker has the stroller out and ready for me by the time I reach the door, and I buckle the little man inside.

We're out the front door and strolling down the street in seconds.

The sun is warm against my skin, and I welcome the glow.

We walk for a half mile, and I hold my breath as we reach the stop sign at the end. Mason and the others' beach house is just across from it, familiar cars sitting in the driveway.

I gnaw on my inner cheek. It would be rude to walk past without saying hello and awkward if I tried and they spotted me out the front windows.

My decision is made for me when a horn beeps behind me, and I look back to spot Noah pulling up against the curb.

He smiles and hops out, his oldest friend, Paige, climbing out the passenger side door.

He walks over, smiling wide as he lowers in front of the stroller. "Hey, buddy. Did you come to play with your favorite friend?"

I laugh and he looks up with a grin, but only for a second, his hand outstretched to Deaton.

"High five," he encourages, lifting Deaton's hand and slapping it into his own so it makes a light clapping sound.

Deaton kicks his feet excitedly, drool dripping from his lips.

Noah smiles softly, his eyes holding my little boy for a few silent moments before he clears his throat and pushes to stand. "Here, let me help get him inside," he offers.

"Oh, no, I'm not dropping him off yet. We're having a little mom and son day first."

"Isn't every day a mom and son day?" Paige teases, stepping up to wrap me in a quick hug. "Hey, girlie." She smiles sweetly.

"I heard you rented a studio down the street. Congratulations."

Paige shrugs like it's no big deal, but the blush on her cheeks says otherwise. "I want to turn it into a rec center, but I have to figure out all the ins and outs. Until then, private lessons on the weekends will cover the bills." She laughs.

Noah smiles, glancing from the front door to me. "You realize if she finds out you walked by and didn't come in, she's going to be sad. Not sure I can have that." He's teasing, but he's also not wrong.

"Just remind her she's picking him up at six thirty, and I think she'll be okay."

Noah sighs dramatically but grins afterward. "Come on, Paige. Let's go break my girl's heart."

I wave and walk away as quickly as possible, turning down a side street that takes me in the wrong direction, but it's better than someone catching up to me.

I don't want to hurt anyone's feelings, but I need some time with just me and Deaton.

Especially today. The fifth of July.

The day he arrived in Oceanside exactly one year ago.

He only came here because of me.

I am the reason he's dead.

————————

You must really enjoy torturing yourself.

That's the unwelcome thought that bursts through my brain the moment I step from the car and onto the beautiful rocky winding path. It's lined with lilies the color of pomegranates, each bundle tucked gently into little silver vases, lilac ribbons tied around the centers. The flowers lead to a massive arched doorway that's propped open, revealing an even bigger hall in the center, more lilies trailing down each side.

The man at the door smiles and greets me, extending his

arm out to welcome me inside, but before I can step through, an older woman rushes out and latches on to my wrist, dragging me forward.

"Oh, thank goodness! We're thrilled you could make it. Everyone has just taken their seats, and dinner's being served. There is a seat and plate for you as well. I hope you like salmon. I'm Evelyn, by the way. Mother of the groom."

"It's nice to meet you. I'm Payton."

"Yes, we heard so much about you. I tell you, Mia has been a lifesaver."

She leads us through a side door that takes us through the kitchen, and I smile politely as we slip past the chefs hard at work with what looks like a dessert course. As we step through the swinging doors and into the reception area, my feet slow of their own accord until I've fully stopped, gawking at the wide-open space.

Fifteen to twenty round tables litter the floor, leaving a bit of space open in the center, likely for the bride and groom's first dance or to view the wedding party table that sits up higher than the rest. Glass vases of different heights rest in the center of each one; lilies, this time white, burst within them, sitting on a bed of what looks like diamonds. There doesn't seem to be an open seat in the place. There's a charge of happiness in the air, and when I glance up at the wedding party table, finding the bride and groom tilted toward each other, moisture builds in my eyes.

I don't realize I'm taking backward steps until Evelyn turns to me and tips her head.

"Did you leave something in the car, hon? I can ask the doorman to retrieve it for you."

Clearing my throat, I do my best not to give away the panic rising within me. "No, I was going to go ahead and pull my camera out here and sneak some shots as I make my way around the room."

"Perfect!" The woman claps in delight. "There's a name tag and a seat for you in the front right corner."

I thank her again and turn to the side, then busy myself in my bag in hopes that she goes back to enjoying the party. She does, and I suck in a breath of relief, pressing my back against the dark corner of the wall and taking a moment to breathe.

It's fine. You're fine. Everything is fine.

It's not like a wedding is something I've ever thought about before. At no point in my childhood did I sit around and plan for my own, so this should be simple. Easy.

I'm here to do what I love, and I'm going to do it well, because despite how fucked-up I am in the head right now, I know I'm good at this.

This I can do without ruining everything.

Jesus, projecting much?

Oh my god, okay. Snap out of it.

I can do this.

So I reach for the numb switch in the back of my brain, flick it on, and get my ass to work.

Surprisingly, the evening goes by in a blur, and even more unexpectedly, I'm having a great time, smiling at the crowds as I make my way through, taking shot after shot of everything I think will be a warm memory.

Ten o'clock rolls around, and I note nearly all the older family members have called it a night, leaving what appears to be the bride and groom's friends, or maybe cousins or siblings as they all seem to be around the same age. As if it were the plan all along, this is when the real party begins.

The guests go crazy when the bride reappears in a shorter, slinkier white dress, and even the music ramps up to what I imagine one would hear in a nightclub downtown.

Alcohol flows faster, people get louder, and I already know these will be the photos that make the newlyweds laugh when I send over the files in a couple of weeks.

Before I can exit the dance floor, a guy with blond hair grabs my free hand and spins me around, laughing all the while. He's not kind of rude or sloppy but clearly intoxicated and having a good-ass time, so much so his mood is infectious. I can't help the smile that breaks across my lips, and I give in for the remainder of the song, dancing like nothing else matters.

The song ends pretty quickly, and he gives a drunken bow before turning toward the bar.

As I make my way toward my designated seat, I catch a glimpse of red. My head jerks to the left to find Mia showed up after all.

She's all dolled up and glancing around the room, so I jump from my seat and rush over, but before she sees me, her ex sees her, instantly commandeering her attention.

Sneakily, I raise my camera at the two, grinning at how obvious they are.

They are 100 percent making up tonight.

"I could have called that." His whisper warms my skin, rolling over my ear and down my neck like an uncontrollable heat wave.

My eyes are still pointed through the lens, every muscle in my body going tense. It takes effort, but I manage to slowly bring the camera down, tucking it to my chest as if to shield what beats beneath it.

He steps around, my eyes and only my eyes slicing to the left the moment he becomes visible in my periphery, tracking his body as he places it *right* before me.

As if suddenly starved and aware of what they wish to be fed, my lungs expand with a full breath made up of nothing but Mason freaking Johnson.

My attention immediately falls to the wide stretch of his shoulders.

He's wearing a button-up shirt and slacks, both a charcoal gray in color. He has the top button undone and the sleeves cuffed just right. That dark hair of his is perfectly messy on top of his head, and his fade is as fresh as always. He is handsome and flawless as ever.

And he's waiting for me to look up, so finally, I do.

Deep brown eyes lock with mine, and he smiles, a smile that widens as he looks at the item pressed between us, and I kind of want to run, though my feet don't seem to agree.

"I'm so damn happy for you," he murmurs, moving closer, and I subconsciously turn my head into his hand when he reaches up to tuck my hair behind my ear.

It's curled today, the top half held up high with a small rubber band, two long tresses left out in front and curled to match the rest. I'm wearing a tan dress, one of my old ones that's made of stretchy material, even if it was designed to be loose, and I layered an ivory sweater over it in an attempt to hide the fact that the seams are threatening to burst. If they haven't already.

A loud squeal sounds, and I blink out of the moment, looking from Mason to find Cameron, Brady, and Chase walking up, all dressed to impress.

"God, this is gorgeous!" Cameron beams, hugging me quickly before tossing her arms around Brady and Chase. "How do my dates look? Hot, right? I told them I would cockblock all night long if they ditched me before I found a single man of my own in here to keep me company."

"You are not finding a random man to do a damn thing." Brady glares, but Cameron just pushes up on her toes, her lips pressing to Chase's then Brady's cheek.

I swiftly snap a photo, laughing at her brand of crazy. "What are you guys doing here?"

Cameron shrugs. "Austin called a couple of hours ago and said the groom was ready to get out of here but didn't want the open bar to go to waste, so I guess the wedding party called some friends. There's a few more cars pulling up." She looks around, spots the bar, and promptly drags both Chase and Brady away. "'K, love you, bye! We're getting drinks before the line gets long!"

Chase gives me a playful eye roll as he walks away, and I smile, looking back to Mason.

Before I can say anything, I catch a glimpse of the bride past his shoulder, and sure enough, she's tucked under her husband's arm, sneaking toward the door.

I sidestep Mason and bend down on one knee. I get their shoes, peeking out between their guests on the dance floor. I get their hands tangled together and the kiss he presses to her knuckle. I even get the quick ass squeeze he thought no one saw, and just before they meet the opening to the hall, I shift a little more, catching their departure at an angle that opens up the shot to a full view of the room.

And then they're gone, and a long sigh escapes.

Mason's hand slides into my view, and I look up at him with a smile I can't contain. It must be a cheesy one, because he chuckles as he tugs me to my feet.

"You look happy," he says so softly, so torn by the idea as he reaches out, his knuckles brushing my cheek.

Tingles erupt over my skin, and my chin falls to my chest. "Mase..."

So many unspoken words hang between us, but when the song changes, a low, rumbling tempo taking over, the only ones that leave his mouth are three words that have left his lips before.

"Dance with me."

My head snaps up.

Dark brown eyes stare down at me. He's smiling easily now, but the uncertainty in his gaze isn't missed.

I shouldn't. I should make an excuse and walk away, so why do I set the camera down on my chair and offer him my hand when he's yet to extend his?

You know why...

The smile that curves his lips makes the decision worth it, and I can't help but laugh when he tugs me forward, spinning me silly until we're on the farthest, darkest edge of the dance floor.

Smirking, he tucks me in close, and my arms go around his neck in a practiced move, my wrists resting high on his shoulders.

We sway silently, and before I realize it, my eyes are closed, and my head is pressed against his chest.

His heartbeat thunders against my cheek, and I breathe deeply, pretending we're in a different time and place altogether.

A place without guilt or fear or regret.

That place does not exist.

CHAPTER 8
MASON

Before, July

As soon as the gang is sitting down, the food spread out along the table, I step up to the end of it. "So, plan for tonight." I clap my hands, making sure everyone's paying attention, but quickly point my focus to the tiny blond. My smile spreads slowly. "Pretty Little here has never been on a walk on the beach at night. That's a crime. So I wanna take her."

A smile tugs at her lips, and her man whips his head my way. He glares, and I wink at the little fucker. I don't know why, but I kind of enjoy messing with him, but there is a point to it. I gotta see how he reacts.

Will he be as douchey as his khaki shorts and collared shirt?

Will he slide right into our crew like he was born to be there the way the girl under his arm has?

I scoff to myself. *Doubtful.*

But if she likes him, I probably will, too. Maybe.

Not that I'll tell him that.

The little laugh that leaves Payton tells me his scowl isn't a constant thing, but she did run away to California without telling him and ignored his calls for a week, so it makes sense. At least he cares enough about her to show up. I should give him points for that.

Nah. Still don't like him much.

I glare right back, fucking with him some more. "Guess you can come. If you can keep your hands to yourself." I look pointedly at his arm around her shoulder.

"Mason," Parker warns, already fully used to my shit. He's hot for my cousin, after all.

"My hands stay where they belong—on her. And I'll take her on that walk, but you're welcome to come if you feel like showing us around."

Huh. Okay, he's got balls.

Jury is still out on how big.

I look to Payton, who tries to hide a shocked smile against his puny chest.

"All right, kid." I fight a grin when his eyes narrow at the word *kid*. "You've got sport. We'll play your way for a while."

Ari sighs and taps his shoulder. "Sorry, Deaton. But you're screwed. When Mason decides he cares, he's a thousand percent. No chill factor. Sorry to say…but he never lets up."

Everyone looks my way, so I force a grin. "She's my sister from another mister," I pop off, clearing my throat after. That was a stupid thing to say, but whatever. It's probably true anyway. That's how things are with Cameron. She's Ari's best friend, therefore she's family. Can't let anyone fuck with family.

"How old are you?" Chase pipes up, staring at Deaton with a blank expression.

I smack Chase's arm, nodding my approval at his question, and join in on the glaring.

"Seventeen," Deaton answers, unbothered by all the third degree he's been getting since he arrived in town.

Parker never got on our asses about the whole taking him down in the sand thing, so it's safe to say they didn't tell him. Probably too embarrassing for him, getting blindsided like that.

The dude should really pay attention to his surroundings. It's no wonder he's a wrestler and not a football player. He probably can't handle focusing on more than one person at a time.

"She's sixteen." Chase frowns.

Almost seventeen…

"I'm aware." Deaton pulls her closer. "Been in love with her since she was thirteen."

Chase nods, glancing over at Payton a moment before looking away.

But what the fuck, in love since thirteen? Ain't no way…is there?

The only thing I loved at thirteen was my PlayStation remote, pizza, and football.

I eye the pair curiously, and I don't realize my head is cocked as I stare until my sister's hand comes across the back of my skull, knocking me out of it.

I grin her way, and she rolls her eyes.

Oh yeah, and I love my family, but my sister the most. She's the be-all and end-all of my existence. My only purpose outside of football.

Without the two, I'd just be a dickhead who laughs when he's stressed and smiles when he wants to punch something but can't. Ari is the softness I don't have but wish I did.

That's okay, though. It just means when life is tough, I get to be the rock she needs.

And I need to be needed.

Maybe it's a brother thing or a twin thing. Maybe it's just a me thing, but I don't do well when I'm optional. It's why I was the best high school quarterback in the state two years running.

You don't *need* a backup quarterback. The position exists as a precaution, a *just in case*, and yeah, more often than not, that backup straps in and hits the field a handful of times a season, but the starter?

That number one slot?

You *need* that fucker.

And all my life, that fucker has been me because I make sure it is. I bust my ass all year long so there is never a doubt in anyone's mind.

"Okay, they're all overprotective fools, nothing new. Now, can we eat?" Cameron whines.

Everyone gets seated, and I quickly squeeze my ass into the seat right across from the happy little couple.

I stare at her until she looks up, then smile around a mouthful of burger.

"So, Deaton, where did you sleep last night?"

My sister slaps her forehead, and the others groan. But Payton?

Payton shakes her head, a small smile she tries to hide around her fork.

Satisfaction flickers through me, and I settle into my seat.

Mission accomplished.

PAYTON

Everyone is chatting among themselves as we follow the path of the sand closer to the pier. Mason and Lolli had been dying to go on that walk he talked about all day and finally got it started. Not sure why he's so excited, but maybe he just really wants ice cream like Lolli does. We've been walking for about ten minutes now, and she's mentioned it twice already.

I look down at my hand, fingers laced with Deaton's, a tension between us that's not normally there. He keeps peeking at me from the corner of his eye, so I give in and face him with what I hope is a reassuring smile.

"I love you, you know," I whisper, and Deaton looks over at me with kind eyes.

"I know." He presses a kiss to my cheek, and we both face forward.

Things between us feel a little fractured, which scares me.

For years, he's all I've had. My brother moved in with my dad, and my mom refused to allow me to see him, and then he didn't

73

fight to make sure he could. Then she ran off my friends and did her best to do the same with Deaton, so it's been hard.

He's been the only person I could lean on for so long, my best friend, and it feels unnatural for us to have colliding mindsets. I know it's my fault and he's just worried. I also know the longer I avoid the conversation he's dying to have, the worse it will likely get, but I sort of dropped two giant bombs on him in one day, and I'm a little afraid to find out if I'm the one holding the detonator or if he is.

I need more time, and while I want to be pissed that he doesn't want to waste another second, I can't be. As much as I don't want to talk, I get why he needs to, but unfortunately that doesn't make it any easier. Even now, in a group of ten or so, he keeps trying to whisper things, and I keep jumping into other people's conversations to avoid answering.

It's obvious as hell, but he doesn't call me out, just shifts his arm to rest on my shoulder instead.

The chatting of the others continues as we near the pier, the night growing louder around us when Mason jumps ahead, forcing us all to pause where we stand so he can have center stage.

"Ah shit." Mason claps, a glint in his eyes when they find mine, and somehow, I know he's coming for me before he even moves. He is facing us, the festivities a few yards behind him, and his attention moves to Deaton. "All right, big D—that's for Deaton, so don't be getting a big head."

Oh my god. A blush heats my cheeks instantly, and when Mason spots it, his grin grows, so I drop my gaze to the sand.

"Lemme steal your girl for a minute." Mason motions to the band taking the small stage. "Promise I'll give her back. I just want all the credit for this one."

"Maybe you should back off a bit, Mason." Chase frowns, the others shooting looks his way.

His best friend glares at him, but he dismisses him quickly when Deaton's arm drops from my shoulder.

"Nah, man. It's cool." His soft hand folds into mine, and he pulls it to his lips, kissing my knuckles. "If she wants to, she can, obviously. But I appreciate you not being a dick for once."

I smile at Deaton, knowing I'm the only person aware he's so far from the possessive type it's not even funny. He's enjoying playing with Mason, and I think it's adorable.

My brother's little friend group is kind of intimidating, even for me. They're all super close and from what I can tell, in each other's business but not in a shitty, judgy way. In fact, it seems to be the opposite, but who knows? Maybe they all talk shit about each other behind one another's backs.

Yeah, that seems more realistic...or maybe you're just so used to shitty people you don't know how to spot good ones?

I swallow, refocusing.

Deaton looks to me when I remain silent, so I plaster a fake smile on my face, hating how my thoughts and experiences always slacken the rope I'm forever climbing, putting even more distance between me and the rest of the world no matter how desperately I try to climb to its top.

Thankfully, Deaton is on the same side of that wall as I am. It's why he and I work so well. It's how we connected, alone and searching for a way out.

Pushing onto my toes, I kiss his cheek, muscles tensing as his fingers skim over the exposed skin of my stomach. Baby.

There's a baby in there.

Our baby.

Oh my god, I'm sixteen and pregnant.

Our eyes lock, and a softness falls over his, one that has panic rising in my throat, but then Mason's hand slides into view. Slowly, I tear my gaze from Deaton's to meet his.

Mason lets out a low chuckle, tipping his head with a grin that draws a small smile to my own lips. "You with me?" he asks, and I get the sense he can see it, my need for an escape.

I sweep a hand toward the band, and the two of us fall in step together.

"Hey, Mason!" Deaton calls not five seconds after we break from the others. We glance back, and Deaton's eyes lock with mine. "You got my family in your hands."

My lips part, my heart pounding wildly. That burning sensation I hate pricks at the backs of my eyes, so I slowly face forward, breaking the connection, and after a silent moment, Mason does the same.

I don't know what he's thinking, but I don't care enough to ask, and we don't speak as we move closer to the giant circle of string lights and laughter. The band members have taken their spots behind the mics, and as the song playing ends, the DJ welcomes them back to the makeshift stage.

They waste no time before strumming on their guitars, playing an acoustic version of "Feels" by Kiiara.

My lips curve, and then a wide chest is blocking my view.

I look up to find a grinning Mason, his arms outstretched as if he's midwaltz, minus the dance partner. "Dance with me."

With a spirited sigh, I take his hand and place the other on his shoulder, his other gently landing on my waist. We step to the music, at least a dozen others around us doing the same thing, though not separated like they're at a middle school dance the way we are.

My eyes keep going back to the band, and I watch the lead singer's fingers as they drift across the strings of his guitar in fluid motions. Up and down, ring finger to pointer to middle, and too many other various versions to track.

"So you've got a thing for musicians, do you?" Mason follows my line of sight "I'm telling Richie Rich."

My chuckle is low, and I shake my head, looking up into Mason's brown eyes. "No, I don't have a thing for musicians, and sorry to burst your bubble, but Deaton isn't the jealous type."

"Clearly," he scoffs, and I roll my eyes playfully.

He's not being an ass, just teasing, so I ignore his Richie Rich comment.

He's not wrong, though. At first glance, Deaton screams money. He looks like the typical private school kid with khaki shorts and a Hollywood smile. His skin is flawless and his eyes the color of dark chocolate. His family has more zeros in their bank account than all the James Bond movies combined, but none of that matters to him. In fact, he hates it. Hates his family.

I'm all he can count on in this world, same as he's been for me.

Sure, I have my brother, but after my dad left my mom, everything changed. I was too young to choose, and she tore me away from everyone, threatened them if they had any contact with me, and since she no longer had my brother's life under her sharp, wide-stretched claws, she took mine.

She stole my dad from me, then my brother and my friends. She even took my body, molding it into what she wanted it to be. She left me with nothing but a sick, twisted need for her acceptance. For the love she refused to give.

It wasn't until I found Deaton that I realized it wasn't that she refused but rather that she had no idea what the word even meant. Strangely, neither did I until I felt it for myself.

The love I've come to know is supportive and kind. It's safe and…honest.

"Hey." The softness in Mason's tone catches me off guard, and I look up, waiting for him to tell me everything will be okay, that having a baby is a blessing, even at sixteen, even if I haven't decided what I'm going to do. "Want me to kick his ass?"

My muscles freeze instantly, and then an unexpected laugh falls from my lips, his words the furthest thing from what I imagined. Mason starts laughing, too, and when he stretches our hands high above my head, I let him twirl me around a little.

Maybe things won't be so bad after all.

Maybe Deaton and I could really keep and care for this baby.

Or maybe I'll screw it all up and end up just like my mother.

CHAPTER 9
PAYTON

Now, July 5

"I've wanted to dance with you like this since that day." *Mason's* confession slams into me, and I think a small gasp slips through my lips. "I didn't know it then, but I did."

His mind strayed just as mine had, and it's as confusing as it is predictable.

As comforting as it is overwhelming.

"I miss you," he whispers, and my eyes fly open.

My breath hitches and I tense, but his hands continue sliding along my lower back, the heat of his palm calming and rattling at the same time.

"Mason, please."

He's quiet for several seconds, and I realize we're no longer moving but standing still as the room moves around us. He pulls back, his thumb gliding along my jawline, those dark eyes locking on mine in desperation.

Tension tugs at my ribs, and I squash my thoughts, but it's too late, and now my pulse is jumping higher and higher. It's fucking *flying*.

"I can't do this." I tear away, rushing over and grabbing my camera, hastily stuffing it in my bag.

Mason appears beside me, gripping my shoulder gently, but I spin away, and what was meant to be a brisk walk turns into a full-on run. People turn to stare, but I ignore them, pretending not to hear the harsh slap of his shoes following behind.

Brady catches my eye on my exit, and he abandons the girl he had pinned to the wall in a heartbeat. I don't know what he sees, but I know the moment he realizes I'm not the only person running out of the party. His gaze flicks behind me, widening before slicing back to mine.

He gives a curt jerk of his chin, and I'm out the door but not before hearing the scuffle behind me.

There's a bit of a crash, followed by a shout. "Let me go!"

"Can't."

"Swear to god, Brady!"

The door slams closed behind me, and I dart to the left, doing my best to disappear into the darkness in case the quarterback escapes the arms of his lineman.

Unfortunately for me, I wasn't fast enough, and Brady must have underestimated Mason's need to get to me, as footsteps pound the payment at my back. There's no escaping now, so I brace for the onslaught.

"I said I can't do this!" I shout, preparing to throw out any excuse in the book as I whirl around, but the words die on my lips, my mouth clamping shut.

Mason isn't behind me. Chase is.

He jerks to a stop, his palms rising as if he's just come across a wild bear, but when my shoulders fall with instant relief, he tucks his hands in his pockets, offering a gentle smile. "Hi."

"Hi."

He glances toward the parking lot and back, a single brow raised. "Wanna get out of here?"

"Yes."

Just like that, he turns, and with eager steps, I follow.

79

Chase drives for several minutes, coming to a stop on a dark street in front of one of those giant, industrial-style rolling doors.

"Are you selling me off to drug lords?"

He doesn't respond, just chuckles and hops out. Reluctantly, I follow, running to catch up with him and crossing my arms as we walk toward the building.

"I feel like a guy in overalls with bodies buried under his porch is about to walk out with a wrench in his hand."

Chase throws his head back on a laugh, glancing my way with a grin. "That's oddly specific."

"My imagination is pretty thorough."

Shaking his head, he steps inside first, and I stick close behind.

Thankfully, it's not so terrifying once we enter. There are actual lights on the inside, but the small vacant desk that comes into view is kind of concerning.

My steps slow, but then low voices reach us, and I look to the far right to find a few people kicking back on a sofa pushed up against the wall.

They look up as we enter and smile.

"Hey, welcome to Riot and Rage," the guy says as the girl climbs to her feet.

"You guys come to let off some steam?" she asks.

I look to Chase, who grins from me to her. "Yup. For two, please."

"You got it."

Ten minutes and a scary release of liability form later, we're standing in the center of a giant room wearing goggles, gloves, and coveralls so long I had to roll mine four times.

A bat hangs from my hands, and a crowbar hangs from his.

There are random doors and mismatched lamps sitting atop hideous end tables. Mirrors hang in a mess of discoordination from one wall to the next, and there's an ancient flat-screen sitting in the center, just right there on the hard floor.

"So…" I draw out, tucking the bat to my chest. "What now?"

Chase smiles, then turns, bringing the crowbar down on an old fax machine.

I yelp as little plastic pieces fly every which way, my jaw dropping with a laugh a moment later. "What the…"

"Did you think we were coming in here to decorate?" he teases, spinning and taking out a lamp. He moves silently from item to item, a shadow falling over his features as he goes.

I glance around the space, unease settling in my gut.

A loud groan escapes Chase, so I peek behind me, finding him heaving over a broken picture frame, the random couple's smiles purposely scratched out, and it clicks.

This place, it's set up for very specific reasons, filled with all the things that can morph in your mind into exactly what you need them to…the object of your inner issue, daring you to destroy it.

To take it by the horns and snap it right off the bull's head.

I turn, my eyes immediately going to a long mirror on the wall opposite me.

It's wide and framed in cheap plastic, smudges of who knows what decorating the center. I walk closer, my hands shaking as I pause directly in front of it.

My eyes lift, catching on the girl on the other side.

She's…broken and weak. A screwup. Fat by other people's terms.

She's everything her mother said she'd be…

My jaw clenches, and I close my eyes, tension radiating through my every pore.

A warm hand brushes against my back, and my eyes fly open, meeting a pair of green ones in the mirror. After a moment, Chase nods and steps back.

It takes me a second to mentally check out or maybe check back in, I don't know, and face my reflection.

I'm not cowering in a corner, begging for someone's approval.

I'm not killing myself to fit someone else's standard.

I'm not the girl I used to be.

I think I'm better.

I lift the bat, shattering the image, staring as piece after piece of the girl before me disappears until there's nothing but a dingy white wall in its wake.

The broken shards crunch and crash to the floor, and an unexpected laugh leaves me. I look over my shoulder, my smile far too wide as I meet Chase's gaze.

He smirks, and then it's on.

We take our weapons to everything in the space, trading and tossing, and it's fucking liberating.

I can't wipe the grin from my face, and when we're done, kicking off our coveralls, I finally pause a second to breathe, take Chase in, and start laughing.

He raises a brow, and I shake my head, my hand going to my stomach I'm laughing so hard now. "What's so funny?" he asks.

"Us. This." I motion between us, moving my hand up and down. "We literally came from a wedding. You're wearing slacks and a button-down with black smears all over your face and you have a mace ball perched on your shoulder like it's normal. I'm in a dress with curls that took way too long and more makeup than I've worn in a year, holding a freaking sledgehammer. We look like Harley Quinn and The Joker."

Chase laughs, too, and then throws his arm over my shoulder, leading us back toward the front. "Nah, we look good." He beams, and my own mood matches.

Not even the cold night air slapping me in the face as we exit can kill the buzz in the air, and it's still just as present when, thirty minutes later, we're seated on the tailgate with milkshakes and a basket of garlic fries.

I sigh for what seems like the millionth time, and Chase just chuckles beside me.

"I take it you've never been to a rage room before?" he asks, tossing me a hoodie before yanking one over his dress shirt and closing the cab doors.

He rejoins me, and I take a break from my shake to answer.

"Definitely not. My mother would have an aneurysm at the mere mention of it. She was a 'work your frustrations out in the gym' kind of woman, but you know, only if it's me. Anything to get me to burn off calories, even if I hadn't consumed any that day." I frown, thinking about it. "She never worked out and looked flawless all the time. It was annoying." I look up suddenly, wincing. "Sorry. I'm always such a mood killer."

"Nah," Chase disagrees with a smile.

"What about you? Beat things up often?"

He digs a spoon into his sundae, shaking his head. "Never needed to before. I get to knock people around or get knocked around on the field enough."

I tip my head at him. "Usually."

He looks over, pausing with a spoon at his lips.

"You *usually* get knocked around enough that it helps *tame the beast*." I try to make light of the subject that's not really light at all.

It sort of works, and the chuckle that leaves Chase is only slightly strained.

"Yeah, I guess you're right." A heavy sigh escapes him, and he frowns at his pile of caramel syrup as if it's personally offended him. "Usually."

Lifting my camera from where it's sitting in my lap, I hold it up and take his picture.

Chase's head snaps up, a small glare fixed on his face.

I shake it back and forth. "Because you look so tragic. I figure I'll show you this when you're back to your happy-go-lucky self."

"I'm not happy-go-lucky."

"Yeah, you are." I pause, testing the waters a little to see if maybe he wants to talk about it. "Or you were, but not so much lately."

Chase's brows dip even lower, but his features quickly go blank as he faces forward. "It's not what you think," he finally says.

"I mean, it would be okay if it was." I lift a shoulder. "If anyone knows how little sense the way missing or wanting someone you can't have messes with you, it's me. Half the time, I feel like a rubber band, stretching and stretching, only to snap right back to where I started with a sting that wasn't there before. It's...exhausting." I tense, peeking at him from the corner of my eye to find him staring. "I didn't mean to throw that at you. I'm fine, really. I'm just—" Cutting myself off, I turn to Chase, my lips flattening, and before I know what I'm doing, I'm running my mouth to him once again. "That's a lie," I tell him. "I'm not fine. Sometimes things feel okay, but I'm never *fine*. I don't even like that stupid word. Fine. What does it even mean?"

I stand up, pacing the length of the bed of the truck.

I never thought things could get worse, but here I am, twelve months past what I thought was the worst day of my life, and guess what? Things. Are. Worse.

Things are worse, and like my mother always said, it's all my fault.

My life is crumbling at my feet, and I'm the one holding the hammer.

I'm losing it.

A flash blinds me, and I look to Chase in confusion to find his phone in hand, a soft smile on his lips. "Because you look so tragic right now. Figured I'd show it to you when you're back to your *pretend* happy-go-lucky self."

It takes a moment, but a laugh leaves me, and I drop back onto the tailgate and bump his shoulder the way he did mine last time.

Picking up my milkshake, I give it a little swirl before taking another drink.

We sit in silence for a while, and it's nice. Relaxing, even if I did have a moment a handful of minutes ago.

I'm so lost in the peace the night provides, I jolt when the warmth of Chase's skin brushes against my own. My eyes fly to his, but his are on his knuckle as he drags it along the side of my mouth.

A small frown builds, and when he looks up, he lifts his hand to show a dab of ice cream before he uses a napkin to wipe it clean.

I hold my shake out in his direction. "Wanna trade?"

Chase looks down at his sundae, a glare growing before he passes it my way. "Yeah." He sighs. "I think I'm ready for something new."

The way he says it, I'm not so sure he's talking about ice cream, but that's none of my business.

I take the sundae and eat every bite. Tomorrow, I'll regret it, but isn't that the story of my life?

I used to think I was a model of self-control.

I'm not.

I'm a mess of self-sustaining tendencies and destroying everything I touch.

I'm a damn plague.

CHAPTER 10
MASON

Now, July 9

"We're having tacos."

"I'm tired of tacos."

"Who gets tired of tacos?"

"The people who have to cut all the toppings up every time, that's who."

"Well, maybe if you paid attention when Noah's teaching Ari tricks in the kitchen, you wouldn't be stuck with the shitty tasks no one else wants and you can't fuck up."

Brady dodges Cameron's right hook with a laugh, throwing her over his shoulder right there in the middle of the store.

Ari sighs, shaking her head at our friends as they disappear around the aisle, Cameron cussing him out all the way. "Bet you five bucks he's taking her to the cookie aisle as an apology."

A smirk pulls at my lips. "I'll keep my five, thanks."

Noah walks up, locking his arms around my twin's middle. "You two really are best friends if food works to get both of you into b—"

I raise a brow at him, and he pivots.

"Brunch."

Fighting a smirk, I point to Chase as he steps up. "We'll get the meat. You two get the veggies."

Chase rubs the back of his head. "I need some things for my protein shakes…"

"Chase and I are on fruits and veggies, then." Noah looks to Chase. "You ever tried adding peanut butter powder instead of peanut butter?"

Chase glances away, and I swear it's a shame thing. He can't quite meet Noah's eyes without flinching, but he knows it's his own doing and mans up every time. "Does it help thin it out more?"

"Oh, yeah, man." The two start walking, Noah talking as they go, and Ari and I stare after them until they're gone.

She looks to me with a half smile and leads us toward the meat counter. "Noah hates the tension in the room when Chase is around."

"A little tension is good for Chase. He can't be let off the hook too easy, and he doesn't want to be."

"And that's exactly why Noah hates it. Chase is punishing himself, *distancing* himself. It's not right, Mase. He's family, too."

An uncomfortable sensation builds in my gut, just like it does every time I think about how my best friend tried to get in the middle of my sister and Noah when the couple was at their most vulnerable. The truth is it sickened me to see him go after her when he did, especially after learning he had his chance and blew it…but at the same time, a small part of me understood.

Or maybe that's a new revelation, considering.

All I know is if before I was against doing something a little less than honorable to get what I wanted, I'm not anymore. You'll never change the score if you don't dare to make the pass, right?

I want the girl, and I'm not sure there's a move I wouldn't make to get her.

"Are you still mad at him?" my sister asks.

Pulling a deep breath in, I slowly let it out, a small shake of my head following. "I was pissed, but I think I was more disappointed than anything, and not because of what he was doing.

87

It's like I've said before. Chase is a good man. I know that, you know that, and we're all young. There's a lot of shit we're going to fuck up along the way. What I didn't like was that he had you and only decided to do something real about it *after* your accident."

Panic pricks at my skin at the thought of everything that went down just seven months ago. I thought I was losing my sister, my twin, and for the first time, no matter what I did, I couldn't protect her. I failed at my position, and I damn well knew it.

And then she healed, and I realized something.

My sister had someone who meant everything to her, who wanted to give her the world, and that meant she didn't need me anymore.

Football was over for the season, so they didn't need me either.

I was floating away, and only when a certain strawberry blond was around did that sense of worthlessness deflate.

I don't know why it's there in the first fucking place. I hate it, and it makes no sense.

My parents loved the shit out of us, raised us well, and had our backs no matter what. They came to all my games, and we had more family time than not. We weren't neglected or expected to raise ourselves once we were old enough to know how. I had friends, and I was as happy as any other kid who had a good home like mine.

Regardless of all that, though, I was still the "big brother." The only brother.

My dad lost his sister when he was young, and after I heard the story of how she was killed by a car while riding her bike, I saw the sadness and fear in his eyes, and I knew I had to be the protector. My family needed me to shield our home from that same fate, because we wouldn't survive a loss like that.

I wouldn't survive, so watching over her became my job. If she fell off the swings, I was there to pick her up. If she was scared, I would make her feel safe. If someone pushed her, I put them on their ass. There was no me without her, at least not until football came along.

Only when I was on the field did I discover I was capable of caring about myself, too, and it didn't take long for us all to realize I was better than most in the sport. Suddenly, not only Ari needed me, but so did my team. It was like the other half of my brain sparked to life.

Just like that, I had two purposes in life, and I fucking thrived on that fact.

"Trauma affects everyone different, Mase," Ari whispers, bringing me back to the conversation at hand. "You can't blame them, hate them, or turn your back on them. The same way people process differently, they heal differently, too." She looks my way, and I meet her gaze. "And some take a lot longer than others."

A scoff leaves me, and I fight a smile. "Really? Just gonna leave that line hanging and hope I bite?"

Her brows draw in, worry blanketing her features. "Are you going to?"

A small scowl builds, and I look away. I hate that she's concerned for me. She shouldn't have to stress herself out over me and my shit.

Sighing, I change the subject. "I'm headed back to campus in the morning. Coach has a new trainer on staff he wants me working with. The team's due back from break in a few days, and I guess since I'm the new Noah, it's my job to make sure shit's dialed in before they get there."

Ari waits, hoping I'll at least touch on what she was not so subtly trying to say, so I try to find a way to say what Ari thinks she knows without confirming or denying.

"Last year, I was champing at the bit to get there, and last night, I was sitting around trying to think of excuses my coach would believe so I could stay here a little longer." My frown doubles. "Last summer, I felt good about the future, but I didn't come back to what I left here last time." I glance her way from the corner of my eye.

Ari's face is full of understanding, and a small, sad smile curves her lips.

The line moves, and then it's our turn, so we face the butcher with tight grins.

I don't even hear what she ends up ordering, the sudden ringing in my ears is too loud.

I have to leave tomorrow, and I'm fucking terrified.

Too fast, the next morning rolls around, and when I walk out to my truck with my duffel hanging from my fist, my fears are validated.

Because unlike the last time, there's no pretty little blond standing beside the hood with a baby carriage, just making sure she gets the chance to say goodbye.

It's just me.

Me and the overwhelming sense of fucking *failure*.

"Last one, Johnson!" Coach Rogan shouts from the sideline.

I line up with the cones, dashing forward, only to cut back into the pocket. Assistant Coach Davies shoves out his pad from the left, and I roll right, evading. I dash to the marker, pull my arm back, and fake a pass, then return to the start.

I drop back, sling myself to the left when my secondary coach, Coach Nichols, approaches my right, my feet cutting across the grass. My arm shoots out, and this time, the ball launches from my fingertips.

A whistle is blown loudly, and I spin with a pant.

"Coach." My hands go to my hips, my neck stretching to

allow my lungs a deeper breath. "I got more in the tank. I can go another—"

"Just because you can doesn't always mean you should. What did I say about releasing?"

It's a rhetorical question, so I don't bother with an excuse as to why I let the ball fly.

"You're on a detailed workout for a reason. Stick to it. We'll see you back here before dinner for your brief with Coach Manu. Shower and recovery. After that, head over to get your meals sorted with the dietician. They should have everything settled. You just need to make your selections and replace what you might not like."

"Yes, Coach."

He eyes me a moment before nodding. "We're counting on you, kid. Now get out of here and get cleaned up."

"Yes, Coach." A bolt of electricity fires in my bones, and I give a curt nod. "Thank you."

They're counting on me.

They need me.

Mason Johnson.

I tear the towel from my shorts, swiping at the sweat rolling down my face and the back of my neck. A satisfied exhale burns its way past my throat, my workout having really done me in good, and I chuckle at myself.

I feel good. I've never been in such good shape in my life, and I'm so fucking ready for the season to start. This is everything I've ever wanted, and I'm going to show this team and everyone else why I deserve to be the guy who leads them to victory.

My head is high, and I can't stop the smile on my lips as I strip down, turn on and step into the cold spray of the shower. My muscles tense for a moment but relax a second later. I press my palms to the cool tile and let the water wash the sweat off my skin before turning to lean my shoulders against the tile.

My eyes close, and a laugh escapes. Man, this year is bound

to be epic. My best friends and I are going to do everything we talked about at twelve years old: start together on a D1 college football field in front of hundreds of thousands of screaming fans, be it in person or on TV. Avix University is top tier, the record Noah led us to the last few years earning us that prime-time spot.

Now it's my turn.

I'm the man they'll lean on.

The crowd will wear my number proudly on their chests.

I need to get Pretty Little a season pass.

My face falls instantly.

With jerky movements, I wash up, get out, and head back to my locker. Digging into my bag, I yank on a fresh pair of boxers and some navy Avix U sweatpants. My phone is in my hands in seconds, my frown doubling as I glance down at the screen.

Zero missed calls, no new messages.

I drop onto the bench seat, opening up my and Payton's message thread, nothing but blue bubbled texts for pages and pages, dating back to May, the newest the one I sent this morning.

It wasn't over the top, and I wasn't prying. Neither was the one I sent last night when I was alone in my room.

Me: I'm back on campus.

Me: Good morning. Tell Little D hi for me.

With a sigh, I back out, checking the rest of my notifications and finding Cameron posted a picture on Instagram this morning. I click on the icon, and the image appears. I jerk upright, glaring at the screen.

It's a photo of all the girls at the café down the road from the beach house. They probably walked there like we all used to. Cameron is taking the shot, Mia and her on one side of the table, Lolli, Ari…and Payton on the other. And at the end of the table is one of those old wooden high chairs, my little man perched right inside it, a blanket tucked against his back. He's smiling, too, his fingers stuck halfway in his mouth, and my eyes soften at the sight.

He's so damn adorable, his dark curls all over the place and hanging over his forehead. I scroll to the next picture, and a weighted warmth falls on my chest. He's got the little football Lolli bought him in his hand, my signature right there in the shot as he tucks it to his chest.

Maybe the little man will be a running back when he gets older.

The next shot is taken from high above, showing only their hands and the plates they ordered. A scowl pulls at my brows, and I tug the screen closer. Payton's pretty pink painted fingernails are delicately placed at the edge of her plate—which is nothing more than a pile of fruit. That's not what has my blood pressure rising, though. It's the phone that's sitting right beside her on the table.

The phone that she would have seen my message on last night or woke to this morning.

That she's seen and ignored all my messages and calls on for months now.

After everything that happened between us.

And then even after all that, when she stopped ignoring me and broke her silence on the Fourth.

After she gave in again and let me hold her on the dance floor four nights ago.

I swallow, my leg bouncing anxiously.

She's letting me go, I know it. I fucking feel it, and it...hurts.

I don't want to do this.

I can't fucking do this.

My mind is screaming, my adrenaline spiking, and it's too much.

I need to clear my head. Again.

Shoving my earbuds in, I start a random playlist, toss my shit in my bag, and throw it over my shoulder. I shove through the door of the school gym dedicated to athletes alone and move over to the treadmill.

I hop on, hit the incline, and turn the thing to max speed.

System of a Down screams angrily in my ears, and I bob my head, pumping my arms as if trying to scale a fucking mountain that seems to double its height every fucking time I reach the top.

I run and run, and I don't stop until my knees buckle and I fall, flying backward until my spine slams into the weight machine behind me.

I groan, dropping my head back, but I don't get up.

I sit there glaring at the man in the mirror, wondering if he's enough to get all he wants out of this world.

All the while knowing damn well he might not be.

I might fucking not be.

CHAPTER 11
PAYTON

Now, July 10

Ari gives Deaton another kiss to the cheek before wrapping her arms around my neck for a quick goodbye, and I do my best to keep smiling. Cameron is next, and then they're piling into the car.

"Bye, girlie! Chat soon!" Cameron blows a kiss, hits the gas, and they're off, officially leaving me and Deaton alone.

Their car doesn't even make it to the stop sign before my lips begin to quiver, and my arms tighten around my son. I walk swiftly into the house, closing and locking the door behind me and bouncing him in place a moment while I try to gather myself.

Everyone is gone. All of them.

This is what you wanted, I try to remind myself, but it doesn't feel like what I want.

Or maybe it's that it's not what I need. I don't know, but I'm alone. My brother and Kenra are gone, Lolli, Nate, and Noah with them, the group headed over to the Tomahawk headquarters, where Noah will get settled into the apartment closer to the NFL practice field. Nate's going to share with him since he's a sophomore at the University of San Diego this year and isn't required to stay in the dorms. None of them are coming home tonight.

Everyone is back to normal life, college, work, playing for a professional freaking football team, and here I am…essentially in the same place I was last year, on this very day.

Two point five seconds away from a nervous breakdown, overflowing with anxiety, pain, confusion, and, the worst of all, wishful fucking thinking.

Last year, I stood in this very place in the entryway, though it was the one next door, and wished Deaton would stay, that we had more time so I could talk to him about where life was going to take us now that we were pregnant. But his brother showed up, and he said he had to go home or his parents would come and make things worse. He promised everything would be okay, that we would figure it out and he'd call me when he got home.

Today I'm standing here wishing for nearly the same things. That he didn't go and we had the time to talk, that I got the chance to tell him I wanted to raise the baby together and I was just afraid, that I wasn't going to give our son up for adoption, and that he would get to be the father he wanted to be the moment he learned I was pregnant.

The only difference is last year, everyone was here, so I wasn't alone when the call came through to say there had been an accident and we needed to get to the hospital as quickly as we could. Ironically, the call wasn't even for me but for Nate, because his sister was in the same car Deaton was that night.

Today, I am alone…because no one realizes what today is, which is understandable. No one was affected by the loss of the boy I loved the way I was. I'm sure it was hard on his parents in one way or another, as horrible as they were. Considering how poorly they treated him, they don't deserve this frame of thinking, but I have to believe they mourned him in some way, that they experienced some sort of loss and sadness. He deserves to be missed, and I'll do everything I can to make sure he's never forgotten.

My son will know his father even if he never gets to *know* his father.

One year.

It's been one full year without you, and it still feels like yesterday.

Deaton's little hands come up, pressing into my cheeks and squishing my lips, and a choked sob slips past them. Thankfully, the wateriness of my smile is missed by my baby boy, and when he smiles back, there's nothing but joy and his big blue eyes. I tug him close, pressing kisses to the side of his head as I play with the dark curls that mirror his father's.

Pulling a deep breath into my lungs, I take one single second to settle myself, and then I put on my happy face and bounce my little boy around the room.

We play with his plushies and then his blocks. We go down to the ocean and dip our toes in the water and have lunch on the patio.

I selfishly try to keep him awake as long as possible, and he makes it well past his nap time, but when he starts to fall asleep in his high chair, I suck it up and lift him into my arms. We settle on the couch, because I can't stand the thought of putting him down, and he quickly falls asleep on my chest.

Within minutes, my mind is spinning once more, and the panic is back so strong, I nearly choke for air but do my best to keep my heart rate steady, since his little cheek is resting against it.

Tears fall from my eyes, the saltiness slipping between the cracks of my lips, and I drop my head back to keep them from landing atop his head.

Lifting my phone into the air, I hastily scroll through the contacts, pausing when I reach his name. My eyes squeeze closed, and I shake my head.

You can do this. You can get through today. Get through today, and tomorrow will be better, and no one has to know.

I drop my phone to my side, but after a moment, I pick it back up and send a different message before I can think twice.

I toss my phone and forget about it, cuddling my son tight. Thankfully, he stirs only forty-five minutes later, his little head popping up with a grin.

"Hi, mister man." I kiss his cheeks and change him, and we settle on his nursery floor.

We read a couple of books and sing along to a couple of shows. We take another walk, a longer one this time, and then we have dinner, just the two of us at the kitchen table. We take a bath and stay in there until we're cold and shriveled, and it's not long until he's rubbing at his eyes some more.

This time, I know I can't hold him as he sleeps. He'll be out all night now.

I rock him slowly, and all too soon, his little snores sound in my ear. With shaky limbs, I push to my feet and ease him down into his bed. After one last longing look, I turn on the monitor and close the door.

And then I collapse against it. I drop to my ass, my head falling into my hands as a sob racks through me uncontrollably, shaking me to the bone and leaving me gasping.

I grip my throat and shove to my feet, stumbling through the house and out the back door. I rush to the railing, clutching it with both hands as I bend at the waist, my head hanging between my extended arms, and I cry.

Cries that are interrupted by the soft shuffle of sand.

My head snaps up, and every muscle in my body locks tight.

Mason stands there, still in his practice gear, cleats and all.

"Mase..." My voice breaks.

He climbs the steps slowly, a soft smile on his lips, his arms hanging at his sides stiffly, as if he wants nothing more than to reach for me but isn't sure if he should.

All worries wash from my mind, and I throw myself into his chest.

Instantly, his strong arms wrap around me, holding me close, his cheek resting against my head.

"I've got you, Pretty Little. I'm here," he whispers. "I've been here."

Confused, I pull back and look up at him.

98

A tender smile tugs at his lips, the longing in his gaze almost too much, but I don't look away. His hand comes up to cup my cheek, and his voice is raspy when he speaks. "I came as soon as I could...just in case you needed me."

I latch onto his wrist, holding on for dear life.

He knows. He remembered what today was. He knew how hard it would be for me.

He remembered for me.

"This is why you've been distant," he guesses.

I nod, unable to form the words and unwilling to admit he's only partially right.

"I should have realized, and I'm sorry I didn't. I just got in my head and thought maybe you changed your—"

"Payton, you back here?" a voice calls from the side of the house, and both of us freeze.

Mason goes rigid against me, and when I look up, his eyes are staring to the left. I follow, spotting a head of sandy brown hair.

Chase jerks to a stop, his brows drawn in confusion as he looks at the two of us.

"Uh...hey." He nods at Mason, and slowly, his eyes come back to mine as he lifts the little bag in his hands. "Brought the shakes."

I swallow, fingers digging tighter into Mason's top.

"What's going on?" Chase asks cautiously, his eyes moving back to his best friend's.

Tension tugs at my chest, and I force myself to look to Mason, but his eyes are still pointed at the newcomer.

"What's wrong?" Chases pushes.

Mason's muscles flex against me, and my stomach churns at the blank sheet of his expression.

"Mase," I breathe.

Gently, with movement so slow it tears at something within me, he removes his arm from around me and his hand from my face, and lastly his fingers latch around my hand, untangling my grip on his wrist. He steps back, and only when no part of him is touching me do his brown eyes drop to meet mine.

"You called…him?" He speaks the words so low, I almost miss them. With a slight shake of his head, he stumbles back a step.

"Mase."

He looks away.

"Mason."

He shuffles farther away, and acid bubbles burst in my gut. When his cleats meet the sand, he starts to run.

I jerk forward, a barbed wire wrapping around and puncturing my lungs. Panic sets in, and I launch myself toward the stairs "*Mason!*" I scream.

But he doesn't answer.

He's gone now, too.

I fall to my ass and cry until I pass out.

Just like I did on this very same night *exactly* one year ago today.

CHAPTER 12
PAYTON

Before, July

Numb.

I feel…nothing.

"There's been an accident."

Nate's voice plays on repeat in my head, over and over, and it doesn't stop. Not on the three-hour drive to the hospital, not in the elevator on the way up to the fourth floor.

Not when my brother whispers words I don't hear in my ear, and not when Mason bends and puts himself eye level with me. His are sloped, lips moving, but if he's speaking, I have no knowledge of it.

"There's been an accident."

"There's been an accident."

"There's been an accident."

A hand settles on my shoulder, but I pull away.

I can't feel. If I feel, the numbness will go away. If the numbness goes away, the worry will come and ruin everything. That's what Mom always said to me, right? Worrying is a worthless emotion that does nothing but destroy and prevent. Be cold, and you'll get further in life.

It's probably bullshit, much like every other word that trips from her poisonous tongue.

At some point, we arrived at the hospital, though I have

no recollection of getting out of the vehicle. All I know is I'm standing at the start of a short hallway, three giant, crimson letters painted onto a pair of double doors glaring back at me that read ICU.

We've been called to the intensive care unit.

I'm so stuck in my own head, I don't realize I've yet to step from the elevator until the doors begin to hide the ominous acronym. Darting forward, I stop it with my shoe, then slip out, realizing the others are all huddled at the end, a woman with brown hair I've never met now with them.

My steps are slow, and with each one taken, the numbness begins to crumble. Little by little, my taut muscles reveal themselves, the ache between my shoulder blades deep and uncomfortable.

My body is rigid, my jaw clenched tight.

"Mom?" Ari shouts, and I jolt at the sudden sound.

Everyone turns to find two women running down the hall. They have to be someone's mothers.

My thought is proven right when one wraps her arms around Nate, the other Ari, and that's when their sobs reach me.

My arm shoots out, and I grip onto my brother's wrist. In my periphery, I watch his head turn my way, but I couldn't look away from the women if I tried.

This is off.

Something is wrong.

They're crying, yes, but there's a hint of something in their eyes.

Hope.

They have hope.

Kenra's mom and aunt…have hope.

Nate pulls back and looks down at his mother. "Ma?"

Tears slip from her eyes, and she swallows. "They said they lost control of the car, flipped it into a ditch."

"No," Parker rasps, and warm liquid coats my nails where they're pressed against his skin.

102

My brother starts to say something, but Nate cuts him off with a scream.

"Mom!" Nate shouts, scared for his sister. "Is Kenra okay?"

"Yes, sweetheart," she whispers. "She's okay." She glances this way, toward Parker. "But we're not in the clear yet. She's unconscious. They're running tests."

Relief fills the hall, the others dropping against the wall and clutching their chests, but the woman's words have the opposite effect on me.

Dread, cold and vivid, courses through me, and my limbs begin to shake.

"You!"

The shrill voice is one I could never mistake, and every vein in my body goes cold.

I can't look, don't dare to, and my heart pounds in unison with every click of heels against the floor.

Her shadow falls over me, and there's suddenly no hiding. Her eyes stab at mine, the hatred within them hard to miss.

"Excuse me, miss. I—"

Mason's voice cuts off in the exact moment a cold, cosmetic hand whips across my face so hard, I can feel the imprint left behind like the heat of a branding iron pressed into my skin.

I don't flinch nor look away, but everyone else? They flip the fuck out.

They scream and shout, and when I pull my head forward, moisture pricking my eyes from the sting, I find Nate has Deaton's mother's arms restrained behind her back.

Parker tugs me a few paces away, and Mason steps in front of me, blocking me from the vicious woman's view, but the numbness, it's completely gone now, and a wave of unease crashes through me.

I stumble, my back hitting the wall.

"Payton?" My brother's worried voice breaks through the ringing in my ears.

103

He moves in front of me, but my eyes slide to the left, once again landing on the double doors at the end.

ICU.

Mrs. Vermont.

"There's been an accident."

"She's okay."

My limbs give out, and I'm falling because I just *know.*

I feel it in my bones, in my heart.

His absence. His sweet soul and whispered words.

His promise.

He promised he'd be back.

"Payton!" Parker screams, falling with me. Mason is there, too, maybe someone else. "Payton, talk to me."

My vision blurs, my eyes closing as my hand subconsciously moves to my belly. It shakes but presses against the soft, stretched skin there hidden behind a hoodie.

Did you leave me all alone?

"This is *all* your fault, little girl," Mrs. Vermont screeches. "Every time you think of my son, remember that. I told you you didn't deserve him. This must be the world's way of proving me right."

My chest cracks open.

"Whoa, what the fuck, lady?" Mason glares, and his mother instantly tells him to stop. "Uh-uh. No way, Mama. This lady just—"

"This lady just lost her son, Mason." His mom's whisper might as well have been spoken into a microphone. Because there it is.

The confirmation.

He's…gone.

My organs squeeze the life out of me. I'm choking on nothing, shaking and convulsing, tearing in fucking two.

But I don't think I'm moving.

My brother reaches down, pushing the hair from my eyes, and his touch stings like a live wire. I'm screaming, but no sound leaves me. I'm being electrocuted from the inside out. I must be.

More voices join us then, but all it sounds like is water in my ears.

Suddenly knuckles are under my chin, and my eyes are lifted to meet a pair of green ones.

Parker says something, and Chase nods. In the next moment, the burn of the cold floor disappears, replaced with a hint of warmth. My eyes open again, and I'm in the air.

I think I hear screaming, and then…nothing.

———————

The soft murmur of voices splinters through the darkness, and I wince at the sound, my head pounding with the threat of an oncoming migraine.

Fingers brush along my hair, and my own sink farther into the material beneath them.

"Peep," my brother whispers.

My eyelids feel like weights, but I somehow manage to lift them, slowly meeting his gaze as he kneels before me.

"Parker…" I blink in confusion, the arm wrapped along my middle tightening, but when I shift, they loosen, and I throw my own around my brother. "Can I go home? *Home to your house* home?"

"Are you sure, Payton?" he asks.

He says something else, but I don't hear it. I'm already nodding.

"I'm sure. I don't want to be here." I can't be here. "Please."

"I'll take her home. Stay with her."

My muscles tense, and I pull away, slowly looking behind me to the person whose lap I'm sitting on.

My brother asks, once again, if we're sure, but Chase doesn't look his way, just offers me a small smile. "Yeah, man. I got her."

My ribs rattle, a chill breaking over my skin. He sat with me this whole time?

How long has it even been?

Chase gives me a small nod, and then he pushes to his feet, not asking if I want to be put on my own. He carries me from the room the same way he held me inside it.

My lips start to tremble, and I squeeze my eyes closed.

I don't want to see the hall.

I don't want to see the others.

I don't want to do this without you, Deaton.

Tears leak from my eyes, and Chase's arms tighten around me.

And because the universe decided I wasn't beat on enough for the day, the only person worse than Miranda Vermont makes her presence known.

My mother is here, and by the sound of it, she's been waiting for a while.

"Where the hell is she?" her threatening voice shrieks. "I gave her long enough."

"She needs to be with people who care about her right now," Parker snaps. "Not someone who treats her like a puppet."

My body bounces slightly with Chase's advancing steps, and I close my eyes tighter, refusing to look her way. I can't face her, not right now, not when I know what I would see.

Victory and *I told you so.*

Suddenly, Mason is in front of me, staring down with an overwhelming sense of helplessness. He gives me a small nod, then turns, standing at our side in silent support as my brother faces off with our mom.

"Put her down," she seethes. "She needs to learn to live with disappointment. It's *life*. And we're leaving."

"She's not going anywhere with you," Chase warns calmly, and then suddenly Brady is here too.

Emotions well in my throat at a fast rate.

Support.

Safety.

Loss.

Emptiness.

Shock.

Absolute devastation.

I can't keep up.

I gasp, and Mason's hand shoots out, pressing to the spot on my back below Chase's elbow. A silent, unspoken *I've got you* passing from his skin to mine.

"Put. My daughter. Down," my mother demands yet again.

"Get the hell out of here, Ava," Parker growls. "Now is not the time for this shit. For once in your life, be a good mother, and let her have some time before you start your shit again. Please."

I curl into myself even more, because I know what he might have forgotten.

There isn't a decent bone in her body.

"Time for what?" She proves my thoughts right. "It's not like it happened in front of her, and she's sixteen! So her little crush is no more. Not my problem! Deaton is dead. She'll get over it!"

My lips part, desperate for air, but the knot in my throat denies it, and I feel my face burn with the lack of oxygen.

"Oh my god!" someone shouts, and I peek left, spotting the woman who must be Nate's mom charge toward mine, but her son blocks her before she can lunge at my mother.

Guilt burrows its way into my bones. Her daughter wouldn't be in that room if it weren't for me. Kenra brought me to California.

Deaton followed.

This is all my fault.

Uncontrollable, gut-wrenching sobs burst from my throat. I might be screaming.

Shadows crowd me, telling me the boys have moved closer, but I can't see them. I don't hear them.

My vision is full of broken glass and mangled limbs.

I see Deaton's bloody body as he screams in my face that this is my fault.

That I ruined his life.

That I ruined everything.

The next thing I know, the cool night air whips me in the face. My body trembles, and then my ass meets something cold. The arms releasing me slip farther away, but my hands snap out, clinging to them.

"Please," I beg.

They come back, holding me tighter this time, and the last thing I hear before I pass out again is "I'm not going anywhere, I promise."

It's like a sledgehammer taken to the last of my strength.

Deaton made me a lot of promises before he left.

I refuse to accept, let alone make, any more.

My boyfriend is dead.

I wish I were too.

CHAPTER 13
PAYTON

Now

The sweet sound of my little boy's whimpers has my eyes opening.

I frown my brain taking a moment to realize where I am, and my gaze finally snaps to the monitor on the coffee table before me. My muscles settle, a soft smile covering my lips as I stare at my sleeping baby boy on the screen.

I lean forward to grab it but freeze instantly when something tightens around me. My head snaps down to find an arm wrapped around my middle.

Mason.

Chase.

Deaton…

The night comes rushing back, and I swiftly tug myself off the couch, glancing back just as his eyes open.

"Hey." Chase eyes me warily, moving into a sitting position on the couch.

"Hey," I breathe, meekly tucking my hair behind my ear as I glance away. My eyes fall to the bag sitting at the edge of the table. I drop my chin to my chest, guilt settling over me as heavy as always.

"What time is it?" he wonders, his voice groggy.

We both look to the clock on the back wall.

It's just after three in the morning.

Chase swipes his hands down his face and scoots to the edge of the cushion, snagging his phone from the floor.

I bury my face in my hands. "God, Chase I'm so sorry. I shouldn't have asked you to come like that. You just got back to school, and you have shit going on and—"

"No one forced me to come here, Payton." When I look up at him, he continues. "I know what it's like to have a lot of people who love you and still feel like you have no one to talk to."

"You can talk to me if you want."

His lips curl to one side. "I know."

We stare at each other for a long, quiet moment before I finally speak.

"I never got to thank you."

He tips his head. "For what?"

"For that night," I whisper, tugging at the hem of my hoodie. "I was a disaster, and your best friends needed you, and you just... stayed with me, the whole time. You probably think I was too out of it to know, and most of it is foggy, but I remember you being there. So thank you."

Chase gives an understanding smile, but that smile slowly fades, and he curses as he looks away. "Today is...or was..."

I nod, dropping my head back to look up at the speckled ceiling. "One year since he was taken."

"That's why Mason was here." It's not a question. Neither is what he says next. "And you didn't call him tonight."

My eyes sting, but I swallow the self-pity, undeserving of such a thing, and shake my head.

Another curse leaves him, and this time when he looks at me, there's something deeper in his gaze. "I have to go." He swallows, looking off. "I don't want to, but I have to."

Something tells me his decision to leave isn't just about the time, but I don't mention that.

"I know. Thank you for coming. Sorry for turning back into

the girl I was that night. I thought I had a handle on her, but... well." I shrug.

Chase nods but sits there for several long moments in silence before rising to his feet. He opens his mouth to say or ask something but seems to change his mind. "We'll talk soon?"

My eyes grow cloudy, but I agree. "Yeah. Talk soon."

With that, he walks out the front door, and I lie back where I sit, my eyes closing.

That night at the hospital flashes through my mind, the days, weeks, and months that followed rolling right behind it, and a heaviness settles over me, but somewhere in that stormy cloud of pain and confusion is a tender touch of something else, like silk sewn beneath a weighted blanket.

I thought no one knew what today was, and I didn't want the worry—or pity—of mentioning it.

But someone did know.

He knew. He knew and he came.

"Just in case you needed me." His raspy, raw voice flows through me, bringing the warmth I've missed back to my shredded soul. Of course the moment it does, guilt rides right in like liquid nitrogen and turns it to ice.

Fighting a scream, I punch at the carpet beneath me, my teeth clenching as I throw my hands through my hair.

Chase was freshly showered in sweats and a hoodie.

Mason still had his cleats on his feet.

He came straight here. He came for me because he knew how hard today would be.

The look on his face when he saw Chase will haunt me endlessly.

Mason came *just in case* I needed him.

Chase came because I asked him to.

My bottom lip trembles, and I wish desperately that things were different.

I have to remind myself this is for the best. Self-preservation at its finest.

Or worst, depending on how you look at it.

Maybe now he'll realize I'm not worth the wait or the trouble. He has his whole life ahead of him. I'm on the cusp of eighteen with a baby and a questionable future. He's the starting quarterback for Avix University and an NFL hopeful.

A smile graces my lips, a tear slipping down my cheek. God, I'm so proud of him.

He's living the dream he shared with me, and I couldn't be happier for the man who brought me back to life without my realizing it.

You don't deserve happiness. Not when you stole that chance from Deaton.

Brick after brick falls on my chest, crushing my lungs until I'm gasping and falling onto my hands and knees.

I pant and cry, and eventually...I pass out.

MASON

Coach blows the whistle, and I drop back as my receiver zips down the field, running his route. He does a little stutter step, as if juking a defender, and the ball sails from my fingertips. I watch as he slants right, the ball dropping straight into his arms. A perfect fucking pass.

I step back, and my alternate slides in, my lips pinching tightly as he does the same, and then I roll in again. This receiver is slower than the other, his footwork not as smooth, so I hold a split second longer, then fire.

Catch.

"Better hope your line is strong, Johnson." Alister Howl, the wannabe me taunts, stepping into the pocket. "Wouldn't want you to get sacked and break some more ribs. Or was it the shoulder?"

Before I know I'm doing it, I'm jerking toward him, but my jersey is caught around the neck, and I'm tugged back.

My eyes snap up, staring at the familiar green ones through the dark blue face mask.

"Don't." Chase snaps around his mouthpiece, scowling from me to the new fucking punk. "*Focus.*"

I scoff, tear away, and slam my left shoulder into Alister hard enough to make him stumble.

"Bitch," he hisses, looking away when Coach's head snaps our way.

The asshole has an issue with me, and he made it obvious on day one, but hey, I'm the guy he has to beat if he wants a spot on the roster that's worth a damn. Assuming that's what's got his jockstrap twisted so tight.

Again, a receiver runs his route, my feet moving without thought, working on muscle memory.

Money shot.

I shuffle back, swiftly pressing my chest into Alister's as he slides forward. "Don't worry, backup boy. *My line* is fucking *solid.*"

He glares, angrily snagging a ball off the cart and stepping up again.

Chase flies down the field like a demon on wheels, nailing his route, but Alister misjudges his speed and distance. Chase is standing there waiting for the ball to drop for a full second.

Alister spits on the ground, and I know Chase is smirking around his mouthpiece.

He's always got my back.

My glare is instant, images of last night flashing through my mind, and I clench my teeth.

So, what, he's got her back now, too?

Since when?

Why?

Why am I being such a bitch about it?

I want her to have all the support she needs and more...but I want her to want it all from me first.

I thought she did.

I pick up another ball and go again. And again.

I was the first to hit the field, and three hours later, I'm the last to step off it.

"You good?" Brady asks when I finally walk into the locker room, his bag already packed and hanging over his shoulder.

"Yup." I move right past him.

"Want me to wait?"

"Nope."

I keep going, stepping right into the shower, and I stay there until I'm pruned.

When I move back into the row of my locker, both Brady and Chase are sitting there playing on their phones.

They waited for me.

The tension in my chest eases a bit, and I can't help the small smile that pulls at my lips as I tug on my clothes. This is what friends are for, to understand that even if you say you don't want them around, they know you're better off when they are.

Brady can tell I'm off today, and Chase likely thinks he knows why.

I kind of want to scream and yell at him, demand answers, but at the end of the day, I'm too fucking scared to hear what they are. We've fought enough this past year when everything went down with my sister, and I can't afford that shit right now. I love the little prick like a brother.

Once my bag is stuffed with my shit, they stand.

"Pizza with the girls?" Brady raises a brow.

"Pizza with the girls."

As we walk out, I can't help but remember the time I had pizza with a different girl.

That was the night I realized she wasn't just the girl I wanted to be there for.

She is so much fucking more.

CHAPTER 14
MASON

Before, July

My hands are trembling with rage, my joints aching from how tense I've been clenching them for the twenty-minute ride back to Nate's.

My eyes keep jumping to the broken little blond in the back seat. She hasn't noticed me staring, she's so far gone right now, stuck in her own head that must be full of nightmares at this point. She's dealt with so much in such a short span of time.

All in a month's time, she discovered she was pregnant, found the courage to escape a toxic home, got confronted by the boy she left behind, *lost* the boy she left behind when he came for her, and then her mother, who she ran away from, tried to rip her from her home just hours after.

I could not believe the way that woman acted toward Payton. Never in my life have I ever witnessed a parent act that way.

She spoke as if her baby girl didn't just have her heart ripped from her chest, if only from the guilt alone. From what I've learned about Payton, Deaton was the only person she had in her corner back home. She was more or less alone.

I'll be fucking damned if she ever feels that way again.

But now this?

I'm seconds from shoving my fist though the window from the mere look of defeat on her pretty face.

This just confirms what I'd already began to suspect. Deaton's family is as bad, if not worse, than her mother. I mean, goddamn. Who the *fuck* sends a photo of a casket holding the boy who passed to the girl who lost him…after refusing to include her in his funeral? I thought it was the lowest they could get, keeping it a secret just so she couldn't be there, but this?

This is some twisted psychological warfare.

My eyes lift again, her blank expression causing my pulse to pound heavy in my ears.

She's being mentally tortured, and it's killing me in ways I can hardly understand. It's deeper than I have words for and heavier than I would have thought possible. I quite literally *feel* the ache she's gotten good at hiding, and she *is* hiding.

Pretty Little's trying to be so strong, fighting the voices screaming in her head.

I wish I knew what they were saying so I could find a way to stop them. I would take it all away if I knew how.

By the time we pull up to the house, my nerves are on fire.

Everyone opens their doors but me, and when I look up in the mirror this time, Payton's eyes lift, latching on to mine. For a split second, her mask crumbles, her pretty face contorting with pain. Her blue eyes are begging for something, but I don't think either one of us knows what it is she's asking for, and then she blinks.

Just like that, the mask is back, and she's climbing from the Tahoe. Payton avoids everyone's gaze, and we all hurry after, Parker tugging me back to allow a few feet of space as if not to spook her. I shrug him off but stay at his side, looking his way when his arm comes down on my shoulder.

We follow behind, her feet picking up speed until she's separated herself from us completely, the door to the room she's been staying in shutting with a soft click.

A split second later, a shrill scream fills the air, reverberating across every wall and slamming into my eardrums like knifes, cutting me, making me bleed. At least that's how it feels. Like a physical pain without a wound.

I do the only thing I can think of.

I send a message in our group thread.

Me: Mama. You need to come. Payton's breaking and I don't know how to fix it.

I stare at my screen, and not five seconds later, Dad's response comes through.

Dad: on our way, son.

The smallest of weights lift from my shoulders, and for the next hour, we sit around, the others in the kitchen, Parker and I taking turns pacing the space in front of Payton's door. He walks off a few times, but I can't bring myself to move. It's not until my sister comes back for the third time to offer me something to drink that I climb from my spot on the floor and follow her toward the others.

I'm not in there for five seconds when another angry cry rips from down the hall.

We wince in unison, unsure of what the right thing to do would be but needing to do *something*.

"This isn't good for her." Chase shakes his head, his face taut with unease.

I drag my hands down my face to keep from matching her screams, the helplessness eating me up too damn much. My sister shuffles closer, and I look her way, finding the same broken expression written across her face.

I know what she's going to say before she says it. It's not a twin thing, either; it's a *we were blessed with a family who is there for us always* thing. I try to offer a reassuring smile. "They're already on their way."

My smile does nothing for either of us, and when her eyes begin to mist over, I wrap my arms around her with a sigh.

"Is she going to be okay?" Ari asks.

"Yeah," I assure her, even when I have no clue if it's the truth. How could she possibly be okay after all this? Anger cuts through me, and my jaw clenches.

"What mother would hide something like this?" she whispers.

"She's not a mother." I glare at the ocean outside the large bay window. Mrs. Vermont is as bad as Payton's mom. "She's a heartless *bitch*. Payton is carrying a piece of that woman's son." I shake my head in disbelief, knowing how my parents would treat her if it was their grandchild she was carrying. Shit, how they will treat her now when she's but a friend. "She should be worshiping the girl, begging for forgiveness for treating her like shit their entire relationship." I swallow. "She's not a mother."

With that, I go back to my spot on the floor beside Payton's door. I'm not sure if I fall asleep or if my mind is running so fast that the time has lapsed, but the next thing I know, my mama's face is in front of me, her soft hand on my arm.

"I've got her, baby. You can take a break."

My head falls back to the wall, and I stare at the best woman I know. The most selfless and kindhearted soul, the woman who made my sister the angel she is. Heat pricks at my eyes, and my mom's face falls. She cups my cheek, staring at me as if she sees something I can't. Knows something I don't.

"Oh, honey," she finally whispers, holds on a second longer, then kisses my temple.

Slowly, she stands and slips inside Payton's room.

I roll to the side, pressing my ear to the door to listen, my heart pounding in my chest.

Will she be angry?

Kick my mom out?

Scream and yell and want to leave because not one of us knows how to mind our own business in this house? Because

118

we don't. We're meddling motherfuckers and probably always will be.

Soft whispers reach me, followed by soft cries, but these are different. They're tears you shed when there's someone there to hold you through the pain.

I want to hold you…

I blink at the thought, my back going ramrod straight as the realization slaps me in the face.

I want to be the one to hold her.

Oh.

Shit.

———————

Payton's door opens, and my mom slips out, her eyes slightly puffy and a look of exhaustion tainting her soft features.

"How is she?" I wince at the stupid question.

Obviously, the answer is *real fucking shitty*. Still, my mom offers a smile. "She slept for a while." When she lifts the plate in her hand, I see it's still piled high with my dad's cooking. "She didn't even take a bite."

"She has to eat."

"She will, baby. Just not right now. I left some snacks by her bed, just in case. Water and some candy."

I nod, my eyes closing for a moment, and when I open them, both my parents are standing there, staring down at me with soft expressions.

"I take it you're not headed back to the house with the others tonight?" my dad asks.

I shake my head. "Nate won't care if I camp out on the couch." *Or right here.*

My dad's knowing smile tells me he's fully aware of what I didn't say.

"Mase…" my mom begins, but Dad wraps his arm around her,

and they share one of those parent looks. When she faces me, her smile is a gentle, slightly concerned one. "I'll come check on her later today before we decide if we're heading back home or not, okay?"

I nod, climbing to my feet to hug them both, and watch them disappear around the corner. After I hear the gang say their goodbyes, Nate, Lolli, and Parker appear. They don't say anything, just nod as they shuffle by like zombies and close themselves inside their rooms.

The house goes quiet, and suddenly I'm wide awake. I look to my phone to find it's well past four in the morning. We've been up all night.

Sighing, no sooner do I settle against the pillow my dad propped behind me at some point and close my eyes than a muffled sound comes from inside the room.

Footsteps pad across the carpet, and I jump to my feet, my hand wrapping around the knob. I wait a moment, then gently rap my knuckles against it. She doesn't say not to come in, so I cautiously turn my wrist, pushing it open to find her sitting in the chair in front of the window.

There's not much to look at from this angle, but she can at least see the light starting to peek through the darkened sky. When she turns my way, there's a definitive *thunk thunk* in my chest, and I rub at the spot.

Her cheeks are blotched red, her big blue eyes low and defeated, but when her lip curls into a small smile and she says, "I knew it was you," a tiny spark flickers across her eyes.

I force a smirk I don't feel and put more pep in my step than I feel. "Oh yeah, and did you know I was coming in here to steal you away?"

She stares a moment, and tension wraps around my shoulders as I prepare for her to tell me to leave, but she doesn't do that.

Payton stands, slides her feet into a pair of fluffy slippers, and walks past me. She pauses at the door, finds me over her shoulder, and says, "I hoped as much."

With that, she walks out, and I hurry after her.

Like a couple of kids doing something they shouldn't be, we tiptoe toward the front and silently slip out the door. We're loaded in my Tahoe and out onto the road in less than a minute.

She doesn't ask where we're going, and I don't feel the need to fill the silence in the car, so we sit in it all the way to the only place open around here at this time of night. Or morning, technically...Peppy's Diner.

Inside, we find a booth in the back corner and sit down.

Payton looks around the place, taking in how busy and loud the diner is at this hour, and finally, a smile she doesn't force tips her lips.

She needed a little chaos to pause her own.

"Okay." She looks up, a little light in her gorgeous eyes. "I say we get stuffed pancakes...and the cheese pizza."

A laugh leaves me, and something stirs in my stomach when her mouth curves even higher.

The cheese pizza here is disgusting, probably microwaved, and I don't think this girl has ever eaten stuffed carbs in her life, but I couldn't disagree with her if I wanted to.

So long as I have a say, she's getting exactly what she wants. Always.

It's not until the untouched pancakes are cold, the last piece of pizza hanging from her fingertips that she sighs and looks my way again.

"I haven't told anyone yet, but..." She stares into my eyes. "I'm keeping the baby."

The conviction in her tone is gripping, and I stare right back. "It means a lot that you trust me enough to tell me."

Her lips twitch, and she nods.

"We'll all support you in this, you know. No matter what," I add.

She nods again. "This is what I want, and not just because—"

Not just because Deaton died.

Reaching across the table, I put my hand out, and tentatively, she presses her palm to mine. I give her a little squeeze, trying to pretend like I'm not all tied up at the fact that she told me before she told anyone else when I am.

"The reason is yours alone, Pretty Little. You don't have to explain yourself to anyone."

Her face softens, and then a large smile blooms across her pillowed lips.

"What?"

"I was sitting here wondering what you were going to say after I told you, and the conversation we had in my head went a lot like this."

A low chuckle leaves me, and I sit back when she reaches for her fork and stabs into the ice-cold flapjacks, cutting off and taking a giant bite. I watch her every move, a smile tipping my lips.

"Nice to know I'm predictable," I tease, unable to find the strength to look away from the girl and not wanting to regardless.

"Not predictable." She speaks low, her eyes coming back to mine. "Just...*Mason*," she says as if it explains it all. She looks out the window then, the sun having officially risen.

I raise a dark brow, and when an airy laugh leaves her, I feel like I'm fucking flying.

She's feeling a little better, and I had a hand in that. Me.

From there, the conversation switches to random topics, and I sit back, indulging her every question, happy to be the center of the distraction she's after.

It's not until we're parked outside Nate's that her spirit dims again. It's in the way she hesitates in the passenger seat, staring at the porch of the beach house in heavy defeat.

"I never got to tell him," she whispers suddenly, her chest expanded with a strangled breath. "Deaton died not knowing what I was going to do."

"He knew." Her eyes come to mine, and I lean closer. "He loved you, Payton." I hold her gaze steadily, and her lips tremble through a broken smile. "*He knew.*"

Slowly, she nods, and her muscles ease before my eyes, as if reassurance from my lips is enough to help put her mind at ease, if only for a little while. "Thanks, Mase. You're a good friend."

What if I want to be more?

CHAPTER 15
MASON

Now, August

Arms crossed, fingers digging into my biceps, I glare at the little fucker on the field.

Originally, I had agreed with Coach's plan to use the second string to start us out. Toss them out there, throw off the opposing team, let them think they have a shot for a quarter of a quarter, and then make the swap. Show them what we really got and crush their little dreams of leaving here with the victory.

Now I wish I would have pushed back, because *of course* this dickhead hits the field in my position and does what he damn well pleases, game plan be damned.

The plan called for a pick play, and his receivers executed perfectly, feet flying forward, one putting himself in the defender's path, leaving the other wide open, but what does the punk do?

He tucked and ran, doing all he could to show off his twinkle toes. He cut man after man, not only picking up the first down but an extra six yards on top of it.

The crowd cheered, he got hyped, and Coach tore into him from the sidelines. Alister looked our way with a nod, threw out some excuse he knew we couldn't hear, took the next play call, and went back into the huddle.

Next play, same thing, but this time, instead of juking the outside linebacker who came down on a blitz, flying right toward him, he leapt into the air, coming down over his head. He gained three more yards.

Everyone went wild that time, and instead of tuning them out and focusing on the task at hand, the freshman fame chaser turned to face them, threw his hands up, and begged for more.

He's a fool, and a move like that will end his career before it even begins.

Jump too low, too late, or too high, you risk getting flipped in the air and landing wrong. Break your wrist or injure your arm for a bit of crowd chasing, and it'll be game over.

Coach Rogan and I look at each other at the same time, both shaking our heads. The clock ticks down, and finally, it's time. I tug my helmet on and get ready to take my position. Because it is *my* position.

All eleven of our boys on the field jog off, the first-string crew jogging on for the first game of the season.

Alister slams his shoulder into mine as he passes, and our glares meet. "Let's see if they like you half as much as they like me," the smiling bastard spits.

"Don't worry, second string." I smirk, snapping my chin strap. "They won't see you enough to like you."

Alister's face falls, and I spin, laughing to myself as I join my team on the field, and the second my feet plant on the turf, all thoughts of him fall away.

This is it.

I look across my teammates' faces, each of us nodding, all of them waiting for my instruction, eager to follow my lead, to take themselves where I need them and make the play happen. The air is charged, and call me Electro, because I'm powered the fuck up.

This is what I've been waiting for.

What I've trained my whole life for.

I'm the starting quarterback at a D1 college, and I'm about to show every person in this place exactly why it's my picture hanging in the halls.

And that's exactly what I do.

I ball out, all my boys right there with me, and by the time the clock runs out in the fourth quarter, the scoreboard reads thirty-four to thirteen, Avix U Sharks.

I'm keyed up, jumping with my teammates as we enter the tunnel like a pack of wild wolves after a hunt. We're loud and rough, laughing and joking, blasting rap music in the locker room as we listen to Coach deliver a fiery speech that has us banging our lockers in victory. When he leaves us, the speakers bump even harder, and we go about our own business.

I pull my phone from my locker, my smile wide.

It falls a split second later when my eyes focus on the screen.

There's a message from my dad, my sister, and even Lolli... but nothing from the girl who started a routine I clearly became dependent on.

After every game last season, Payton would message me, without fail. If she was able to watch, it would be a joke about home runs or nothing but net, playing up her lack of knowledge of the game that she knew drove me crazy. If she didn't, she would search for the results, coming back with a sassy little remark, and I just knew she was smirking that cute little smirk when she sent it, usually because she was teasing me, talking about how so-and-so's tight pants being the reason the tackle was missed that led to the game-winning touchdown she found on the *Avix Inquirer* Instagram page. None of it made much sense, and I knew she understood more than she let on—I spent a ton of time breaking it down for her, after all—but that was the fun of it. Playful teasing *she* started. It was our thing. I never wondered if her message would be waiting for me. I knew it would.

It was a guarantee.

Keyword *was*, my man.

Frustration claws at my skin, and I toss my phone in my locker with an angry huff, doing a double take when I spot Chase a few lockers away, grinning down at his screen.

Without realizing I'm doing it, I'm rushing over, tearing the phone from his hand. "Who are you talking to?" I snap.

"Bro, what the hell?" He yanks it back, shoving me away, but not before I see the name on the screen.

Guess Lolli messaged him, too.

Chase studies me with narrowed eyes, but I spin away, squeezing my lids closed a moment.

I don't hit the showers.

I grab my shit and get the fuck out.

PAYTON

Lifting my camera, I follow the newest addition to the team as he flies off the starting line, sprinting to the end and blowing his opponent out of the water.

I'm pretty sure it's in good fun, a locker room bet maybe, seeing that they tugged their pads off their shoulders and dropped them to the turf.

He spins, smiling as he swipes his hand through his dark hair.

The team is shouting and shoving on number thirteen, heckling him for losing to the new guy, I'm sure, but Noah only shakes his head, walking over to where the receiver coaches have gathered.

It's late August now, more than a month since the one-year anniversary—such a ridiculous expression—of Deaton's death, and I'm feeling a little more like myself again. The weeks leading to that day were unexpected, the months before that even more so.

But what a beautiful mess it was.

I shake off the thought.

After Deaton died, I was stuck in a state of disarray. Confused and unable to get past the shock of it all. For the longest time,

I didn't quite feel real. A few months after his death, I found I wasn't crying every single day anymore, and the days I realized this, I'd cry out of guilt.

Who did I think I was, walking around and having lunch with my friends, taking breathers on the beach while he was lying cold in a coffin?

A sharp pain flickers through me, and I wince.

It's such a strange thing, to lose someone, and as sad as it is, I'm kind of seasoned in it as if it's a sport I willingly participate in. Technically speaking, I lost my dad when he divorced my mom, which led to losing my brother. I lost my friends when my mother began to meddle in my life, and I lost my free will at the same time. I lost my senior year when I got pregnant, and then I lost Deaton.

Every one of those instances, I mourned in one way or another. I knew I had to take it a day at a time, and I did. Slowly, things got better. I could think of him and smile or laugh, missing him without complete misery.

But the one-year mark of his death? That was like nothing else I've experienced, and I can't pretend it doesn't have something to do with an entirely different dark-haired man.

Regardless, it was as if after a year of compartmentalizing, my boxes were full, the overflowing weight too much to hold strong. They tumbled to the floor with a heavy crash, the latches splitting from the locks and pouring over me until I was a body with no heart, lungs with no air.

I felt dead inside, guilty beyond measure.

He was dead, and I lived a whole life in one year's time.

I carried a baby to full term. I got my GED. I started an internship at the job of my dreams, and I made it to my eighteenth birthday with a little less weight on my shoulders.

I created a home in the home my brother and found family offered me. I took their hands, and I held on for dear life.

Instead of sinking under at the thought of Deaton, I trained my brain to swim, to tread the endless waters of grief until I found a way to breathe easier.

I untied the rope around my wrists and broke the surface of my woe whirlpool. I had a little boy to bring into this world, to protect and cherish, and a fractured girl wouldn't be strong enough. He deserved more. So as time passed and I discovered where the light I felt within me was coming from, I leaned in ever so slightly.

It wasn't my intention to fall off the cliff, but I did.

I fell headfirst, but I never hit the ground.

Strong hands held me steady.

It didn't take long for the guilt I lived with to grow from a warm, wieldy pit in my stomach to a volcano of vast proportions.

It doesn't make a whole lot of sense. I mean, he's dead, right? So what does any of it matter?

I'm here, and he's not.

A humorless laugh leaves me, and I shake my head, lifting my camera once more and peering through the lens.

If only it were that easy, girl.

"Shoot, I am late!"

I whip around, smiling wide at the sight of Ari.

"Hey! I didn't know you were coming to town today." She beams, skipping down the steps and throwing her arm around me. "I was hoping I'd catch their practice, but looks like they're about done."

Both our eyes move toward the field, and as if an invisible string is tied from her to him, Noah looks up into the stands in the same exact moment. The smile that breaks across his lips has us both laughing, and a softness blooms in my chest, a teeny tiny thread of jealousy tugging within me.

It takes her several seconds, but she finally looks my way again. "So you're back at work?"

"Thank god for that," I admit with a light scoff. "Too much time on my hands without it."

She tips her head, eying me for a moment. "Have you ever thought about taking courses at the college? Maybe they have some photography or business classes that could help?"

Tucking my hair behind my ear, I shake my head, snapping a few shots of the running backs and their coaching staff as they close out their day.

"My internship comes with full-scale training in the equipment and software, and now that I'm on year two, I'll be working on the film side as well, moving into live shorts for social media."

"How exciting!" She lights up, and when she looks out at the field, a softness falls over her. "I wish I could just…be out here with him every day."

"Why don't you transfer to USD with Nate?"

She lifts a shoulder, not taking her eyes off the blue-eyed, black-haired man ahead. "I was more thinking along the lines of…dropping out."

My eyes widen, and she laughs lightly, shrugging once more.

"I never wanted to go to college anyway, but I knew I should. Now, though? After everything that's happened?" She shakes her head, emotion heavy in her voice, and I don't know if she realizes it, but her palm presses to her belly. "I just want to be where he is."

I can understand that. She almost lost the love of her life in a completely different way than most, but still she almost lost him. She understands, now more than ever, that life is short, and we should spend every moment we can with the ones we love most.

Unless you know what it feels like to lose that person for real and are certain you couldn't survive it a second time…

I swallow, glancing at Ari once more. "Does he know?"

Her smile is sassy now. "That man knows everything I'm thinking with one look." She sighs sweetly. "He's just waiting for me to be the one to say it first." She looks to me then. "It's funny how the literal opposite he is of my brother."

Both of us laugh at that.

"Yeah, Mason is…"

"Mason" we say at the same time.

We grow quiet, and when I drop down onto my butt to pack my things, she follows.

"The boys played their first game today," she whispers, and the note of caution in her tone has my muscles bunching. "Mason threw for over three hundred yards."

Unease stirs in my gut. I don't know exactly what that means, but she says it with a tentative pride, so it must be good. Does that mean he won his first game as a starting quarterback?

Anxiety tugs at my conscience, my eyes slicing to where my phone hangs around my neck. Did he check his phone after?

I'm sure he did, but he's probably way too excited to notice I didn't reach out. If they won, I mean. He's the starter now. Things will be different for him this year. Busier.

He's the man everyone will look to. The one they'll chase after.

The one the girls will want.

"I have to go." I jump up, offering Ari a quick hug.

Her lips curve, a question in her pretty brown eyes she doesn't ask. "Maybe I'll see you before I head back to campus on Sunday?"

"Maybe." I nod. "Have fun at Noah's game this weekend."

She nods back, and I spin, quickly escaping before anything else can be said.

But before I head into the child center at the team's headquarters, I pause outside the door and pull up Instagram. The *Avix Inquirer*, the newspaper page dedicated to Avix University, pops up, and the photo brings tears to my eyes.

It's him. Of course it's him.

His hair looks nearly black, from sweat or water I couldn't say, but it looks good on him, the front tips flat against his forehead. His jersey is littered with green stains, the giant number four in the center having met the field at some point today. He has his helmet lifted high into the air in victory, but it's the familiar cocky tilt to his lips and wild gleam in his dark eyes that has me inhaling deeply.

131

I don't have to read the headline. It's clear as day he came out on top.

Backing out, I tap the search engine and type out the question burning in my mind.

What are the average yards thrown in a college football game?

I wait and wait, and when the answer pops onto the screen, a mixture of sorrow and happiness flickers through me. Closing my eyes, I take a deep breath. "Way to go, Superstar," I whisper.

Maybe one day he'll forgive me for the mess I've made of us.

Or maybe he'll become so famous he won't even remember my name.

Maybe that will be for the best.

Maybe Mason and I aren't meant to be, and there's someone else out there who can give him what I can't and better.

The mere thought is as devastating as the others.

Maybe I'm an idiot, and the story of us is not that serious.

CHAPTER 16
MASON

Before, September

She's so beautiful.

Her hair looks longer and a little lighter than it did over summer. FaceTime calls don't do her justice, and we've had plenty of those.

It's nothing like sitting across from the ocean-eyed blond who talks with her hands and expresses every word with her whole body. She looks…happy. Smiling and laughing.

What makes it even better is every ounce of her attention is locked on me.

Fuck, I like it.

"Oh my god, and when you did that thing where you pretended like you were going to throw the ball and all the other guys slowed and you just ran right past them to the end?"

My smile is fucking geeking, face hurting from its force, but I can't stop. "It's called the end zone," I tease.

"I don't even care what it's called. It was so badass!" She chuckles, finally taking a breath as she reaches for her cream soda.

A low laugh leaves me, and I can't stop staring. Her cheeks are flushed, eyes bright with life, and I wish I could see her this way every day.

I wish I could see her every day, period.

"So can we say you're an official football fan now?"

A playful scowl crosses her face, and she sits back in her seat. "Too soon to say. It was my first game."

"Come on now, Pretty Little. Don't play." I lean forward, dropping my forearms to the table between us. "We both know you watch me all the time."

She pretends like she's making herself gag by pointing a finger in her mouth as she sticks her tongue out. "Someone is full of himself."

"And someone is very well aware of this fact and likes me anyway." I grin, and she laughs, shaking her head.

"You're all right." She eyes me a moment, fighting a grin by pulling her lips between her teeth.

I raise a dark brow, and she rolls her eyes, that smile breaking free once more.

"God." She tilts her head. "I don't know how the girls have dealt with you for so long."

"Stick around and find out. It's hard not to love me."

The words are intended as a joke, but when she flushes and looks away, a strange sensation zips through me, all the way down to my damn toes. I can't name it, but I don't hate it. Quite the opposite, in fact.

The gang's voices grow louder as they come back from the arcade section of the pub, so I set my water down and stand, not ready to share her just yet. *Or at all. Ever.*

"Come on."

I offer her a hand, and she hesitates, glancing at the others briefly before taking it. I haul her to her feet and lead us toward the back door. We step out onto the patio and start cruising down the street.

Away from the chaos of the night, I take a deep breath.

"It's really pretty here," she murmurs after a few silent minutes, leading us onto a little bridge, a small stream running beneath it.

I nod, agreeing, still surprised she and Parker drove out to catch the game today. I wasn't expecting it. In fact, they didn't tell any of us. We found out after the game when we walked to Chase's truck and there they were. Cameron left with some girls from her dorm, Ari had already taken off back to her room, something she's been doing a lot lately so I don't even know if she's aware they're here tonight, but Payton hasn't asked about the girls so…maybe she came for me?

As far as I know, she doesn't talk to them on the regular like she does me, so does that mean I'm right? Did this gorgeous girl come to my college today just for me?

It's a little stressful how much I want the answer to be a hard-ass yes.

Payton turns to look at me, tipping her head.

"What?"

"You got quiet," she says softly. "You okay?"

I chuckle, licking my lips as I look off. "I'm good."

"Promise?"

My lips twist up, and I nod. "I promise, Pretty Little. Better than good, in fact."

She stares for a few seconds before glancing back toward the creek.

I do the same, noting the length of it. "I've never been out here, actually."

"No?" She sounds pleased.

Does she like that I'm here with her first?

Fuck, bro. Chill.

You sound like a bitch. It's a creek, hardly even that, not Niagara Falls.

"I stick to campus mostly."

"Such a good boy, Mason Johnson."

"I didn't say that," I tease, giving a devilish smirk.

She chuckles, looking away. "No, actually I bet you're not."

A small frown builds across my brow at her words, even if they are just in response to mine, but I was being a blatant flirt, and I think she might have taken it differently.

I want to tell her I'm not out here chasing a good time, nor am I allowing myself to be caught by someone else who is.

It's strange to say, but I'm not the same guy I was when I met her a couple of months ago.

Something changed, and it might have everything to do with the girl standing beside me.

Payton stares out at the night, and I watch as her hand falls to her belly.

I wince, waiting for the stiffness to settle in her shoulders as it usually does, but it never comes. In fact, she smiles, spreading her fingers out wider. It's really good to see.

Her belly is bigger now, a perfect little basketball you can't even see from the back. It looks hard and painful, and suddenly, I'm anxious.

"We should go back. Sit you down and put your feet up or something, and I can get you some ice or a heating pad or whatever and—"

My rambling dies on my lips the second her little palm presses to my chest. My eyes snap to the contact, the heat of her skin somehow seeping through the thick material of my hoodie. I swallow and ever so slowly lift my gaze to hers and hold it there. The humor in her blue eyes fades by the second, a subtle but not missed shift happening around us.

Her lips part, and in what I might call slow motion, her hand draws back, and the weirdest fucking thing happens.

I physically *miss* the way it felt. Literally. I frown, and she drops her eyes to the ground.

When she lifts her head again, it's with a soft smile, but there's an uncertainty to it this time. I don't like it. Want to take it away.

So I step forward, grab her hand, and put it back, holding it there.

"Don't shy away from me, okay?" I don't know what the words mean, and by the way her features pull, she doesn't either, but they feel right, so I keep going. "Anything you ever want to say to me, to tell me or show me or ask me, do it. No matter what's going on in that pretty little head of yours…don't shy away. Not ever from me."

"What if what I want to say will upset you?" she whispers.

My pulse pounds harder, and I try not to overthink that. Try and fail. "Say it anyway."

"Are you sure?" She bites her lip.

Shit. Am I? The fuck is this twisty shit going on in my stomach right now?

I shift her, putting her back to the bridge, her front to me, suddenly needing her to say whatever the hell is on her mind. "Say it."

She nods, looking away, then peeks up at me through her lashes. "I…"

Here we go.

"I think the other team had better uniforms."

I tense and then throw my head back on a laugh, Payton joining in at the same time.

"You should have seen your face." She giggles. "You looked like you were expecting me to say the end of the world was coming and you'd never get your day in the big leagues."

"That's baseball." When her mouth tugs to one side, I narrow my gaze. "But you knew that…"

"I did." She smiles, proud, her blue eyes shining.

Before I can stop myself, before I even realize what I'm doing, my knuckles are sliding across her cheek.

Payton's lips part on a gasp. It's soft, nearly unnoticeable, but it happened.

Heat zips through me at the sound, and I tense.

Our gazes lock, and she smiles timidly, her hard belly pressed to my abdomen. Slowly, the hand that was holding on to hers rises once more, but before it reaches its destination, my eyes snap to hers for permission.

Payton nods, pressing on the back of my hand until my palm meets the cotton of her shirt.

I hold her eyes a moment, then drop them to the contact.

"It's…"

"Weird?" she impishly adds.

"Nah," I whisper, sliding my hand along the perfect curve. "I guess I thought it would feel hard, and it does, but it's also, I don't know. Soft?"

"You should feel him kick."

I smile at that, looking back at her for a long moment, overcome with concern. "You're getting close, huh?"

She nods, then stiffens, making me more uneasy. "December's not so far away anymore."

"Tell me what you need."

Her eyes pop up.

"Tell me what you need," I repeat.

Payton's grin is soft then. She shuffles a bit so she can step away, and my hands fall from her. She starts walking back the way we came, and I fight the urge to hold her still.

I don't want to go back inside.

I don't want to share her with the guys.

It's irrational and ridiculous, and I roll my eyes internally.

"I'm good, Mase. Nothing to do but wait for him to be ready to meet the world."

There's a sorrow in her tone I don't like, so I wrap my arm around her shoulders and tug her close.

"Well then. In the meantime, let's go back to our earlier conversation where you tell me how awesome I am at football… even if I'm the second-string quarterback and only played for two minutes the entire game."

Payton laughs loudly, and when she looks up at me with those big blue eyes, I can't look away.

"Well, go on, then. Talk me up."

"You're insufferable."

"I think you like that about me."

Smiling, she shakes her head and faces forward. "I think you've got a big head."

"I most definitely do."

She looks down, humor shaking her shoulders. When she finally glances back, I give her an expectant expression, and she sighs.

"Fine." She tugs away, clearing her throat as she makes a fist, bring it to her mouth as if it's a microphone.

I chuckle, and she covers her face.

"OMG. I can't do it if you tease."

"Okay, okay." I raise my palms, clamping my lips shut.

Her eyes narrow, then she clears her throat again.

"Avix University took the win tonight, a feat that wouldn't have been possible without the one and only Mason Johnson!" She speaks animatedly, flinging her free hand all around. "Mason played like he was made of *magic*. He's like no others we've seen, with an effortless elegance about the way he moves. The man is fluid in every shift of his body. Precise in every intention. He's what dreams are made of, Avix U's very own Greek god!"

She's laughing by the end of it, this time covering her rosy-red cheeks with both hands.

"Damn, woman." My grin spreads. "I'm impressed. You know jack shit about football and made that sound good."

A shy sort of smile curls her lips, and she lifts a shoulder with a shrug. "I wanted to be a reporter when I was younger. I might have spent a lot of time practicing in front of the mirror."

"Obviously." She scrunches her nose in a feisty little scowl, and I keep going, liking how playful she's being tonight. "And, hey, you nailed everything about me. I actually am the shit...again even if all that wasn't true and I only played for two minutes."

"There were only four touchdowns made tonight, Mase. It took your team the entire game to make three. You made one in less than two minutes." She glances my way. "That's something to be proud of."

Her words sink deeper than they should, all the way to a part of me the praise of others has yet to touch. It's...a lot. A sort of tense feeling, one wrapped in confusion and laced with a small sense of panic.

Does she really think all that?

Was that just part of the fun?

Does she like watching me out there?

Bro. Chill.

I laugh off the feeling and start walking, Payton falling in step at my side.

"Careful, Pretty Little. Wouldn't want you to give me a big head or anything."

"I think that ship has sailed."

"Then you must be the captain."

Payton peeks my way with a grin. "Whatever you say, Superstar."

I say I might not be the only one in this...

CHAPTER 17
PAYTON

Now, September

My nerves are a wreck as I load Deaton into his car seat, passing my bag to my brother when he reaches for it.

"You sure you want to ride all the way in the back?" he asks. "We can put you and the car seat in the middle row, shove Mason and Chase in the third row."

"Their legs would hardly fit, three seats back there or not. Besides, this way I have room for the diaper bag beside me, and if I need to change him, I have space and don't have to get out when we stop."

"We could make the boys ride with Brady and the girls," Kenra singsongs. "Ari and Cam are going to be annoyed when I tell them the boys are riding with us. We all know they are expecting them." She buckles up and glances back, tossing a toy at me. She smiles. "You forgot this on the couch."

I force my lips to curve, staring down at the plush football... that I purposefully let fall from Deaton's fingers before we walked out.

Deaton spots it instantly and makes little grabby hands, so I pretend to tickle him with it, handing it over.

"Hey, the girls know the name of the game." My brother smiles, moving to the driver's side and sliding in. "First to the finish line gets the prize."

"How were they supposed to know the boys already asked to ride with us? Better yet, why would they want to when Brady is taking his Bronco?"

My brother meets my eyes in the mirror, and I quickly look away.

"Don't know," he says. "But we were still on the group FaceTime call making the plans to go when Mason texted he was riding with us. Chase asked a couple of days later." He shrugs, pulling from the driveway and heading to the others' beach house down the road. "At least this way it's fair." He smirks when his girlfriend smacks his arm.

Last week, Ari realized Avix U's bye week landed on the Labor Day three-day weekend, giving the boys Saturday to Monday off practice. She nearly passed out at how excited she had gotten, declaring we would all be headed to Nevada for Noah's game. Well, everyone but Lolli and Nate, seeing as he has a game of his own this weekend.

It's a six-hour road trip.

Cue the anxiety.

We pull up along the curb, the others already outside, loading up. The second Brady realizes the boys are ditching him, leaving him in a car full of girls, he grins.

"Oh, fuck yeah." His excitement throws me off, but he just chuckles, poking his head inside my brother's SUV so he can see me. "Sure you don't wanna ride with us, Payton baby? No boys, which means all the good gossip is about to pop off."

"You sound really excited about that."

"Oh, I am. I'm the only fucker who minds my business. Ask Ari. I knew all her shit before the others, and did I say a word? Nope." He smirks.

"Too bad you ratted us out every single time we went to a party without you in high school!" Cameron shouts.

"That's 'cause you had no business partying with our friends. They were assholes." He smiles. "Last chance, mama bear." He looks my way. "You staying with the broody train or jumping on the booty train?"

I chuckle. "Broody train?"

His face goes serious. "Dude. Mason's got a whole goalpost up his ass. Been that way since school started." He looks over his shoulder, considering his words. "Maybe before that..." When he looks back, his eyes narrow. "Hmm."

"I'm good," I rush to say.

His gaze narrows some more. "Uh-huh." He points at me, and I feel like a child scolded.

It's ridiculous.

"Move, asshole." The man of the hour appears, and Brady backs up with a smirk.

"Paige! Get your little ass out here, or we're leaving you!" he screams.

"Oh my god, Brady!" Ari hisses, her tone low. "She's never going to like us if you keep...being you." She finishes with a laugh, rolling her eyes. "Just ease up on the *baby* this and *do as I say* that. 'K?"

He lifts Ari off the ground, pressing a wet kiss to her cheek. "Sorry, Ari baby. No can do. Paige!" he shouts again, throwing his head back with a laugh.

Paige does come out then, and I can't help but notice how pretty she is.

I think she might have cut her hair since I saw her last, the beautiful, golden-blond locks reaching just below her shoulders, curling outward to give her an even more porcelain-doll look. She's nearly as short as I am but petite, with the body of a ballerina and the poise to match. Her posture is everything my mom wished mine would be, and her smile is soft, as are her features. She's fairer than any of us, her cheeks tinted with a natural blush. When she smiles at Brady, he slaps a hand over his heart in pure, purposeful dramatics.

My eyes fall to the others.

Mason is staring, too.

My gaze slides back to her, taking in her white sundress, her flats the same bright blue as the flowers decorated across it. She's like a walking doll. Chase shifts in my periphery, his eyes narrowed in her direction.

The radio flicks on, and I jolt in my seat, my eyes snapping forward, finding Mason staring at me with a blank expression. Slowly, his eyes slide to his friend outside the car, and I take that moment to sink farther in my seat.

Thankfully, everyone piles in, and I focus on giving Deaton all my attention. We play peekaboo and tickle monster. He spends at least ten minutes holding on to my finger, lifting and lowering it over and over again as his little arms flail.

I clap a few times, and he smiles, sticking his fingers in his mouth and making a little squeal. I laugh and hold my hands before him. It doesn't take long for him to understand, and he grabs my fingers, pushing them together, helping me clap.

"Your turn, mister man." I take his hands and clap them together.

He kicks his feet with excitement, making soft cooing sounds. I let go, hoping he'll finally figure it out on his own, but he just reaches for mine again. We go back and forth for several minutes. Trying something new, I clap his hands a good five times, making animated smiles and sounds as I go. On the last clap, I let go but leave my palms hovering close to his own, and he instinctively follows the rhythm, his hands meeting in the middle with the softest little *clap*.

His blue eyes widen, as does my smile. He tries again, missing the first time and then again, *clap, clap, clap*.

"You did it!" I shout, my heart freaking melting when a laugh bubbles from his throat.

Both Chase's and Mason's heads whip around, both men pushing up in their seats to get a look at his face. I spare them a smile, quickly looking back to Deaton.

144

He claps again, so happy at the sound he's creating that he keeps laughing, his little face turning red.

"How is this the cutest fucking thing I've ever seen?" Mason stares intently, his best friend chuckling at his side.

"'Cause it is." Chase reaches back, brushing his fingers along Deaton's curly hair.

Mason watches his friend's every move, his frown deepening by the second. He, too, reaches back then, the frown wiped free when Deaton instantly wraps his fist around Mason's pointer finger. He drags it right into his mouth, slobbering all over him before Mason can pull back.

"Always straight to the mouth, huh, my man?" Mason laughs, retreating slightly, and then he's on his knees in his seat, stretching his torso over me.

I press against the seat, trying to disappear, but there's nowhere to go, and then he's *right there*, his face inches from mine, brown eyes as stormy as ever. I hold my breath, shocked at what he's doing, panicking over the others seeing. But then his hand comes back up, and in it is the little plush football Deaton tossed a while ago.

Eyes still locked on mine, he passes the toy to Deaton. "Here you go, little man," he murmurs, finally pulling back.

He spins in his seat, and I sink in mine, my cheeks burning. I don't have to look up to know someone's eyes are on me. I don't know whose, but I feel them.

I peek to the screen on my phone.

Only four more hours.

Fuck my life.

———————

It's after dark when we pull up to the pump at the gas station. Ahead of us, everyone piles out at once, stretching and walking our way.

My brother gets out to pump the gas, and the others peek in, whispering when Kenra puts her fingers to her lips.

"He's sleeping?" Ari coos, cupping her hands to look at him through the far back window before sticking her head back in her brother's door once more. "How's he done on the drive so far?"

"He's been fine," Mason answers before I can, and I frown.

"If crying for forty minutes until he was hiccupping in his sleep and freaking Mason out means *fine*, then he did perfectly fine," Chase teases, leaning away when Mason reaches over to punch him on the arm.

"I did not freak out," he snaps.

"No? You only stared at him for fifteen minutes after, checking his pulse when he got too still."

Cameron and Brady laugh at him, but his sister practically has hearts in her eyes.

"Hey, his head kept falling over!" Mason defends. "I had to make sure."

"His mama was right beside him." Chase fights a smile. "You were being ridiculous."

"It was sweet." The words leave my mouth before I realize I'm speaking, and Mason's head yanks my way.

His eyes pierce mine, something flashing behind his dark orbs, but the spell is broken when Cameron starts talking.

"'K, well, we're starved, and there's, like, fifty thousand fast food options here. We figured we'd grab and go, save some time," She hooks her long arm around Ari.

The others pile out, and when I hold back, Parker leans in the door. "You staying behind?"

"Yeah. It's a miracle he's sleeping still, now that the car stopped, so I don't want to wake him if he's not ready."

"We'll grab you something."

I nod, and he closes the door, locking us inside.

I stretch out on the seat, arching my back and rolling my neck.

146

Moving so my legs are over the seat in front of me, I close my eyes, taking advantage of this moment alone, knowing I might not get many others over the next few days.

Just when my muscles begin to relax again, Deaton's soft clap has my eyes snapping open.

I giggle, staring at my little boy and moving over, taking him from his seat.

"Well, well. Aren't you a master at that now." I hold him up, and he stretches his arms up high before locking his legs and jumping up and down on my thighs. "Someone's excited, isn't he?" I kiss his cheek, dropping onto my knees in the small leg space I have. "Hate to have to do this to you, but we've got to get you changed."

Surprisingly, Deaton doesn't fuss, just stares up at the seat belt, trying to wrap it in his tiny hand as I get him all cleaned up and changed into a warmer sleeper.

Setting him on his feet, I keep one of his hands in mine to help steady him and let him lean his weight against my legs for support. I dig a jar of baby food from the bag and the small container of mashed bananas. He only takes a few bites of the chicken and rice concoction but devours the fruit. Just as I get to the last bite, he starts to fuss, rubbing at his eyes again, and starts tugging on me.

"Okay, little man. Okay." I pull a bottle out, hoping he'll take the formula okay, since I've only stopped breastfeeding for a handful of days now.

Of course, the change in our routine isn't settling for him, and he bats it away several times, whimpering slightly.

The door opens then, and I look up to find Mason there, an Arby's bag in his hands. He looks tired, almost worn out as he holds it up without a word, and I force a smile, accepting, fully aware of what's inside it without him saying a word.

"Can I hold him a minute?" he asks, quickly adding, "You can run in, use the restroom, stretch or whatever."

"He's a little fussy…"

Mason pushes the seat forward, then walks around and takes Chase's seat, reaching back with open, expectant arms.

Slowly, I pass Deaton over, not looking back as I climb out of the car.

I take my time, use the restroom even though I don't need to, and walk the aisles since no one else is standing around the car yet. I grab a cream soda and a pack of cheese crackers before heading back outside.

Kenra and Parker are standing by the pump now, Ari waiting to climb back into the Bronco after Cam.

"They're so sweet." Ari beams my way just before pulling her door closed.

I frown, looking to my brother and his girlfriend, but they're both just leaning against the hood, playing on their phones.

I open the SUV door to climb in but stop short.

Mason is passed out in Chase's seat. The bottle I left him with is half-empty in his hands, Deaton curled up on his chest, sleeping like a little angel.

My features pull, something in my chest doing the same damn thing.

Despite myself, despite the pain and anger sparking within me, I can't deny there's more.

They look so peaceful.

So...precious.

They look like father and son.

The thought splinters through me, shattering the shell of respite I'd built back up.

With jerky movements, I push the seat forward and begin to pull my baby from his arms.

Mason's grip tightens around Deaton at first, his eyes snapping open with a glare, but the moment he realizes it's just me, his hold eases, and I swiftly take my son back. Silently, I climb into the back seat, buckling him back into his car seat.

Just as I get settled, Chase reappears. He sees Mason in his spot and goes around to the other side.

"Here." He grins, passing back a cream soda and a pack of cheese crackers.

A small chuckle leaves me at the sight, my muscles locking when, in my periphery, Mason's body shifts this way, but I don't look at him.

I thank Chase and sit back, hiding my own snack in my bag so he won't feel bad, and cover my head with a blanket to pretend I want to try and get some sleep.

Yes, it's a coward's move, especially when I know I won't be able to sleep for several more hours.

Still, I sit there silently, breathing through a mask of fleece until the car rolls to a stop and my brother announces we've arrived.

That's when I learn about the sleeping arrangements.

If I thought this trip was going to be tense before...

It just went into overdrive.

CHAPTER 18
MASON

Now, September

"Ninety-seven, ninety-eight, ninety-nine..." I reach my goal, then do two more. I quickly pop up from the push-ups and jog in place for thirty seconds. My shoulders ache, my core muscles pulsing, but I drop back down again, this time into a five-finger plank.

The burn in my abdomen is intense, but I breathe through it, counting down from forty-five, then hold a little longer before collapsing on the mat.

"You've been in here for almost three hours."

I push up onto my ass, folding my arms over my bent knees, and look toward the door.

Chase shoves off the frame, slowly stepping into the garage of the Airbnb we rented. He glances around, noting an elliptical, a treadmill, and a station of free weights. "So this is the *home gym included*, huh?" he says, quoting the ad.

I scoff, nodding toward the bucket in the corner. "At least they have mats to put down. Saw a couple of jump ropes in there, too."

Chase nods, moving over to the treadmill and climbing on. He ties his hoodie up over his head and starts with a slow jog. "You skipped breakfast."

"I had a protein shake."

"You went to bed without talking to anyone last night."

"I was tired. Why you so worried about me?" I snap, shoving off the ground and pulling my shirt over my head. I use it to wipe the sweat from my face.

"Because I see what's going on." When I say nothing, he adds, "You didn't come to class on Thursday. We had a test."

I look away, wrapping my T-shirt around my neck, and move for the door.

"We're here to relax and hang out with our friends a couple of days, Mason."

"I'm aware."

"Don't fuck it up."

"Me?" I whip around. "What could I possibly do to fuck it up?"

He eyes me a moment, increasing the speed he's running at and hitting an incline. "You're in your head. You have been for a while. I'm not sure what's going on exactly, but I think I know enough, and you're running toward ruin. Try to let it go."

I scoff, turning my back and heading for the door. "I bet you would just love that."

"What's that supposed to mean?" he shouts after me, but I close the door.

The house is quiet aside from the TV running in the living room, Kenra asleep on the couch.

Grabbing four cold water bottles from the fridge, I down one and carry the other three toward the room down the hall. With a soft knock, I push the door open.

Brady is out cold on the twin bed on the right side of the room, his skin clammy, while Cameron and Paige are sitting up on the other bed. Cameron has a box of tissues and a blanket wrapped around her, reading from a school textbook, while Paige is staring at the TV that has no sound coming from it.

Fuck, I guess I should have brought my books, too. Not that it would help. There's no way my professor lets me make up the test, not when I'm already behind in her coursework. I grit my teeth, pushing the worries aside, and meet the girls' gazes.

"Hey." Cameron smiles through a light cough.

I wiggle the water bottles. "Brought you guys something cold to drink." I set them beside her and look to Brady. "He good?"

"He's been snoring like a bulldog for the last two hours." Cameron shrugs. "So he's alive at least. Thinks he can sleep off the ick."

Paige laughs, then groans, her hands flying to her temples. "I'm so sad. I can't believe we're going to miss the game tonight. Who gets sick sitting in a car for six hours and doesn't get better when they get out of it?"

They were hoping the vomiting was from car sickness, which neither usually gets, but all three woke up feeling just as shitty as they did when they went to bed.

"There will be plenty more games to go to. Just rest, maybe try to sleep it off like Brady."

Both girls push out their lower lips into a pout, and a grin pulls at my lips.

"Let me know if you need anything. One of us will make you guys some food before we leave."

"Noah's not here to work his magic in the kitchen." Cameron throws herself back dramatically. "So, my sweet Paige, that means all we're gonna get is canned soup."

"I can bring it to you cold."

Cameron gives a fake smile, fluttering her lashes. "Canned soup will be just fine, please and thank you. But if you don't mind, I'm climbing in bed with the beast. He's burning up, and I'm freezing."

Shaking my head, I go to step out, but Cameron pops over to the door, grabbing the frame, so I pause in the doorway.

Her smile is softer now as she looks up at me, whispering, "You okay, Mase?"

Tension tugs at my chest, and I force a nod, but I can feel

the frown along my brow dig deeper. "Yeah, I'm good. Perfect. Fine."

She tips her head slightly, reading the lie on my tongue easily enough. "Sometimes people fight against things because they're afraid of how they'll play out."

For a moment, I'm stuck staring at her, but then I manage to force a laugh. "I have no idea what you're talking about, girl. Go on. Get in bed with Brady. Feel better, okay?" I think I manage a grin and then softly close the door behind me.

The minute it's shut, my face falls, and I squeeze my eyes closed.

Get a grip, my man.

Sighing, I head upstairs. I go to enter the room I was moved to, but my hand won't wrap around the handle. I move past it into the bathroom for a cool shower.

My muscles bunch under the spray, slowly easing with each passing minute. I take a deep breath, trying to block out the stupid thoughts racing through my head.

So Chase bought Payton a soda. Big deal.

I'm sure Ari and the others know her drink of choice, too, just as I know what they like. Sure, I've known them for most of my life, but that doesn't make a difference, right?

Yeah, it's normal to notice things like that.

What's *not* normal is the ghostly color she turned when Ari announced the room changes, since the others got sick on the last half of the drive.

It's not like she has to share with anyone. She just got moved from the one downstairs she was originally going to stay in to the one upstairs where us boys are, and only so the baby would have less chance of getting sick. Instead of still sleeping close to the sick girls and Brady.

Yeah, that puts her right next to me and Chase, but so what? Maybe she's just worried the baby will wake us up?

Chase sleeps like the dead, when he sleeps at all, so I doubt he'll even notice. He'll stick to the living room, watching ESPN like he does back at the dorms, only going to his room to sleep.

Me? I'll be waiting, okay, hoping, to hear that little cry that tells me they're up. I want to hold him, and I need a minute alone with her.

Might have to yell at her, I don't know yet, but she's going to talk to me.

She needs to tell me we're on the same page.

That she didn't change her mind.

Shit.

What if she did change her mind?

Wrapping my arms around Ari, I lift and spin her in the air. "How'd you like that, baby sister?" I shout, the hype real and the two beers I had while waiting for Noah to get here warming me up. "Your man just won his team the game!"

"And not one but two touchdowns!" Brady, who says he sweat out his sickness, screams into the air, turning to a group of random strangers walking into the pub, wearing jerseys. "Hey. Number nineteen is my girl's man. You see him out there?"

The women giggle and walk off, but Brady isn't deterred, telling everyone in the vicinity Noah Riley is a badass and entirely spoken for.

Noah drops his eyes to the floor at the praise, quickly stepping up and demanding his woman back. The second Ari's on her feet, he's got her wrapped in his arms, and I turn away when he bends down to whisper something in her ear.

Love the guy…but she's still my sister.

As I swing around to face the others—we're cooped up in the back corner of the only restaurant in walking distance to both the stadium and the rental—a frown pulls at my forehead.

Payton passes Deaton off to Chase, heading toward Brady

154

when he calls her name, and I reach Chase just as the other two curl around the corner.

His eyes pop up, and he leans back slightly, not realizing I was so close as the smile he had pointed at my little man fades. "What's up?" His brow furrows.

"Give him to me." I reach out, but Chase doesn't pass him over right away, so I take a step closer.

Chase shakes his head, as if just realizing what I said. "Yeah, man. I was going to order some more wings or something anyway."

He passes him over, but Deaton's still between us when Payton reappears.

She steps up, taking him from both our hands. "Thanks," she mumbles, sliding between our chests to get to the others, but I gently wrap my hand around her upper arm, halting her movement.

Her eyes snap my way, pleading and flicking to Chase for the briefest of moments. "I'm going to go sit by Ari and Noah. He wanted to hold him, so…"

I want to hold him.

I miss him. Can't you see that?

My fingers twitch against her soft skin, and it takes ample effort to let go, but I do. I step back, my jaw clenched so fucking tight I might need a dentist after this shit.

It's fine.

No big deal.

Noah and Ari lost so much, it's good for them to bond with my little guy.

Besides, I'm still his favorite.

Everything is fine.

When I face forward again, Chase is still there.

He eyes me warily, keeping his voice low as he leans in. "You good, brother?"

"You gonna stop pissing me off, *brother*?"

His head jerks back, and I curse under my breath, lurch past him, and head to the bar on the other side of the room, taking a minute to settle myself. Or trying, at the very least.

It helps that the place is packed to the brim, especially since the bartender doesn't bother or forgets to ask for my ID—not that it would matter, because I have a fake one that hasn't failed me yet—when I order two pitchers of cheap beer.

The waiter follows me back to our section, setting several chilled mugs beside the pitchers, and I look up at the others with a forced smile.

I meet Noah's gaze first. His head is cocked as he stares at me, Deaton jumping up and down in his hands, his little feet smaller than the cardboard coaster he's kicking around. Ari sits at their side, concern written in her gaze.

My attention falls to the tabletop, and I fight the scowl threatening to take over.

Am I being that transparent here?

What do they see when they look at me?

A man who isn't wanted?

Fuck.

I grit my teeth and pour the golden liquid into a mug, offer it to my friends.

Every single person passes, and my pulse jumps in my throat.

Fuck it. Whatever.

I drink the glass myself. And then I drink another.

And another.

A while later, a smile breaks across my face.

Who finished the other pitcher?

"Guess I didn't have to drink alone after all." A chuckle leaves me, and I glance up when Brady drops beside me. "My man!" I shout, wrapping my arm around his shoulder and yanking his big-ass body closer. "I fuckin' love you."

"Ditto." He chuckles low, placing his forearms on the table and coming so close my vision crosses a bit. "You feelin' good over here?"

"Fuck yeah." My body seems to sway a bit, and I laugh again, lifting my glass. When nothing comes out, I bring it before my eyes. A frown is instant. "Who drank my beer?"

Brady scoffs, bumping his shoulder into mine. "Might wanna slow down, my boy. Long drive back tomorrow."

"I don't have to drive." I shrug, thinking about the long-ass way here. "I just gotta sit there in my seat. Get ignored some more."

Brady glares, and when I look up, Payton is staring with a turbulent expression.

Is she sad? Mad? Worried? I don't know, but if I know her like I think I do, she's a bit of all three. But why? I'm the one dying over here.

It's my chest she's cracking open and my heavy beating heart she's tearing out, one tug at a time. And for what?

Or is it *for whom*?

No. It can't be.

But what if it is?

The alcohol in my system brings my blood to a boil at the sideways thoughts, and my eyes narrow on the pretty blue ones holding me hostage.

"Hey, Brady." My voice carries over the noise, my gaze locked on my girl. "What's Payton's favorite thing to drink?"

"What?" he chuckles.

Payton's eyes fall then, and guess who walks up behind her? I glare at my other best friend, but I repeat my question to the one at my side. "Her favorite drink. What is it?"

"Uh...Dr P?"

My limbs shake. "Wrong."

Chase shakes his head, dropping down on the bench-like seat beside her, and she faces his way, answering whatever question he asks.

"Dude," Brady whispers. "What am I missin'?"

He might keep talking. It's hard to tell when my eyes are locked on the Chatty fucking Cathys a few spots over.

157

What could they possibly have to say to each other?

Chase hardly talks to any of us anymore, ever since he realized his mistakes with my sister.

I thought he felt like shit, that he was embarrassed by his actions and couldn't face us because of his own inner bullshit. That sounds like the Chase I know.

I love that fucker. Die for him if it came to that.

But maybe I was wrong.

Maybe he's being sneaky.

Maybe they both are.

Payton's tense laugh reaches me. It invades my mind and sweeps through me, the sensation calming and *right*, but then my brain catches up.

He made her laugh.

He made her laugh, and she won't even talk to me.

She's talking to him.

He knows what she likes to drink.

"Are you two fucking?"

Gasps and sputtered curses fill the air, but I hold the gaze of the girl who's breaking my fucking heart here.

"Tell me the truth."

"Mason. Please," she whispers, but her eyes scream so much more.

They tell me how disappointed she is, how out of all people I should know the answer to that question. That I shouldn't have to ask it in the first place.

But I do.

"Did you make him a promise, too?"

"Stop," she begs.

"Did he tell you that—"

"You're drunk, man. Just quit talking before you say somethin' you regret." Chase steps around the corner. "Let's get you back to the house, huh? You need to—"

"You need to stop trying to get with girls who aren't available!"

158

Payton turns beet red, Ari gasps, and Noah's eyes grow wide.

Brady steps up with his hands raised. "All right. Enough. Let's take a breath here, and—"

"Fuck you, Mason." Chase cuts him off.

"Nah, fuck you!" I shoot to my feet, my arm shooting out to keep balance. "I'm trying to talk to her."

"Not like this."

Rage rolls through me, and even my spine starts to shake. "You think you can speak for her?"

"You guys," Brady tries again.

"At least she's *speaking* to me!"

My fist flies so fast no one's stopping it. My knuckles come down across his cheek, and Chase's head snaps to the side.

Instantly, everyone screams and shouts.

Security barrels over, and I hear my friends yelling, but my feet are already being dragged across the floor. I'm eating a mouthful of dirt in seconds, my head pounding, vision as foggy as a winter morning.

Someone helps me to my feet, and when I look into Chase's eyes, I yank away.

"Get off me, man."

"I'm helping you, jackass."

"No, you're fucking with me. Everyone is."

He shakes his head, and I stomp my way toward the Airbnb, the soft murmurs and footsteps of the others not far behind.

When we reach the door, I stumble to the side, letting someone else open it.

No one bothers to tell me to come in, so I let it get shut in my face, wondering when the wall behind me is going to stop wobbling.

Who knows how long I stand there, but eventually a waft of warmth greets me as someone steps out.

"Oh my god, your hand." Soft fingers brush my wrist, but I yank it back.

"Don't pretend to care." I blink, pretty blue eyes coming in and out of focus.

"That's not fair," Payton whispers.

"You know what's not fair?" I rasp, my head rolling to the opposite side, lids too heavy to keep open. "What you said and what you're doing. You're killing me." I breathe, forcing my lids to open and meet the prettiest eyes I've ever seen. "I'm fucking dying here, baby."

Her beautiful face is blurred, so I raise my hand to make sure she's really there, that I'm not imagining it. The second my knuckles meet her silken skin, I jolt. Pain slices through me, and I stumble away in panic, gripping my wrist.

"Fuck." I look at my hand, but there's too many fingers there. "Fuck, fuck, fuck!"

I jerk, stumbling into the house, and manage to find my way to the bathroom.

I struggle to reach the faucet of the sink, finally figuring out how to get the damn thing on and shove my hand under the stream. "Shit!" I yank it back, the water too hot.

I reach up again, but soft fingers gently curl around my shoulder, sliding down my spine, and my head falls to my chest, the sensation shutting off everything else. All I feel is her.

God, I want more.

"Let me help you," she murmurs.

"You can do whatever you want to me, Pretty Little. Anything. Always."

Payton grabs my other hand, leading me who knows where, but I follow like an eager pup, and then I'm sitting on something soft. My eyes close, only opening again when a cooling sensation meets my knuckles.

Strawberry-blond hair and puffy pink lips hover above me, like my own little angel.

"Where's my little man?"

"Sleeping. I laid him in the playpen before I came back outside to get you."

I nod, my head turning when the bed shifts. Payton sits on her knees, gently setting the bag of ice over my knuckles.

Several quiet minutes go by before she speaks again, and when she does, it's a low, torn whisper that claws at my insides. "I know things are…" She shakes her head, unsure what the right word is or unwilling to say it.

It doesn't matter though. None of it does.

This girl could stick a knife in me, marry my best friend, and disappear for a decade, and so long as she came back for me in the end, it would. Not. Matter.

Only one thing does.

My fingers stretch under the Ziploc covering them, the tips brushing against her bare knee.

Slowly, her eyes come to mine.

I blink through the fog in my vision, trying to control the alcohol bobbing in my brain so I can hold her gaze. I reach out, tucking the loose strands of her hair behind her ear, my palm lingering in the spot.

Subconsciously, Payton turns into my touch, her eyes closing. "Mase."

"I fucking miss you."

Her whole body quakes.

"Can I hold you?"

She sucks in a choppy breath, those blue eyes on me.

"Please, Pretty Little…" My eyes start to close, my words more slurred than the last ones. "I need to hold you."

"And I need to take care of you," she murmurs.

My mouth curves at that, and I fall into my memories of the first time she spoke those words to me, desperately holding on to what happened afterward.

My life changed the last time she took care of me.

Everything changed that day.

But what will I wake up to tomorrow?

CHAPTER 19
MASON

Before, November

Tugging my sweats on, I towel dry my hair and step out of the hotel bathroom. Noah's chilling in the same spot I left him, grinning at his phone like a fool.

"That better be my sister you're smiling at, dick." I hear her laugh and grin to myself as I slide back into the bathroom to brush my teeth.

When I come back, Ari's girlish squeal fills the room.

"Ah shit, you told her, didn't you?" I shout, popping my head beside Noah's to catch a glimpse of my sister on the screen.

"Holy shit!" She beams, Cameron crowded beside her.

"I know." A chuckle leaves me, and I give a playful glare when tears fill her eyes. "Knock it off."

"Oh my god, Mase." Her tone is thick with emotion. "You're going to rock it."

"Love you, girls."

"Love you!" they shout.

I heave a long sigh, stepping out into the hall before I, too, get emotional. That would be embarrassing in front of my captain, but aside from that, I don't want to get sappy when I'm juiced like this.

What I want is to share this with the first person who came to mind when I learned the news.

I pull her name up, anticipation firing inside me with each ring, but when her voicemail picks up in the end, a defeated breath pushes past my lips. I kick off the wall, ready to head back to the room, but before I make it a single step, my phone is ringing, a picture of an unsuspecting blond staring out at the ocean lighting up my screen.

"Pretty Little," I answer.

"Superstar."

My lips curve, and I can picture her smirk. "Why didn't you answer my FaceTime call?"

"Not everyone can look as perfect as you all the time."

"I mean, duh." She laughs in my ear, and I lean back against the wall. I like her laugh. "If everyone could, my superpowers would be insignificant." I pull the phone way, hitting the FaceTime button again. "Answer, Pretty Little. I wanna see your face when I tell you what I called to tell you."

"You just want your way."

"Also true." I chuckle, nodding at two of my teammates when they walk by and moving so I'm a little farther down the hall. "Come on now, and don't tear your lower lip apart thinking too hard about it."

She goes silent, and I smirk to myself. A moment later, I'm accepting her video call.

She pops up on the screen, her head propped up on a mountain of pillows. Her face is makeup-free, hair spread out around her and wet from what I'm assuming was the shower, if her pink pj's tell me anything.

She looks as perfect as ever.

My smile is ridiculous. "Hi."

"Hi." She smiles back, shaking her head. "I never thought a pregnant belly would help hold things for me, but a little extra blanket and boom. Hands free." She wiggles her fingers, and a low laugh leaves me.

I can't help but note the color in her face and lax expression.

She's having a good day. No dark circles or redness around the eyes. I don't think she cried today, and damn if that doesn't send a sense of pride through me. She's strong, and I hope she's starting to realize it. "You look good."

She scoffs, pushing herself up and holding the phone back to show me her swollen belly. "I look like I swallowed a watermelon and got stung by a hundred bees."

"Watermelon is my favorite."

"And the bees?" She lifts a brow, her playfulness making me all the more eager to share my news.

"What are you doing tomorrow?" I ask, knowing she's going to roll her eyes cause we both know she'll be watching my game, if only to text me something in her brand of silly afterward.

She smiles, and I wait to hear it. "Actually, I'm going with Lolli to watch Nate's game at USD."

My face falls instantly.

She sits up, a small frown pulling at her forehead. "Why? What's up?"

"Nothing." My answer is too quick, and worry washes over her, her mouth opening, but I quickly add, "Hey, I've got to go. Don't think about me too long, all right?"

She doesn't buy the grin on my face, but a small smile does curve her lips. "In your dreams, Superstar."

We hang up, and I wonder what she would say if I responded with *more often than not*.

Sleep doesn't come so easily after that. I'm too keyed up, an anxious excitement blending with the bitter taste of disappointment knowing my girl, I mean Payton, won't get to see me in action.

Sure, she'll catch the highlights like always, but it's not the same. I want her to hear the roar of the crowd and know she's sitting on the edge of her seat when I step out on that field. 'Cause there is no doubt in my mind she would be, just like my sister and Cameron will.

Or are right this minute, because it's time, and nothing is going to sour this moment for me.

Let's.

Fucking.

Go!

I growl, stretching my lips out along the mouthpiece as I bob from foot to foot, hopping high into the air to the heavy beats blasting through the stadium speakers, but it's go time now.

Slowly, the music fades, the crowd goes crazy, and I watch with sharp eyes as Jency Fayo, our kick returner, catches the ball and dances his way down the field. He jukes left, then right, spinning until he passes the thirty-yard line. The defenders come at him from every direction, and he goes down at the twenty.

A hand slaps my shoulder, and I look over.

Noah grins, shoving me forward. "Take it home."

"Let me show you how it's done, pretty boy." I smirk, and Noah chuckles goodheartedly, not in the least put off by the fact that I'm starting in his position today.

We couldn't be more different in that sense. He's mentally secure in what he does and has to offer.

I know I'm good but have no greater fear than falling over the edge of insignificance.

I need to do well, show Coach he made the right choice when he offered me this position, knowing his star player won't be coming back next year.

None of my hard work matters if I'm not wearing that C — marking me team captain— on my chest next season, when Noah retires it on his way to the NFL.

None of it.

I jog out alongside our starting offense, and the second my cleats hit the turf, all the noise falls away, my brain fires on a hundred, and I become the fucking game.

The call is given, the team lines up, and my nostrils flare as I drag in a long lungful of charged air. I give the signal, and the ball is snapped.

It's a good fucking snap, the leather between my palms, the laces tingling against my skin.

The call is meant to confuse the defense, my side shuffle and the drop of my wrists leading them to believe we're going for a quick toss to the running back. They shift, my line holds strong, and I step back, firing down the field. My receiver is wide open, and the ball drops into his open gloves with precision. He's taken down instantly, but that don't matter.

The crowd goes wild, the chains are moved, and it's first down, Sharks.

We jog down the field, bending into position, ready to get the next play underway. This time, the snap goes a little high, forcing me to call an audible and change the play on the fly to maximize the potential of success.

The O line opens up a gap, and I break through, my legs pumping, ball gripped tight. The safety drops down, and a linebacker charges from my left, so I propel my feet faster, getting one extra yard before sliding onto my side.

The whistle is blown, and I pop up, tossing the ball to the ref.

First down again.

Fuck. Yes.

The coach gives the next play, an outside slant, the target being the deepest corner of the end zone, and I'm going to make it happen.

We get set. I line my boys up and step back.

"One! One!" I look left, then right. "Set, hike!"

I drop back, focused downfield, shifting on my feet as I get ready to bomb it. I draw back, knowing without a doubt this ball is gonna land between ten fingers with ease.

My arm whips forward, and I don't see the moment my line collapses. I'm blindsided. As hard as a bull, I'm slammed on my right side. My body bends, and in the same moment, a second body collides with my left. My lips pull back, pain exploding in my ribs. I briefly register my feet leaving the ground. The crowded stadium whips across my vision as my helmet is thrown from my head seconds before my body slams into the ground, emptying my lungs and turning the whole world black.

It's no wonder people go mad after long stints in the hospital. The incessant beeping of machines alone is enough to drive you insane, and if that doesn't do it, the pitying looks from the nurses will.

Outside of a quick phone call to let my family know I'm alive, I've spoken to no one over the last twenty-four hours.

My team is already back on campus, preparing for a long day of practice tomorrow, and I'm sitting in a fucking wheelchair at an airport. The gang thinks my cousin is picking me up, but I lied to my sister when I told her that.

I can't face any of them right now, especially Nate when I saw the score from his game. He slayed, and I got fucking filleted.

My cousins likely think I'm headed back to my parents' house, and my parents think I'm headed to the beach house where my cousins can help look after me. I don't plan to tell anyone, and I'm hoping the others won't find out I'll be staying just down the road. I don't need their help or pity during this *mandatory recovery period*.

That's right. I've been benched, deemed useless to my team.

Not my team. *The* team. The team I'm technically not a part of for the next who the hell knows how long.

Who gets injured on the first drive of the first game they start in at a higher level?

Weak, slow, worthless fuckers, that's who.

A familiar truck pulls up, and my buddy jogs around, but I

don't meet his eyes. I can feel him staring though, taking in my injuries and this chair I don't need but am required to sit in so long as the team facilitator is standing beside me.

The second he pulls open the passenger door, my glare grows deeper.

"I can open a door." I push to my feet, forcing myself to stand tall. My ribs scream in protest, but I don't show it.

Duke lifts his hands and stands back, watching as I walk toward the vehicle, my hoodie tight due to all the bandages wrapped around me beneath it.

My shoulder is on fire, burning like a dozen branding sticks are pressed into my skin, but I hide that, too. I climb inside and don't look his way when he glances over.

Duke is a cool dude, a surfer we met years ago who gives cheap lessons off the pier. Sure, I had to pay him to come get me, but I like it that way. Now I don't feel obligated to talk, and he's perfectly happy to sit back and listen to the soft rock bullshit he likes so much.

Needless to say, the ride is a long one filled with nothing but shitty music and an overwhelming array of emotions, the easiest of those to hold on to being anger. Anger is good. I might buckle under anything else, but at least rage can be funneled into something else.

When we pull up to the beach house, he parks in the damn grass, getting as obnoxiously close to the front door as possible. He's grinning when I swing my scowl on him, and I almost relax, but the tension doubles when I struggle, and he quickly looks away.

Sighing, I face him with a forced smile. "Thanks for coming, man."

"I was free, so no big." He shrugs. "Let me know if you… Just call if you want."

I nod, climbing from the truck, every inch of my body object-ing. That's the only reason I don't get pissed when he carries the small, worthless duffel I had taken on the away trip. There's nothing in there but a toothbrush, some deodorant, and the pills the doc sent me home with, the clothes I'd brought for the ride home already on my back. I don't even have a phone charger.

He doesn't try to come in, and I don't bother with an invite, just close the door and hide myself inside.

With each aching step, I curse the world a little more, determined to make it to the kitchen for a glass of water.

By the time I get one filled, my limbs are shaking, and it hurts to breathe. Pushing off the island, I head back for the living room. I nearly pass out from the throbbing in my temples, my hand shooting out to grip the wall, but of course, my dominant hand is what goes out to save me, sling be damned.

"Ah!" I scream in agony as my shoulder erupts in flames, and this time, my knees buckle.

The glass falls from my fingertips as my body goes down. It shatters across the tile floor, and I slam into the broken shards, screaming again when my rib seem to crack a little more.

"Fuck! Fuck! Fuck!" I shout, kicking at the wall, my head lolling to the side.

That's when I do a double take, my entire body freezing in horror, gaze focused out the floor-to-ceiling window of the back deck.

One the other side, big blue eyes stare back at me in shock.

PAYTON

My mouth is hanging open, my limbs frozen as I stare through the clear glass.

Mason.

He's...here.

Why is he here?

He squeezes his eyes closed, and mine fall. The blood on the floor is what snaps me out of it, and I jump up, my camera tumbling to the wooden deck beneath my feet as I dash for the slider. I tug, but it's locked. My eyes snap up to him, but he's facing away from me now, so I run around the wraparound porch. Thankfully, the front is open, and seconds later, I'm barreling into the house, coming to a screeching halt when I reach the kitchen.

"Oh my god." My hand drops to my belly, worry washing over me and completely unsure of what I'm really looking at. "Mase."

"Leave."

My head snaps up, our eyes locking, and he gives me a look I've never seen from him.

Anger. His lip is curled, teeth clenched, and there's a dark fire in his brown gaze.

I move closer.

"I said leave," he snaps, his head yanking in the opposite direction.

I bend down in front of him, one hand holding on to the island to keep me steady, my other trembling as I reach out and brush my fingers over his knee.

Slowly, he glances over, and the bravado falls instantly. "Please leave," he whispers, his tone so desperate, something stirs in my chest. "I can't stand you seeing me like this."

"Well, we have to get even, don't we?" I whisper, smiling softly when he frowns. "You've seen me a heck of a lot worse."

A hint of a smile tugs at his lips before it's gone. "So you're saying this is only fair?"

I shrug, and he drops his chin to his chest.

"Can I help you stand? You may or may not have glass sticking out of your ass."

Mason huffs a laugh, and instantly his back bows, a harsh wince whooshing past his lips. He starts panting, and worry claws at my throat.

He's hurt, that's obvious. But how? When?

I stand, tugging gently on his left hand, seeing as his right is cradled to his chest, but he doesn't budge, instead yanking back with a look of horror on his face.

"The baby." He shakes his head.

"If I feel like I'm straining myself, I'll stop. Trust me." I reach out again, and Mason's jaw twitches.

Slowly, he allows me to take his hand, but he gives me little to no weight, his nostrils flaring with his own exertion. He turns slightly as he stands, leaning a hip against the island, and I shift behind him. I glance at his back, and there's no glass in his sweats I can see, so I shuffle closer, hoping he'll lean on me at the least.

"Be careful," he whispers. "Don't get glass in your feet."

I look down at the sandals I'm wearing but say nothing as I try to slide under his left arm, but he doesn't allow it, shifting away and moving ahead at a slow pace.

His posture is rigid, his fist bloody and clenched. I follow behind as he makes his way toward the couch and eases himself down.

A harsh breath hisses past his lips, and he drops his head back with a pant, as if it took all he had in his tank to get there.

My heart rate picks up, concern consuming me. He's so pale, no sign of the forever tan I know him to wear, and his face is scrunched in pain and misery. Before I turn to a pile of panic, I rush back into the kitchen, snagging the first aid kit.

When I come back, Mason glances my way from the corner of his eye. "I'll be fine. You can go."

I lower onto the cushion beside him.

"I'm serious, Payton."

I fold my feet under me.

He faces forward with a frown. "I'm tired."

"I could use a nap." I tip my head. "I mean, you're just a little bruised. I'm the one carrying around a bowling ball."

A grin splits his lips, and he jerks, his hand flying to his ribs. "Fuck, it hurts to even think about laughing."

I say nothing, and after a stretch of silence, he sighs and holds his palm out.

Gingerly, I take his hand, using a pair of tweezers to remove two small pieces of glass, and then wipe the skin clean. The little cuts aren't big enough to need a Band-Aid, but I add one anyway because they have little footballs all over.

Mason glares at the small white strip, and realization hits me hard and fast.

Oh my god, *football*.

My eyes fly to his face, and when he looks at me, it's with a loaded expression I know all too well. It's panic and pain. It's fear and loss laced with utter disappointment.

And it's all pointed right back at himself.

I have a million questions, and based on his next words, it must show.

"I'm guessing you haven't talked to the others?"

I wince, feeling a little guilty. "I'm sort of…hiding out."

He turns his head my way fully, worry etched in his brown eyes when he's the one who's hurt. "What happened? What's wrong?"

Something stirs in my stomach, drawing a sort of tension there. Mason is sitting here, hardly able to move a muscle, and he's worried about me?

"I'm fine," I manage to whisper.

Now he glares, and a low chuckle leaves me.

"Honest."

"Tell me anyway."

I fight a smile. Even in complete disarray, he's still got his bossy boy edge. Or man.

I peek at him a moment, taking in his sharp features and vivid dark eyes.

Yeah, he's no boy.

Clearing my throat, I focus on his hand. "So my dad showed up out of the blue." I pause, scoffing as I unfold my legs to get more comfortable. "Well, supposedly it was out of the blue. I grilled Parker, and he swears he didn't know Dad was coming, but I feel like that's a lie."

Mason nods slightly, waiting for more.

"Anyway, he asked me to dinner, and I felt like I couldn't say no, so I ended up agreeing, canceling on Lolli last minute."

"And?"

I smash my lips together. "And I wish I hadn't." I frown. "It's just that we're not what I would consider father and daughter anymore, you know? When my mom refused to let him see me after he left her, he didn't exactly go out of his way to try to get around that. But now that *I* got out of that house, he's been around, if only over the phone since he still works as much as he did when we were kids. I do appreciate the effort, I guess, and I love him in a way I could never love my mom, but I lost him a long time ago. I learned how to be fine with that." I shake my head, looking away.

"What is it?" he asks.

This time, I'm the one who drops their head back. "He asked me to move in with him. Says he has room for me and the baby and—"

"No."

My eyes flick up to his, and his gaze narrows further.

"You can't go. Don't go."

My stomach stirs with something unnamable yet familiar, and a heat touches my cheeks. "I don't want to. I like it here." I peep at him to find a strained expression on his handsome face, like he wants to say something but isn't sure what would come out if he opened his mouth.

"Anyway," I quickly continue, "he took me to this cute little restaurant in Santa Monica, and when he dropped me back off this morning, I just…walked over here. Lolli's and Kenra's cars

173

were both parked in the driveway, and I didn't feel like talking.
I've been sitting on the back patio all day."

"Did you eat?"

"I'm fine."

"Did you eat?"

Fighting a smile, I look up into his brown eyes. "Yes, I ate."

I hold his stare, and with every moment that passes, a deeper
sense of torment creeps into his gaze. He wants to talk, but he
can't quite form the words yet.

It must be bad.

The last thing he needs is to feel forced to chat when he isn't
ready. I would know. So I take a page from the Mason Johnson
playbook, prop my head on my fist, and say, "Want me to kick
his ass?"

I don't know who "he" is, and clearly a fight didn't do this to
his body, but the line I borrowed from him does its job.

Another pained laugh escapes him, and he turns to me with a
wretched smile, borrowing a line just the same. "So how boring
is photography?"

"Well, Superstar." I shift toward him. "Let me tell you *all*
about it…"

174

CHAPTER 20
MASON

Before, November

*I wake with a wheeze, pain cording through me like venom enter-*ing the bloodstream, making it hard to fucking breathe. My entire body aches as if I were hit by a dump truck, then tossed into it with a load for compaction.

My lungs can't stretch past half-full, and my ass is sore from being in a sitting position all through the night. I turn my head, my jaw clenching at the strain it puts on my shoulder, and I spot my phone on the nightstand. I try to reach for it, but it feels like I'm being torn in two.

"Fuck," I pant, and the short gasps only make everything hurt even worse. "Ahh," I groan as I toss my legs over the side of the bed, taking short and quick exhales as I tug myself over until my feet can reach the floor.

My eyes squeeze closed, and sweat beads at my forehead from the little exertion. I'm so fucked, my muscles screaming ten times louder today.

My attention falls to the wraps along my ribs, and I glare at the sling holding my throwing arm against me.

Images of the moment before my body was thrown into the air flash before me, and I grind my teeth. I should have seen them coming. Evaded. Cut in the other direction or threw away the ball.

I should have dipped or ran or… "Fuck!"

Shaking my head, I stretch my left arm out, my limb shaking as my fingers brush the edge of my phone. My cheeks expand from the effort, and I have to slip a little more off the mattress to grab it, but I can't get a good grip. It falls to the floor with a thud.

"God damn it!" I scream, just as muted shouting reaches my ears.

My head snaps toward the bedroom door, and with slow movements, I push myself to my feet.

I release a sharp exhale, the stretch of my stomach almost opening my lungs up a little, but the pressure of my broken ribs creeps in a moment after. The pain's too much, so I stand still a moment, trying to focus on the sounds coming from outside the room in order to forget the knife fight happening inside my body. At first, I think I'm hearing things, but then it sounds again.

My brows dip, and I drag my ass from Ari's room, my temporary room since mine is upstairs, and head toward the living room. As I come around the corner, the giant television stares back at me.

My eyes snap across the screen, taking in every detail, every player, and slice back just in time to watch as my body flies into the air, spinning from hits from both directions. My helmet is torn off on impact, and I'm slamming onto the turf with a thunderous boom.

There's a sharp gasp, and I realize it's not coming from the replay.

My head jerks left.

Payton stands at the edge of the couch, fingers pressed to her lips, staring up at my seemingly lifeless body on the screen.

I must move, because her head suddenly yanks my way, and she pales, fumbling with the remote to turn it off, but I reach her before she can, wrapping my palm around hers.

Big blue eyes fly up to mine, tears and an apology written within them.

"I'm sorry," she whispers.

"For what? Caring enough to want to know what happened?" I hit play, my gaze moving between hers and the announcer's worried words playing from the speakers around us as I give her the real details. "Two fractured ribs and a sprained shoulder."

Her lip trembles, and there's a whole other kind of pain behind my ribs.

"Don't cry." My free hand lifts of its own accord, thumb trailing along the soft plumpness of her mouth. "Not for me. I can't take it."

Her attention falls to my body, fingers coming up and gingerly touching the wraps across my skin. She traces every inch and starts to shake a little. "Are you okay?"

With one finger beneath her chin, I tilt her head up, our gazes connecting.

I was planning on saying something, but the second those big blue eyes collide with mine, my train of thought disappears. All that's left is this deep-seated need to touch my lips to hers. To press farther against her and see how close I can get, though I'm already aware the answer would be *not close enough*.

I need more.

I *want* more...and I don't think I'm the only one.

Her fingers fan out across my chest, the tiniest part of her pinkie now pressing to the naked skin just above my wraps, and fuck me. A shudder slashes through me.

Something shifts in her gaze, and the world falls away—my injuries, the pain. The crushing sense of loss.

It's all gone.

She's all that's left.

My hand glides along her jaw until I'm cupping her cheek in my palm.

She doesn't blink, just stares straight into my eyes with this endless intensity. Her lips part, pretty blue eyes widening as her fingers bite into me a little more, and all I can think is *Yes. Dig them deeper. Mark me more.*

My muscles clench, my pulse jumps, and then something knocks against my stomach. Once. Twice.

We both freeze. A small frown pulls at my brows, and then it happens a third time.

Slowly, I look down. "Is…is that…"

"Yeah," she whispers, my free hand already on its way to her pregnant belly.

She takes half a step back.

I take a full step forward, pressing my palm against the front, and the baby kicks again.

A smile breaks across my face instantly, and I look at her.

There are tears in her eyes again, but there's also more. Something deeper.

Something almost…raw. It thumps against my chest walls, a sensation too profound to put into words yet too delicate to understand.

It's heavy and light at the same time.

A weightless force, drawing me to her.

Calling me to her.

My torso tips, my upper body curling over her tiny frame. A hiss instantly whooshes past my lips, my muscles screaming in disapproval, my body having moved on its own without thought or care to its condition.

Her eyes fly wide, and she pulls away, blinking rapidly. "Oh my god, you need to sit down."

She goes to step by me, but my good hand flies out, latching on to her before she can. She gasps, looking up at me with a desperate sort of confusion, the same emotions flitting through my own mind, but I don't care to listen right now. Not to my body or my mind.

"Pretty Little," I rasp, her mouth the North Star to my broken compass, leading me fucking home.

"Well, fucking, *well!*"

Payton literally jumps at the sound of Lolli's voice, and both of us look toward the back door.

Payton smiles sheepishly, and I frown at my cousin's girl.

"I brought French toast." Lolli smirks, holding up a plate of food. "Unless of course you're hungry for something a little more..." Her saucy tone trails off when she notices my bandages, her face pinching with worry.

I tense instantly, heat crawling up my neck, and I go to turn away, but then the little blond beside me jerks forward, using her tiny body to try and hide my much bigger one from view. Like she's protecting me, and just like that, the black cloud hanging over me turns a lighter shade of gray.

"Thanks, Lolli," Payton says swiftly, rushing her way and taking the plate from her. She sets it on the counter with one hand, clasping Lolli's bicep with the other, shocking the shit out of me when she leads Lolli all the way to the door, gently nudges her out of it, and, with a tone that brooks no argument yet somehow still holds gratitude, says, "I'll let you know if we need anything else."

Alone on the other side of the glass doors, Lolli gapes from her to me, but Payton's not done. She yanks the sheer curtains across the window, closing us off completely before she spins to face me.

And I'm. Fucking. Stuck.

She holds me captive as she walks back this way, tucking her long blond hair behind her ear with one hand and snagging the plate of food with the other. Payton grabs my fingers, and I let her lead me to the couch, where she shoves some pillows in the corner. She doesn't let me go until I'm sitting back against them, and then she lowers onto the coffee table in front of me.

She bends, digging into something at the foot of the couch, and when she says "Open," I don't question her.

I open my mouth, and she drops two pills inside before lifting a cup with a straw to my mouth. My lips wrap around it, eyes on hers the entire time.

I release it, and she grabs the plate, setting it on my lap.

"Here." She pushes to her feet, rushing toward the back door. "Now that they know I'm here, I'm going to go home and grab some things."

I watch as she slides her feet into a pair of sandals, my pulse beating a little harder at her words. "Things?"

Her head lifts, gaze finding mine over her shoulder. "I need to take care of you." A small frown pulls at her brows. "Please don't say you don't need me here."

"I want you here."

Her hand freezes on the handle, and for a moment, she just stares.

I didn't mean to be so blunt, but there it is, and my response has nothing to do with my injuries.

In truth, she's the last person I want to see me like this, all busted up and weak, yet somehow, at the same time, the reality of my situation is a little less devastating when mixed with her presence. Like maybe my entire world *didn't* come crashing down and maybe this *isn't* the end of it all. Sitting in that hospital, I felt like my entire life had fallen apart. It was all I could think about on the trip back to Oceanside, how things might have changed for me forever.

That I'd lost everything I worked for, my future included.

Then there she was with big blue eyes and the softest fucking touch I've ever felt. She sat beside me and smiled, and everything else fell away because it was a real smile. One without all the pain I've watched her carry the last several months.

I knew right then I not only wanted her to stay, but I needed her to. I just didn't know if I could say that to her, so when exhaustion hit and the pain doubled, I used it as an excuse to go into another room. I would have rested on the couch next to her, but I didn't want to have to watch her walk out.

Yet here she is, still here hours later, and she's not asking if she can stay.

She's telling me she's going to.

A ripple rolls through me, realization breaking through the last layer of fog in my mind.

There's no more *maybe*.

No more *I might*.

All that's left is I am.

Because I *am* completely fucking gone on this girl.

I don't know how it happened, and I don't care when.

All I know is she snuck up on me, and I'm not mad about it.

Someone's shouts intrude from outside the cracked-open door, and the moment is broken.

Payton slips onto the back patio, and I drop my head back with a huff.

The minute I'm alone, it's like the light she brought left with her. All the negative thoughts come rolling back, coiling around my limbs like a snake has snatched me as its prey.

Fangs forge their way into my lungs, and I gasp. I blink, but the haze won't clear, my heart now working overtime, threatening to tear through my rib cage. I try to swallow, but knots form in my chest, panic threatening to suffocate me where I sit.

I'm an athlete who can't play. A student who can't go to school. A man who can't protect.

I'm completely. Fucking. Useless.

CHAPTER 21
PAYTON

Now, September

Pressure falls heavy on my chest, and I reach up as if rubbing the ache away was a possibility. It isn't. I should think pain is something I would be used to by now, and maybe in some ways, I am. I am in the sense that I know when I open my eyes in the morning, pain is quick to follow whatever sensation I wake to, and when I lie down at night, pain is the last thing I remember.

Sometimes it's a hollowness that seems never ending, one that grows, chipping away at the density of my bones, leaving me brittle. Other times it's like an avalanche, and I go tumbling, buried under mounds and mounds of pressure.

Then there are the times when it's but a tangled web in my mind, memories and moments spun into fear and fate. I'm caught in a loop of *damned if I do, damned if I don't*, and I don't know how to get out of it.

I don't know what's right and wrong, and lately, I wonder if I even care.

I should, but do I actually? Or is it some sort of societal ideal that frowns on falling for someone new so soon after losing the person you promised yourself to that has me messed up?

The truth of the matter is none of that makes a difference, because the damage is already done. There is no stopping it, no backtracking or changing what I feel for the man before me, and that means all that would be left of me if something went wrong is an entirely different dose of heartache and everlasting pain.

I couldn't survive that. I can hardly handle this, and it's my own doing, so I can't even begin to imagine all the ways in which I'd crumble if I fell at his feet and then something swept him away.

My eyes trail over Mason's features, and I reach out, running a shaky thumb along the tension lines between his dark brows. They shouldn't be there.

Mason, if nothing else, is a worrier and stress case. Almost always, his thoughts are made up of someone else, something I'm sure has only gotten worse after Ari's accident. He was known to pick apart his performance with a fine-tooth comb or kill himself with concerns over what his sister had going on or his parents being too far for him to get to if they needed something fast.

But these lines, now nearly ingrained in his handsome face, didn't invade his sleep before.

Yet here he is, out cold on a bed that isn't his in a town we don't live in, with deep creases lining his forehead and a tight pinch to his perfect lips. I can't pretend I'm not the reason behind the restlessness he's experiencing. I'm causing him pain, and that makes me sick to my stomach.

What's worse, Mason looks thinner, his hair not as trim as normal and his usually smooth face littered with a shadow of stubble. I glance to his hand, the ice pack I brought in sliding more and more off his knuckles with each uneasy twitch. There are even slightly dark circles beneath his eyes, telling me he's not sleeping like he should.

Gingerly, I open my palm, pressing against the heat of his cheek. Mason leans into my touch instantly, and sharp prickles sting behind my eyes when a ghost of a grin appears.

"My Pretty Little," he slurs, his lashes fluttering, but his eyes are too heavy to raise. "Why's she doing this to me?"

I clamp my hand over my mouth to keep the cry threatening to slip at bay and cautiously push to my feet, my eyes trailing over his pale face as I take backward steps toward the door. I pull it open as slowly as a snail, stepping out before looking back inside one last time, and when I close it, I take a moment to lean my head against the frame.

It's as if an anchor is tied around my neck, tugging me farther down by the second. My emotions battle for dominance: guilt and sadness, confusion and regret. But it's the overpowering sense of longing that burrows me deeper into the sand, because what right do I have to miss someone new when I'm supposed to be missing someone else?

I want to rewind time and speed it up at the same time.

I want to go back and shield him and jump forward and walk away.

More than that, I want the exact opposite.

I hate what life has done to me, but I hate myself for what I've done even more.

A soft clink of glasses snaps me out of it, and I take a deep breath, blinking several times to clear my head before stepping from the hall into the open kitchen area of the rental.

Everyone turns the minute I appear, varying expressions of concern on each of their faces.

"He's asleep," I whisper, offering a small smile as I cross into the space to join them, Deaton's baby monitor sitting right there in the center of the table.

The sight makes my heart beat a little faster, and I'm forced to blink the tears away all over again, because my god, I've never known such real friendships existed. I never have to ask for their help or support. They give it freely and without fail. Without expectation.

Brady pulls out a chair beside him, patting the cushion, and Ari scoots the bowl of chips closer to the center.

I lower into the seat, a heaviness on my chest as they end whatever card game they were playing and redeal to include me.

It would be a lie if I said I'm the only one who feels the

tension in the air tonight. With Paige and Cameron still feeling sick, Ari worried about her brother, and likely all of them trying to work out what exactly happened at the pub tonight, the mood has turned sour.

It's clear everyone only rallied to make sure Mason was okay, especially when we don't make it through a full game of Uno before we're calling it quits and Ari and Noah are jumping up to make us a late-night snack.

I trudge over to the couch to get more comfortable, and I can't help but stare at the couple hovering over the stove.

Noah slips behind Ari, wrapping his arms around her as he holds her hand in his, a pair of tongs tight in her fist. He helps her flip a slice of Spam, then turns his head, whispering something in her ear, and her head falls to his chest in silent laughter. The spatula is set down, and slowly she spins in his arms, their lips meeting in a soft kiss. I should look away, but I can't.

There's just something so pure about the sight that a small flicker of hope warms my bones. They just stand there, staring into each other's eyes with a look akin to longing, which is crazy because they're together. But I guess that's the thing about finding that one person who was meant to be yours.

There's no such thing as too close.

No such thing as too much.

No such thing as letting go.

That warmth turns to ice, and I swallow to settle the sting.

A coffee cup slips into my vision, and I blink, looking up into a pair of green eyes.

Chase is wearing a tight expression, his smile forced and eyes a little…sad. "Don't torture yourself with that view," he whispers, peeking quickly into the kitchen. "It's just warm tea."

A small smile pulls at my lips, and I take a moment to smell the herbal aroma steaming from the mug. "Thank you."

He nods, and I can't help but glance toward the kitchen once more.

185

Ari's sitting on the edge of the counter now, Noah between her legs, eyes intent on her as she tells him god knows what, but the look on his face, it's complete and total awe.

The man is enraptured. Midsentence, he reaches up like he just can't help himself and takes her face in his hands. He doesn't say anything, and she just smiles in return.

Sighing, I look back to Chase.

He lifts a brow, speaking in a hushed tone. "It's like watching a chick flick in real life, isn't it?"

"What do you know about chick flicks?"

"Do you have any idea what Cam and Ari put us through growing up? Forcing us to sit through romance movies was their favorite form of blackmail when they'd find out we lied about going out so they wouldn't ask to come."

"Why not just let them tag along?"

"You mean aside from Mason being a protective asshole when it came to his sister?"

A smile breaks across my lips, and the two of us laugh. I can't help but notice he doesn't seem all that bothered by the happy couple, even if there is something troubling him. He could have easily gone to bed to avoid this altogether, yet here he is, sitting beside me in perfect view of the girl who, once upon a time, wanted to be his.

And when Noah looks this way with a smile, calling out, "Hey man, want to come grab a couple of these?" Chase grins and hops up, strolling right in there. He brings back two skewers stacked with cubes of pineapple and fried Spam.

I take a bite, rolling my eyes to the sky dramatically, and Chase chuckles. "Why is this so good?"

"Why is he good at everything he does?" he mumbles.

My head snaps his way, and when I find him grinning around a mouthful, I'm the one who laughs.

After the quick treat and low conversation about the drive home tomorrow and where they want to stop this time for food, everyone decides to head to bed.

Instantly, my mind jumps back to the heavy part of the evening, and I push to my feet.

I don't know what my face shows as I say good night, but Brady is suddenly at my side. He kisses me along my temple and whispers, "It ain't your fault, baby girl. The man's in his head. It's been a hell of a year for us all, you more than most, and under all that mess he's making, he knows that."

He smiles reassuringly, but all I can do is nod and accept the hug he offers.

I know once I close the door behind me, locking myself inside my room, I won't be able to sleep, but I'm simultaneously afraid I will sleep just fine and what that will bring.

My eyes fall to the playpen beside the bed, zoning in on the full head of dark curls and puffy little lips parted with soft snores.

I run my hand up and down Deaton's back, patting his butt a couple of times before tugging the blanket a little higher on his shoulders.

If I close my eyes, I can picture his dad here with me and what he'd say, but his voice is a little harder to reach for new conversations, only words he's spoken to me able to play out in my mind.

Brimming with guilt and desperate for connection, I lower onto the bed, fold my legs beneath me, and open my laptop, hovering over the folder icon for a long moment before squeezing my eyes closed. I click on the little blue folder, counting to five before opening my eyes.

Hot tears pool instantly as hundreds of small frames pop up, nearly every single one a shot of Deaton's face—not little Deaton but his daddy.

There's us at thirteen playing in the pool and us at fourteen sneaking onto the carousel ride at the county fair after being told we were too old. Us at my house and at his. School dances and his family's fundraisers. At wrestling meets and the stupid pageants my mom forced me into.

A choked laugh leaves me as I scroll past the photo I took of him from the last pageant I was ever in. Deaton found me crying in the changing room after an epic fight with my mom over a half-eaten apple she found in the trash can—because how dare I eat so many carbs before the swimsuit segment? When I refused to come out, he put my swimsuit top on over his tank top and danced around the room. It was ridiculous and so out of character for him, but I smiled and laughed, and he said that was the point. He was good at that. Taking my ugly life and painting it pretty.

He was my best friend.

I keep going, memories assaulting me with each flick across the touch screen.

Walks in the park and trips to his family's cabin when he would steal the keys. The day I got my license and the day he failed his driver's test for the third time. The first day of junior year and the pep rally I shot for the school newspaper's article on the football team...

I swallow, my heart rate jumping and sending a hint of panic through me.

Football games and walks on the beach and dancing to no music at all...

My eyes squeeze closed, warmth rolling down my cheeks.

The boy who died and the man who's still here...

I gasp, eyes flicking to the ceiling as I inhale deeply.

With shaky hands, I close out of the little blue folder, holding my breath as I locate a second, this one buried within several other files, forcing my clicks to be deliberate and never by mistake.

I open it up, and tears fall without fail.

The very first image in the gallery isn't of me and Mason.

It's just him, sitting on the back deck of the beach house, his head tipped back against the cushion...my son held tight in his arms with a fuzzy blanket wrapped around him. Fast asleep.

They were both asleep, and I can't help but notice how not a single line is to be found on Mason's expression. He's blissfully passed out, my baby boy wrapped in his strong arms.

My eyes flick to the thin wall separating me from Mason.

He's *right there*. He's within reach. All I have to do is go to him and end this.

My feet carry me to the door before I realize it's happening, and slowly, I tug it open.

"Hey."

I yelp, my hand flying to my chest, eyes narrowing on the dark hall.

Chase's grin comes into view as he comes closer. "Sorry, I thought I heard you up, and I couldn't exactly sleep either," he whispers.

"If only we could sleep half as good as Deaton does," I tease, glancing back at my sleeping baby. My eyes fall to the open laptop, then bounce to the wall Mason is behind once more. "Umm…" I face forward, pressure pulling at my muscles as I force my feet still when they're desperate to move toward the man in the room next door.

"It's not too cold out. Want to sit outside for a bit?" Chase offers.

I hesitate, trying to fight the irritation sweeping over me while wondering if I should simply tell him no and march myself right into Mason's room, his best friend's eyes on my back be damned. I would be in there already had he not appeared, lowering myself onto the mattress beside Mason and…

I swallow.

And what, Payton?

Forget you have to protect yourself, shield your son from the devastation you'd be left in if…

Chase's smile falters a bit, and I shrug off my thoughts. It's not his fault. He's being thoughtful, offering me an escape from my thoughts with the presence of good company.

"Yeah," I relent, a bitter taste on my tongue as I grab the baby monitor and a blanket, allowing him to lead the way. At the end of the hall, I glance back, staring at the outside of Mason's door for a moment.

It's for the best.

Filling my lungs with air, I spin to follow Chase out back.

I set the monitor on the little table and watch Deaton's chest rise and fall a few times before looking up at the sky. We're both quiet for a long while, and I know when he finally turns my way, he has questions.

"Mason hasn't been himself for a while now," he says instead, green eyes holding mine.

I nod. "He's…angry."

Something softens on Chase's face, and slowly, he shakes his head.

"Nah. He's not angry. Trust me, I've been on the receiving end of that a couple dozen times." His chuckle is light but as heavy as the sigh that follows. "This is different. I was hoping he just needed a break, to forget about all the pressure he puts on himself. You know it's half the reason Ari demanded we all come this weekend, right?" He looks my way. "Noah bought her a plane ticket originally, but she wanted to get Mase off campus for a bit. Group shit and game nights usually do the trick."

I swallow, hoping he doesn't notice.

"I can imagine it would." I nod, a fragile smile pulling at my lips. "You know, I never had a game night before I met you guys, and now it's like a regular thing. I find I look forward to it."

"No?" He frowns slightly. "What did you do with your friends on nights in?"

Bitterness coats my tongue. "I didn't exactly have any that lasted beyond elementary school. My mother's bullshit was too much for most, and if the girls my age didn't care, their parents did."

Chase nods. "Okay, so what about you and Deaton?"

I wait for the sharp pain of guilt at the mention of his name to slice through me, but it never comes. In fact, that never happens when I talk about him with Chase. It's…nice.

I can't help but wonder if it's because being with Chase

doesn't overpower my thoughts the way a certain someone seems to without even trying.

I consider his questions, thinking back to the days he and I spent together, and a small frown builds when I come up blank. It shouldn't be such a difficult question, right?

We were in a relationship. That should say it all, so why am I drawing a blank?

He'd come to me when he couldn't stand to be at home, and I would do the same, which was often for both of us. Angry, sad, or lonely, we'd seek each other out.

Pressure builds in my chest, and I shake my head at the way that sounds. As if we were nothing but the stability and support the other craved. A product of convenience. We weren't.

Right?

What did we do when we hung out?

Faintly, I answer, "I don't know. Talk shit about our families, play on our phones." A small smile tugs at my lips, and I look his way. "Make babies apparently."

Chase laughs at that, his head falling back slightly, and he shifts to face me better. "Apparently."

My smile holds, and I nod. "He was a good guy. Kind and gentle. Never pushed or picked fights. Yeah." I pause. "He was good."

"He must have been."

I look to Chase, and he continues. "You loved him, so he must have been."

We stare at each other a moment.

"You're worth someone's love, too, you know." I take a breath, adding the second part in a low tone. "She just wasn't the one meant to love you back."

Surprisingly, his lips pull into a smile. "I know."

"Are you sure?"

Chase chuckles, slowly pushes to his feet, and moves for the door. "Trust me. I'm sure," he says, glancing my way with a look

I can't quite decipher. "I'd better head in. I'm behind the wheel tomorrow for Brady."

I nod but don't rise, and Chase smiles softly.

"Good night, Princess Payton."

I meet his eyes in question, and his mouth pulls to one side.

"It's better than Princess Puke," he jokes, and a tired chuckle escapes.

He leaves, and it's not until the door is closed behind him that I realize I didn't want him to go, though even once he does, my feet don't carry me inside.

Brady's words from earlier come back and begin to loop in my mind.

He was right, it has been a hell of a year. Longer than that in my case.

If that much could change in twelve months plus time, who knows what the hell could happen in a single season, and fall is fast approaching.

I wonder what life will look like come winter.

Nothing could have prepared me for the answer to that question.

CHAPTER 22
PAYTON

Before, November

"Nate helped set up the nursery, and Lolli and I washed all his little clothes a couple of weeks ago. Everything is ready for him, but he seems perfectly happy squashing my lungs."

Deaton links his hand in mine, chuckling softly. "Pretty soon, he'll be here, and you'll be wishing for a night of peaceful sleep," he teases.

I smile, running my free palm up and down my belly. "That's the same thing Vivian said." I look up into his brown eyes. "You would like her and her husband. They're nothing like our families. They're kind and loving, and they go out of their way just to be a part of his life." A pinch of sadness makes itself known, but I shake it off. "I wish you could have met Mason's mom and dad. They're good to me. Always checking on me."

"I'm glad you have them," he whispers. "Your new friends, too."

Warmth washes over me, and I close my eyes, snuggling closer to him. "I don't know what I would do without them."

"What would you do without him?"

A frown builds, and I look up.

Deaton smiles down at me, but something rings, and he looks to the side a moment before coming back. "I have to go now, Payton."

"Wait—"

The chirp of my phone wakes me, and I squeeze my eyes closed, wishing my dream could have lasted a little longer, but they never do. I always wake up too soon.

Sighing, I pick up my phone and clear the dumb weather notification that popped up. The time catches my attention—it's nearly ten in the morning already. Mason and I stayed up way too late again watching old VHS tapes and arguing over who played the best Batman. Clearly it was Christian Bale.

"*Shit.*"

The low hiss comes from the kitchen, and I grin, the slight tinge of burnt toast teasing my nostrils. Thank God for the third trimester; no more obsessive vomiting over the subtlest of smells. I scoot to the edge of the cushion, using my arms to help hoist me off the seat.

It's sad how much effort it takes to stand right now, but I guess that's to be expected when you're fifty-plus pounds heavier than normal.

There's a soreness to the pads of my feet as I make my way into the kitchen, and when I come around the corner, I can't stop the laugh that escapes.

Mason's head jerks up, the action causing him to wince.

"You look—"

"Sexy? Rugged? Like a total man's man?" he supplies.

"Adorable."

Mason glares, but it's playful, and I move closer, swiping the flour off his chin.

He grins down at me. "Good morning, Pretty Little."

"Good morning, Superstar. Why are you sneaking around the kitchen with a frilly apron on when you're supposed to be resting?"

"I have rested. For four days, I've rested. I've sat on the couch all day, each day, and I can't do it anymore."

"But your ribs—"

"Are going to heal just as slowly if I'm standing as they will if I'm sitting."

I must be frowning, because the next thing I know, Mason is pushing closer, his knuckle running along my forehead.

"Pretty Little, as much as I like you worrying about me, and I do by the way, you need to stop." His eyes lower to where my hand rests, and small bubbles seem to burst in my belly.

"Worrying about you isn't hurting me, Mase, and just because you say stop doesn't mean I'm going to."

He nods, his attention still locked on my stomach. Suddenly his eyes pop up, and a smirk takes over. "Sit down, girl. I'm about to hook you up."

And he does.

Mason pulls chocolate muffins from the oven and bacon-wrapped sausage from the air fryer, setting it out between us. He toasts a few slices of bread next, without burning them this time, and brings over a bowl of scrambled eggs he had sitting in the microwave.

I can't stop smiling as he comes over to join me. "This looks amazing."

"Good. Eat. We're leaving this damn house today, so we need to make sure the little man is good and fed."

My head snaps his way.

"What?" he mumbles around a mouth full of muffin.

"You really think it's going to be a boy?"

Mason eyes me for a moment, then nods, his features softening. "I think everything happens for a reason," he says gently, his hand tentatively reaching out to cover my own.

My eyes burn, but I don't let the tears come. I'm hit with so much at once, denial and anger weighing down on me with that one line of his, but as fast as those emotions come, they're washed away by a strange sense of curiosity and hope. I'm not sure how I feel about it.

"You think Deaton died for a reason?"

A sorrowful smile points back at me. "I think you lost someone you cared about, but you were given something even more precious in return. So...yeah. Of course there's a baby boy in there, just waiting to meet his mama."

Mason's face grows blurrier by the second, so I look away, focusing on my food instead, and when a hot tear streaks down my face, the bitter cold they normally leave behind never comes.

Because Mason reaches up and wipes it away, leaving nothing but the warmth of his touch in its wake. Like the whip of whimsical wings, a flutter dances across my abdomen, and my limbs lock at the sensation.

My gaze snaps up, catching on Mason's.

"It's okay," he says faintly, as if he knows what I'm thinking.

What I'm feeling.

As if he is feeling the same.

He can't possibly.

Hell, I can't possibly.

Can I?

No.

No, no.

I can't.

I miss Deaton.

I *love* Deaton.

I only want Deaton.

Right?

MASON

She's freaking out.

I don't know if it was us waking in the same house and having breakfast or the comment I made about the baby being a boy. Either way, Payton is in her head, more so than normal.

Her every answer is a single word, and when she looks at me for longer than a second, her cheeks turn a truer shade of pink.

I think it's fucking adorable, which is kind of messed up

considering it's probably a blush of embarrassment and not the sweet, shy little blush a woman gives a man she's attracted to.

I've seen that on her before, because like it or not, she is attracted to me, but this is different. It might even be guilt, and that freaks me out. I can't have her feeling guilty. If she does, she'll pull away faster than a NASCAR pit stop, and there will be no one to blame but myself.

That's not going to happen, though, because getting out of the house is as much for her as it is for me. I might still have wraps around my ribs and a sling rubbing my neck raw, but I can walk just fine, so I lead us from the house and down the road rather than to the sandy beach.

It might be November, but it's Oceanside after all, so the sweats and hoodies we're both wearing are more than enough to keep us warm.

I lead her down a side street that points to a few shops, and we make our first stop in a small candy store.

Payton's eyes light up as she steps inside, her attention going to the giant wall of gummy candies right away. "I would have killed to come to a place like this as a kid," she whispers, running her baby-blue painted nails along the acrylic dispensers.

I grab her hand, lifting to look closer at the color, and this time when she looks up and that blush comes back—it's for me. A thrill of excitement rolls through me, but I tamper it down.

"I found it in the bathroom drawer." She chews at her lips, the unspoken words hanging between us.

It's baby-boy blue.

"I like it."

She looks away, and a smile kicks up on my lips.

"So never been to a candy store, then?" I ask, lifting a giant gummy bear on a stick and showing it to her.

She gapes at it and shakes her head, picking up a tin box full of candies made to look like Band-Aids. She cringes, setting it back down. "Not once. There was one in the local mall back home, but my mom would never let us go in there. She said it was ghastly to even consider such a place. She saw some other kids stick their hands in a jelly bean dispenser once, and I think it freaked her out. That and we weren't allowed sugar."

"Not even Lucky Charms?"

"Especially not Lucky Charms." She smirks, her eyes lighting up when she spots a container of chocolate almonds.

"Seriously?"

Her head whips my way. "What?"

"Almonds?" I make a show out of looking all around the space. "Out of all this, and you pick almonds?"

"They're not just any almonds. They're chocolate sea salt–covered almonds," she teases back, holding them against her chest with a fake pout.

It's so damn cute, I can't help but reach forward and tug at her lower lip.

Her eyes flare, and she swiftly whips around, clearing her throat. "I think I'll get the chocolate cashews, too."

"Yeah." I track her as she makes her way to the other side of the store. "You do that, Pretty Little. Anything you want is yours," I mumble.

"Now that's how you keep her happy."

I look to my left to find a woman around my mother's age. She has reddish-brown hair and a name badge that reads Margo. I smile, moving closer to the counter and checking out their fresh baked goods.

"So you're going to be a daddy, huh?" The woman smiles, and my back muscles clamp tight. "That's so exciting. And it looks like you scored some maternity leave of your own." She jerks her chin toward my sling. "Milk it if you can, honey, 'cause before you know, it will be time to head back to work, and leaving her or that little one will be the hardest thing you ever had to do."

My eyes find Payton across the room, watching as she tucks her long hair behind her ear, and there's a stir in my chest, thick and heavy, and I swallow down the knot threatening to form in my throat. "Yeah," I rasp. "You might be right." The bell on the door chimes, and I snap out of it, facing the woman with a tight smile. "Can I pay for this and what she has now?" I lift the giant gummy bear I'll never be able to eat and set it on the counter.

"You got it, stud."

We're out the door in two minutes, all possible awkward conversations between the two of them effectively prevented.

I don't know why I didn't correct her about the baby, but she kept talking, so I just...didn't.

Didn't want to.

Fuck.

"Hey, you okay?" Payton asks, already popping her treat of choice into her mouth.

I force a smile and nod but frown down at her treats when she tears into another. "You need to eat lunch before all that."

She rolls her eyes but grins as she slides closer so she can tuck the almonds in the bag I'm carrying. "Fine, feed me then, Superstar."

So I do.

We walk a little farther, deciding on a small Mexican restaurant with outdoor seating and a view of the ocean. It's perfect for what I had in mind, so we wait for one of the tables on the patio's edge to open before sitting and ordering our meals.

Payton only makes it through half of her fajita bowl before she's sitting back with a satisfied smile, her eyes soft and trained on the waves ahead.

"I really like it here," she says softly, her blue eyes finding mine. "I don't think I would have been able to go back home even if...if Deaton hadn't passed."

My smile is small. "Maybe he would have stayed, too," I offer, hating the bite of acid that coats my tongue at the thought and feeling guilty for it happening at all.

It's so fucked-up, and I could never say it out loud but...

I'm happy he's not here, but I'm not happy that he's *gone*.

It's a dickhead way of thinking, but it's still the truth.

I wish she still had him so she wasn't hurting or confused or heartbroken that her son would never know his father…but I also wish I could hold her how I want and touch her in ways I don't think she's ever been touched.

I don't know if I would have fallen for her had he stayed, but I don't see how I could have avoided it. Not that I would have ever done anything about it, and there are a lot of things that likely would never have happened had he still been here, lessening the pull I feel toward her. I think. Maybe.

But he's not here, and that invisible thread that tugged me toward her from the start is thickening. It's growing roots and digging deeper.

I can say with certainty there's no stopping it now.

I'm already hers, and while she no doubt has an idea, she's yet to realize how much she truly means to me.

"Yeah," she agrees with a small smile, one that makes me wonder if she believes what she's saying or if she's saying it because she believes she should.

She looks out at the water again, and the lines along her forehead disappear, a serene expression blanketing her features as her palms lift to rest on the highest point of her stomach.

As stealthily as possible, I dig into the backpack I had slung along my good shoulder and click the on button on her camera carefully, popping off the cover on the lens the way I've seen her do a hundred times. I lift it, focusing on her, and press the button.

The unmistakable click sounds, and her head whips my way.

She frowns at first, then a blinding fucking smile curves her lips.

She laughs, then reaches over, taking it from my outstretched hand as if this is exactly what she wanted in this exact second. Her camera, to capture whatever beauty she saw through her eyes out in that water.

Before Payton pulls away, her fingers wrap around mine, and she gives a little squeeze.

I feel it in my chest.

In my core.

In that place in the back of my mind that's begging for this to turn into something so much more.

She is the only beauty I see.

The ending I want.

I swallow as she lifts from her seat, moving closer to the water, and I watch her from afar.

When she finally comes back, she takes the seat beside me rather than across, her big blue eyes lighter than before and locked on mine. "Thank you, Mason." She peeks up at me, a glow in her crystal-blue eyes that keeps getting brighter. She lifts the camera, taking a photo of the two of us, then says, "This was exactly what I needed."

Do you think you could ever need me?

PAYTON

It's a little after midnight when I'm woken by a harsh thump.

I jolt upright, the movement so quick I have to close my eyes to fight off a wave of nausea, and I notice the light shining through the jack-and-jill bathroom and into my temporary room.

Mason had decided to take Cameron's room, so when he insisted I take Ari's, the room on the other side of that connecting bathroom, I had to agree.

I sit quietly, waiting to see if maybe he just dropped something and fell back asleep, but then the sound of running water hits me, and I climb from the bed, moving closer.

My stomach clenches unexpectedly, and it only seems to get

worse with each step. Once outside the bathroom, something has my feet coming to a complete stop.

It must be after midnight by now, seeing as we didn't turn off the movie until after ten.

Why is he up?

Jesus, Payton, he probably just had to pee.

Shaking my head, I spin on my heels, but then I hear something.

Is the shower on?

Did he fall?

I lean closer, straining to listen beyond the spray, and what I latch on to is the sound of labored breaths. They're harsh, hurried exhales. I take another step, just one away from seeing inside, when a low groan sounds, and my feet freeze in the entryway.

Another groan.

My skin prickles, goose bumps washing across my flesh and making me nervous. There's no way he's—

"Fuck," Mason grunts, and I jolt when there's another thud on the other side of the wall.

Like his head has fallen back against it, as if the feelings he's feeling are suddenly too much for him to hold it up. As if he's overcome...

Oh my god, he is, isn't he?

Heat explodes in my core, and my eyes fly wide with shock, the sensation startling but...not unpleasant *or* unwelcome.

What? No!

No, no.

I squeeze my eyes closed, realizing all too fast it wasn't the best decision, as now, hidden in the darkness, desires too daunting in the light come to life, and the most sinfully surprising images flash through my mind.

Mason with his strong shoulders pressed against the wall, eyes closed, and those lush lips parted just enough for his tongue to taste the air. His abs taut and hips thrust outward, those long, lean fingers wrapped around himself as he—

"Payton…"

My eyes fly open, every muscle in my body freezing.

Oh my god, he said my name. He's pleasuring himself, and he said my name, and there's a volcano erupting in my stomach. My hand shoots out to grip the wall, my toes curling into the carpet beneath my feet.

"You can come in."

My back goes straight, my mouth agape. I open and close it several times, but all that comes out is "Uh…"

Come in? While he's—

"I could use the help."

Oh. My. *God.*

He wants me to help?

A million hummingbirds take flight in my abdomen, and I swear my knees start to shake.

Wait. What's going on with me right now?

"I could really use a shower," he rasps.

Just like that, my mouth clamps closed.

Shower.

Shower?

Hesitantly, I mean with the bare minimum of movement, I peek my upper body around the corner, too afraid to look inside but rather finding him in the mirror instead.

My frown is instant.

Mason does have his back against the wall, and his head *is* resting against it, but his good hand is latched on to the clasp of his sling, the shirt he wore to bed tangled all around it.

His sweats are not down, and his dick is, well, most definitely *not* hard and in his hands.

So he wasn't pleasuring himself to thoughts of me?

I feel the scowl before I know it's coming, and then I flush all over.

Why is there a bitter taste in my mouth all of a sudden?

I clear my throat and slip inside. Mason instantly looks away, his cheeks tinged the slightest bit pink, and I realize he's embarrassed.

If there's one thing I've learned about this man, it's that he hates feeling helpless, and he's not a fan of being the one waited on, though he seems to love doting on me.

Even the day I met him, he filled my plate high with breakfast, breaking down the proteins and carbs and all this other crap the dedicated athlete knows all about.

I didn't have the heart to tell him I was well aware carbs were in just about everything thanks to my mother's obsession with my weight or that I wouldn't be able to finish a quarter of what he served me without getting sick to my stomach.

Okay, enough stalling!

I push forward, grab Mason by the waist, and turn him. He jolts at first, then allows me to spin him around, and when I push gently on his good shoulder, he lowers onto the lid of the toilet.

When he finally looks up, his eyes widen, his good hand shooting to my forehead as panic pulls at his features.

"What?" I rush, my own hand shooting up to my cheek.

He frowns slightly, moving the backs of his fingers to my temple. "You feelin' okay? You look like you have a fever, but my hand's kind of numb, so I can't tell if you're hot or not."

I might flush even more as I pull his hand away, turning his head so he can't stare at me and pretending it's so I can untangle his shirt. "I feel fine. Kind of pissed, to be honest."

His head snaps back, eyes narrowed.

Chuckling, I turn his head again. "I am here for a reason, Mase. Did you think I was just trying to get out of my house?"

"Were you not?" he teases back.

Smiling, I tug his shirt over his head and ease it down the sling, letting it land around the clasped part for now.

Mase looks to me as best he can, and I raise a blond brow. "What good am I here if you're not going to use me how you need to?"

Something flashes in Mason's eyes, and he reaches out, his hand planting on my hip.

He gives a little squeeze, and I swear my pulse jumps. "Sorry, Pretty Little. You want me to use you how I want, then that's what I'll do."

There's an intensity in his eyes that holds mine a moment longer than it should. I think I nod, quickly leaning over so I don't have to try and decipher the expression on his handsome face. I work the clasp of the back of the sling and ease it down his body, tossing it to the side.

Mason stretches his neck slightly, but when he goes to move his arm, he can only lift it so high. His jaw clenches, and he looks off again.

"Hey," I whisper, and I don't realize I've gripped his jaw and turned him back to me until his lips part, causing my thumb to slide up his chin, the tip tingling against his lower lip. I yank away, but Mason catches my hand before I can lower it and holds it in the space between us, his eyes locked on mine.

"Say what you were going to say," he whispers.

I smile softly, tipping my head a little. "I was just going to say you're going to get better and remind you that it's only been a handful of days. You'll be out of here and back on campus in no time."

His gaze moves between my eyes, his hold on my hand tightening. "That's the only part I'm not looking forward to."

I cock my head, contemplating the easiest way to remove the bandages. "Going back to school?"

"Leaving here. Leaving *you*."

My eyes snap to his, but I quickly dip them to his bandages once more, trying to hide the smile threatening to slip. "*Such* a kiss-ass."

Mason's chuckle is low, and hesitantly, he releases my hand.

"Okay." I nod, taking in all the bandages across his torso. "So I take it we're removing the wraps?"

Mason blows out a long breath. "I think it's time, yeah. I'm starting to smell myself. Pretty fucking gross."

"Yeah, I thought it was the feta earlier but..."

Mason's arm is quick, fingers flying out and tickling my sides. I jolt backward, laughter spilling from me.

"Kidding. Kidding." I move toward the drawers, digging through them for something to help. "How you still smell like you, I'll never know." Scissors. Score.

I hold them between us, and he spreads his legs so I can step closer, but I shake my head. "Up."

He stands. "Smell like me?"

"Yeah, you know...like summer and citrus or a warm blanket right out of the dryer." I purse my lips. "Maybe turn around so you can still keep your arm steady?"

He doesn't move, and when I look up, he's just staring down at me.

"Mase."

He licks his lips, then nods and spins, and I start with the lowest wrap, gently sliding my finger between the cloth and his skin. Mason shivers, and I smirk.

"Cold?"

He huffs, shaking his head, mumbling something along the lines of "Something like that."

I cut the bottom wrap off, and it falls to the floor at his feet. I suck in a sharp breath through my nose, my eye snapping up to the back of Mason's head. He must hear it, because he turns slightly, but not far enough he can see my face.

There're dark, purplish-yellow bruises all along his spine, and when I cut off the second set of wraps, they only get worse. They're everywhere, in every shape and size all over his sides and wrapping up and around his shoulder.

"Holy shit," I whisper.

My fingers feather across the markings, trailing along the largest one at his side. Mason spins, and my hand is suddenly pressed to his abdomen. His muscles flex, and I swallow, looking up into his eyes.

"I'm fine," he rasps, his fist wrapping around my wrist. I think he intends to remove my hand, and for some reason, my fingers splay out against his heated skin. His palm slides up until his fingers are lacing with mine.

My limbs start to shake, my breathing picking up, and it's as if his caramel-colored eyes are whispering words not meant to be heard but felt.

I *feel* them.

But what am I feeling?

It's new and...different. It's painfully soft and strangely compelling.

"You don't look fine."

"What did I say?" he murmurs, tucking some loose strands behind my ear. "You don't cry. Not for me."

"I'm not crying."

A sense of warmth gentles his features, and he releases me but only to grip my shoulder so he can spin me until I'm looking in the mirror.

My eyes find my own, the image blurry, because yes, there is definitely moisture in there, but my attention quickly flicks to the man at my back.

He's so much taller than me, the top of my head just above his collarbone. Despite my swollen frame, his cages me in, his shoulders wider and visible behind mine, and when he steps closer, his stomach now pressed to my back, my heart jolts in my chest.

His hand comes around, gently gliding along my stomach as he turns his lips to my ear. They open, and my eyes close, the heat of his breath sending goose bumps down my spine.

My legs are tingling, it's so strange.

I don't hate it.

"No tears for me, Pretty Little...but I'd be lying if I said I didn't like that you care so much. In fact, knowing that you do does something to me."

What does it do to you?

"I'm going to get into the shower now, gorgeous girl, just in case you want to keep your eyes closed."

I swallow, but my eyes, they open without permission, latching on to his.

I can't help but notice his pupils have grown wider, the golden brown now hidden behind a layer of darkness.

Mason takes a step back, staring right at me as he uses one hand to push his sweats to the floor.

They puddle behind my ankles, and my toes curl into the fuzzy mat beneath my feet.

My cheeks are on fire, my eyes holding and following his in the mirror's reflection until he's turning away, stepping into the shower, and closing himself inside it.

The moment he's out of sight, the spell is broken, and I run back into the room, stopping to press my back against the wall.

I pull out the yoga breathing techniques, fighting for long, deep breaths and exhaling just as slowly. It doesn't help.

I lift my shaky hands, staring at them in shock and confusion, then press them to my heated skin, explicitly aware my face isn't the only part of me that's on freaking *fire*, but a part that's been dormant for a while now...if ever woken at all. A part of me I'm kind of scared to acknowledge but can't ignore.

There's a heat bubbling between my legs, threatening to grow into a boil, and my skin is tingly all over. My eyes fly wide.

"Oh my god," I breathe, gently banging my head against the wall. "This isn't happening," I mutter, clenching my eyes closed. "I'm not falling for Mason." I swallow, taking several long lungfuls. "I *can't*."

"Can't what?"

I yelp, spinning on my heels to find Mason standing in the doorway in nothing but a towel, water dripping from every inch of him.

"What?" I think I say.

Mason comes closer, water rolling down his face, his hair so dark from the water it's nearly black. "You said you can't. Can't... what?"

"I...uh..."

His eyes, they're roaming over every inch of my face, and I blush harder.

Can he see it?

Does he know my body reacted to his?

That I kind of want to know what it would feel like to be closer, if only out of curiosity.

Or maybe it's a subconscious need for human contact or comfort.

Or maybe something else entirely...

Shit.

Mason takes another step, and I watch as fresh droplets from the fastest shower known to man slip from his sharp, slightly scruffy jaw onto his pecs. They're impressive, perfectly cut and gleaming.

My throat grows tight, and when he nods his head toward the bathroom, stepping inside, my feet decide to follow, and we don't stop until we're in the room on the other side.

My eyes fly to the plush blankets on the bed, down comforter after down comforter thrown on top. Mason steps around me a moment later, basketball shorts slung low on his hips. Everything burns when I catch the smallest hint of dark hairs peeking out below his navel. And those hip bones, as sharp as a sculpture.

My god, what a perfect prize he would make behind my lens. I could win awards with his flawlessness.

Mason Johnson is...grown. He's not a teenage boy on the cusp of adulthood. No, he's all man. Strong and exquisite.

And shirtless and staring at me.

My head yanks down, chin practically digging into my chest. "Come on."

Oh god. There's humor in his tone.

"Ari's bed can't be as comfortable as this one."

"It's not so bad" comes out before I can stop it, but as I say it, I realize I'm internally searching for an excuse to go back to the room I've been sleeping in. I don't need one, though, do I? Mason asked me to come in here, and I…want to.

So I say nothing else. I climb under the covers, sitting up slightly from all the pillows. A sigh leaves me instantly, my smile wide and turning on Mason.

He chuckles, gazing at me with a gleam in his gaze. "Yeah, Cam's bed is like this back home and at the dorm, too. She has a pillow topper on her mattress and *still* sleeps on top of a down comforter while covered in another. Girl's a brat with a bad night's sleep."

Something hot spears my gut, and I flick my frown away before he sees it.

So he's not only been in Cameron's bed…but *all* her beds.

What does that mean exactly?

I did hear she had a crush on him growing up. Did something happen between them?

Is something going on with them now back at Avix?

Oh my god, Payton, why do you care?

"We used to pile in each other's rooms every weekend, trading off houses each time, for movie nights and pizza. Hers was everyone's favorite."

I look over to find him studying me with a hint of a grin on his lips, like he knows what I was thinking, liked it, and that's why he explained, but that's weird, right?

Mason shifts, facing me as much as possible, so I make it a little easier on him and turn onto my side. He smiles down at me and laughs lightly.

"What?"

"You look cute like this, all snuggled up and shit."

I roll my eyes at his teasing and settle farther into the blankets.

"I would be so much more comfortable if I didn't have a tiny human hanging out in my body."

Mason grins, his eye falling to the large lump of blankets. He stares for a few moments, and then his hand disappears under the comforter. He doesn't just lay it there, though. He slides it farther down until the hem of my shirt is in his hand and he's pushing it up, the heat of his hand pressed directly to my taut skin.

A soft current courses through me, his touch like a tame note of electricity. I pull in a shuddering breath.

I can't *see* where he's touching me, the blanket still up to my chin, but his calloused fingers leave a trail of warmth everywhere they go. He slides his hand from one side to the next, to the top and back down, pausing when he feels a small protruding point.

His eyes pop up to mine, nothing but the light he forgot to turn off in the bathroom cascading over us. "Does it hurt?" he wonders.

I shake my head. "Getting a little harder to breathe now that I'm so close, and my back hurts as much as my feet, but that's just what happens at this point, I guess."

Mason nods, then asks, a little more hesitant this time, "Are you afraid?"

A rush of sadness falls over me, and I look down for a moment, Deaton's soft curls and infectious smile slipping into my mind. A weight falls on my chest when I realize I haven't thought of him much this past week. I wasn't asleep long enough for him to visit me in my dreams, but he will.

He always does.

I don't realize a small grin is pulling at my lips until I look up to find a matching one on Mason.

"I don't think so," I finally answer.

"That's good," he whispers, and I can see exhaustion setting in.

We're quiet for a few minutes, and when he shifts again, his gaze finding mine in the low-lit space, a small smile curves my lips.

His words from earlier are like a warm blanket in my mind, and I tuck my hands under my cheek, staring up at him in the dark.

Not many people at my age know what it feels like to have something, or *someone* in my case, that you love taken from you. It's a fucking nightmare that gives you legitimate nightmares.

It's like being carved to the bone with a fillet knife, but instead of leading you to the good part, all you get is the bad.

The empty.

The bloodcurdlingly bare.

No matter what you add back or pump yourself with, it doesn't go away. Your bones begin to ache with no exertion, and your heart threatens to explode with even the littlest of it.

People think they know how you should act or feel, how long you should mourn, when you should be better, and how hard the entire process will be, but they don't. They couldn't possibly.

Sure, it's different for everyone, but at the end of the day, the base is the same.

You lost something, or something was stolen from you. You want it back.

Maybe it's possible, or maybe it's impossible, but that doesn't mean the person with a chance hurts any less than the person without one. It just means we're human and both must try.

Try and live with the hole, or try and fill it.

Or do nothing and get buried beneath it all.

Mason and me, it's like we're on the same page.

Both holding on to the shovel, but both drowning in a mountain of dirt that doesn't seem to lessen, no matter how many times we scoop.

Mason with his slow recovery, and me with…god, I don't even know how to put it into words.

But with Mason, it's almost like I don't have to. It's as if he already knows.

Maybe because he's lost something, too, albeit temporarily, but still.

Just because our pain is different, that doesn't mean his isn't as deep as mine.

We both may have lost what was supposed to be our future, but maybe there's a purpose behind it all. A way to make us stronger than we would have been.

Maybe what he said to me is true.

"Hey, Mase," I say, even though he's staring right at me.

He blinks, a small smile on his lips encouraging me to say whatever is on my mind. For some reason, nerves swim in my stomach, and when I continue, my tone is so low I wonder if he'll hear me at all.

"If everything happens for a reason, then maybe there's a reason you got hurt."

Mason's eyes move between mine, and when he speaks, it's in the softest of whispers. "I think *maybe* you're right."

CHAPTER 23

MASON

Before, November

Rolling my shoulder forward three more times, I take a deep breath, thankful that such a thing is even possible. Injured ribs are no joke, not that this shoulder shit has been much easier.

I roll my shoulder backward, the tenth rep causing me to grind my teeth. At least I can lift my arm up and over my head now. We'll just pretend there's not a small strain when it's near full extension. That and I'm sure my ribs are not yet back to 100 percent, but at last I can breathe easy now. I can bend and twist, and that's good enough for me. For now anyway.

It's been a hell of a recovery period. Weeks of stress and fear and anxiety, of mental torture.

My eyes slide to the blond five feet away. She's bouncing on an exercise ball in the corner, her eyes pointed at the TV, where reruns of *Forensic Files* are playing on a loop.

Weeks of me and her and no one else.

That familiar sense of rightness I've come to know when she's near flows through me, a heavy weight following closely behind.

My time with her is almost up, and as much as I want to get back on the field, the thought of leaving her brings back the claws of panic, and that's just at the thought. I have no idea what kind of games my mind will play once I actually go. I've become a bit dependent. Maybe it's the twin in me. Maybe it's her.

When she's not in the same room, I seek her out.

When she's asleep, I'm waiting for her to wake.

When she's looking at me, I'm fucking mesmerized.

She's more than I thought I'd ever find, and she's not even mine.

I mean, in my mind, she is. She *has to be.* There's just no other option, but that's my mind, and while I like to think I have a damn good idea I know what's going on inside hers, I can't say that for certain. Even if she now looks at me in a way she didn't before.

As if our minds are linked, her head turns my way, catching me staring. The soft smile she gives has my heart pounding. It's pretty strange honestly, but it's there, this incessant thud beneath my rib cage.

"You're quiet today," she murmurs, carefully climbing to her feet and walking over, her eyes trailing over my bruises, all now mostly faded into nothing. Her gaze moves back to mine. "What's the matter?"

"The others will be here soon."

Her lips curve higher. "Don't sound so excited."

"What if I said I'm not?" A small frown of confusion builds across her brow, so I add, "I don't want you to go."

Her smirk is playful. "Mason Johnson, are you saying you like me bossing you around?"

I push to my feet, and her head tips back to follow. "I'm saying I like *you.*"

She laughs. "I like you, too."

My head is already shaking, my feet shuffling closer. "No, Pretty Little." I run my knuckles along her jaw. "What if I asked you to stay the rest of the weekend? I'm moving up to my room tonight. You could stay with me in there like you've been staying in Cam's room with me."

Her cheeks pinken, and I need to get a grip, because the sight has my dick throbbing in my sweats. How can I, though, when I know where her curious little mind just went?

It's right there, in the gloss of her gaze.

She's thinking about how we've woken tangled in each other for the last several days, each morning more and more wrapped together, now that I can actually lie on my sides or flat on my back. Each of those mornings, my body knew exactly what it wanted, and there was nothing I could do to stop it. This wasn't the standard morning wood; this was *I want the girl in my arms with every fiber of my fucking being*. Because, god damn it, I do, and I'm tired of telling myself I shouldn't.

The first day, she practically sprinted into the bathroom, locking herself inside.

The second, she blushed like crazy but didn't run.

But the third? The third she pressed back against me, a tiny gasp she doesn't know I heard heating me from the inside out. Even now, my blood is running warm at the mere thought of it. It was the sweetest sound, and I'm *dying* to hear it again. And again. And sure, one could argue she didn't mean to rub her ass over me, but I'm thinking she did. Even if subconsciously, she still did.

I won't get the chance to hear that gasp again tomorrow, though, not with the others due to arrive today. So yeah, I already knew before asking my question what her answer would be, and her next words are only further proof that some part of us, be it big or small or steadily growing, is connected. We *are* connected.

"Parker's been hounding me about coming home." She tells me what I already knew.

Still, I argue. "He's a half mile down the road."

"Exactly." She grins. "I'll only be a half mile down the road." She holds that grin all the way through. "I'm sure you won't miss me too much." She says this but with a flicker in her eyes I don't miss.

Sadness.

Dread.

You don't want to go, do you, baby?

"You know if there is anything you need, anything that you

want, anything *at all*, I'll give it to you. You know this, right? That if I'm physically capable, it's yours. You just"—I lick my lips, moving closer—"just ask. Or take. Or—" I break off, shaking my head.

"Mase?"

"I'm messing this up, aren't I?" I step back, running my fingers though my hair. "I'm trying not to scare you, but I'm fucking dying here, Pretty Little."

I wait for confusion to cross her face, but it never comes.

My eyes narrow, watching as she swallows, and fireworks light me up on the inside because hot damn. She knows.

She's not confused.

She fucking *knows* what I'm feeling, and she's still standing right here.

Fuck it.

I rush for her, her eyes widen…and a car door slamming in the driveway serves as a shield between us, jolting me in its invisible trap.

My face falls, and hers points to the floor.

That's it. My time is up.

The others are here.

I look to the garage door, considering waiting until they come in and track us down, but then I hear a soft laugh that has a smile crossing my lips regardless of the situation.

It only grows wider as I step from the garage into the house and over to the front door, Payton quietly following behind. I yank it open just in time to catch Noah saying "Best thing I ever did was miss that pass."

I grimace at the sight of my sister in his arms, but I can't help but grin.

"And here I was thinking the best thing you ever did was toss me on the bed and—"

Okay, yeah. No.

"Don't finish that sentence." I cut her off, but my tone is playful if anything.

Ari whips her head around, hitting me with a bright smile. She kicks so Noah will set her down, and she's rushing for me in the same breath.

I don't have time to brace, groaning when she slams into my chest for a full-ass hug.

"Shit. Sorry!" She jumps back quickly.

"It's fine. Come here." I pull her into my arms and hug her tight. And because she's Ari, her sniffles follow soon after. "I'm okay, baby sister," I whisper. "Promise."

"Yeah?"

I nod. "I was fucked up for a couple of weeks, but I'm good now."

"Thank god for that."

My girl lays on the sass, and I glance back to find her leaning against the frame all fucking adorable like. I almost go to her, but Ari beats me to it.

"Oh my god," my sister murmurs. "Look at you."

The two hug, and Payton meets my eyes over Ari's shoulder, playfully rolling hers. "Go ahead. Feel me up."

Ari doesn't hesitate, instantly running her hands along her belly, and the sight shifts some pieces inside me, yet another clicking into place.

My sister looks so honored, a giddy, loving eagerness bright in her brown eyes. She can't wait for there to be a baby in our mix, something she's dreamed of since we were way too young to even want such things, but that didn't stop her from planning for it. She begged our parents to have another one for years, and as soon as we hit junior year of high school, she started talking about how she couldn't wait until one of us had a baby of our own.

Of course we tried to take bets on who would be first, but everyone picked Brady, so the bet never took.

None of us expected a broken blond to join our mix.

Least of all me.

No one is happier than I am that she showed up.

218

The girls I've met on campus this semester, they meant nothing, and going back, I know I won't even be able to entertain the noise. Not now.

Not after the last few weeks.

Last few months?

When is the last time I hooked up with someone? A couple weeks into the semester, maybe? A dumb drunken night that I hardly remember.

I remember every moment I've ever had with Payton, and I haven't even kissed the girl yet.

I'm fucking going to.

The girls are still talking, but I've managed to tune them out, moving to Noah with an outstretched hand. "Riley." I lift a dark brow. "Looks like my sister's still in one piece. This shit serious now or what?"

"It's whatever she wants it to be."

"Good fucking answer, my man." I chuckle, turning to Payton. "Payton, Noah. Noah, Payton."

Noah smiles, giving a little wave. "Hi, Payton."

A teeny tiny pink hue begins to creep up her neck, and I narrow my eyes, taking a half step before I realize it, as if to block his Prince Charming–looking ass from her view, but her eyes are already on him.

"Hey," she says in greeting.

"Okay, intros are over." I frown. "Inside. It's getting cold as fuck out here." I turn, raising a brow at her as I pass her on my way into the house.

I swear she thinks it's funny, and I'm right when she teases, "Ari, did you know your brother is the bossiest person on the planet?"

Her words are purely for my benefit. Kind of like that part, though.

"Yeah, you get used to it." My sister sighs dramatically, and I pretend to groan, flipping her off over my head.

My boys come in, both giving me that unsure, pitying look, but when I only grin, they wipe it away in an instant, coming in for a hug.

"Good to see you, my boy." Brady slaps my good shoulder. "This motherfucker won't shut up about you at practice." He pretends to complain about Chase, but we all know it's his way of letting me know they've had my back. As if I had any doubt.

"Oh yeah?" I grin at Chase. "Miss me, fucker?"

"Nah, just wanted to make sure the other dude trying to show off didn't forget he was nothing but a stand-in."

"My man."

Chase smirks, moving over to say hi to Payton.

I watch as she beams up at him, laughing as he whispers something in her ear. Brady catches my eye, a brow raised, and I wink at the fucker.

"Whoa, whoa—" he starts, jumping out to grip my arm, fully intent on grilling me over what his perceptive ass is picking up on, but I dodge him, quickly whirling around the island.

I kiss Cameron's temple, and she kisses the air in return, already digging into the fridge for something sweet, and I take a moment to look across my friends, all doting on the pregnant girl who's glowing from the inside out.

I can't help the images that flash across my mind of all of us in the future, in this same spot, plus a little blond-haired boy running around.

He'd run up to me and—

A harsh exhale I'd recognize in a room of a hundred catches my attention, my head snapping to the right.

Payton is slowly climbing to her feet, but she only just sat down. Worry slices through me when her hand shoots to her back, the other pushing out to grip the table, and I'm already moving.

Snagging the water she set down, I quickly drag the larger chair with the doubled-up cushions we fixed up for her a few days ago closer.

"I'm fine," she whispers, looking up at me.

Don't lie to me, my scowl screams, and she responds in kind, her little glare replying with *I'm not*. I don't mean to smile, but it grows wider when a low chuckle leaves her. She shakes her head and settles once more.

Fine or not, I stay beside her regardless, and I plan to all damn day.

Because the gang's all here now, and that means soon...she won't be.

Unfortunately, soon comes too quick, and before I know it, I'm lying alone in my bed, staring at the dark ceiling. No matter what I do, I can't get comfortable. The bed feels too big, too... empty.

Jesus, I turned into a sap.

I smirk to myself.

I think I'm okay with that.

I wonder if she's asleep. I look toward the clock, finding it's a little after eleven.

Is she lying restless like me? Wishing she'd stayed instead of going back?

Lifting my phone off my chest, I sigh, scrolling through social media, something I haven't done all week. It's just as boring now as it was then, and I toss it back down, flipping onto my stomach. Forcing my eyes closed, I begin to count down from a hundred. I make it all the way to fifteen when my phone pings.

I jerk up, looking at the screen to find it's from Payton.

Sitting up, I pull up the message.

My Pretty Little: Mase?

I hit the Call button instantly, my pulse jumping faster by the second, because somehow I just know something is wrong.

She answers on the second ring, a soft sniffle tearing into me, and I fly to my feet.

"Tell me what's wrong."

"I'm scared," she whispers.

"Baby, what's wrong?"

Another sniffle, and then a shaky "I think the baby is coming."

I'm already shoving into my shoes and running out of my room.

"I...I need you, Mase," she cries, the sound so fucking soft.

And there it is.

She fucking needs me.

"I'm on my way." I run down the stairs, screaming, "Payton's in labor, and she's scared!"

Just like that, doors open, footsteps pound, and the whole gang is out the door.

By the time we're seated and pulling from the driveway, Ari has Kenra on the phone. Turns out I'm the only person Payton told, even though she was in a room just down the hall from her brother when her water broke.

I'm gonna analyze the hell out of that later, but calling them ahead of time was the right thing to do to get us moving. They are running out the door and jumping into Parker's car as we pull to the curb, but not Payton.

She hesitates, her eyes snapping over and finding mine as I hop from the Tahoe, ditching the driver seat and ready to climb in the back seat with her. It seems she was waiting or expecting that, too, as she didn't dare climb in until I was at her side, my intention clear. Ignoring the frowns from my cousin and her man, I press my body right against hers, our hands clinging together instantly. I don't know who gets behind the wheel of my Tahoe, and I don't care.

My focus is on the girl gripping me for dear life, a nervous expression on her pretty face. She doesn't say a word the entire drive, just clenches her eyes and my fist.

As we pull through the hospital roundabout, Parker and Kenra jump out instantly, and as swiftly as possible, I dart between the seats, stretching out and hitting the lock button on the doors.

As my ass falls back in the seat, I look out in time to see Parker jogging through the double doors, probably to get help or something, but Kenra steps over, tugging on the handle of our door.

"What the hell?" She knocks, cupping her hands and pressing her face to the window to try and see through the tint.

I turn to Payton, take her face in my hands, and tip it toward me.

Her hands come up, wrapping around my wrists, fear written across her face.

"I can't do this," she finally cries.

"Listen to me, Payton Baylor," I whisper, holding her gaze. "You've gone through hell for years, but you fought through it, and in that hell, you found a bit of peace to hold on to in a boy who meant the world to you. And then you lost him." Her lower lip trembles, and I clutch her tighter. "But you're still here, Pretty Little. Pushing and fighting and growing even stronger than before. I know you're afraid, but you're also brave. Braver than me, no doubt, and I need you to know, even if you were all by yourself, the ten of us here nowhere to be found, you could do this."

She shakes her head, but I push on.

"You can. You're the strongest person I know, and you've fucking got this. And if for some reason you need a little help, I'm right here. Hold on to me. Yell or scream or claw at me, tear me a-fucking-part if it helps, and know that I'll still be right here, no matter what. You amaze me, gorgeous girl. You've got me in every sense of the word." I press my forehead to hers, our gazes still locked. "I'm not going *anywhere*."

Big blues blink up at me, a tenderness taking over her tense features.

"Promise," she whispers. "Promise me, Mason. No matter what. Promise me."

A shudder runs through me, my eyes burning as I stare intently into hers. "I promise, Pretty Little."

She stares a moment longer, and then a small smile breaks her lips, a choked laugh escaping. "Oh my god, I'm about to have a baby."

A laugh breaks from my lips, and I look up over my shoulder to see Parker now back with a wheelchair, the others rushing down the path from where they had to park.

I face the angel at my side with a smirk. "Yeah, you are. So what do you say? You ready to meet your little man?"

She licks her lips with a nod, smiling wildly now. "I'm ready."

I open the car door, and in the hospital we go.

I'm *really* fucking glad I gave Payton that pep talk before we stepped into the hospital, because apparently her water breaking at home was just the beginning. I mean, I knew that, but it wasn't until we got up in the room, the monitors all hooked up and the doctor coming in for the second time, that shit got real.

Parker stepped out, glaring at me when all I did was move back a few feet, but that was only for his benefit. The doc told him to wait outside, and I'm not sure why the woman didn't tell me to go, too, but she didn't. The only reason I moved at all is because Payton gave me a small nod.

Maybe because she didn't want to hurt her brother's feelings, or maybe it was because the doctor threw Payton's gown up to her waist like she was simply looking under the hood of a car, but either way, I slipped out.

Of course, the second Parker and the others turned around and a nurse came out the double doors blocking her from me, I snuck through them before they could close. I went right back to her bedside, ignoring the looks Kenra was shooting me from Payton's opposite side. I was so fast, only out maybe a solid minute, that the doc hadn't even had time to stand from her little rolling chair.

I don't know what it was they put in Payton's IV, but it's been only five minutes now, and the whole-ass game has changed. Payton's contractions have finally started, and according to the nurse with her head between her legs right now, she's moving at an accelerated rate.

It's absolute fucking torture.

She's crying, gripping the bars on the side of the bed, and writhing in agony, tears fogging her ocean eyes. She can hardly sit still, and I'm as useful to her right now as a condom would be.

But I don't move from my spot at her side. I wouldn't dare.

Not when every few minutes, she lifts her pretty head to look at me, as if to make sure I'm still there.

I swallow, moving with the nurse toward the door, and whisper, "How much longer?"

She smiles brightly as she pulls her gloves off and tosses them in a red bin. "Any time now, hon. Just keep doing what you're doing, and you'll get to meet your little one soon."

"Mase."

I whip around to find her hand outstretched and hurry back.

I press my palm to hers, and it's she who links her fingers around my own. Her eyes close, and I look over at Kenra.

She's got her lips pursed, but I shake my head, bending to rub my free hand over Payton's forehead, blowing cool breaths along the sweat beads building there.

"It hurts," she cries, squeezing me tighter.

"I know. I know it does, but you're doing so good."

She starts to scream, her entire body coiling and shoulders caving in. She pants, gasps, and thrashes against her pillow. "I need to… I don't know. I think…"

The nurse runs back in, lifts Payton's gown, and I wait for her to panic or scream for help.

The crazy woman in lime-green scrubs smiles at us and says, "It's time."

We all freeze. I look from Payton to Kenra to Payton.

Payton's eyes are wide, her lips trembling as she looks from my cousin back to me.

They both look at me as if I've got all the answers, but I don't have shit. I'm fucking terrified here. "Should I get Parker?" I take a guess, thankful when she nods eagerly.

"Please." She gives one more squeeze before releasing me. "I want him here, too."

I'm already moving toward the door when she shouts. "Wait!"

The panic in her tone wraps around my shoulders. I jerk around again, ready to run right back. Hell, I'll do circles right here in this little room if she wants me to.

"You promised," she rasps, fear glittering in her gaze.

There's a heavy knock in my chest, and I nod. "I'll be right back, Pretty Little. *Right back.*"

She drops her head to the pillow, nodding as she squeezes her eyes closed, and I book it down the hall, pressing the button on the automatic doors, but there's no time to run into the waiting room, so I shout from the other side. "Baby's coming!" I clap, but I don't wait around to be sure Parker heard, spinning on my heels and jogging back toward room 227.

Parker's right behind me, and he moves for her right side, but that's my side and I hold still, so he goes to stand behind Kenra, reaching past her to gently brush Payton's arm.

She looks to each of us, then back at the doctor, nodding as the doc explains what happens next.

And honestly, I'm shitting my pants right now.

Her legs are up, feet locked in these scary-ass metal things reminding me of those contraptions Forrest Gump had on his legs when he was a kid, and there's an operating tray set out with all sorts of shit like a horror movie prop setup.

Yeah, I'm freaking out, and I'm guessing it's obvious seeing as nurse number two steps up beside me and whispers for me to breathe.

So I listen, dragging in a long shaky breath as I look back to Payton.

"Okay, Payton, I'm going to count back to one, and on one, you're going to push for a full count of three, okay?"

"I don't know," she whines, squeezing her eyes closed.

The doctor looks up at me, an expectant expression on her face, and my eyes widen because what the hell, man? What am *I* supposed to do? I don't know shit about shit and—

Payton starts to cry, and panic bubbles into my throat.

Spinning, I face her, grip her hand, and squeeze. "Hey, Pretty Little, look at me."

She does, tears slipping down her cheeks.

"Little man is ready to meet you." I nod, catching the doc's eyes a moment, quickly refocusing on Payton. "And I know how much you've been waiting to meet him, too, so what do you say, hmm? We ready to do this?"

Her lips press tight, those big blue eyes locked on mine, so fucking trusting and afraid at the same time, it shreds me to the bone.

I move her hair from her face, tucking it behind her ear the way she likes to do. "I'll be right here the whole time."

Slowly she nods, and together, we look to the doc.

"Okay." The doc hunches down slightly. "In three, two, one..."

Payton groans, her teeth clacking as she shouts through them, her body curling up into an impossible crunch. Her face starts to turn two shades too red, and Parker and I lock eyes, fear and uncertainty burning like lava in my veins.

"Good," the doc praises, and Payton falls back against the bed, panting. "A few more like that. Deep breath. The next contraction is already coming. Get ready in three, two, one..."

"Ahh!" Payton shouts, clenching again, her hand shaking, nails digging into my skin.

My jaw is locked, and I'm fucking sweating.

Payton settles again, her breathing all over the place, and those teary eyes find mine once more.

"You're going so damn good," I rasp.

"I can see the head," the doc announces.

"She can see the head."

"Two more and you get to meet your baby."

"Two more and—"

The doctor snickers, and I clamp my mouth closed, gaze snapping around the room.

Even Parker is smirking, his gaze narrowed, though he quickly points it back to his sister. "You're so close, Peep. Come on."

"And three, two, one…"

Payton pushes, her shoulders trembling and legs shaking with the force.

"The head is out. Another push."

"I can't!" Payton cries.

"Come on, Payton," the doctor encourages calmly. "One more."

Payton shakes her head, dropping it back and shouting into the room as her body locks tight.

I lean over, pressing my forehead to hers, and our eyes meet.

"Payton, you need to push." The doctor is a little more urgent this time.

Payton's lip trembles as she stares at me, her head moving back and forth.

"Yes, baby," I breathe. "You can do this. Come on, Pretty Little. You're so close. Show me how strong you are. How fucking brave." My lips slide across her cheek, and she cries harder. "You can do this. Let's go."

Slowly, she nods and starts to push. Her features pull tight, the cries of a warrior slipping from her lips, sweat rolling from her forehead and mixing with mine, but I don't dare move. I hold her eyes, and with our gazes tied, pulses pounding dangerously fast, we hear it.

The softest, craziest fucking sound I've ever witnessed.

228

A little broken cry.

Awe. Complete and total awe, that's the expression that blankets her face.

Her entire body goes limp, tears streaming down her face at an unstoppable rate.

Slowly and with a bit of fear I didn't expect, I face the doctor, vaguely aware of Parker and Kenra telling Payton how proud they are and how good she did.

My eyes lift, locking onto a little head full of dark hair. Even covered in…whatever that is, it looks curly and perfect, and I swear to god, my heart, it jumps in my chest. Jumps, skips, and then shifts.

A hole opens up inside me, the teeny tiny little thing the doctor holds up slipping inside and filling it right back up.

My vision blurs, my body frozen in place.

Parker says something, walks by, and the nurse steps up, but I can't hear her.

All I hear is *him*.

It is a boy. A little baby boy.

It's like time doesn't exist and the world stopped spinning, and all that's left is him…and her.

Slowly, I turn, and as if sensing I was coming, her eyes move to meet mine in the same instant.

She smiles, and I hate the weight within it, but there's so much joy there, too.

"You were right," she whispers, blinking heavily. "It's a boy."

I'm not aware I've moved until her face is in my hands, my lips coming down on hers with such intensity my entire body vibrates. "Congratulations, Pretty Little," I whisper against her. "You're a mama now."

"I'm a mom now," she breathes, a slight tremble in her smile.

I push the hair from her face, and her eyes close, exhaustion setting in. Not a moment later, the nurse nudges my arms with her own.

"Come." She dips her chin, so I spin, stepping beside the tiny little table they've laid the little guy out on. The doctor is talking to Payton, and I try to focus on what the nurse is saying, but I can't.

"Why is he crying?" I ask, my hands lifting to touch him, but fear tethers around my muscles, holding me back. "Don't cry, little man" I swallow beyond the knot forming in my throat. "Your mama's waiting to meet you, and you're gonna scare her," I whisper.

Suddenly, his wails soften, and my pulse hammers in my chest when he starts to blink. Just like that, his little eyes open, and all the air whooshes from my lungs.

"He's…perfect," I rasp, then notice the scissors held out before my hands.

My eyes snap to the nurse, and she smiles, pushing them into my palm. "Cut right here, daddy."

My knees shake, white flashing behind my eyes. This is…

I don't have words for what's happening inside me right now, but it's big, life-fucking-changing, and when I open my eyes, looking into his, everything inside me shifts. It rearranges, twisting, turning, and tightening. It clicks into place.

My lungs open up, and the air tastes different.

Daddy.

My vision blurs, and I reach up, running a shaky hand over his perfect little cheek.

Oh my god.

I…I *want* to be his daddy.

CHAPTER 24
MASON

Now, September

It never gets easier.

In fact, it only gets worse. Every. Single. Time.

It's to the point where I can hardly sleep and forget to eat. I'm choking down protein shakes just to keep enough carbs in my body to keep it moving. It's no wonder I got so trashed off the beer. I can't remember eating anything yesterday, and who knows when I ate before that?

I close my eyes, taking deep breaths to keep from puking this vanilla shit all over the cab of my Tahoe.

It's just after two in the afternoon, and there's but a single car in the practice facility's parking lot, most people not set to head back to campus until later this evening since we don't report for official practice and classes until tomorrow.

That's when the others will be back, tomorrow morning. The plan was to head back to the beach houses this afternoon when Noah had to catch his quick flight back to the team's headquarters. Then tomorrow morning, we'd get up and make the drive early.

I was supposed to have one more day with my little guy.

One more day with her.

My jaw clenches, and I shove the door open, stepping out into the frigid morning air, tugging my hoodie up.

I couldn't face her this morning. Couldn't face any of them, and since Little D was asleep in the same room as his mama, I didn't get to say goodbye.

The thought has my pulse pounding in my ears.

What if that's the story of my life? A constant goodbye.

Quick visits that are over before they start, like a distant uncle or, worse, family friend.

I'm not just a fucking friend.

I'm more.

You thought you were more.

"Fuck," I curse, quickening my pace and focusing on the echo of my own footsteps in an attempt to drown out my thoughts, but it's to no avail.

There may as well be a megaphone pressed to my ears, screaming out all the ways I've fucked up, but the *fucked-up* part about it?

I have no idea what those things are. There has to be more than I realize, right? For her to pull away after everything. For the ache that enters her eyes when she pretends not to watch me with Deaton. There was always that sliver of inner pain there. It's the same tangled expression that would enter my father's eyes when he'd watch me and my sister do something he and his sister did as kids before she passed, but inner pain or not, Payton never pushed.

In fact, she did the opposite. She kept me close, called first, and hung up last.

She'd run to me and jump into my arms when I'd sneak a short visit I didn't tell the others about. Now she hears me coming and off she goes, a sudden appointment or event or urge for a coffee she can't make herself.

But why?

What happened?

Where did I fuck up, because I must have, right?

Or maybe she can see through me and knows I'm not as

confident as I like to make people think. That I do feel fear and I do have insecurities.

It just so happens my biggest one might be the very reason things have veered so far off course I'm running circles around my damn self.

Maybe I'm not enough, or maybe I'm simply not needed.

Why would I be?

What do I truly have to offer her?

I'm not even fucking there. I'm stuck three hours away for the next two years, and that's if I go to the draft after my junior season. And if I do get drafted, I'll be off to who the fuck knows where after that, but the odds say it will be farther. Somewhere I can't hop in my truck for a quick visit.

The best I'll be able to do is see their faces over video, but who's to say I'll even be given that?

The girl won't even take my damn calls anymore.

So yeah, maybe it's not that I'm not enough or needed but not worth the trouble at all.

Pushing the heels of my palms into my eyes, I growl in frustration, shoes pounding heavily against the concrete until I'm breaking out into a full sprint, tearing down the long hall, and shoving through the metal door at the end until I'm stumbling through, out onto the open field.

I gasp, hands falling to my knees as my lungs threaten to seize.

Behind me, the door slams against the wall with a resounding ricochet, and my eyes snap to the field just as the figure in the center of it comes into view, whipping around and glaring this way.

My brows snap together, and my spine shoots straight.

Alister fucking Howl stands at the fifty-yard line, a bag of balls at his feet and half a dozen spread out on the field. He stares for a long moment, then pretends I'm not even here, spinning back around and firing a bullet toward the end zone. It's fast, straight, and a perfect spiral, not unlike a pass I'm known to make.

I was out getting drunk and acting like the sentimental prick I am and punching my best friend in the face for buying a soda, and this guy's here on his days off, working on his game.

Anxiety falls over me like a tsunami, preventing me from breathing and sending panic through my every pore. My eyes fall to my hand, the knuckles swollen and bruised, an ache that burns all too familiar.

You're fine. Everything is fine.

I step farther into the afternoon sun that's scarcely peeking out between a layer of clouds, and I keep moving until I've reached the sideline benches. I don't look his way, but I can't help but watch his every pass thrown from the corner of my eye as I stretch.

A few minutes go by before he's stalking closer.

I wait until he's nearly reached his bag, sitting on the ground four feet from me, before I take off around the track. At some point, Alister packs up his shit and disappears, and I keep running.

I run until my legs begin to shake and my lungs start to shrivel, and then I push beyond the burn. My speed increases, my arms pumping wildly as I round the track for what must be my ninth mile. I've run farther distances, but that was when I kept a steady pace, so when my body starts to rebel, I have no choice but to listen.

My legs give, my knees buckling, and I just manage to veer to the left, falling onto the grass.

My stomach muscles convulse, and I start puking, nothing but vanilla protein shake and stomach acids. Maybe a little beer.

I heave and heave, my vision spinning and calves burning as I throw myself onto my back, fighting for air my lungs refuse to give. Lying there, I stare up at the cloudy sky and out at the empty stadium seats.

It's like an omen, the emptiness around me, a glimpse into the future I'm headed toward.

One without the girl.

Without the boy.

Without the game.

Who knows if I'll even finish college at this rate? Nobody gets to keep a sports scholarship if they're booted from the team for bad grades.

Closing my eyes, I replay my last game, tracking my movements as if watching from outside my body, picking apart my every step until I'm fully immersed in the game, every other part of me fading to the background.

It works.

It works until I get to the third quarter, and the ball is snapped, but instead of a rough brown leather pressing into my palm, it's a fuzzy little football with red ink penned into the side.

My lips twitch. My little man loves that damn ball.

My eyes flick open, and I sigh.

What the fuck am I going to do?

The harsh bang on my window has me jolting, my glare swinging to the side. It's black out, so I blink a few times, and then his face presses closer, a hard glare etched across his face.

"Fuck," I mumble, turning on my Tahoe and unlocking the door, fighting against the throbbing of my every muscle. It feels like woodpeckers pecking at my damn temples, and I groan.

"You dumb son of a bitch," Brady starts in the second he throws the door open, locking himself inside with a purposeful slam and sending those woodpeckers into a frenzy.

Alcohol, a long-ass drive, and a three-hour run do not fucking mix.

I drop my head back against the headrest, gripping the wheel for something to focus on, and a jolt of pain slices down my arm. I jerk, fighting back the nausea and blinking through the haze that slips over my vision.

235

My eyes snap to my throwing hand, and my pulse hammers harder. "Fuck."

"Yeah, oh fuck, you fuckwad." Brady glares. "The hell was that last night?"

"Nothing." My lips press into a firm line, and I turn away, reaching for a bottle of water, my eyes falling to the tiny bottle of orange pills I found beside my bed before I took off this morning, the sight sending pain of a different kind through my chest.

I know it was Payton who left them for me.

Sighing, I face Brady, but I can't make myself ask.

He scowls but swipes it away a moment later. He always has been the most perceptive of the three of us. "She's the one who realized you were gone first."

A flicker of something sparks in my chest, and I face him better.

"She thought Little D would help cheer you up, took him in there the minute he woke, but…"

That spark is snuffed, and acid is poured down my throat, eating away at my insides.

She brought him to me?

She fucking came to me, with him, and I wasn't there.

I slam my fist down on the steering wheel, and a scream leaves me. "Fuck!" I yank my hand to my chest, my eyes flying wide.

"Goddamn, Mason! What the fuck!" Brady slides over, gripping my wrist and pulling it closer. His eyes widen, moving from me to my hand as he shakes his head. His jaw clenches, and he squeezes his eyes closed. "Get out," he snaps.

I don't argue. I get out, swapping spots with him, and notice Chase is here too, his truck parked beside mine.

I can't quite see inside it, but when he flashes his lights, I nod, and he's pulling out before Brady takes the driver seat, getting us onto the road.

"Chase didn't want to stay behind?" I grumble.

"Don't ask stupid questions," Brady snaps. "You know we came the minute we realized you'd left early."

Brady doesn't head to our side of campus, instead leading to a drugstore. Neither of us speaks on the short drive, and even after he kills the engine, the silence stretches, though it's him who breaks it first.

"Look, man." He faces me, reaching over to clasp a hand on my shoulder. "You're my brother, all right, and I don't know what's going on with you and Payton, so let me start by saying I love her little ass as much as I love you. But, Mase." He shakes his head. "This is your fucking time. The last ten years, this is what you were working toward, a starting position at a D1 school. Your face on top of the stats pile. Your file on the desk of every head coach in the NFL. You're *right there*, man. Two more years at Avix, and you'll be on your way to the draft. You're literally on the path you've always dreamed of, about to get everything you want."

My frown deepens more and more by the second, and I look to my hand. The swelling in my knuckles seems to be worse than it was earlier, but it's not broken.

"That shit last night could have been worse, and losing it a minute ago didn't do a damn thing to help either." Brady releases me. "I mean, come on, man. You want Alister fucking Howl to take your seat?"

My lip curls, and Brady nods.

"Exactly." He swallows, and I know guilt when I see it, but he pushes past his hesitation, because that's what friends do, and adds, "Payton is strong. Stronger than me, that's for damn sure, and not only that, but she's surrounded by people who care about her. Anything she needs, she can ask any one of them, and they'll be there. Shit, we all will, no questions asked, but..." He pauses. "But she has a future to figure out, and you're already heading toward yours."

My throat clogs, my mouth running dry. I can't swallow past it.

What he's saying, it's all true. Payton does have an endless support system, and she doesn't have a clue where life will take her from here. She's just trying to make it one day at a time.

My time already started, my future just over the hill, waiting for me to climb to the top and grab hold.

He's saying I should let her live her life and figure out what she wants along the way.

It would be fair.

It's in part what I've been doing, albeit reluctantly.

But what Brady doesn't know, and if he did he would *never* say what he just said, is that my future did start.

It started last year when I first met the blond-haired, blue-eyed girl with the weight of the world on her shoulders. I knew the minute she showed up in Oceanside that I wanted to know her. There was an instant need to protect her, and at first, I thought it was because she was Parker's sister, therefore she was family, and family looks out for each other.

However, little by little, things shifted. I was a controlling asshole when it came to protecting my sister, but I was a feral fucker when it came to Payton.

I didn't just *want* to make sure she was okay, I *needed* to, and just like that, the mountain I've been climbing widened its peak. It stretched, creating more space, so I could be standing there at the top with my hands outstretched, waiting to take hers once she reached it.

And we were on our way, moving at a steady incline, side by side.

But now?

Now she feels farther away than before. It's as if halfway up, her path split, taking her in the opposite direction.

I would give anything to lead her back.

The reality of the situation is this.

I had a dream, but that dream has changed.

It's not about me and what I want anymore.

Or maybe it is.

I don't want a ticket to the top anymore.

I want three.

PAYTON

I hug the girls, smiling as Cameron, Ari, and Paige all take turns peppering Deaton with kisses and promises of seeing him again soon. Cameron jogs around the car, and I look to Paige when she speaks.

"Lunch when I come back to check on the studio in a few days?" she asks, closing the car door and leaning against the open window.

"Can't wait."

She smiles, dropping back in the seat and glancing down at her phone.

Ari steps up next, hugging me. "Love you, girlie. Remember, you can call me if you want to talk."

I swallow, forcing a smile as she pulls away. "Let us know you made it back safe?"

She eyes me a moment, then nods, a smile breaking across her lips. "Okay. Off we go."

I give one last wave, turning away as they say bye to Kenra. I head straight to my room, plopping on the bed and settling Deaton down beside me.

"Can we sleep for a week now, mister?" I tickle him, laughing when he drops his face into the pillow and wiggles his little body.

The light knock against the frame has me looking up to find Cameron standing there.

"Hey." A small frown pulls at my brows.

"Hey." Slowly, she steps into the room, but it's when she glances over her shoulder briefly that a knot forms in my stomach. "Look, you know we love you guys, but we love Mason, too."

239

Anxiety builds, my throat growing tight at the implication. "Cam…" I start to lie, but she shakes her head.

"What the hell happened, Payton? He was on top of the world when we went back for our spring semester, and then summer hit, and suddenly he was different, so…what happened? And don't say you don't know or it's not about you. It is. I saw it back in November before Deaton was even born, and I see it now. Something happened between you two when he came home with his injury, didn't it?"

Tears build in my eyes, and hers blow wide open.

"I knew it!" She frowns. "He's in love with you, isn't he?"

"Cameron, please," I beg in a whisper. "You can't tell anyone. It's…complicated."

Air whooshes from her lips, almost as if in relief, and she rushes forward, dropping on the bed beside me. "He loves you, and you broke his heart."

My muscles lock, and I wait for her to yell at me, so I'm shocked when her arms wrap tight around me and she tugs me into her chest.

"I never meant to hurt him," I admit, pulling back and running a hand over Deaton's curly hair. "There's just"—I swallow—"so much at stake."

When I look up at Cameron, there's a sympathetic smile on her lips, but it's the words she leaves me with that are sure to haunt me.

"I would argue that there's so much to lose." She pushes to her feet, squeezing my hand before letting it fall. "If you go too far down this road, you will."

CHAPTER 25
PAYTON

Before, February

Warm lips press to my collarbone, and a smile tugs at my lips. I *stretch my neck, allowing him more access, and his mouth curves against my skin, his hair tickling along my ear and making me giggle.*

I shift in the bed, spinning, and he takes me in his arms, holding me tightly.

"It's time to wake up, Payton."

"Just five more minutes."

"That would only make you want five more," he whispers. "Come on, time to get up." He tugs at my hands, but I just twine my fingers with his, reveling in the warmth.

Finally, my eyes open, locking on to a perfect pair of brown ones. "Good morning, Deaton."

His eyes slope at the sides, his voice low. "Good morning, Payton."

"I miss you," I whisper. "I don't want you to go."

"I know." He nods, his voice fading. "But it's time to get up now."

"Wait." I swallow, reaching out when he begins to blur. "Wait!"

I fly up in bed, blinking around the room when a soft cry reaches me.

I look to the side, smiling down at my son in his bassinet, his big blue eyes wide open, tiny fingers in his mouth.

Warmth spreads through me, and I swallow past the melancholy my dreams always seem to leave behind, yet still, every night, I look forward to them.

To seeing his face and hearing his voice.

"Someone's awake early," I murmur, leaning down and lifting him into my arms.

He stretches, his little butt pooching out and tiny arms lifting above his head in the most adorable way.

There's a soft knock on the door, and my brother's face appears.

"Hey." He slips inside to rub his hands over Deaton's curly hair. "I thought I heard someone."

I grin, allowing him to take my son in his arms, and I stand, grabbing what I need to get him bathed and laying out an outfit for him to wear today.

"I'm working from home the next couple of days. You can always leave him here with me, you know."

I nod, frowning at my own wardrobe options—or lack thereof. Literally the only thing that fits that's not part of my maternity donation pile are sweats and two pairs of leggings that are pretty much stretched thin at this point.

I sigh, digging a pair of fake jeans from the maternity pile and picking from the load of old T-shirts Mason gave me when nothing else would fit over my stomach. My stomach that's now three months postpartum and still looks as swollen as it did the day Deaton was born. Well, give or take a few inches.

"I know, but the day care center is a perk of the internship."

"That doesn't mean you have to use it."

"Yeah, but it makes me feel like I'm…I don't know, doing things on my own, you know?"

Parker nods, making ridiculous faces at his nephew, who tries his best to reach out and grab him but hasn't quite figured out his hand and eye coordination yet.

My phone buzzes on my nightstand, and I don't have to look to know who it is.

It's always the same person, every single morning at nearly the same exact time.

I ignore it for a moment, but Parker clears his throat.

"I take it you know Mason is calling?"

I nod, tossing a pair of socks beside my jeans and top, then reach over to grab my phone. "I do."

"You gonna answer it?"

"Why wouldn't I?"

Parker lifts a brow. "'Cause you haven't yet, and your cheeks turned pink when I mentioned whose name was on the screen."

A chuckle escapes me, and I raise two brows right back, pressing the Answer and Speaker button all in one.

"Someone was about to get in some serious trouble here, Pretty Little."

"Don't you have class or something?" My brother scowls at the black screen.

Mason chuckles, and I quirk my lips to one side. "Don't you have work or something, old man?"

Parker scoffs, crossing his arms.

"Course I have class," Mason says. "I'm on my way. This is my pep talk time."

"She doesn't need a pep talk."

"Who said she did? I'm the one about to take a fifty-question exam. Feel bad for me, Parker, 'cause your sister won't."

Parker rolls his eyes, but a smile pulls at his lips as he passes Deaton back to me and walks out.

I drop my phone into the baby shower caddy, heading into the bathroom.

"He's gone."

"Good. Let's start over." Mason pauses. "Good morning, Pretty Little."

I shake my head with a smile, turning on the water. "Good morning, Superstar. Test today, huh?"

"Yep. It's going to be a rough one, and then Coach asked to

243

see me, which is weird since it's February, and we only really see each other during weight training."

"Maybe it's about next season?"

"Maybe. Guess we'll see. Now, you know what to do."

I roll my eyes even though he can't see, but then I give him what he wants. I test the temperature, then situate Deaton in his bath, clicking the button to swap to FaceTime, something we've done every day since the gang went back to campus for their spring semester.

His face pops up on the screen, and something knocks in my chest, my cheeks warming at the unexpected sight, but I say nothing as his view isn't of me. He smiles wide at Deaton and starts talking as if they're having a full conversation.

As if Deaton has any idea what's going on at all.

Mason jokes with him about his morning workout, and when Deaton flaps his arms in the water, Mason's smile grows wide.

"Dang, my man, look at the guns on you." He chuckles, and a low laugh leaves me.

"He's getting chubby, isn't he?" I tickle his belly.

"Nah, he's getting strong. Tell her, Little D."

Deaton splashes some more, and for a moment, I wonder if he does know he's being spoken to.

Mason smiles, and when he looks directly into the screen, as if he's looking right at me, my cheeks burn for some reason.

I swallow. "Why are you shirtless?"

The smirk that tugs at his lips is deadly, and I almost roll my eyes again, but something forces them to stay locked on the screen.

Man, he's...ripped.

I clear my throat.

"Had to get an early morning session in. My meeting with Coach is at my normal training time, so here I am." A whistle blows in the background, and his head jerks left, hand lifting to cover his eyes.

"Johnson, the fuck you doing?"

Mason grins, looking back at the screen. "Oops. I'm caught. Let me see you before I go."

I shake my head even though he can't see. "Get back to it, Johnson."

He laughs. "Yes, ma'am." Mason looks at the screen a moment longer, then nods. "All right. We're on for our call tonight? I… uh…" He looks nervous all of a sudden, his gaze straying from the screen, and I bite my nail in response.

Mason swallows, a serious expression now on his face. "I have something to tell you. It's… I want to look at you when I tell you, though, okay? So tonight, FaceTime, me and you?"

My pulse patters beneath my skin, and I shift anxiously. Trying to tamp down my suddenly rising anxiousness, I tease, "Don't you have better things to do at college than sit on the phone with me on a Friday night?"

"Ha!" Mason tosses his head back obnoxiously, his smile far too cocky. "Cute. That's cute." But that cockiness falls away in an instant, and what's left is a timid grin that has my blood pressure rising. "Tonight, gorgeous girl."

He hangs up, and I stare at the blank screen longer than I should.

MASON

"I don't know about this, Coach. I mean, I know I look good, but are you sure I can't get in trouble for this kind of thing? Feeling a lot like undercover *Playboy* but, you know, the one for girls."

Coach just chuckles, tossing me a second bottle of some shit that's suspiciously close to lube if you ask me. "Enjoy it, son. Any minute now and a pretty little thing is going to walk through that door. If you ask real nice, maybe she'll help rub it on your back."

I scoff. "Yeah, you say that until a dude with big beefy hands and a monster's build walks in."

"I've never heard them described as beefy, but I guess I don't hate it."

My muscles freeze, and oh so fucking slowly, my head turns, attention pointing over my shoulder.

Like in my damn dreams, there she is, standing in my gym and smiling like the Cheshire Cat.

My eyes trail over her, locking on to the fact that she's wearing my old high school football shirt, the chest stretched mouthwateringly tight over breasts, now even fuller than before. She shifts on her feet, and I notice the camera bag hanging from her shoulder.

My smirk is slow, and I spin to fully face her. "Are you shittin' me? Am I being punked? Hallucinating? I gotta be imagining this, right? Ain't no *way* you're here right now."

Coach knocks me on the shoulder, but I don't break eye contact with the girl. "Beefy fucker, my ass," he mumbles, then he might as well turn invisible, because I couldn't tell you if he stays or goes. All I see is her. In. My. Gym.

Well, the athletic department's gym at Avix, but tomayto fucking tomahto.

She does her best not to smile, squashing her lips to the side and tethering her fist tighter on the strap of her bag with each step I take closer. And I'm moving in on her fast.

I get about two feet from her and raise a brow, and there it is.

She laughs, lowers her bag to the floor, and throws herself in my arms.

Her hands wrap around my neck, mine her waist, and I lift her up, spinning her in circles, her airy laugh echoing around us.

When she pulls back, she smiles, but just as fast, her nose crunches up and she pushes off. "Oh my god, you're sticky."

"Yeah, the chick setting up the lights and shit said I had to be shiny."

"And you, what, used the whole bottle?"

"Bottle and a half." I frown.

Payton laughs loudly, glancing around the room, her gaze pausing on Jeremy, one of the Sharks star receivers Chase competes against, and Fernando Blanca, a beast of a lineman, the other two from the team Coach asked to be a part of this little project. Her brows raise when Fernando tugs his shirt over his head, and I glare, slipping into her view.

"So. I mean, what the hell?"

Payton grins, gesturing to her bag and the badge I didn't notice hanging around her neck. "Avix asked Embers Elite to be the official photographer for a new project they're testing. I don't know much about it other than it's for your school newspaper's social media pages. Today is football, tomorrow baseball, and then basketball."

Tomorrow... Wait.

"You're staying here? For three days?" My brain catches up to me, and I look behind her. "Where's Deaton?"

Her features soften at his name, and she tucks a few loose pieces of hair behind her ear, the rest piled high in a ponytail on her head. "I just met up with Cam at the child development center. I almost turned this down because I wasn't sure about the situation, but Lolli suggested I call Cam first, and thankfully she was eager to take the weekend to get more of her volunteer hours in. She'll be there with him each day, and the shoots are only for three hours, so it's not like he'll be there too long and—"

"Take a breath," I tease, my knuckles grazing her jaw before I can stop myself.

Her cheeks grow warm, and she drops her chin to her chest, so I let my hand fall.

"He's in good hands there. Especially with Cam."

She nods, sighing and looking past me. "Well, I'd better go meet the crew and get set up." She pauses when she realizes I'm still staring and narrows her eyes. "What?"

247

"My mind is blown. I can't believe you're standing here right now." I laugh. "And wearing my shirt, no less."

"Well, nothing else fits, so…"

"Good. I hope nothing else fits ever again and all you get to wear is my shit."

She shakes her head in amusement. "Go wipe some of that stuff off. It's going to dry and be useless by the time I'm ready for you anyway."

With that, she walks off, and I watch her go, yet another shuffle and shift stirring in my chest, another piece sliding into place.

My puzzle's got to be nearly complete now, right?

We're here at Avix. Together. All three of us.

That's got to be some kind of sign.

Payton steps up to who I thought was the photographer, and within a moment, she's swarmed, her short little body buried behind half a dozen others from the school paper.

A hand clamps down on my shoulder, and I look to find Coach standing there with a brow raised. "Go on, kid. Get some push-ups in, and get those veins bulging. Wouldn't want to look like the skinny one in the pictures next to Blanca."

I glare, and he laughs, shaking his head as he stalks off toward the long table covered in finger foods. Pretty sure it's intended for the staff, but that doesn't stop him.

Shaking off my thoughts, I do exactly what Coach suggested, adding in a solid hundred crunches before those big blue eyes find mine in the crowd, calling me over without a word.

Too bad Jeremy and Fernando are called on too. I smirk when I glance at Jeremy, his chest, arms, and overall physique smaller than mine, but a frown digs at my brows when I face Fernando. Fucker's added a good twenty pounds on since the end of the season, and in all the right places, but she doesn't like that big, buff look.

She likes trim and tapered, wide shoulders, and a core

248

that looks painted on…if I do say so my damn self. She likes, well, *me*.

I glance her way, narrowing in on the pink of her cheeks as she looks at the three of us through the lens.

Right?

"Okay, Payton, we want at least a dozen group shots to pick from and then double that for the individuals. We'll be featuring them come summer, trickling them in to help build excitement for next season. And if there's one thing the *Avix Inquirer* readers love, it's abs, so don't hold back. Move them where you want them, and let us know when you're done. Kari and Leddy are working lighting, so just do you, and they'll follow your lead."

Payton nods, the slight press of her lips letting me know she's a bit nervous, but then she blinks, straightens her shoulders, and hot damn. She transforms.

One minute she's a blushing, shy little thing, and the next she's bossing a two-hundred-and-sixty-pound man around like no one's business.

It's a damn good look on her, but I'm not the only one who thinks so, and when it's Fernando who goes first for his solos, he's a smirking bastard, staring her right in the eye the entire time.

I stand to the side, arms crossed and glare intact, listening as she instructs him, praising when he does what he's told, but when she asks him to twist his torso slightly while keeping his hips facing forward, he pretends like he don't get it.

"You'll have to show me, sweetheart. I'm not sure what you mean." He grins, and the fucker ain't ugly.

But he is lying.

I've seen his Instagram. He's a thirst trap pro. Loves the mirror.

Payton steps away from the tripod and onto the small rise of the set. Her hands move out, and she directs him without touching him.

Fernando's eyes are on her face, and he smiles wider. "Like this?" He doesn't even move.

"No." Payton chuckles, and this time when her hand goes out, her fingers press to his upper abs. "Twist here. It will define the abs more, and keep facing forward."

My teeth are grinding together, and I take a step forward when his hand shoots out, wrapping around her wrist as he does what she asked.

Payton's eyes snap my way instantly, and that is the only reason my feet freeze in place.

She knows I don't like it, doesn't she?

Knows I want his hands off her and hers off him.

"Like this?" Fernando smirks.

Anger and jealousy start to boil in my blood, and my foot starts tapping.

This is her job. She's working.

She's not touching him because she wants to.

I close my eyes, counting to five, and when I open them, she's behind the camera again.

Jeremy goes next and listens a hell of a lot better, and then it's my turn.

I step into the lights, standing tall, and wait for her instructions.

"Uh…um." She swallows. "Okay, straight on first, and then slow shifts to each side, hips staying in place."

I'm a good fucking boy, doing exactly what she asked, my eyes locked on hers through the lens the entire time.

"Holy shit." The lead editor of the *Avix Inquirer*, as she introduced herself earlier, steps up, staring at the sample screen to the left. Her eyes move from it to me and back. "These are just…yes."

Payton's eyes snap up over the lip of the camera, and I wink at her.

I don't know what those images show, but I know what I was thinking about the entire time she was clicking that little button.

Me and her.

Her and me.

Every which way our bodies could move and how well she'd

250

listen if it were me on the other side of this little situation. How bad I want to get her in front of a camera lens so she can see how I see her.

Literal, utter perfection.

A fucking mirage I want to capture and keep. Spoil. Fucking ravage.

A flush works its way up Payton's neck, and I chew the inside of my cheek to keep from smiling. I'm standing here alone under bright-ass lights in nothing but a pair of navy football pants, undone in the front to show my black briefs.

I lift my left hand, run my thumb knuckle along my lips, and watch as her chest rises, the flash flickering over and over and over. My teeth sink into my lip next, and she drops her gaze to the floor, but only for a split second, and then she's back, gripping her camera and tugging it from the tripod. She steps right once, twice, and my head follows, my body staying stationary, and I swear she shudders.

"Done," she calls out suddenly, and then she spins on her heels, her steps carrying her across the room and through a small door in the back of it.

Chuckling to myself, I step down, moving over to my bag in the corner.

I pull my pants off and slip into a pair of track pants, and I no sooner get the shirt pulled over my head than a familiar voice reaches me.

"Hey, stranger."

Fuck.

I turn to find Allana, a girl I met at one of the football parties when I first got to Avix. "Allana, hey, how are you?"

"Good." She reaches up, her hands drowning in a baseball hoodie, and tucks her blond hair behind her ear. "I called you a couple of times. You know, after."

I clear my throat, offering a soft smile. "Yeah, I'm sorry, but I'm...not single anymore."

Allana nods, opening her mouth, but when my eyes slide away, tracking Payton as she steps back into the room, Allana looks back to me. "Yeah, of course. Well, I just wanted to say hi. See you around."

I nod, glancing her way briefly. "Yeah, see you around." I stuff my things in my bag, meeting Payton halfway.

She's beaming, and the expression makes me laugh.

"Have fun?"

"That was so awesome! They said they love what they're seeing. I mean, it's only the sample sheets, and none are edited but—"

"But I'm flawless and don't need any edits."

Payton's lips smack closed, and then she laughs loudly, and when she loops her arm through mine, pride and something else thump behind my ribs. I take her bag and heave it over mine.

"Come on, Superstar." She drags me along. "Let's go get Deaton, and you can walk us back to our room."

"That sounds like the best idea I've ever heard."

She smiles, but of course on our way across campus, Fernando spots us and jogs over.

"Hey, photo girl."

"Hey." She smiles.

"Think you could show me some sneak peeks?" He presses closer, and I push her back, glaring harder when he smiles my way.

"Not a chance." She laughs. "I mean, if I want to get fired, sure...but I don't."

"Fine, fine," he teases, reaching out and flicking her ponytail. "Maybe I'll see you around."

"You won't," I snap. "Go the fuck away."

Payton blushes, but my teammate only laughs, winking before sauntering off like the shithead he is.

I heave a sigh, watching him with a glare. "He's a jackass."

We start walking again, and Payton laughs, shaking her head.

"He's not so bad." My eyes move her way, and she glances

over. "If you think college athletes are bad, you have no idea. The egos only float higher at the next level."

That's right.

She's an intern for hire at Embers Elite, the official photographer of the pros. She's around men all day.

Older men.

Pro fucking players.

Before I know what I'm doing, my hand is pressed to her ribs, and I've spun us, backing her up against the wall of the child development building.

Her head presses softly to the old brick, and I'm on her.

Payton gasps, and my eyes slice to her lips, zoning in on the little part between them, and my tongue suddenly feels too heavy. It wants to slide out and slip between her lips. To taste her.

I need to taste her.

"Mase," she whispers.

"I don't like when other men look at you, and I hate when you look at them." I lean down, lowering my forehead to hers. "I'm a man. A stupid, possessive one who wants you all to himself."

Another gasp, this one deeper, rawer, and my eyes flick open as I realize what I just said.

I pull back, needing to know what her eyes are saying.

They're wide and wanting, and once again, I'm locking on her pouty, pink lips. "Pretty Little," I all but beg.

I lean in, and a door slams at our side, making her jump.

Her head whips away, and it feels like a sharp slap across my cheek.

Fuck.

I swallow, running my hand through my hair when she squeezes away from me.

I open the door for us, unable to meet her eyes fully. "Come on, Pretty Little. Let's go get Little D."

Unfortunately, Cameron has him all packed up when we get there. He's already fast asleep in his carrier, a blanket softly laid over the top, so I don't get to play with him on the short walk to her room, a small studio-like place in the staff quarters reserved for guest speakers and, well, photographers, I guess.

He doesn't wake when she transfers him to his playpen, already set up in the corner, and with every passing minute, my limbs grow heavier, so I finally face her and say, "I don't want to leave."

Payton smiles up at me, her head tipped to the side. "Why would you leave?"

My brows go up. "You want me to stay?"

"You act like you'd listen if I said no."

My grin grows quickly, and I face her fully. "But are you saying no?"

Her eyes narrow playfully, and she crosses her arms, but I grip her biceps and give her a little shake.

"Come on, girl. Let me hear it."

She chews her lower lip, but that smile breaks free, and she laughs. "Hey, Mase?"

I'm full-blown smirking now. "Hey, Pretty Little."

"Do you want to stay with us tonight?"

Us.

Not just her. Them.

Us three.

I don't bother answering. I toss my shit in the corner and pull up DoorDash.

I'll be damned if we leave this room tonight.

I'm not sharing her attention with anyone.

Not even the delivery driver.

CHAPTER 26
PAYTON

Before, February

"Bye!" I call over my shoulder, slipping out the gym double doors and coming to a complete stop.

Mason and his parents are all standing there with grins on their faces.

Vivian throws herself at me, hugging the life out of me, and Evan comes up next, his hug just as warm but less fierce than his wife's.

"Someone's missed you," he teases as he pulls away.

"I don't think it's me she misses," I joke back, and when Vivian claps her hands, eyes big and eager, I share an *I told you so* look with her husband.

"Can we go get him now?" she nearly begs, hands folded like in prayer and all.

I look to Mason, and he winks.

"She thought she'd get some kind of perk with Cam in the building, but they wouldn't let any of us through the gate." He frowns then. "You should really put me on the list Cam was talking about, just in case."

"Sure thing, Superstar." I chuckle, handing off my camera bag when he reaches for it. I turn to his parents. "What are you guys doing here?"

Vivian loops her arm in mine, a sneaky way to quicken my

speed, and it warms my heart to know how much she cares for my son. Maybe even loves him in the way my own mother should.

Not that I'll ever give her the chance.

Not that Vivian is his grandmother or anything but…

I swallow, shaking off the anxiousness threatening to slip in, and focus on the now.

And right now, I am happy to see them.

"Well, it's been a while since we've made it down for a visit, and when we heard you were here, we figured we may as well come where you are and see our kids, too."

"Hey," Mason pretends to complain. "You'd rather see her than me and your sweet princess baby girl?"

"Oh, please." His mother raises a brow, and I laugh as it looks so much like her son. "Noah is glued to Ari's side after everything, and she likes it that way, and you…well, yeah, I'd rather snuggle with that baby boy and let you two run off and do you sort of things."

My eyes snap to Mason's.

Us sort of things.

Oh my god, she knows?

Wait. Knows what?

There's nothing to know. Right?

As if he can read the jumbled thoughts I hardly process my damn self, Mason smirks and looks away. "That sounds a lot like an offer to babysit."

"It is, even though I should want to punish you, you brat."

"For what?" Mason gapes, blinking innocently.

"You know what! Don't think your aunt didn't call and rub it in my face."

Mason goes stiff, eyes everywhere but on us. "Okay, Mom."

His dad glances my way from the corner of his eye, and I grow even more suspicious.

"Don't 'okay, Mom' me. My only baby boy went all the way to Alrick on his free time instead of coming home to see me?"

My head whips his way. He runs a hand over his hair, peeking at me briefly before shrugging off her words.

"It was…a quick trip. Sudden and—" He cuts off, swallowing.

"You went to Alrick?" I ask, unable to hold the question back.

When did he do that? We talk every night and every morning. We text throughout the day, most days anyway. He never said a word.

Sure, his aunt and uncle live there, and that's where his cousin Nate grew up with Parker and me, but…he went to my hometown and didn't tell me?

"Did you go to pick up some of Nate's stuff, or Parker's?"

He still won't look at me, and then we're in front of the child development center.

Clearing my throat, I tell the others I'll be right back, running in to get Deaton.

He's wide awake this time, and I lift his tiny self into my arms.

"Well, hello, handsome." I rub my nose along his. "Someone is here to see you."

"He is literally the cutest thing in history." Cameron sighs, staring down at him with gleaming eyes. "I want one, but, like, not yet. I'll just play with yours and the dozens in this class until then."

Chuckling, I buckle him in his seat, and she rolls over the stroller, helping me lift and clip it into place.

"I take it Nana Johnson is stealing him?" She smirks.

"Nana?"

She shrugs. "Cute name for a grandma, don't you think?" She smiles, then someone calls her name. "Duty calls. Literally." She snags a diaper from the tray on the wall. "See you tomorrow!"

She takes off like nothing. Meanwhile, I'm halfway to panic, but when I step outside and join the others on the grass, the mere expression on, well, every single Johnson face is enough to drown it out.

It's clear as day how much my son means to them.

They love him.

Mason loves him…

I swallow, catching his eye, but his smile quickly moves back to Deaton as his mom lifts him from the seat I just put him into.

"Okay, shoo." She turns away from us. "Call me later. Or don't. I assume all we need is in the bag."

I open my mouth, but only a laugh comes out, and I nod. "I mean, yeah." I look to Mason.

"You can't have him all night." He frowns. "I hardly got to play with him, and they leave tomorrow."

"Uh-huh. Bye." And off they go, my infant son in their arms.

My shoulders fall, and I sigh. "Well, shit." I glance up at Mason. "What now?"

He frowns after them for a moment but then swings his head my way with a grin.

"I've got a few ideas." He takes my hand, and I let him lead me where he wishes.

———————

"Absolutely not."

"Absolutely *yes*. Come on, girl. Get that booty in here before I lift and lower you myself."

I chew my lip, eying the ATV with distrust. "There's roll bars."

"What are you, a girlie girl or something?" he teases, well aware of my pageant days, forced or not. "Come on. I'll even let you drive."

"Hell no. Then we'll really be in for it." I look to the other couple climbing into one on the left and say screw it, settling into the seat and strapping myself in. I glare at the man beside me. "If we flip over…"

"Don't worry, baby. If you get hurt, I'll kiss it better."

He's teasing, but his words are like a flame across my skin, and I face forward to hide it just as he slams his foot down on the gas.

I hold on tight, stiff as a board for the first minute or so, but then I start to relax, and fear turns into fun, leaving me laughing. I knock my shoulder into his. "Go faster! We've almost got them!" I shout over the whine of the engine.

"Hold on, Pretty Little." Mason floors it, whipping us through the grassy track, dirt kicking up and hitting the goggles on my face.

I'm suddenly super glad I put on the ski goggles like they suggested. We thrash through the brush, and I squeal when we are airborne over the next blind hill, coming down in a bouncy crash without missing a beat.

We're coming up to the end of the path, a giant checkered flag coming into sight, just as the other ATV barrels through the split in the trees across from us.

They look our way, and we look at each other.

"Go, go!"

"I'm going! We're winning this one!" he screams.

We skid and slide, flying toward the end with squeals and shouts of excitement.

We miss the mark by three seconds, taking second place.

"Noooo!" I shout, my palms slapping at my goggles, and Mason laughs at my side, nudging me with his shoulder and helping me with the buckle.

The other two are cheering, the guy lifting her on to his shoulders for a victory dance that's a little obnoxious but in a fun way I wish was us.

Mason must see it, because the next thing I know, his arms are wrapped around my knees, and I'm hoisted into the air. He pumps his fist, shouting and cheering, and my eyes are wide behind the mask.

"Stop it," I hiss, smacking his head.

"Fuck yes, second place!" he screams.

The couple ahead frowns our way, shaking their heads as they trudge up the short dirt path, but Mason isn't deterred.

He keeps celebrating until finally I cave, cheering and laughing with him.

Only after I give in does his laughter morph into a deep chuckle, and he slides me along his body until the tips of my shoes meet the ground. His arm stays locked around my lower back, and he lifts his goggles, then mine, before tugging our masks over our heads.

He grins, and it's ridiculous. He has a full-on dirt mustache and dirt glasses, and I have the sudden urge to wash it away.

In a hot shower.

Just the two of us.

Mason's smile slowly falls, his brown eyes darkening, and I swallow at the sight.

Suddenly, he licks his lips and looks away. "Come on, Pretty Little. Let's get cleaned up and find some food."

I have no idea how dirty we actually got until I look down at the photo the souvenir lady took of us at the end. Thankfully, the place has an outdoor shower, so we rinse quickly, and I put on a pair of extra sweats he had in his trunk with one of his university hoodies.

Instead of going out for dinner, we order from the small pizza pub near campus and sit on the grass at the edge of the school.

"Hey." I remember suddenly. "The other morning, you said you had something to tell me, but you wanted to see my face when you did, and then we only had a chance to text before bed. What was it?"

Mason freezes midbite, then chews it as slowly as humanly possible. After, he takes his soda and brings it to his lips for another snaillike moment, and I realize he's delaying.

He's nervous, and now I'm nervous.

"Never mind." I shake my head, picking at a piece of pineapple. "I'm sure it's not that big a deal and—"

"It is." He cuts me off.

My eyes snap to his, and everything about Mason softens, even his tone, now so low I hardly hear it.

"It is a big deal."

I swallow, shaking my head, now absolutely certain I don't want to hear it. "You don't have to tell me."

He's nodding before I'm even done. "I do. I do because it's…" He trails off, closing his eyes.

My heart starts to pound in my chest.

"It's about why I went to Alrick."

A knot forms in my throat. "Oh" is all I can manage to squeeze beyond it.

Mason wipes his palms on his sweats and reaches out, taking my hands in his. He gives a gentle squeeze, and when my eyes meet his, he tries to smile. Tries and fails.

"You're scaring me, Mase."

"I found him," he whispers, his Adam's apple bobbing harshly.

My pulse roars in my ears, too afraid to read into his words but fucking terrified I've misunderstood at the same time. "Found who?" I rasp, pretending there is more than one person he could be talking about when we both know there isn't.

Mason tips his head, the saddest yet most tender curve to his lips. "He's at Carmichael Cemetery on Fredricks Street."

I stop breathing.

My vision blurs.

I freeze.

My heart jolts, maybe even stops.

Hot streaks roll like waves down my cheeks, and I can't think. Can't hear or see.

So I close my eyes, and behind my lids, there he is.

The warmth of his smile and the calm of his eyes.

Deaton…

I choke, gasping for air as I stumble to my feet and walk away.

Mason calls out, but I don't stop. I break into a run, and I keep going.

I run and run and run until I can't run anymore, and then I collapse, but not against the ground.

No, he'd never allow that.

Strong arms catch me, lowering with me, and then I'm cradled in warmth. Cocooned in it.

He found him.

Nearly seven months ago, Deaton was buried without my knowledge. I wasn't invited, and I wasn't allowed to attend. I was to blame for his death after all, so his family taunted me, sending me the image of his casket and refusing to tell me where he'd been laid to rest.

I cried myself to sleep for weeks after that, the gaping hole in my heart widening with the knowledge that I'd never get to say goodbye. Knowing he'd never have a visitor because his family didn't care. The boy who gave me my little boy would be forever alone, and there was nothing I could do.

But the man beside me...

I lift my head, blinking through the storm in my eyes until a soft brown pair comes into view.

Mason.

My lips tremble, and I clench my teeth, my face falling into his touch when his hand lifts.

"You did this for me."

"Have you not figured it out yet, Pretty Little?" Mason presses his forehead to mine. "I would do anything for you."

My emotions rage, and my heart twists, full of fear and relief and a million other things.

We stare at each other, and when his mouth parts, my eyes fall to his lips.

Reaching out, I run my thumb along his lower one, my entire body shaking.

This man, he's been my rock. My friend. My savior.

My new favorite person.

He's not just Mason.

He's my Mason.

I look back and forth from his eyes to his mouth, pulse pounding out of control as I lean a little closer.

My eyes close, and his soft whisper rolls across my skin.

"No."

I tense, gaze flicking to his pained one.

He shakes his head, desperation and sorrow in his tone. "No, baby."

"Mase," I cry.

But Mason only shakes his head, pressing his forehead to mine once more. "I want you to have to kiss me because you can't stand the thought of not," he rasps. "I want it to be desperate and urgent and necessary." He swallows, whispering, "But I want it to be *mine* and *only* mine."

Not his.

That's what he doesn't say.

He wants this, this surreal, gravity-defying connection that's tethering us, but he wants it to be real. Ours.

More tears fall from my face, and when Mason tucks me to his chest, I burrow even closer. His arms tighten around me, and he holds me to him, rocking us back and forth.

I have no idea how long we stayed sitting there, but not once did his embrace slacken, and not once did his whispered words of reassurance pause.

Mason gave me something that means more to me than he could possibly understand.

Then again, maybe he does.

Maybe he knew exactly what it would mean to me, and that's why he did it.

Just for me.

Out of the kindness of his heart.

To show me how much he supports me.

How much he cares.

I care about him, too.

A lot.

More than I've allowed myself to admit, but I...I don't know how long I can fight it, this consistent tug that begins and ends with him.

What if I stopped fighting?

What if I let go and let life lead me where it may?

What if I give in and he leaves me, too?

But what if he doesn't?

CHAPTER 27
MASON

Now, October

My hand is fucked. Every time the ball presses to my palm, the ache reaches deeper. How I managed to do so much damage is beyond me. Chase didn't even have a black eye, just a swollen cheek, and I get a fractured knuckle?

Not that I know for certain. There's no way in hell I'm going to go to the doctor, not when the only insurance I have is athlete insurance covered by the school and it could get back to my coaches, but I know something is wrong.

I can hardly make a fist. Thankfully, I don't need to in order to throw a ball, but it's getting harder to hide. We've got a tough game this week against a team we lost to last year. If I can win this, if we can win this, it will be the first W over Oregon in five seasons, ending the damn losing streak.

Coach says I'm gonna make it happen, and I'm determined to prove him right, which is why my hand's shoved in a bowl of ice, my skin screaming in protest as I glare across the room at my sister, Cameron, and Paige as they fight over how to fry a damn tortilla.

"What the hell is the issue?"

All three scowl my way.

"Noah said," Ari begins, and the other girls groan dramatically.

"Noah isn't here, Arianna." Cameron frowns at the stove. "We're dropping it in the oil folded."

"If you fold it, it will break." Paige puts her hands on her hips. "You have to put it in flat first, flip, then fold."

"We need to heat them first, then fry," my sister argues. "Brady, tell them!"

Brady's brows jump, and he looks from the TV to me to them. "What Ari baby said."

"You don't even know what she said, you big dummy! You just like to argue." Cameron shakes her head. "I'm doing it."

"Paige is right," Chase pipes up.

"Oh, since when are you team Paige?" Cameron quips.

Chase's head has never popped up so quick. "What? I'm not!" He frowns, though his eyes stay locked on Cameron rather than looking at the blond who is now staring down at her fingernails.

Cameron smirks, a challenge in her eye I'm not sure I understand, and when I look to Chase, his are narrowed in on our friend.

Finally, he huffs, shaking his head. "Whatever, but it's going to split if you fold it first." The other girls glare, but Chase looks past them to the stove. "And I'm pretty sure you have to start over now, because your oil is smoking."

All three look to the stove, freaking out in unison.

We chuckle, refocusing on the game film and starting back at the top for the second time tonight.

The game is tomorrow, and if we want any chance of pulling this off, we can't miss a thing.

Chase huffs, shaking his head. "I'm not seeing any tells. The running backs don't even shift. They give nothing away."

It's true. They have no tells. Their heads don't pull, and their feet don't point any which way that could lead you to connect the dots and anticipate the play call. The quarterback doesn't double tap the ball or lift his foot to indicate any damn thing. They're stone still, staring straight ahead until the snap.

Sighing, I sit back. "I can get us down the field, but in the end, this one is coming down to defense."

"You're going to have to go with the handoffs as much as you can, brother." Brady motions toward my hand. "You talk to Coach about the plan yet?"

"Far as he knows, I'm good, but I did put it in his head that they expect us to pass most of the game, so he's all for the run plays."

"Good, good." Brady nods, and Chase echoes his agreement just as the girls walk in with plates of food.

None of us comment on the fact that we're now eating with microwaved flour tortillas rather than fried corn ones.

"I can't believe you're playing on Halloween." Cameron bites into her burrito, talking around a mouthful. "That blows."

"The fact that you can still get your mouth open that wide with all that food in it means you know how to, too," Brady teases, laughing and dodging her backhand when she stretches her long-ass arm across the coffee table.

"Speaking of Halloween." Ari smiles. "How cute is Deaton's little costume!"

My brows snap together, and I look to my sister, but she's looking at Cameron.

"I know! I told her she should add a little war paint under his eyes, but she said that's just a football and baseball thing." She shrugs. "Still be cute."

"Little dude's gonna be a buff little badass when he gets bigger." Brady stuffs his face, eyes on the TV.

My appetite is gone in a single instant.

So they've all seen his costume. His first Halloween costume.

They've seen it, and I don't even know what it is.

A bitterness coats my tongue, and I lift my water bottle to my lips, trying and failing to wash the taste away.

My sister nudges my ribs, and my head snaps her way, but it's Paige who discreetly opens her phone, setting it on the carpet beside my feet.

My eyes fall to the screen, and there he is, smiling all big and bright, and goddamn if the murkiness in my mind doesn't grow a little lighter at the sight.

He's wearing what looks like overalls but a spandex version, his name printed across the chest in the same font as our university hoodies.

He's wearing a singlet.

He's a little wrestler, and when I look to the second photo, zoomed in to only show his shoulders, printed proudly across the back is Vermont.

Because that's his last name.

He's not mine, and as much as it pains me to think it, I don't think she'll ever allow him to be.

Not that I'd ever want to take big D's place. I wouldn't. I don't.

But little man has four sides, right?

Why can't I have one?

Why can't I have her?

I push to my feet, excusing myself for a minute, and step into the hall.

The door opens a few moments later, and surprising me for a second time, it's Paige who joins me.

She smiles softly, propping her shoulder against the wall, her body facing mine. "She didn't send them the picture."

I look at her from the corner of my eye, and she shrugs.

"I made the costume. Dropped it off when I went to check on the progress of my studio last weekend. She only just tried it on him today and...well." She shakes her phone in the air.

"You made it?" I ask, surprised and trying not to read too much into her explanation.

So Payton didn't send it to everyone but me. That's good.

But why *didn't* she send it to me? She must know I'd want to see. We talked about it once...when we were still talking.

"I did. I make the costumes for my dance students all the time. It's cheaper that way, and the kids in my classes can't afford to be there, let alone to pay for something they'll never wear again." She smiles. "Although this was my first time making anything wrestling related, and to be honest, I don't know much about it... but I was a little surprised to learn wrestlers have numbers."

I chuckle despite myself, shaking my head. "You're right, you don't know much. Wrestlers don't have numbers because while they are part of a team or club, it's a solo sport. No need for numbers when it's just you and the other guy on the mat."

Paige makes a face of confusion, but the pinch of her eyes tells me she's not all that confused, and the simple "huh" that leaves her is even less convincing.

I raise a brow, and she giggles, but the playfully patronizing way she pats my chest on her way back inside tells me it's at my expense.

A moment later, my phone pings, and I pull it up. The number isn't one I have saved, but I know it's Paige when I open it, her first text telling me so.

Unknown: stole your number from the group thread.

Before I can respond, a second message comes though, this one the image she showed me inside of Deaton smiling wide at the camera, his big blue eyes as bright and glacier-like as his mama's.

"Hey, little man," I murmur, gliding my thumb over it a moment...but then my eyes travel lower, and I see something I missed before.

My spine shoots straight, and I push off the wall, dragging the screen closer but zooming out as much as the image allows.

How did I miss it?

Right there on his chest is a number, stitched in big block letters to match his name.

The number four stares back at me, and all the air leaves my lungs, because holy. Shit.

That can't be a coincidence.

It's not random.

The number bolded on his chest is the same one I'll be wearing on mine tomorrow...when he'll wear it on his.

He's going to wear my number as I wear it.

My eyes burn, and I clutch my phone tighter.

Baby, did you do this for me?

I squeeze my eyes closed, breathing through the thin thread of hope threatening to take over.

When I first left for school last summer, after Deaton died, we talked a few times that first month, then weekly, and that quickly turned into every damn day.

I liked it like that. I *want* it like that.

But the girl has gone radio silent on me, and I haven't figured out what to do other than let her. I stopped hounding her because I didn't want to push. That's what Noah did, right? When things got tough with Ari. He gave her space and waited like the saint he is.

I'm not like Noah, though.

I'm not strong enough for this shit.

I'm freaking the fuck out and constantly stopping myself from walking out of class, driving my ass to Oceanside, and forcing her hand. I've almost done it. Four times now, I've found myself sitting in my driver seat, keys in the ignition, but each time, something's held me back.

The sad part is I'm pretty sure it's not my deciding to give her the space she's clearly after.

No, it's straight-up fear.

What if it's not a little extra space she's looking for...but a set of shears to cut us off completely? If I go to her and make her talk to me, she could say those words.

Call me weak, which wouldn't be a lie.

I'm already weak when it comes to her, so if she cuts me out, it will only get worse.

My eyes fall to the photo again.

270

This means something, though, doesn't it?

She told Paige what she wanted, and what she wanted was my number included with his name.

She didn't tell me, didn't show me, but maybe she will?

Maybe tomorrow when I get off that field, I'll have one of those texts from her, the ones I looked forward to all last season but have yet to get this time around.

———

Too bad when the end of the game comes, the only messages I have are from my parents. Suddenly, the epic win under my belt and relief in my hand, thanks to the cortisone shot my trainer gave me after Coach saw me wringing it out on my way off the field, mean jack shit.

The weight on my chest is heavier than I expected, a fucked-up sense of dread burning through me like whiskey without a chaser.

My restraint slips, and I send a message of my own.

Me: Happy first Halloween, little man. I wish I could have seen you tonight.

I hit Send and toss my phone in my bag, where I plan to leave it for the night, the thought of no response too much for me right now.

There's a huge after-party happening tonight to celebrate the end of Oregon's reign over us, but I won't be there.

How can I celebrate a win when I'm drowning in the weight of loss?

I need to get some shit off my chest, have a conversation I should have had a while ago, and I know just where to go to have it.

———

My phone rings for the third time, but I ignore it, just like the others, and finally put my Tahoe in park.

The minute my seat belt is thrown off, my skin pricks with nerves, and I close my eyes, dropping my head back against the headrest. My knee starts to bounce, and the ache in my hand decides to flare up again, likely from the death grip I had on the wheel the whole drive.

Our quarterly check-ins from our professors went in this morning, and I know the minute I get back to campus I'll be fucked in yet another aspect of my life, but I'm not going to worry about that right now.

I drove all through the night for a reason.

Pulling in a lungful of air, I step from the vehicle. As if this shit wasn't ominous already, a storm cloud rolls overhead, rumbling its warning of what's to come.

I've never been real good with warnings, though. Never been able to switch to chill mode like my friends. I run at a hundred all day, every day, in every aspect of my life. It's likely what got me here, and while I can't say it's a comfortable place to be, I wouldn't trade it. Incessant, overbearing sense of fucking failure or not, I want every part of it.

It can only be a fraction of what she's felt over the year, right?

My feet meet the curb, and I look to the sky, praying for the first time in a long time I'm not making a mistake, while knowing he and I would be the only people aware of it if I were.

Before I can bitch out or tell myself this is stupid and solves nothing, I push forward, counting the rows vertically, then horizontally until I'm stepping in front of a stone plaque, so large I could have spotted it without the map ingrained in my mind.

Sighing, I drop onto my ass, hanging my arms over my bent knees as I stare at the wet green grass near my feet.

"Hey, man." I clear my throat, blowing my cheeks up with air and releasing it slowly. A dry chuckle leaves me, and I wince. "This is fucked-up," I mumble, shaking my head.

I nearly stand but grit my teeth and talk myself out of it, instead sitting there silently for way too long. So long, the rain spills from the clouds, falling over me and adding to the weight I'm already carrying.

"You don't want to hear this, do you?" I mumble. "You don't want to hear how the girl you left behind has become the most important person in my life. Or that I think I felt it even when you were the one holding her hand while I watched from across the beach like a fucking creep." I pluck a piece of grass and toss it. "You don't want to hear how in the months that followed your death, she was breaking over and over again because all she wanted was to have you back, and all I wanted was to take your place. I wanted her to let go of you so she could grab on to me." A revolted chuckle leaves me, and I look away. "Fucked-up, right? What kind of man falls for a girl who's already on her knees?"

I stare at nothing for a long while, images of her flashing through my mind from the first day we met to the night I slipped out without her knowing and everything that happened in between.

"I didn't know what I was doing, and I didn't know how to stop it. Believe me, I tried. When I first got to Avix last year, I masked it all. I smiled and laughed. I went out and did the whole college thing, but when morning came and reality set back in, she just…slid right back into my mind. I tried to give her space because I was here and she was there and our lives were so fucking different, but it didn't matter, and sooner than she was ready for, I was all in.

"No one knew." I scoff. "Shit, most still don't. They suspect, but they don't know the half of it. I'm different now. Better because of her." My lips twitch. "Better because of him."

A low laugh leaves me, and I shake my head.

"He's something else. Big and strong. He looks just like you, man, but with his mama's eyes." I blink hard, taking a deep breath, looking up at the cold stone before me with a smile. "I think you would have hoped for that."

I read over the words written before me.

Deaton Vermont, son and brother. Loved by many and lost too soon.

It says nothing about his legacy, the only person who truly loved him and the little boy he left behind, let alone never got to meet.

I blow out a long breath, tamping down my anger, and pull my wallet from my pocket, taking out one of the copies of the little picture I had printed, the first and only thing I see when I flip open the old leather.

I run my fingers over the number on his chest, wishing I'd thought to print the back side that showed they share a last name. His real dad's name.

His only dad?

I focus on Deaton's chubby cheeks, the tight squish of his smile making my own wobble. With shaky hands, I stretch out, leaning the little photo against the headstone, the sight forcing me to look away to get myself in check.

"I…uh…" Fuck.

How is it so hard to talk to someone who can't even talk back?

Blowing out a long breath, I force myself to keep going.

"I know he's yours. He's every bit you as he is her, and I'll never forget that, not for a minute, man. I can promise you that, but…I love him like he's my own, and I know I'll never stop. You have to know I didn't plan on any of this, but it happened, and I don't know what to do." I clench my teeth. "She's pulling away, and I'm losing my mind. I'm losing her, and that means I'll lose him, and that right there makes me feel like I'm fucking dying." I wince at my word choices but can't take them back, because it's true.

Nothing that mattered before matters anymore. Not without her.

Not without him.

I swallow, shaking my head and whipping the rain in my hair with my hands.

I look down, whispering the words aloud to the only person who could possibly understand.

"I love her, Deaton. I love her with everything I am, and I'm so fucking fucked because I know now what I missed then. That no matter what I do and no matter how much time passes, she'll never truly love me back, because at the end of the day, I'm not you. You left, but she didn't let you go. She's holding on with all she's got, and I can't even hate you for it. I want to, but I can't. If she loved you this much, you must have been one hell of a guy, because she's...an anomaly."

My anomaly.

She's my everything.

Yet she's not even mine, is she?

"So what do you say?" I look at the headstone once more. "Do I learn to let go or keep fighting?"

Thunder breaks from the clouds then, and the rain pours in heavy streams.

I close my eyes, pointing them to the sky.

Yeah, that's what I was thinking, too.

She's inside me now, and no matter how sharp the blade, nothing is cutting her out.

All I can do is weather the storm and hope when the clouds clear and the sun rises, I'll still have the strength to stand.

Even if it's not at her side.

With a sigh, I pull out my phone. "Okay, Big D. Time to teach me a little something..."

CHAPTER 28
PAYTON

Before, March

One week.

One glorious week of doing absolutely *nothing*.

It's exactly what I need after the last couple of months I've had. The internship kept me busy and bouncing around each day, which I'm grateful for. I've learned so much from it, and I've already made it halfway through the online, go-at-your-own-pace courses they enrolled me in, but I am so ready for all the free time I'm about to have with my son.

My hours are still just part-time, so he's only in the organization's care center or with Lolli for four hours, five if I count drive time, a few days a week, and I only do my course work once he's asleep for the night, but oh my god. It's going to be so nice not having to jump up first thing every morning and get our asses together.

I understand now why in all the movies, the moms are up and ready before the kids even roll out of bed. We need that precious silence as much as we need the chaos that follows.

Warm coffee in one hand and monitor tucked beneath my arm, I slip out the back door. I flick on the gas firepit and drop onto the little couch on the back deck, gazing out at the early morning ocean.

I bring my cup up, taking a long whiff, and a smile crosses my face. "Early morning breeze, coffee, and warm fire is my exact idea of spring break."

"And here I thought I would be the highlight."

I jump at the sound of his voice, my coffee spilling over the edge slightly. My head whips around, spotting Mason on the sand, only his head visible through the planks of the high deck.

"What the heck?" I squeal, setting my mug down and running to meet him at the stairs.

I don't know what comes over me, but I jump, knowing he'll catch me at the foot of the steps.

My legs wrap around him, and he laughs, jogging up with me in his arms, his lips pressing to my cheek before he pulls back.

"Damn if that wasn't the exact greeting I was hoping for."

"Why are you here?"

He raises a brow, looking to the monitor on the table, Deaton still fast asleep in his crib.

I roll my eyes, wiggling until he reluctantly sets me on my feet. "I mean aren't you supposed to be getting on a plane right about now?"

"Oh, that?" He smirks, moving into the house and straight over to the coffeepot to make his own cup.

I trail his every move, following him back out to the patio and lowering into the seat I jumped from when he plants himself into the space beside it.

"Are you going to talk now?" I playfully scold.

Mason lifts a finger, takes a sip of his coffee, and nods his head. "You're right. This is my kind of spring break."

I glare. "You were supposed to be headed to Mexico."

"Was I?" He tips his head, laughing when I smack him playfully on the back of it. "I heard Parker was able to get off and he and Kenra decided to go, too, which meant—"

"I am fine on my own, Mason." I frown.

"—that I had a chance to have you two all to myself, and I took it," he finishes as if I didn't speak.

Damn if I don't get all warm and fuzzy at that. God, I'm such a girl. "Stop."

"I'm serious." He grins, eyes traveling over me like he knows I'm happy about this. "Cashed in my plane ticket and got something better."

"What could be better than a trip to Mexico with your friends?"

"A trip to Disneyland with my girl."

His eyes widen as if he didn't mean to say that and before I can respond, not that I have a response other than the blush I'm trying to fight, because *oh my, I don't hate the sound of that.*

I should, right?

Wait.

"Did you say *Disneyland*?"

Mason grins wide. "Better soak up these next two days of early morning breeze, Pretty Little, 'cause the three after that, that breeze will be rolling in on a balcony overlooking downtown Disney."

I try to rein in my excitement, I really, really do, but I can't help the squeal that escapes, and I dive into his arms, hugging him tight.

When I pull back, I realize I'm half in his lap, and his hand is running up and down my spine.

I chew my lip, and Mason leans forward.

My lips part, but Mason reaches past me, handing me my mug.

"Here you go," he rasps, tucking it into my hands.

I take it and face the water, but I don't move from his lap, and he doesn't ask me to.

We sit there in the early morning, enjoying each other's company in complete and utter silence.

It's the most relaxed I've felt in weeks.

But there's something about Mason that soothes me, isn't there?

Something that's always there beneath my skin, hovering. Heating. Reminding me of the man who's had my back when he didn't have to.

"I'm happy you're here," I admit.

His lips slide along my temple, and he whispers so low, I'm not so sure he intended for me to hear. "Where you are is where I want to be."

I close my eyes at the thought, basking in the warmth his words bring.

It's going to be a good week.

"Come on, come on. It starts in five minutes." I drag Mason by the wrist, literally, and he chuckles all the way, Deaton strapped to his chest in the little carrier he demanded I let him buy on the drive out here.

"You know, for a girl with face paint on, you're kind of bossy."

"Because a unicorn horn and glittery rainbow cheeks deem me a sweetheart." I laugh. "If I miss this, you're gonna get it."

"Kind of tempted to make us miss it just to see what that means."

I don't have to look back to see if he's smirking. I know he is.

"Keep it up, Johnson, and I'll steal all your blankets tonight."

The chuckle that leaves him is dark, and I don't dare peek his way, realizing it was not the right thing to say and well aware my chest is on fire right now.

We make it to the gate with two minutes to spare, only for me to learn the lightning passes come with a grace period in case you are, in fact, late. Oh well, I wasn't about to risk it.

We're pretty much at the front of the line and stepping into the large bucket-like contraptions faster than I expected.

Mason chuckles suddenly, a soft and airy sound, and I look over to find him staring.

"What?"

His lips are curved to one side, and he shakes his head. "I like how excited you are for this ride, as if there isn't a Ferris wheel in Oceanside you can go ride anytime you want."

"Oh, Superstar, you haven't put it together yet?" I grin, unclipping my travel case and pulling out my camera, pointing my finger at the sky before us.

Mason looks out, and slowly, the other side of his mouth lifts. "Well, hot damn."

I nod. "We'll have the best view of the sunset, and if I timed it right yesterday, on our second round up, we'll be at the very tip-top, but it's not only that." I turn and tip my head over my shoulder. "Look."

"Man." He nods, eyes roaming over both of the parks in view, the lights from the rides starting to glow brighter with the movement of the sun. "You really do have the eye of an artist."

I smile behind my lens, snapping a few images of the park from up high, my eyes flicking to the sky every few moments just in case. As predicted, the sun is nearly halfway disappeared just as we hit the very top and the cart pauses for the change in riders below.

I click and click and click, smiling at the sight. Just as I go to lower my camera to my lap, I hear Mason sigh. It's a long, gentle sound, and when I look over, my stomach flutters, a silky shuddering that melts my muscles.

My son is asleep, still cradled in the carrier strapped to Mason's chest. Mason's lips are settled at his hairline, resting there adoringly, his palm pressed to the curve of his bottom as he stares silently out at the pinks and blues in the distance.

It's a beautiful sight, a hundred times better than the setting sun I was so desperate to see and one I know I want to hold on to, so I shift my camera to capture it. The moment it clicks, there's a matching sensation that takes place behind my ribs, a soft, shadowy shudder I can't quite put my finger on, but warmth

280

washes over me, and I smile at the two, camera clutched tight between my hands.

I'll look back on this moment with the fondest of memories.

A man and a little boy.

A father-and-son moment any mother would love the opportunity to catch. And me—I'm glad I have someone in my life who holds my son with the same thread of care as I do.

And Mason does.

He holds him like he doesn't want to let him go.

He holds him like he loves him because he does.

"Thank you," I find myself whispering.

Mason's head snaps my way, as if for a moment he forgot where we were and that I was even here. When he really looks at me, his expression morphs from confusion to something...more.

"For?" he asks softly.

It's a fair question. We both know there are a million things I could be thanking him for.

Like the incommensurable gift of Deaton's grave location, and that very first day I arrived in Oceanside. For this very moment.

For all the time, thought, and care in between.

"Everything." Keeping my eyes on his, I lay my head back on the cart, my vision blurring, but for once it's not in sorrow. "You mean a lot to me, Mase." *More than you know.*

"You mean a lot to me, too, Pretty Little," he whispers.

You love me, don't you?

I swallow hard, the question sudden and the answer terrifying, because as my mind conjures it, the answer isn't one that needs to be spoken. It's obvious.

Mason Johnson is in love with me, and I think he has been for a while now.

I wonder what Deaton would say if I told him this when I see him in my dreams tonight. Would he be angry? Happy?

I honestly don't know, but I like to think it would be the latter.

Mason stares into my eyes, so much written in his deep brown irises, but he says nothing, just places his hand on my knee in offering, and something inside me liquifies.

Reaching out, I cover his hand with mine, our fingers threading together in a perfect little fit.

I close my eyes as we grow closer to the ground, settled in a way I'm not sure I've ever felt. "Okay," I rasp. "We can do whatever you want to do now."

Mason squeezes my fingers.

We stay on the ride two more times, and somewhere in the back of my mind, a low, loving voice I know all too well whispers...

What if this is a ride you never get off?

MASON

After two long days in the park, we only lasted until after lunch on the third and final one, deciding to head back to the hotel to hit up the tiki-style restaurant beside the pool for an early dinner.

We order a few items from the appetizer menu and sit out on the patio, the weather in March as nice as it is in May here, with maybe a little less heat depending on the day. When Payton comes back from the restroom, she spots the two frozen daiquiris in front of our plates and raises a blond brow.

"It's little man. Makes people think I'm older," I tease. "Well, that and the fake ID Brady got for me."

Payton laughs, shaking her head and eyeing the fresh, fruity drink before her. "What if they ask for mine?"

"Just pick up Deaton, and she'll forget all about it."

"Doubtful." She chews her lip, gingerly reaching out for the drink, but pushes it my way with a small smile. "I appreciate it and it looks amazing, but I can't have alcohol quite yet."

Leaning forward, I push it right back. "I know. That's why yours is a virgin and mine is not."

She stares for a moment, and then a smile spreads across her face, and she yanks it back. "Well, in that case." She takes a long drink, wincing. "Oh my, good, so good, but holy brain freeze."

Chuckling, I slouch in my chair, spinning the little toy hanging from the arc of Deaton's stroller again and again, loving the squawky sounds he makes as he does his best to grab it. He's kicking his feet like crazy, and I can't help but reach out and tickle the bottoms.

"Oh, so you're ticklish, huh, little man." I tickle up his thighs and back down.

He squirms and stuffs his hands in his mouth, smiling around his chubby fingers and sending drool down his chin.

I smile, and when I feel her eyes on me, I glance up.

Sure enough, she's staring, straw stuck between her lips, hair lying down her back for the first time in a while.

I reach out, tugging it gently, and her mouth curls over the straw, a softness settled across her.

"He likes you," she says.

"Pshhh." I grin, looking back down at my guy. "Of course he does. I'm his favorite, ain't that right?" I lean in, pretending like he's whispering something. "Oh yeah? Well, let's see." I play it out, winking at him for show, and then I thrust my hand out, tickling his mama along the ribs.

She squeals in laughter, tossing her head back, fingers wrapped around the drink. I bend in more, pressing my fingers high on her ribs, and she twists and shifts, her ass sliding right off the chair, but I catch her, half standing over her as I tug her back up. The move has me leaning over her completely, her head dropped back, staring up at me with innocent yet *indulgent* eyes.

Yeah.

She feels it. This intangible marking, like the laces of a

football, weaving us together to create the perfect placement. The perfect pair. We're tied in a way neither of us expected.

A way I can't fight. Don't want to.

I lean down, eyes closing as I press my lips to her cheek, inhaling her and holding on for a moment longer before I lower into my seat once more.

When I look up, her cheeks are as red as the lipstick she put on to match the ears on top of her head, and I can't help but wonder if every part of her changes colors this way.

Heat builds in my core, but thankfully, Deaton starts to whine, and I snap out of it, quickly rushing to unbuckle and lift him into my arms.

Little man goes silent instantly, laying his little chin on my shoulder, taking a fistful of my shirt and tugging it to his mouth.

Payton's chuckle is soft, and she shakes her head, taking the last wing from the plate in the center. "Such a spoiled little guy."

"Say, 'Damn straight, Mama.'"

Payton raises a brow, and I laugh louder.

"Okay, so my baby vocabulary needs some work, but I think I'm doing a pretty good job."

Payton chews her food, looking away for a moment, but when she goes for another drink, I see the smile she tries to hide, and I take it as a nonverbal *Yeah, Mase, you are.*

Deaton starts rubbing his face along my shoulder, kicking a little more frantically, and I look her way with worry.

She smiles, whipping her hands up and pushing to her feet. "That means he's ready to eat."

"I can feed him." I glance into the bag sitting under the stroller, looking for one of the bottles, but there's no more in the side pocket. I look up at her, and her cheeks tinge pink.

"I, um, forgot my pump, and we used all the formula I brought at the parks the last few days so…"

I replay her words a few times, and it finally dawns on me:

She needs to feed him, as in…with her body. I think about last night and yesterday morning, how after I got out of the shower both times, she was burping him, and I realize she's only been breastfeeding when I've been away or occupied.

Why does that bother me?

I clear my throat, fighting off the sense of…I don't even know what, and add our room information to the bill the lady set down before standing with him in my arms.

Silently, we make our way back to the room, me holding Deaton and her pushing the stroller.

People smile at us as they walk by, and the little kids stare at him like he's a toy they wish they could play with, and it all fills me with a sense of pride I may have no right to feel but do.

It doesn't hurt to pretend, right? If in my head I also see us as the little family these strangers see when their eyes are on us.

Man, is that fucked-up?

"Do you think we could go down to the spa?"

My mind clears, new images replacing the others, and the idea of a man rubbing his hands all over her has me frowning. "I mean, I can give you a massage if you need it. My hands are strong."

While she blushes a bit, she also smiles. "No, like…the hot tub spa?"

"Oh." Now the images in my head? "Ohhh."

Payton laughs, and I swear she knows what I was thinking. Maybe even likes it, the thought of a man getting jealous over her.

No, the thought of *me* jealous.

"I mean, I didn't bring a suit or anything, but I have a pair of spandex shorts I can wear, and we leave tomorrow, so I can just wear this top in." She looks to the T-shirt she's wearing, a frown on her face.

I can see the moment she starts to change her mind.

She fiddles with the hem, tugging it outward so it doesn't press against her newfound curves and starts chewing on her lower lip. "Actually—"

"We are definitely hitting up the hot tub, even if we have to wrestle some ten-year-olds for a spot by the jets."

Payton looks my way with a knowing smirk.

"I don't have trunks either, so basketball shorts it is, and you can borrow one of my tops if you want."

"I might just take you up on that." She grins, heading out of the elevator before me and moving up toward our room.

We step inside, and I talk a bunch of nonsense to Deaton as she stacks pillows on the freshly made bed before moving over to me to take her son into her arms.

I try to busy myself, but we picked up before we headed out this morning, and the maids were already here, so I'm moving around aimlessly. I dig in my bag for clothes to get wet in, change, and take too long in the bathroom to kill time. I move to my suitcase once more, folding and refolding my clothes.

"Mason."

"Yeah?" My voice is scratchy, so I clear it and try again. "Yeah?"

"Sit down," she says softly.

Finally, I look up at her, and my shoulders ease when I spot the blanket thrown over her shoulder, the baby hidden behind it.

"Are you blushing, Mr. Johnson?"

I scowl, and she chuckles, dropping her back onto the mass of pillows behind her.

"I am not blushing." Okay, so my face does feel a little warm. Sighing, I raise a brow, and she smiles, but it grows a little anxious as I lower beside her. "Okay, I've never actually seen anyone breastfeed before so...I mean, yeah, I guess I was a little nervous, but only 'cause I didn't want to make you uncomfortable."

She nods, peeking under the blanket before looking back. "Yeah, honestly, it was kind of awkward at first, especially at the hospital. The nurse would just...walk in and stare to see how he was doing and make sure he was, well, you know, that it was all going how it was supposed to. Maybe it seemed strange to have people watching because I was young or maybe because it was new, I don't know, but after a while, it just felt natural." She shrugs, glancing over at me.

"Can you feel him?" I wonder. "I mean, does it hurt or..."

"I know when he's eating and when he stops, but it doesn't hurt, not anymore. Like right now," she says softly, then her arms start to move under the blanket, and instead of his little toes poking out beside me, a bit of dark hair appears. She's switched sides. She looks at me then. "How come you're not nervous with him?"

"How do you mean?"

"I mean to hold him or play with him. I swear Parker freaks out if he moves in his arms, and don't get me started on Nate. He goes stiff and starts to panic if he cries for five seconds."

"I hate that they see him more than I do." The words fly out before I realize they're coming, and my eyes snap her way. "I mean..." I try to backpedal.

"You meant what you said." Payton's features are soft as she whispers, "You hate that they see him more than you can." She chews on her lips, gaze moving between mine. "I like that you hate that."

"You do, huh?"

She nods. "I like how much you care. How often you call to talk to him, even when he might not know it. I like how you check in on him, sometimes without saying a word about me."

"I'm always wondering what you're doing and wanting to check in on you."

"I know, and I like that, too."

A question that's crossed my mind pops up, and I force myself to ask it. "Do you think Deaton would have liked me much?"

I don't know what I expected, but Payton's smile spreads wide, and my heart thumps heavy in my chest, doubling when she says, "I know he would. I talk to him about you sometimes, in my dreams I mean." Her cheeks pinken, but I don't have time

287

to consider why she would be embarrassed to admit that, because she just admitted that.

She talks to him…about me.

That's no small revelation.

That's a gauntlet thrown into still waters, creating a rippling effect that expands to the very edge of who I am and what this means to me. A complete change in the foundation of what I feel for this girl is built on.

My eyes hold hers, and then a tiny hand appears, fist latching on to the edge of the blanket covering her and tugging it down until his little face appears.

His eyes snap up to mine, his mouth, still wrapped around his mama, curving into a gummy smile before closing around her once more.

My eyes lift to hers, and when I find hers already on me, I reach over, running my thumb along her lips. "I—" *want to kiss you so fucking bad, Pretty Little.* I swallow. "I'm going to step out on the balcony," I say instead.

I see a flash of disappointment sparking in her baby blues, but I can't think about that right now, so I convince myself I imagined it.

Outside, I take a deep breath, trying to calm the wild waves of emotion raging inside me. When I lift my head, I let my gaze travel over the place, the pool and play zone quieter than it was last night and the restaurant twice as busy as earlier. But what really gets my attention is the rope lights to the far right, what looks to be a reception in full swing.

"I guess this is what they mean when they say fairy-tale wedding?" Payton steps up, folding her hands over the railing. She must see the question, answering before it's asked. "He's out. Not sure I have the heart to put him in the stroller to make it to the spa, though."

I shake my head. "Leave him. He had a long day, taking pictures with characters and all."

"Oh yeah, he must be *so* exhausted," she teases back.

I slip my hand in my pocket, pulling it out and holding my fist up between us. "I got you something today."

A small frown builds across her brows, but her lips twitch in excitement as my fingers uncurl, her eyes locking on to the small blown-glass item in the center of my palm. Her lips part, and when she reaches up, her gaze meets mine first, asking for permission.

I nod, and she gently takes it from my hand, tilting hers from right to left, smiling as the glass glimmers from pink to blue, depending on where the bit of light around us hits it.

"It's so pretty," she says softly.

"It's a lotus flower."

She inspects it more closely, her fingers gliding along the smooth edging.

"The lady said they grow even in the worst condition because they're resilient and strong, just like you." Those blues meet mine, holding with an intensity that has my palms sweating. "The petals, they close at night, only to open again the next day. It's like coming out of darkness and finding the light again."

Payton stares at the small flower with what can only be described as longing. She tucks it close to her chest, her eyes closing before reopening and lifting up to meet mine. "Thank you, Mason. It's…perfect."

I nod, watching as she sets it on the small table beside us, turning to face me in a way that has me doing the same, her head tipping back and smiling a soft sort of sly smile that has my skin prickling.

She glances toward the party below and back. "You gonna ask me to dance, or is that only when the beach is involved?"

Heat spreads through me, and I wrap my arm around her back, yanking her to me so hard she gasps, her palms slapping at my chest on impact. Slowly, her arms slide up, wrapping around my neck, and I press her even closer, bending so my head can rest along hers.

The music is soft but reaches us easily, and we sway to the beat.

It's hard not to listen to the lyrics of "What's Mine Is Yours" by Kane Brown and imagine it's playing just for us.

I didn't know I was a sap like this. I used to tease my dad when he'd talk to my mom like he was reading from some book of poetry or roll my eyes when he'd refer to her as if she was this angel sent here just for him, but now…I get it.

I understand the feeling of utter perfection and raw need, because this girl, she is that for me.

She's light and sun and reason.

It's like despite everything that's transpired and all the hurt that she went through, it happened for a purpose, to lead her right here. Right to me.

My arms tighten around her until we're flush against each other, and hers do the same, her palm pressing and sliding along the back of my head. The feeling is so fucking foreign, a shiver runs through me, and I know without a doubt I will never find this anywhere else.

I don't want to.

I really need her to be mine.

Please, baby, be mine?

As the song comes to an end, I slowly release her, and with every bit of space that grows between us, a weight drops onto my shoulders.

I try to smile as I back away, doing all I can to slip past her without touching her, because it's all too fucking much.

It's too much and not enough, and I might be freaking out a bit. I sidestep into the room, but then her little hand presses to my abdomen, halting me.

Every muscle in my body freezes, nothing but my eyes able to move, lifting and locking with hers.

Her fingers are trembling, little creases forming between her brows as she shifts on her feet until she's facing me fully.

I don't move.

Her other hand finds mine at my side, her touch so fucking soft as she takes it, lifting until it's pressed against her chest.

Her heart is beating out of control, not unlike my own, and when she steps closer, my chest inflates, a heavy pounding echoing in my head as I wait to see what happens next.

The hand on my stomach glides higher so it's in the same place on my body as she placed mine on hers.

She swallows. Her lips part, and she whispers, "Hey, Mase?"

I say nothing, just wait.

"I...I can't stand the thought of not."

It takes me a moment, two really, but then her words register. They were mine after all.

I close the last bit of distance between us, my hands falling to my sides. "Well then, Pretty Little," I rasp, my voice too thick, need coursing through me like never before. "You know what to do, don't you?"

"I'm scared."

"Not as scared as I am."

"What if I hurt you?" she asks quietly.

"I'll forgive you."

"Promise me," she whispers. "Promise me, Mason."

"I promise you, baby."

She surges onto her toes, and the world fucking stops.

Sparks fly, fireworks boom, and the brassy note of a trumpet blares.

She fucking kisses me, and it's soul-wrecking. Bone crushing.

She's ruining me with nothing but her luscious lips.

They're pillowy, thick, and full, and so goddamn soft, like clouds of silky sweetness.

She tastes like sugar and honey and mine.

My arms wind around her, and I don't know what I'm doing until I feel the glass against my skin, her back now flush against it, my need for her to be close taking over.

She arches into me, her tongue chasing and tangling with mine, the sweeps delicate but daring, long strokes and needy flicks. And when a low, whiny whimper slips from her mouth into mine, I have to grab on to the wall to steady myself.

My body is fucking shaking, an overwhelming sense of rightness I couldn't explain if I tried consuming me, burning me alive from the inside out. I'm on fucking fire. It's sensory overload and endless suspension. It's an electric current that only she can charge, and it's coursing through every fiber of my being.

It's fucking *us*, and if I have any say in this world, it will never change, because my god.

I get it now. This right here, this is why I exist.

It's why my family bought a house decades ago in a little town called Oceanside and why a girl named Lolli became best friends with a boy named Parker. It's why she fell in love with my cousin Nate. To lead them to Oceanside.

To lead *her* to *me*.

She might have had more than one purpose in life, but the reason for that is clear to me, and he's sleeping but five feet away. But I was sent here with one purpose, and that is to love them both as if they're mine.

In my eyes, they are.

I won't let anything come between us.

I won't love anyone the way I love them.

I couldn't possibly.

I can only hope she feels the same and that she knows I love her son like he's my own. He may not be my blood, but that doesn't matter. He's still mine, and if this changes things, if tonight means they're becoming mine for real, he's the only little one I want for us. It will be just us three forever. He will never have to wonder if the lack of blood we share leads to loving him differently. It doesn't. It won't.

Maybe I'm getting ahead of myself, but how could I not?

I've waited for this moment for months, and it's here.

The girl of my dreams is in my arms, her mouth pressed to mine, heart beating wildly and showing no signs of stopping.

I hope she doesn't.

I hope she kisses me until her lips go numb and exhaustion sets in.

I hope her lips stay on mine until her knees give and I get to lift her in my arms, just to lay her in the bed we're sharing.

And then I hope when she finally does fall asleep, I'll be the one she sees in her dreams, the way I have no doubt she'll be in mine.

She *is* the girl of my dreams.

Please let me become the man of hers.

CHAPTER 29
PAYTON

Before, March

"I wish you could have seen the sunset the other night. It was like *being in the clouds."*

"I saw."

Smiling, I look over at him, his brown eyes shining. "You did?"

Something in his face softens, and I turn toward him, reaching out to take his hand. "Of course I did. I was with you, baby. Always will be."

"I wish there was time to take Deaton to the beach before heading home. He's obsessed with the water. He is so going to be one of those beach boys when he grows up."

He reaches out, his warm palm pressing against my cheek. "I look forward to seeing that."

My heart aches, and I reach for him, running my hand through his dark hair. "I miss you."

He smiles wide, and I blink slowly, the image of him starting to blur.

My eyes open, and I look over just as Mason kills the engine, finding we're back at his beach house. "Hey, sleepyhead," he whispers, nodding toward the back. "Little man slept as hard as you. He didn't make a sound the entire drive."

My mouth tips up at the corners, and I unbuckle, stretching my limbs. "That's because we woke up at an ungodly hour to beat the traffic."

"If you thought I was going to waste any of my last day sitting on the highway for hours, you were wrong, Pretty Little. We're doing our last day right."

He climbs out, and I follow, trailing his movement as he makes his way around the car. With every step he takes, my stomach flutters, feelings I haven't felt in a long time and some entirely new ones, swirling low, low, and lower. Nerves I'm not accustomed to tickle along my spine, and I chew on the inside of my lip, my eyes lifting as he steps into my space.

I forget to breathe as he leans in close, his palms planting on the glass windows at my sides.

"This is how it's gonna happen," he whispers. "Brunch, bathing suits, beach, bonfire."

I swallow, pulling in a lungful of air as I drop my head back, dizziness settling over me—a result of his nearness. "Is that right?" I manage to say.

Mason presses his body to mine, his smirk shamelessly mischievous. He opens his mouth, and mine parts, and then he pushes off, yanking open the back door and disappearing inside.

I'm stuck where I stand a moment longer, and I don't miss the raspy chuckle he lets out.

God, he knows what he's doing to me.

What the hell *is* he doing to me?

My nerve endings are firing, and I'm antsy all over, and I just woke up. I feel like I could run for miles, and I hate running. It's a last resort or something I force myself to do when cardio is in order.

There are other forms of cardio, girl.

Oh my god. My face flames at my own thoughts, and then of course, Mason's face appears again, Deaton in his arms, sans car seat. He lifts a brow, but there's a knowing grin tugging at his lips.

I spin on my heels and head for the door, pretending his laughter doesn't reach deep down inside me. He passes me the keys, and I fumble with the lock, half paying attention to what I'm doing, half caught up in the conversation he's having with my son.

"And after that awful flavorless oatmeal stuff you somehow drank quicker than the bottle, we're putting on your new Buzz trunks. I think you'll like 'em. I'm more a Woody kind of guy myself, but…maybe that's a conversation for when you're older."

"Oh my god!" I laugh, whipping around to face him and nearly stumbling over the threshold of the door.

Mason throws his head back, laughing. "I knew you were eavesdropping."

"You're right behind me." I playfully roll my eyes, stepping into the house.

"True, but it took you about five tries to open the door. Reminded me of one night over summer when me and the others came home drunk. Pretty sure I fell off the porch trying to open it." He chuckles, then stops midthought. "Or maybe that was Chase."

Now I'm laughing, shaking my head before tossing myself onto the couch. "Okay, who's making breakfast?"

"The fact that I burned the toast last time means I say we both figure it out together."

"I can cut fruit. Fry bacon or make pancakes without screwing them up? Not so much."

"Hmm." He drops onto his back on the carpet, setting Deaton on his chest and holding him up so he can stretch his legs and pretend to stand. He smiles up at him, moving him around like he's dancing. "How about scrambled eggs with cheese in a tortilla? We can't fuck that up too bad, right?"

I roll onto my side, propping my head up as I watch the two of them.

Mason is just so natural with him. He doesn't get frustrated or hurry to hand him back. It's quite the opposite, in fact. When he fusses, Mason comes running, reaching for him and carrying him off. When he's hungry, Mason asks if there's a bottle, wanting to feed him himself. When he's tired, he tucks him to his chest and walks back and forth until his little eyes close, and even then, he doesn't put him down. He sits down, keeping him tucked against his chest.

Against his heart…

Mason looks up at me, and I blink a few times, realizing he's waiting for a response, but I forgot the question. "What?"

He chuckles, lifting Deaton into the air and laughing when he squeals and smiles wide. A long drop of drool falls, and Mason jumps, but it still catches him in the neck.

I laugh, rolling over, and he reaches over, gripping me by the hoodie.

"Oh, this is funny, huh?" he teases, tugging me from the couch until I'm bumping into his side. He drops Deaton onto my chest, then bends his neck, running it along my cheek.

I squeal, wiping at the wet spot and rolling halfway away without letting Deaton fall.

When I look back, Mason is propped on his arm, leaning over the both of us.

Suddenly, the room grows quiet, and when he leans forward, I hold my breath, but his lips don't fall on mine. They press to Deaton's temple and hold, his gaze never leaving mine, a tenderness tucked deep inside, and I feel it all the way to my toes.

My lips curve, and his follow.

We sit there for a little longer, neither of us in a hurry for the day to begin, because the sooner it does, the sooner it's over. Or at least that's the thought that crosses my mind when the food's been made, the mess cleaned, and we're all set up closer to the water.

I wish I could slow time down, because as I look over at the man tugging the little hat lower on my little boy, I realize I don't want today to end.

I don't think I want any of this to end.

I want to do it all over again tomorrow.

And again the day after that, and *that* is terrifying.

Because what happens if it's all taken away?

What if I start to fall in love with him and then lose him?

What if the first part isn't a what-if at all?

There's tension in the air, and it's not going away.

In fact, it's getting stronger by the minute, like a storm on the horizon. I feel it coming, sense it in the air, but I don't react.

Deaton's been asleep now for a few hours, and the outside air grew too chilly, even with the help of the fire, so we're back inside the house. The big-ass house that no one else is in.

It's just me and Mason on the couch, a random movie neither of us has ever seen playing on the big screen. We're sitting beside each other, bundled in the same blanket with our legs outstretched on the coffee table he tugged closer. His left arm is thrown across the back cushions, his fingers teasing at the edge of my shoulder, and I curse myself for not putting a hoodie on after the shower. Why I went with a tank top and sleep shorts, I don't know.

Or maybe I do, because while I'm brimming with an anxiousness that makes me want to jump and run, I'm also melting at the feeling of his rough fingertips against my skin.

I don't even know if he knows he's doing it, but he is. He is and has been for twenty minutes now, and I swear, the goose bumps covering my flesh are going to become permanent if he doesn't stop soon, but I don't want him to stop. I want him to slide a little lower. Scoot a little closer.

I want him to kiss me again.

My muscles clench, and I curl my toes in my socks, shifting slightly beneath the blanket.

Mason moves, too, a little closer.

My eyes stay glued to the TV, and the anxiousness in the pit of my stomach doubles when I realize where the scene is leading.

Mason catches on at the same moment I do, his fingers freezing against my upper arm as the man on the screen gently pushes

298

the girl against the wall. His hand disappears under her shirt, and I inhale, my eyes tracking the movement and snapping up to the woman's face when her breathy noises flow from the speakers.

My core clenches, and I swallow, my heart rate spiking, beating so hard I'm scared he'll hear it, that he'll know what's happening inside me.

And what's happening inside me?

I'm coming alive, sprouting from nothing and desperate for the heat of the sun.

For the heat of *him*.

I lick my lips, and Mason's fingers start their little dance all over again, trailing up and down, a little farther each way this time, and I gasp, staring at the couple as they move to the edge of the bed.

Before I realize what I'm doing, my legs are rubbing together, chasing the friction I suddenly *desperately* need.

Mason's fingertips bite into my skin, and a low whine builds in my throat, slipping free. Instantly, I'm flying to my feet. I race from the living room into the kitchen and bury my head inside the fridge.

I inhale deeply, welcoming the cold. My eyes close, and a shaky exhale escapes.

Then his chest is pushing into me from behind, and I jump, my head snapping up, but I don't look. I can't.

This is...too much.

It's nowhere near enough.

Shit. I swallow, panting now.

Mason's hand comes around, pressing to my upper belly, and I allow my body to fall back into his.

Those perfect lips find my ear, and I feel them part, the heat of his breath sending a shiver down my spine.

A small groan leaves him, but he swallows it away, whatever words he planned to speak dying on his lips. Instead, he takes the lobe of my ear between his teeth, and my center spasms, clenching. I might whimper. He drags them along the skin before releasing me, and I swear I'm floating.

I can feel him against me. He's turned on. Hard and long and resting against the highest curve of my ass, his fingers biting into the softness of my stomach and sliding south.

I want to spin around and press into him.

I want him to reach between my legs and feel how much I want him, too.

I do. I want him more than I've ever wanted anything.

The thought has me tensing, and Mason goes taut behind me.

Slowly, he releases me, the heat of his body retreating and leaving a coldness in its wake.

I whip around, unsure if I want to reach for him or run, but the expression on his face tells me I can do whichever I want and he'll understand. It makes me want him even more, but I'm afraid.

The feelings washing over me are like nothing I've felt before. Ever.

Not even with—

No.

No, no.

This isn't about before. This is about now, and right now, I…

I swallow, stepping forward.

Mason steps back.

I move again, and he turns, his eyes blown black and locked on mine as he blindly moves back into the living room. Like a magnet to metal, I follow.

Fireworks burst beneath my skin, sparking and heating every part of me as I wait to see what he does next, and then he lowers back onto the cushion, those brown eyes holding mine prisoner, an expression so damn deep, there are no words fit for it.

I don't even know what's about to happen here, but I trust this man more than I trust myself, so when his eyes fall to the place at his side, I lower my body into it.

The gap between us is a little wider than before, but it seems intentional, so I sit, a ball of fire in my stomach, and wait to see what comes next.

Mason turns to the screen, rewinds it to the moment the man presses the girl to the door, and then he hits play.

I suck in a breath, head snapping in his direction.

His attention remains glued to the TV, and ten seconds in, he lets his head tip back just enough where he can keep his eyes on the screen, his hips gliding down the cushion the slightest bit.

My eyes fall of their own accord, locking on the bulge pressing against his sweats.

My thighs press together again, and all the air whooshes from my lungs when his hand slides down his hoodie, his palm pressing against his own length.

My body shakes at the sight, and our eyes flick to each other.

In the background, the woman moans, and I bite at my inner cheek.

Mason holds my gaze, giving the slightest of nods as his features tighten, his fist closing over himself from the outside of his clothes. His eyes close, and he faces forward.

My entire body vibrates, and slowly, my hips slide down to match his, my head falling back just the same.

He peeks over, but only with his eyes, and I watch, mesmerized, as his teeth sink into his lower lip, making me wish it were me sinking my teeth into his flesh. Slowly, his gaze slides back to the couple, who are now peeling the clothes from each other's body.

Their noises grow louder, and with each sound they make, my pulse jumps higher.

The man lowers her to the bed, slipping between her legs, his lips falling to her exposed breasts.

Mason groans softly, and it's a shot of adrenaline in my veins.

That ball of fire is a raging inferno, and I need to put it out.

I need him to put it out.

God, I need—

Mason grabs the blanket that fell to the floor and gently lays it over us, and when he shifts, a hiss leaves his lips, and my clit throbs with need.

The blanket starts to move, up and down, up and down, and when I look to his face, his eyes are closed, those lush lips parted. He's pleasuring himself with long, leisurely strokes, and I cannot look away.

He moans, and I nearly shatter, my hands shaking as I dare to follow his lead.

I push my shorts down, my chest and cheeks burning with the blush of all blushes, and then my fingers brush over myself. It's the barest of touches, yet my hips fly off the cushion, the need so strong I can't breathe.

I gasp into the room, my eyes flying to the TV when a long, loud moan fills the space.

The man is fucking her now, his body rolling and hips thrusting slowly.

Suddenly, it's not two strangers on the screen.

It's me and Mason.

It's my body bare beneath his.

He leans in, licking along my neck, and I shake.

He grabs my thighs, rough and hard, and I moan.

His body lowers, covering me like a warm, weighted blanket I need more of.

I drag my nails along his back, desperate to bring him closer, and he presses my knees open wide.

He buries himself inside me, driving deeper than I've ever felt, and I start to shake.

Mason groans and I whine, my eyes flicking open and realizing it wasn't part of the fantasy.

My eyes slide his way, the blanket having fallen with our movement, exposing his wrists but nothing more.

My eyes are glued on him, my hand following his rhythm, and my stomach muscles tighten, my breathing growing choppy.

I want to feel him.

See him.

I want to taste him.

The thought is so tantalizing, the pulsing need to do exactly that so foreign, I choke on air.

My toes curl into the blanket, and I give a tiny tug.

The fleece hiding him from me falls to his thighs, and my face grows beet red.

Mason's hand is wrapped tight, his dick silky and solid and swollen in his fist. The tip is glistening, a thick gleam slipping down the head, and when he takes his thumb, brushing it over the wet spot, I moan, licking my lips.

His eyes snap to mine, and my entire body quakes, my core locks, pleasure bursting low and all the fuck over, but my hand won't stop.

And neither will the feeling.

Mason runs his tongue along his lower lip, and my hips fly up, chasing something, chasing more.

I need more.

His pace quickens, his hips raising with each long pump, and then his eyes widen, his muscles growing tight, and I clench my eyes closed, my own hand moving faster.

A second wave is about to crash.

"I don't think so, baby," he groans. "Let me see you."

I listen, and when his free hand falls into the space between us, I press mine into it.

"All I'm thinking about is you." He squeezes, flipping our hands so his is on top, shoving our fisted connection into the couch as pleasure bursts within us, and I can see it.

His body pressing me into the bed. Burying me beneath his large frame. He's so big.

Everywhere.

And I want him all over.

His hold starts to shake, and I pant into the air.

Our eyes are locked, the girl on the TV screams, and we both shake, hips jolting, bodies shuddering.

Long white ropes pulse from his dick, and I stare, the twisting and turning in my belly a full-blown whirlpool. I might drown.

Suffocate.

My lungs are drained, my body so tight it feels like it might snap, and then it does.

It shatters into a million tiny pieces, every single one laid out at his feet like I'm a peasant making an offering to the king.

I wait for the awkward silence to follow, but it never comes.

Mason sits up, shuffling around a bit as he cleans up, and then we're lying side by side, tucked in each other's arms, the movie still playing in the background.

I'm not sure how much time goes by, but when I wake in the morning, I find that I'm alone.

With a frown, I sit up, stretching, and follow the sounds coming from the kitchen.

As I reach the threshold, my feet pause, the sight a soothing, settling one.

Mason is sitting at the table, Deaton's high chair pulled in close, a baby spoon pressed between his fingers.

He notices me instantly, his eye snapping up to meet mine.

The man smiles, and I feel it in my soul.

"Looks like mama's awake, little man. What do you say? Should we tell her about our plans?"

Our plans.

His and Deaton's and mine.

Heaviness falls on my chest, but hovering above it is a little white light, a soft tendril of what could be. Or maybe of what is.

I smile and step into the room. "Okay, boys. Lay it on me."

CHAPTER 30
PAYTON

Now, November

Pulling up in front of the Avix U football house, I put the car in park, my eyes gliding toward the white wooden door.

The last time I walked inside there, Mason led me by the hand.

The last time I walked out of there, it was with tears in my eyes...

"Hey." Chase leans forward, his soft tone slipping through the memory, and I turn to face him. "You sure you're okay?"

"Yeah. Yeah, just a long day," I lie.

"You know you can come in if you want. We're allowed guests."

A derisive laugh leaves me before I can stop it, and I nod. "Yeah, I know."

He nods, and when he opens the door, I climb out, too, meeting him near the hood. "Thanks for lunch."

He grins. "Thanks for going for sushi with me. No one else will."

"I mean, I did order a California roll, so it doesn't really count, but..." I tease, smiling a little when he laughs.

"If you're up for it, I'm free again tomorrow."

"Maybe," I joke. "But if so, I'd say it's my turn to pick."

"As long as it's not pizza. I'm pizza'd out. That's all everyone seems to get in this house."

"I'm sure I can be a little more creative than that."

Chase grins, but that grin falls right off his face, and two point five seconds later, the reason why reveals itself.

A big white Tahoe appears, and then *he* steps out.

If I could sink into the dirt, I would, but my feet are frozen, my eyes glued to his face, waiting for the moment he looks up.

It only takes a second.

His head lifts, eyes finding mine without effort.

His feet stop moving, his limbs locking in place as a thunderstorm of confusion, concern, and cold hard resentment rolls across his face. He looks...bad. Worn out and pale.

I try not to stew on the fact that no one saw him all night and the fact that his clothes look well worn, as if he's had them on for longer than today, but the pit of dread in my stomach only grows wider, even if I'm the one who dug the hole to start.

I take a half step forward without meaning to, and it's like I reached out and touched him. He jolts as if burned, his head falling back, and he looks up at the sky, seemingly searching for an answer he desperately needs.

"Mase," I finally call.

His head snaps forward, and slowly, he heads this way, his eyes not once traveling to his friend beside me. "How long you been here?"

"I—" Shit. "Friday." I manage to force the word, quickly adding, "I looked for you, but—"

"But you didn't call."

In my periphery, I notice Chase looking between us. "I called," he says. "Ari, too. And Brady."

Mason just keeps staring right at me. "You didn't call."

Up close, the dark circles beneath his eyes are so clear. Too clear. "Where were you?"

"There was someone I needed to talk to." He faces away, then mumbles, "Not that it made much of a difference."

Something coils around my spine, a sense of unease sweeping

306

over me that I can't quite put my finger on. "Mase." I try again, stepping toward him. Suddenly, I really need to know. "Where did you go?"

"Do you honestly care?" His response is swift and gut-wrenching, as is the glare he throws my way. "Do you care where I went, what I did, who I did it with?"

"Mason," Chase begins but cuts off when Mason's gaze pins him with a clear warning.

My lips press together, a familiar burn building behind my eyes.

He looks away, creases forming along his brow. "Where's my little man?" His eyes pop up to mine, following when I glance at the car, the Embers Elite logo scrawled across the back door.

He swallows, leaning toward it, maybe without realizing. "Can I at least say hi? Or…bye?"

Finally, he looks my way again, and this time, my lips do tremble. But I nod.

Of course I nod.

He doesn't wait for another second.

He turns, opens the door, and closes himself inside.

MASON

Big blue eyes find mine the second I slip in, and when he smiles, the hint of two tiny teeth beaming back at me, it's like every bit of tension drains from my body.

My muscles ease, my heart grows full, and I can't help but smile through a laugh. "Hey, big guy." I tickle his toes, and he laughs so easily, so loud and fucking adorable, that mine doubles along with it. "Did you get even bigger?" I lift my hand, and he slap his into it, doing it over and over and giggling at the clapping sound. "Yeah, you did. Look at that big ol' hand." I grin. "You'll be palming laces in no time."

He starts kicking, his lips moving a mile a minute in full-on baby talk.

I can't help it. I take him from his seat, my eyes springing up when he launches to his feet.

"Dang, boy. You're strong, aren't you?"

He claps. "Ma, ma, ma, ma."

My hands tense a moment, my smile spreading slowly. "You got that one down solid now," I whisper. "I bet you're talkin' like crazy now, huh, Einstein? What else can you say, hmm?"

Suddenly, he whines, arm stretching and pointing over my shoulder.

"What is it?" I spin for a better look, laughing when I find his little plush football. "Did you throw this sucker that far? Sheesh. You must have an arm on you."

I tickle him with it, and he starts laughing.

"Ball, ball, ball, ball."

"That's right." I can't stop smiling, even if *ball* from his little mouth sounds more like "buh" than anything, but it's obvious what he's trying to say. "That's a football."

"Ball, ball!" He claps, yanking and pressing the plushy to his face and biting on it, two little half teeth sticking out from his lower gums and a couple that look about ready to break through the tops.

My body falls against the seat, suddenly deeply aware of the remarkable, precious little thing in my lap. My little man is growing, more and more every day, and I'm missing it.

The weight of a thousand possibilities, none of which end well for me, falls on my shoulders. I hug him to me, my damn heart skipping a fucking beat when his little tiny palm pats along my shoulder like he knows. Like he's comforting me the way I should be there to comfort him.

The way I want to be.

"You're my favorite person in the whole world, you know that?" I whisper, fighting off the sting creeping behind my eyes. "I miss you, Little D. Every day."

He turns his head, and a broken chuckle escapes when he presses an open-mouthed kiss to my cheek.

"Thanks, buddy. That's exactly what I needed." I grip his hand, smiling at him, and he starts jumping up and down in my lap all over again.

The door opens then, and I tense, my grip tightening around him of its own accord.

I meet his mama's eyes, breaking a little inside at the sadness in them.

What are you sad for, baby?

For you?

For me?

Payton breaks our stare, blinking as she glances off. "I'm here for some more work with the *Avix Inquirer*. They have some new ideas they want to try out and asked for me again, so…"

Pride swells, and I offer as much of a smile as I can muster. "That's good, Pretty Little. I'm happy for you."

Her brows pull tight, and she nods. "Anyway, I'm staying at the same place as…last time. Maybe you want to—"

Come over? Be with you for a while? Hope sparks…

"—take him for a little while? You could bring him to me in an hour or two, whenever you want to, really."

That hope is snuffed out, buried beneath boulder after ten-ton boulder.

I regard her closely, a pit of emptiness gnawing at my insides. "Without you?"

Payton drops her eyes to the ground, and I watch as tears slide along her cheeks.

But they make no sense to me, so I don't fold to the overwhelming need to protect. To safeguard her and hold her tight. I don't go to her, wipe them away, and beg her to let me make her feel better.

All I do is nod, climb from the car, and tuck my little man to my chest. Reaching back in, I snag the diaper bag off the floor-board. I say not a word to her as we slip past, ignore Chase's questioning look on my way, and walk right into the football house, disappearing into my private room up the stairs.

I want to be angry.

I want to scream and yell and demand a reason for all the shit she's not saying, but as soon as the thought comes, it washes away, because my boy is in my arms.

At least she gave me this.

Just like that, my mind completely resets, and for the first time in a long time, unwavering contentment flows through my veins.

This is what I want.

Afternoons with my main man, doing nothing and every-thing all at once.

"Okay, little man." I toss a blanket on the floor, throw some pillows around it, and set him on his butt, dropping to my belly before him. "I watched some of your pop's tournament videos with him, and I think it's time I show you a thing or two. What do you say?"

Deaton sprays me with spit, speaking in some foreign baby languages before launching at me in a crawl of epic speed.

I laugh as he throws himself half over my body, pushing with his legs.

"Look at you, a natural." I hook his arms around my neck, pretending he spins me, settling him so his legs are sprawled out to the side. "That's a pin! And Deaton Vermont gets the W in the first round." We do a few more moves, my big guy laughing and clapping all the way as we wrestle around the floor. I lift him into the air over my head, using his weight like a pair of dumbbells. "You'll be the best little wrestler the world's ever seen." I smile, making silly faces and fucking melting when he copies what I do.

Twenty minutes or so in, I drop onto my back, having worked up an actual sweat, and laugh as he copies me, lying out flat beside me.

"Can you give knuckles?" I reach out, smiling when he slaps my hand and starts saying "mama" over and over, because that seems to be his favorite word. "Like this." I take his hand and make a little fist, pushing it against mine. "Boom!" I say when our fists touch, and he cracks up, sticking his knuckles out to me over and over and doing his best to mimic the sound I make.

I fold my arms behind my head when he gets distracted, watching his every move as he pushes onto his butt, then presses his hands on my ribs.

"Aw." I pretend he pins me down, and he laughs, shoving up onto his feet and clapping for himself.

Every muscle in my body freezes as I stare. "Holy shit...you're standing."

Slowly, I push into a sitting position, sneakily scooting back a few feet, and spread my legs out on the carpet.

My arms are outstretched and shaking as I stare at this little freaking miracle, afraid he might fall even though he looks steady as a rock standing there. "Little D, are you walking now?" I don't mean to whisper, but the words come out that way.

Deaton keeps on clapping, and then his right leg lifts, planting down a few inches forward.

Fumbling around, I quickly shove my hand in my pocket, snag my phone, and press record before propping it up with some of the pillows to our left, hoping to hell he's in the shot.

My mom is gonna die when she sees this.

Unless she already knows.

Maybe everyone knows *but* me.

Pressure falls on my chest, but when his left leg lifts and he comes even closer, all that washes away.

"Baby boy, you're walking." I smile, holding my hands out.

And Deaton damn near runs forward, clearing the last five

311

steps with ease. He slams into my chest with a laugh and squeezes my cheeks with his slobbery hands.

"Oh my god," I laugh, my arms lifting him from the floor. "Daddy's so proud of y-you."

I don't realize what I've said util the words are out there, and I squeeze my eyes closed, tucking him closer for another quiet moment.

"Ba, ba, ba," he babbles next.

A low, raspy chuckle escapes me, and I spin him, tucking him in my lap as I reach for his bag and pull out the small sippy cup from the corner pocket. "Man, you are getting big. Talking and walking and a big boy cup?" I murmur, handing it to him to see if he knows what to do.

Sure enough, he tips it back, gazing up at me and tugging on my hoodie strings as he takes a few small sips of water.

My hand lifts, and I run my fingers over his soft curls, staring down into his big blue eyes.

This must be what it's like to have to share a child with a second family, like a family of divorce.

Bone-splitting sadness envelops me, and I wince at the literal pain it causes. I can't imagine not being with the mother of my child. It would be pure torture every day knowing you're missing something. I think I'd want to do everything I could to make it work.

I blink, shaking my head.

What the hell am I talking about? That is exactly what's going on here, and I have tried everything. Because I am the other half. Blood or not, he's still mine.

Even if she won't be.

Why the fuck won't she be?

Because you're not enough, and you never will be.

I thought I understood, but I don't.

She promised me.

She promised, and I wish she would have just…not.

312

CHAPTER 31
MASON

Now, November

Turns out Payton's new project is bigger than the last one. Not only was she personally requested for another collab between Embers Elite and Avix, but she's been asked to take headshots of the entire Sharks roster.

Which is why all fuck ton of us, even the guys who have yet to touch a toe to the turf come game days, stood half-fucking-naked in a line half a mile long, waiting for our turn to step in front of the lens. *Her* lens.

I was in the first flow, Brady and Chase right along with me, being that we're starters, but that also meant we were in and out the quickest, the sheer number of athletes overwhelming to look at, even for the rest of the camera and lights crew.

We were brought in, twisted and turned, and shuffled out in an all-business fashion that sent pride through my veins. Because damn, she looks good in her element. Moving and directing and demanding. It's a side of her I haven't quite seen, a new, more polished version of the little photographer I met on the beach a year and a half ago. That internship is helping her find her way, and man, if there isn't a brighter blue shining in her eyes because of it.

Of course, after I was done, I had to stick around. Just in case. So for the last two hours, I've been leaning against the wall not ten feet from the makeshift photo booth, just…watching. Maybe waiting.

Swear to god, if I hear one more son of a bitch comment on her hair, I'm going to shave theirs in the locker room.

My eyes cut to the black curtain ten feet away, a glimpse of her strawberry-golden hair shining through the crack, and my lungs inflate. Her hair is gorgeous, though. It looks like she might have cut it a little, something I noticed the minute I walked in this morning but didn't catch yesterday, since her hair was pulled back in a bun. Not much, maybe just the length of my pinkie, but I won't know for sure until I have it in my hands, testing the length I've become accustomed to.

As soon as the thought hits, it bursts into a cloud of dust, leaving me coughing.

I won't get to run my fingers through the length of her curls this time. No, this time, her trip will play out a lot differently. She won't be coming back with me or inviting me back with her.

"Hey." A soft voice interrupts my thoughts, and I look over to find Allana.

"Hey." I offer a polite smile. "How are you?"

"Fine. Um, listen." She wrings her hands together, eyes bouncing to where the team is lined up and back. "Can I talk to you a minute? Outside?"

A small frown builds, and I look toward Payton. "Can you maybe talk here?" I ask, unsure what we could have to talk about that would require privacy and unwilling to give it. I can't leave Payton in here with all these assholes.

"Listen, I just want you to know that—"

"I don't know. She's a little thick for my taste."

Whatever she says falls flat on my ears at the very loud and purposeful comment. My head snaps forward, narrowing in on the back of Alister Howl's dumbass head, his Ken doll hair sticking out under a hat like he just stepped off the baseball field, not a hundred-yard stretch of green. And yeah, I realize that sounds

314

fucking dumb, but I don't care. He looks like a fool, and I can't stand him or his all-American act.

He's always on me, and I know he's only speaking because he knows I can hear him.

He's seen me with her.

The motherfucker *knows*.

And he proves this when he glances this way, glaring from Allana to me as he adds, "But hey, if she's good enough for one quarterback, she's good enough for another, right?"

I dart forward, shove by a few, and yank on the bill of his stupid-ass Dodgers hat and tug until he's tripping over his own feet, landing on his ass.

He looks up from the floor, the others around laughing and talking shit, but he knows what he's doing. He doesn't even glare. He grins, lifting his hands in mock innocence.

"My bad, Johnson." That grin grows, but there's something underneath it. A twisted sort of hate he's carried since he stepped foot on this field this summer. "Forgot you got a thing for blonds, don't you?" The last words leave him on a snarl.

"Watch your tongue, asshole. Don't test me. Not here." *Not with her.*

Now he does glare, his lips curling as he hops up and presses his chest to mine. "I should ruin this for you. I could, right here, right now."

I don't know what the hell he's talking about, and I don't care. I push forward. "You could try."

He opens his mouth, but Coach appears with a clipboard, and what do you know, his name is called to the curtain.

He shoves me with his shoulder on his way by, and Coach raises a brow, but I only shake my head.

The dude is a punk with a stick up his ass, so who the fuck knows what his issue is.

He steps into the space with Payton, turns, and looks me straight in the eye, and then he closes the curtain completely, erasing the sliver of sight I had.

My fingers curl into fists, and I move forward, but I only make it to the line of red tape on the floor before Brady appears.

He shakes his head, dipping down and speaking so only I can hear. "Don't. I know you want to, but this is her show. Fuck it up, and it's only gonna make shit worse."

Worse.

Worse?

How could this possibly get any.

Fucking.

Worse!

As if the universe is testing me, the answer comes with a swift kick to the nuts not four hours later, in the form of a mandatory meeting with Coach Rogan.

"Alister is starting in Friday's game."

My pen freezes over the paper midsignature.

"Son." He shakes his head, my expression clearly shouting the *what the actual fuck for* question racing through my mind. "You started this time last year over Riley. You know how I do things. Twice a season, every season, the second string is first out." He narrows his eyes, and I know he has more to say, so I sit back, cross my arms, and wait for it. "I want you to work with him tomorrow. No less than two hours. Give him pointers and tips, take him under your wing like Riley did you."

"I'm not Noah, and Alister is far from me."

"He's a football player, a damn good one, same as you."

"He's a dick who wants all the glory."

Coach laughs. Loudly. He pushes to his feet, coming around the desk and tugging open his office door. "We all do, son. Every one of us. Some just hide it a little better." He yanks his head, and I stand. "Watch his film. It'll be in your inbox in the next ten minutes. Now go. And if I call you in here again, you know why that will be."

I swallow, give a curt nod, and walk out, my shoulders tight and head high, but the minute I'm out of sight, they both crumble, because damn it—it's happened.

I knew this was coming, but I guess my mind's been too preoccupied to really process how screwed I'm on my way to becoming. Academic probation.

Academic probation with a sports waiver that affords me two points.

If I fail my next exams, even one, I'm out.

Fucking *done*.

Benched for the remainder of the season and personally placing Alister on the path to the playoffs, an opportunity he didn't earn but would no doubt capitalize on. Any man would.

No one gives a shit who got the team there so long as they come home with the win in the end. If he leads the team to victory, where does that leave me?

Where does that leave my future?

I don't know how I let things get this far. Football has been my life for as long as I can remember, and then Payton came along, and suddenly I had more than the sport I'd dedicated my all to. She became the most important part of my world, and in the mix of what I'd call my heartbreak or fear that she was on her way to breaking my heart by refusing to give me hers, I forgot how important it was to stay strong and steady. Motivated both off *and* on the field.

Because making it to the next level isn't just about me and my dreams anymore. It's about them. Us.

My new dream is to have my girl and our little boy and a family suite in an NFL stadium with my last name on it. To have the means to offer her a happy, fulfilling future where she can travel the world if she wants, taking pictures of all the pretty things she's ever imagined, me and Little D watching from the sidelines with smiles on our faces.

How could I drop the ball so hard? I should have been doing the opposite. Fighting with all I had for what I could control rather than letting it all fall apart by obsessing over the things I can't. The thought of losing a life with her would have still been at the forefront of my mind, so how did I allow myself to fumble so far?

"Fuck, fuck, fuck!" I shout, shoving the door open and stepping out into the cold November air.

"Take it you heard the good news."

You've got to be kidding me. Slowly, I turn my head, and sure enough, there he is, posted up against the side of the building.

I scoff. "Did you seriously wait out here just for this moment?"

His face is blank as he kicks off the wall and steps forward. "Yup."

Spinning, I face him fully, lifting my arms out. "You got something to say to me, Howl, say it."

"I'm just wondering what's so special about you." He pauses. "I've been watching you, asking around about you, and I've found nothing worth repeating."

"That's some creepy shit. Little odd to admit you're obsessed with your captain."

Slowly, he shakes his head. "Not obsessed." He takes a step back, grabbing his bag off the ground. "Disappointed. Maybe even disgusted." His eyes harden, and he gets in my space. "I see what others don't, and you're nothing but a weak prick, failing his classes and fucking up on the field because he can't handle his life off it. I'm glad you're in the position you are. You don't deserve to be—" He yanks his head away then, glaring at nothing in the distance. "Just go fuck yourself, Johnson. Fail and get off campus before you screw up someone else's life."

My frown follows his retreating form, his words a jumbled mess of who the hell knows what.

I've met athletes who thought they were better than the next, who believed they deserved the starting position over the others, and some of them were right, they did, but the proof is always in the game film. It reveals itself.

That's not happening here.

So if Alister is talking about him and me and our position on the roster, he's going to be severely let down, because I am better than him. He won't be able to take my position until I'm ready to pass it down on my exit.

Or bomb your exams.

Shit.

No. That won't happen. I will not fail.

Not in school. Not on the field.

And never with the girl.

If only she'd allow me to show her as much.

———

PAYTON

Three days turned into four, and they've just asked me to stay for another week, all expenses paid. I can't stop smiling, a sense of accomplishment I haven't felt in, well, maybe ever washing over me.

"It's crazy, you know?" I look to Chase and Paige, who were waiting for me outside the building, in awkward silence, I might add. "This feels like the first thing I've done on my own, and I'm not…"

"Not what?" Paige tips her head, books folded across her chest.

I scrunch my nose and face forward. "Messing it up."

"Hey." Chase steps in front of me, his green eyes on mine. "You've messed up nothing since I've known you. Stop telling yourself otherwise. You got your GED, had a baby, and landed your dream job all in the same year."

"Internship."

"Internship that's turned into this." He holds his hands out, and I allow myself to glance across the college campus.

It wasn't too long ago that I wondered if I'd ever even get the chance to go to one if I wanted to, even before I got pregnant. It was never about what I wanted before. It was what Ava Baylor wanted, and Mother wanted a social princess, not an *artsy little brat with unrealistic ideals*. She was so sweet.

Not.

Chase tips his head, and I look back up at him with a smile.

"You know, you're pretty good at this pep talk stuff. Isn't he, Paige?" I look over, finding a curious expression on her face as she looks from me to him.

When she realizes I'm watching, she clears her throat, smiling that stage-like smile of hers. "Sure, if you say so," she teases.

He whips his head her way. "What's that supposed to mean?"

She shrugs. "That you seem to enjoy pumping others up well enough, but when it comes to yourself, you're set to deflate." He glares, and she laughs, lifting her shoulders again. She looks at me. "Sorry again for cancelling today's plans so last minute, but I'll still see you in the morning?"

I nod, watching her walk away, and then the two of us continue toward the day care center.

"Why'd she cancel?" Chase asks the minute she's out of earshot.

"Something about a meeting of some sort. I didn't really ask for the details." I look his way, noting the tug between his brows. "What?"

"Nothing," Chase mumbles, watching her go. "She just gets on my nerves."

A laugh leaves me, and I face forward "Yeah, her never-ending sweetness is a real brain irker."

He says nothing, just continues to glare in the direction she disappeared, so we walk in silence.

Ari texted me this morning, asking what time I would be off so we could all get together for an early dinner, something

320

the others do every week. Now, I get to be a part of it, and that's pretty damn cool.

We get about four feet from the child development center when Chase grabs my arm, halting my movement. I follow his glare to the blond man hanging outside the building, his phone to his ear.

I smile instantly, pushing forward.

"Payton, wait," Chase begins, right as I say, "Alister, hey."

Chase glares harder. This time, though, it's pointed at me. I widen my eyes as if to say *what the heck* and glance back to Alister.

"Thanks for meeting me." I dig into my bag, pull out the form I need signed, and hand over a pen.

Alister smiles wide, maybe a little too wide as he glances from Chase to me. "No problem at all. In fact, I was already headed this way. You know, you should let me take you to dinner sometime so we can talk. I've got some secrets you'll want to hear."

I don't have time to respond before a looming figure is pressing close to my back.

"I warned you." Mason's voice is clipped and full of anger.

Alister visibly stiffens, yet somehow, his smirk grows. "Chill, Johnson. Just helping the girl out so she can finish up and get back home."

What does that mean?

Also...what the hell?

I look up over my shoulder, that familiar ache forming in my chest, but this time, a swift hit of annoyance follows. "Warned him about what?"

Mason doesn't look down, his expression hard and locked on the man before me.

But it's Chase who yanks the paper from the guy and shoves him in the shoulder. "There. You signed. Now bye."

I glance at him, too, tearing the paper from his hands and smiling apologetically at Alister. "I'll text you later."

"What the fuck?" and "Oh shit" are spoken at the same time,

321

and then I'm crowded by both Chase and Mason, but Alister seems to want the escape. Between their shoulders, I watch as his head lifts and he starts running somewhere to the left.

Both boys open their mouths, but I lift my hands. "I was asked to do a full profile on four players, one from each year. Alister is my freshman."

"He is trying to fuck with me." Mason frowns, taking a step forward. "Please, just—"

"Mase." I cut him off, begging him with my eyes not to make a scene. When I cut a quick glance at Chase, he rubs the back of his head and takes off.

Refocusing on Mason, I find his brown eyes are downcast, a wrecked expression carved across his face, and the last two minutes wash away. Instinctively, I step forward, my palm pressing to his chest.

"What's wrong?" I whisper, forgetting what I was originally going to say.

He swallows, bending slightly so his forehead meets mine, but only long enough to whisper, "Everything. Everything is wrong, Pretty Little."

And then he tears himself away, yanking on the tips of his hair as he goes to stand on the steps up ahead. Swallowing, I follow, leading us into the child development center.

Cameron is coming around the corner with Deaton in her arms before I'm even done signing him out. "Perfect timing." She smiles, tucking loose hair behind her ears.

A fake grin pulls at Mason's mouth, and he raises a brow. "Long day?"

"Kiss my ass." She blinks sweetly. "I know I look like shit ran over. Thanks for pointing it out."

"Cameron." A curly-haired woman in her late fifties, June I think her name is, closes her eyes, giving a light shake of her head.

"Oh, Junie. You love me."

"If these little ones go home and start cursing, the only one loving you is gonna be that hunky boy toy you've wrapped around your finger…if he can even find you once you're fired."

Cameron waggles her brows, and the woman huffs, turning back to stacking diapers into trays.

"Boy toy?" I tease, watching as she grabs Deaton's stroller and bag from the storage area. After out little…heart-to-heart? Yeah, we'll call it that. After that, she and I have gotten closer. To be honest, it's nice to know someone is rooting for me and Mason, even if she doesn't know more than the fact that he and I have a connection deeper than friendship.

Cameron smirks my way but doesn't divulge any info on this new guy of hers. She steps up, and I stick my hands out for my little man, a wide goofy smile on my face.

But Deaton reaches out for the man beside me.

My chest warms, and that heat burns hotter when I look over to find a matching smile on Mason's face.

He chuckles, and a knot forms in my throat at the sound. "Come here, my man. Did you miss me?" He kisses his cheek and pretends to bite at his neck.

Deaton laughs, shoving him away with his little hands, all to pull him closer in the next second.

Finally, he looks my way and leans over but doesn't let go of Mason's hoodie strings.

"Well, hi, mister man." I laugh, puckering my lips and laughing when he opens his mouth and presses it over mine in a slobbery kiss.

Mason laughs with me. "We gotta work on that, my boy."

His boy.

I whip away, taking a deep breath as I do my best not to panic, but those words, they just seem to hit harder today. I realize he's being playful in this moment, but I'm not naive to the fact that what Mason feels for my son is deeper than, say, what Brady feels for him.

What does that mean for my son? For the dad he never met?

Forcing a smile, I turn back to Cameron, desperate for a distraction as the three of us make our way from the building. "So, busy day?"

"Yeah." She sighs, pressing on her chest dramatically. "We have a new baby. He's, like, five months I think, and he is so damn cute. He's been here a couple of weeks now, but I swear I'm his favorite. His mom is kind of strange, but she must notice he likes me, because she asked if I could be here on the days he is, and honestly the schedule worked out well enough. It doesn't hurt that his dad is obsessed with me. He *is* single by the way. I made sure." She laughs, and Mason sighs playfully. "Oh! There're the others! Ari, wait the fuck up!" she screams, and I look ahead to where Brady, Chase, and Ari are waiting.

The minute she breaks away, Mason stops, turning to face me. I know I owe him a conversation, but having it means I have to break open a part of myself I've worked so hard to hide. That's the problem, though, isn't it? Hiding. It feels like that's all I do, and for what?

It's hard to explain when it's a me problem, and to get to the other side, I have to find a way to live with my own actions and decisions…and I'm just not there yet. I need to be. For Deaton, for Mason, and for myself. I'm trying, desperately, but every time I think I have it figured out, it all comes crashing down again.

I feel like a ball of mistakes, a snowball sent down the hill that's growing even bigger with each roll.

A million questions flash across Mason's face, the hurt there so heavy I'm sure he's about to ask how we got here, but I'm wrong. The pain on his face isn't related to me at all. It's related to my son, a fact that becomes clear when he says, "You didn't tell me he started walking."

I open my mouth to apologize, prepared to instantly go on the defense, but then his words register, and my face falls. "I… What?" I whisper. My eyes move from Mason to Deaton and back. "He…he doesn't. Hasn't." I swallow, eyes watery and on my little boy. "Mase?" I whisper.

When I look up into his brown eyes, the sight is so tender, the tears fall, and my hand comes up to cover my mouth.

"Oh my god, he walked?"

Mason's smile is as loving as any parent's could ever be as he glances down at the baby boy, not so little anymore, in his arms.

"He did," he murmurs, then digs his phone from his pocket and holds it up. "Want to see?"

I nod fervently, leaning in beside him as he pulls up the video and presses play.

Mason's legs come across the screen, and then there Deaton is, all smiles and big boy steps, straight into Mason's waiting arms.

A choked laugh leaves me, and I look up at Mason with a watery smile, subconsciously pressing myself closer to him. I replay it over and over, taking the phone from Mason's hands the tenth time through and turning up the volume so I can hear the laughter I see on Deaton's face.

"Baby boy, you're walking." Mason's voice is as soft as velvet, even through the phone speaker.

"Wait, Payton, don't—" Mason rushes when he hears himself, reaching over swiftly, but Deaton bends, forcing his hand back.

My attention is locked on the screen, and then I hear it: Mason's whispered words as he embraces my baby boy. "Daddy's so proud of you."

Every muscle in my body locks tight, my eyes glued to the still image at the end of the video and what a moment it captures. Mason's eyes closed, Deaton smiling, his little fists latched just as tight to the man before him as the large hands pressing into his back.

Daddy.

Mason is…

"Oh my god," I breathe. My vision blurs, and I gaze up at the man beside me.

Shadows cast over the space around us, and I'm struck with breathtaking clarity, as clear as it is cloudy. Echoes of regret reverberate around us, dragging me under and lifting me up.

I feel heavy and light at the same time.

All this time, I've stressed and lost sleep over Mason and what he meant to me and what that meant *for me*, but I didn't pause to consider him and Deaton. I mean, I did, but not like this.

I knew he cared. That when he wasn't around, Mason missed him and wished he could be there. I knew he loved him, would do anything for him, but I didn't *see*.

My eyes weren't open, so focused on the facts of what I knew had *happened* rather than what was *happening*.

Deaton didn't have a dad, and that was my fault. I was the reason for that. I led him to California, and he died on his way home.

My son's father died, leaving him without one. He had me and only me. Those were the facts. That is what I knew for certain.

But…that's not true, is it?

It was never *just* him and me.

Panic rises in me, and I take a step back. And then another.

And then I spin, leaving my son in safe hands.

I leave him with his…*daddy*.

CHAPTER 32
PAYTON

Before, May

"He crawled a little yesterday. Backward mostly." I laugh, shifting so I'm sitting up, leaning on the headboard. "But I think he'll have the hang of it soon."

He stands across the room, smiling softly at the sleeping baby boy in the bed. "I can't believe how big he's getting. And so fast. He's going to be running around like a crazy kid soon enough."

I nod, running my hand along his little back. "You know, my mom has never even tried to call. Not that I want her to, but he's just so precious, you know? I'll never understand how anyone could ignore that there's a small piece of them out there they've never met."

"That's because he's not a piece of her." His deep brown eyes meet mine. "He's you, Payton, and maybe he'll be a bit of me one day, too."

"He is," I promise, a small frown building, one that doubles when I realize he's not beside me like he should be. "Why are you so far away?"

My arm stretches out, my hand seeking his, but he only smiles, his head tipping a little. "I'm right here, baby…"

"Ma, mm, mm."

My smile forms before my eyes peel open, locking on to a matching pair of blue ones.

I laugh, grunting when Deaton pushes on my belly and practically throws himself on top of me. "Well, good morning to you, too, mister."

Mason chuckles, reaching over and lifting him off, pushing him into the air and flying him above us like he's an airplane. "Say, 'Mama, we've been up for so long, and we're starving. We want waffles.'"

Tugging the blanket up to my chest, I turn in the bed, meeting Mason's eyes over the covers. "Hi."

His grin stretches, and he leans over, pressing his lips to my forehead. "Hi. I've got you guys here for one more day, and you're wasting it."

I gape, and he chuckles, climbing from the bed with Deaton in his arms.

"Little D is changed and dressed, and he ate half a jar of that nasty oatmeal stuff. My sister's in the lobby with Noah, so we're heading down to meet them by the pond." He buckles him into the stroller as I sit up in the bed, then comes back this way, leaning over me with a smirk that makes my body heat. The heat of his lips washes over mine as he whispers against them, "Get that perfect little ass outta bed, Pretty Little. Your boys will be waiting."

I close my eyes, but the pressure of his mouth never comes.

The soft click of the door follows, and I throw myself back in the bed with a sigh, but I can't wipe the smile from my face.

It's May, which means Mason's semester is almost over. Soon, I'll have him for more than random weekends and holidays. At one point this summer, I'll have him for several weeks straight.

The kindling flame in my belly grows at the thought, and I know if I sit here and think too hard on it, that flame will grow into an inferno. I can't have that.

It's hard enough not to beg him for things he's yet to offer, even if I know it's for my benefit.

He'd give me anything I wanted at any moment. That much I know.

It's obvious and written in the way he looks at me, the way he touches me.

The way he tries his best *not* to touch me.

There's a hint of torture in his dark gaze when we're alone, and it only makes me want him more. There isn't a single part of this...whatever this is between us that isn't terrifying.

We've never really talked about what's happening here, and maybe that's because the words never seemed necessary. We're just so effortless.

We slid right into friendship and, along the way, fell into something more.

Something *real*.

A sliver of guilt slips down my spine, and I tense, taking my memories back to a little over a year ago when my life took its first turn and I found out I was pregnant.

Not long after that the boy I loved left this earth.

It all feels so long ago and like yesterday at the same time.

If anyone asked me then if I thought I'd make it through that first year...well, I would have lied and said yes, but in my mind, I'd be screaming no. That I can't do it and don't want to. That it was all too much, and I wasn't strong or ready.

I would have been wrong.

I might not have been ready, but I was strong.

I am strong.

The man waiting for me downstairs helped me see that.

I owe him more than I'll ever be able to repay for what his presence in my life has done for me.

I don't know what I would do without him.

Maybe you'll never have to find out?

Smiling, I push from the bed, quickly changing and rushing into the bathroom to brush my teeth. It's not until I grab a comb, looking up at my smiling face in the mirror, that my mother's words come crashing down and bursting the little bubble I allowed myself.

She said I ruined her life.

I literally destroyed Deaton's.

What if the poison I seem to carry infects Mason, too?

329

What if, instead of being the positive in his life the way he is in mine, I became the negative?

What if I'm not strong enough to let him go regardless?

No.

No!

I glare at the girl in the mirror. "Don't do this. Don't let her ruin you any more than she already has."

Lifting my chin, I run the gold glittery comb through my long hair, splitting it down the center. I smirk as I make quick work of putting it into two Dutch braids, the one hairstyle my mother hated on me more than anything.

It's petty and ultimately irrelevant, but I don't care.

It feels good to be me, to do what I want, and right now, what I want is to go eat waffles with friends, my son, and the man who makes me feel like I matter.

But there's something else I want, too. Desperately.

I just have to find the courage to ask for it.

I think I might.

It's with that final thought that I slip into my shoes and head out into the hall.

The café is attached to the hotel Noah booked for us, the free nights at this place one of the many gifts he's been given since signing his NFL contract. It's one of those frilly places with teapots and three-tier fancy scones and treat things. I have no idea what it's called, but everything I've tried—and I tried nearly all of it—is delicious. Not to mention the mile-high cinnamon toast waffles Mason ordered. A scoop of fried ice cream on top of three giant waffles? Whoever thought of that needs a raise, seriously.

We finished our plates a little over a half hour ago, but the food coma put us on lockdown, unable to stand from our tables.

The morning sun doesn't help either, but it does feel good beaming down from above.

The café is at the farthest corner of the hotel, surrounded by a massive koi pond with rock waterfalls and a tiny bridge in the middle. There are ducks sitting in the moss, little ducklings learning how to cross from one side to the other.

Deaton is sitting in Noah's lap, Ari right beside them, the three of them taking up the entire bridge. They've been sitting there for twenty minutes now, laughing and talking to Deaton, pointing out the fish below. Deaton's eyes are glued to the water, and when I look to the side, I find Mason's are glued on him.

A small smile curves his lips, and he just…stares.

"Hey," I whisper, and slowly, his head turns my way. "Penny for your thoughts?"

The sharp angles of his face are soft in this moment, and he adjusts his chair so it's facing mine, then bends forward, yanking mine closer.

He reaches out, tugging on one of my braids, and takes my hand. "You can have them for free." He holds my gaze, promising, "You can have anything you want from me."

Can I have your future?

The thought is so sudden I jolt, and Mason catches it, his eyes piercing mine as he searches for the source.

"Mase," I whisper, glancing at the others and back. "What are we doing?"

Mason swallows, his thumb rubbing circles over mine. "Whatever you want."

"But what do you want?"

"You. Him." His answer is instant. Sure.

Absolute.

It's as exhilarating as it is alarming. How could he be so certain? "You're so young—"

"Older than you, Pretty Little."

"You know what I mean," I murmur, my heart rate doubling. "This is my life. I made choices that led me here, and I understand my responsibilities. I welcome them now, but you…" I trail off, Mason's head shaking as if to deny or refute my words, but they're true.

I am a mother.

I have a son.

He is my life, and every decision I make will be with him in mind. Those decisions won't always be easy, and sometimes, they'll be sacrificial, but I am prepared for that. It's my reality.

It's not his.

It doesn't *have* to be his.

"You can walk away anytime you want, you know," I manage to say. "You have no obligation here."

"Stop."

"I'm serious."

"So am I." He frowns, pulling away and pushing to his feet, but only so he can come closer and tug me to mine. His hand comes around me, cupping the back of my neck, and he holds my gaze to his. "My father told me once a man worthy of the woman he wants lives and functions one way and one way only. It made no sense to me before, and I kind of thought he was crazy, but I get it now. He said when I knew, I'd be selfish."

An unexpected laugh leaves me. "That is…not the philosophical line I was expecting. I was waiting for something earth-shatteringly profound."

"My dad is more about action than words." He grins but quickly grows somber once more. "But it's true, Pretty Little. I feel it. When it comes to you, to both of you, I am selfish. I want all your time. All your tears. All your smiles. I want all of you, always, and I don't want to share. I'm a good five seconds from going over there and killing my sister's mood 'cause *I* want to show Little D the fish and the ducks, and *I* want to hold his little hands while he pretends like he's walking on his own across the bridge. Because I'm selfish. Because I know what I want." His eyes hold mine, his thumb running along my cheek. "I want you. Any way you'll let me. Always."

Before I can respond or break down in tears, as I'm pretty sure they're coming, Ari and Noah rejoin us.

The conversation quickly shifts, and for the rest of the afternoon, I find all I'm waiting for is when the three of us can go up to our room, grab our things, and head back to the Avix campus to spend the last few hours we have together locked away in Mason's room.

My lips curve as I peek over at Mason, Deaton now locked in his lap.

I guess he's not the only one feeling a little selfish.

The moment the thought enters, a second, sobering one follows.

I'm not allowed to be selfish.

I have a child to think about.

His future to consider.

To be the best mom I can, to protect him from another potential loss, I can't be selfish.

I have to be self*less*.

———

It's a little after ten when I finally move Deaton into the playpen. I kept him on the bed as long as I could, trying to make sense of the million thoughts and concerns and worries working their way through my mind.

My nerves are wound tight, my hands wringing together as I step back around the small divider Mason put up that separates the living room space from the bed, and there he is, as in tune with me as ever.

Mason sits on the edge of the bed, his shoulders slumped, a dejected expression on his handsome face as he meets my gaze with a small, forced smile that doesn't reach his eyes.

"Come here, Pretty Little," he whispers, holding a hand out and widening his legs so I can slip between them.

I do, the position one of the few that brings us nearly eye level, mine just a few inches above his. His hand comes up, and as gently as ever, he tugs on my braids, a soft smile on his lips. "I love your hair like this."

I love how he loves all the things about me that my mother hated, even a simple hairstyle.

"I know," I whisper.

He swallows, moving the loose hair from my eyes. "Talk to me."

Taking a deep breath, I find the strength to start at the most important yet confusing concern consuming my mind.

"I miss Deaton," I say, meeting his soulful brown eyes.

The moment the words leave me, the rest comes rolling in, a sense of understanding sparking deep in the recess of my mind, making the dread I had over this conversation suddenly shift into confidence, because this must be said.

"I love him, Mason. As in still, and maybe that's because he died as mine or because he gave me that little boy, or maybe it's because I'm just meant to love him forever. I don't know, and I don't care to. It's just what is."

He nods, eyes still glued to mine. "I understand."

I nod back, a little more hesitant with my next words but speaking them clearly.

"When I look at my son, I see his dad. I see him in his smile and his curly hair. The way he touches his face when he's tired and how he sleeps with his hands under his pillows. All these little things, they make me think of him." I swallow. "Even though he's not here, even though I only get to see or speak to him in my dreams, he's still *here*, and it's my job to make sure that doesn't change. I want Deaton to know who he got his name from. He deserves to be remembered, especially in his son's eyes."

Mason's features tighten, but still he nods. "You're afraid having me around will take away from that."

"I know it will," I whisper, and Mason's face falls.

"Payton—"

I hold my hands up. "Please, let me finish."

Mason's mouth clamps closed, unease creating creases along his temples. I want to reach up and wipe it away, but I don't.

I keep going. "I know it will, because yes, when I look at him now, I see the boy I lost, but when I think about his future?" I whisper. "All I see is you."

Mason's eyes spark with hope, his hands shooting out to grip my hips like a lifeline, like I tossed him overboard and, just before he went under, threw him a rope.

My lips quiver, and I reach to take his face in my palms. "I see you, Mase. When he takes his first steps. On the first day of school and at his first wrestling meet. On the sidelines at his first football game and in the passenger seat, teaching him how to drive." My voice breaks, and I lift my shoulders in a helpless shrug. "I don't know how it happened or when, but it's the truth."

"Baby..." He trails off, swallowing, waiting to see what might come next, too afraid, too aware to let the line he's holding on to go.

"I'm scared," I admit. "What I feel for you, it's...different. Too much, maybe, and I"—my voice cracks—"I have a little boy to think about. As much as I want to be selfish, as much as I want to run headfirst and see where this leads, I can't."

Mason's brows are pulled taut, his eyes clouding over as he stares at me, fighting to keep control, but I can see it. I feel it in the shake of his hands on my hips. "What are you saying to me right now, Pretty Little?"

The tears fall, and his face crumples with them. "I don't think I can do this."

He shudders, chin falling to his chest.

"Not yet."

Mason's head snaps up at that, eyes narrowing as he pushes to his feet, backing me up and caging me in. He swallows, hands planting at the sides of my head, eyes locked on the tears rolling over my cheeks before coming up to mine. "Yet," he rasps, his voice thick with desperation. "Yet?"

"I know you said you're ready for this, but this... We jumped without looking. Fell into this routine so fast that I forgot to stop and think. To consider where you are in life and where I am. Deaton has already lost who was supposed to be the most important man in his life. Now he has you, but we can't pretend things aren't complicated. You come see me or I come here, and we forget about everything else, but when Monday rolls around, you'll be sitting in a college classroom, and I'll be nursing a baby boy on a couch on the coast. You're finishing your first year of college, and I just got my GED. You have your whole life."

"Please stop saying that. It's not fair." His dark eyes pierce mine. "I know what I want, and I want you two to be my *whole life.*"

My lungs deflate.

Jesus. This is torture.

My smile is sad. "Maybe that's what you want now, but that could change. You could want kids of your own one day, and then Deaton will be—"

"I won't," he swears. "He will only ever feel how I see him, and how I see him is as *mine.* I won't give him reason to question that. Never. I want to be what he lost because I love him. I want to be the most important man in his life, and I can do that without overshadowing the man who was supposed to be."

"This is what I mean," I whisper. "You are so ready to go all in, and I love that, but I can't. I have to protect him *just in case.* I know it's not fair, but I have so much to learn about being a good parent. This is me trying to do that."

"I need him, Payton."

"I'm not taking him from you. You can see him and talk to him whenever you want. It's just..." Reaching up, I press my palms into his chest. "Mase, you need to do what you came here to do. Play football, enjoy college, and then maybe later—"

"You've said 'yet' and 'later,' but you haven't said what those words mean for us." He scowls, but there's tension he tries to fight, a thread of promise threatening to unravel. "Are you saying no to us, or are you asking me to wait?"

I swallow. "I could never ask you to wait."

He presses into me, his knuckle under my chin, eyes narrowed. "But do you *want* me to wait? If it were up to you, if you held all the cards in your hand, what would you want me to do?"

"Mason."

"Answer me, Pretty Little," he demands. "No what–ifs, no maybes or maybe nots. You can't be selfish, but if you could, if you were, would you ask me to wait? Would you want me to wait?" His voice lowers, breaking with his words. "Would you want me at all?"

There's a crack behind my ribs, an invisible cord desperately fighting for a way to reach for him, begging to tie us together, to lock itself so deep inside him nothing and no one could ever tear it out.

"Mase."

"Answer me," he breathes.

"Yes."

Mason needs no other explanation, that one word like liquid, heated hope, filling him to the brim and driving him forward. His lips crash against mine in a kiss so desperate, I feel the tethers tie him tighter to my soul.

He kisses me like a man possessed. *Obsessed.*

And I think he is.

He takes my mouth with a fiery passion so intense it's like I'm on the outside looking in, the feeling so out of body and intoxicating, I can't breathe. My entire body tingles, my knees giving out. Mason is right there to catch me, wrapping me in his strong, capable arms and caging me closer.

"You have no idea what you mean to me." Mason's forehead presses into mine. "I'm going to wait, Pretty Little."

"It might take a long time."

"I don't care. I'm telling you right now, I could never want anyone the way I want you. This. I can wait. I will wait."

I give a wobbly smile. "I would like that."

A shuddered breath escapes him, visible tension leaving his body at my confession.

"Will you tell me?" he whispers. "When you know you're ready, when you even think you might be, will you tell me?"

"You'll be the first know."

He holds my eyes captive, a sharp fierceness I've never seen before. "You said things won't change for me and D. I'll still see you and him. We'll still talk. You're saying when you're ready, I'll be the first to know."

I nod.

"I need you to promise me." I think I see moisture brim in his brown eyes, but he hides his face in my neck. "Promise me, Payton."

"I promise."

CHAPTER 33
MASON

Now, November

"You have too much weight on your front foot."

Alister scoffs, holding his stance as he fires off the ball, and all I can think is this is a huge waste of my time. I should be studying, getting my ass back on track so I have something to offer, yet here I am. Trying to teach a punk who refuses to learn.

Alister glances back with a smirk, but I shake my head, mimic his position, and send one. After that, I look him in the eye as I move through the motions a second time but with proper form.

"Back leg takes eighty percent of the weight. When I shift," I begin, rotating my hips and pushing off the back leg, "the weight transfers to my front leg, opening up my hips and putting more power behind the ball." I pull back, releasing using the breakdown I just gave, and his jaw clenches as he watches the ball fly, the radar set up on the ten-yard line not necessary to see the difference in power.

"Not everyone has to do things the way you do, asshole."

"It's not how I do things. It's the right way or the wrong way."

"Because you're so damn perfect."

Spinning, I glare at the dickhead. "You want to get better or not?"

"I'm only here because Coach said I had to be. I made this fucking team on my own, and I don't need your help to stay on it."

"No, what you need to do is figure out what it means to be on a team."

"What the fuck is that supposed to mean?" He gets in my face.

I just shake my head at him. "You're unaware, and you don't fucking listen."

"I'm unaware," he deadpans, rearing back and shouting in my face. "I'm unaware? You have no fucking idea how rich that is coming from you!"

He shoves me with his chest, and I shove his ass right back.

"What's your problem, man? You've been on my ass since day one, and I'm getting tired of it."

"Serves you right after what you did!"

"What the fuck are you talking about?" I shout. "I don't even know you, and I didn't get on your ass until *after* you got on mine."

"Yeah, 'cause you're so damn good. Perfect little playboy, huh? You're just a punk fucking with vulnerable girls. Soon as that pretty thing with the baby sees you for who you really are, she's gonna run so fucking fast—"

I headbutt his ass, refusing to put my career in any more jeopardy, especially over this punk, and I'd be lying if I said the harsh crunch of his nose against my forehead wasn't just as satisfying as a fist to his face would be.

His head snaps back, blood sprays, and he stumbles, but I keep at him, yanking him by the collar and dragging him to his feet.

"I warned you once. Do not talk, look, or even *think* about her!"

Alister spits blood in my face. "I'm going to tell her to take her kid and run as far as she can—"

"That is *my kid!*" I scream.

Alister goes stone still, his eyes widening.

I'm shaking I'm so mad. "He is my son, and you will stay *the fuck* away from them both, or so help me, Howl, I will break your

340

arms and then your legs, and then everything you're trying to gain here goes out the window."

"You're an even bigger prick than I realized." Alister swallows, tearing away from me with a tense expression that makes no sense to me. But then he jerks his chin. "Better run after *your girl*, Johnson. Seems something you said pissed her off."

My brows pull, and I look to the left. Sure enough, Payton is whipping the stroller around, practically running back into the tunnels from the track.

"Payton!" I shout, breaking out into a run, but the door swings shut in my face. I heave through it, following her into one of the conference rooms. "Wait!"

She rushes to the back corner, fumbling with the knob, and I know this one locks from the other side.

"I went to see him!" The words fly from my mouth like a desperate plea.

It works.

She pauses, the knob in her hand, stroller half out the door.

Swallowing, I take slow steps forward and repeat, "I went to see him." I watch as her shoulders tighten. "Spent some time at his grave."

She whips around, tears thick but not yet falling.

"How dare you," she breathes, a storm building in her blue eyes. She pulls the stroller back into the room, letting the door close as she advances on me, her voice low. "You had no right."

"I did. I do," I tell her, and her chin wobbles. "You haven't been there, have you?" I ask softly. "I told you where he was laid to rest *months* ago, and you haven't gone. Why?"

"You don't know that," she rasps, arms stiff at her sides.

"But I do." Another step closer. "If you had, you would have left your mark, because that's what you do, but there was nothing. Why haven't you gone?"

"That's none of your business," she whispers.

"I think it is. I'm part of the reason, aren't I?" I take another

341

step toward her. "You feel guilty for wanting to be with me, and you know you can't lie to him like you lie to yourself."

"I am not lying to myself."

"You're torturing yourself."

She swallows, hands fisting. "Why did you tell Alister that Deaton was your son?"

"Changing the subject doesn't help us."

Stubborn as ever, she raises her chin. "Answer me, Mason! Why did you tell him he was yours?"

"Because he is!" I scream back.

Payton shakes her head, spinning around and moving back toward the stroller. "I can't do this. I thought I was ready to have this conversation, but I'm not."

Before she reaches him, I dive forward, jumping in front of her and blocking her path.

"Please move."

"I can't. Not until you hear me out."

"I don't want to."

"I don't care."

"Mason, please."

"I understand the boy you lost is inside you," I say hurriedly. "I understand he's a part of you."

"You don't." She squeezes her eye closed. "You can't possibly."

"I do, Payton. That little boy over there means more to me than anyone in the whole fucking world, and he *is* him. He is his dad, just like you said before. But he can be me, too." I'm all but pleading now. "I want him to be, so what else can I do? Tell me, and I'll do it. Anything. Everything. But you are pushing me away when you promised not to. Overnight, everything changed, and I don't understand. Help me, please. Talk to me, because I'm at a loss here. I told you I'd wait. I want to wait. Five months, five years, I don't care."

"I do!" She throws her arms out. "I do, and I changed my mind. I don't want you. Don't you get it?" She swipes at her tears

342

angrily, her glare heavy and pointed at me. "Have I not made that obvious enough yet?"

"No, you haven't." Her false bravado falls in a blink. "I know you. Better than anyone."

She looks to the ceiling, trying not to cry. "No, you don't."

"Yes, I do." I'm right in front of her now, and when her gaze moves back to mine, it's laced with longing she won't give in to. "Me and you?" I push on. "We were inevitable. This was meant to happen. Written in the fucking stars way back in time if you want to be cliché about it."

"It couldn't have been." She denies my words, but hers hold little conviction. "I could lose you just the same, and then what?"

My brows snap together at that, those words not ones I've heard from her before now. "But we were, and you won't."

"You don't know that. Anything can happen."

My heart pounds in my chest, and I take a step closer. "As sad as that might make you, as hard as the reality might be, it's the truth. I feel it in my bones. You and Little D were meant to be mine, and whether you give me you or not, I'm not going anywhere. Not ever."

"Don't say things you have no control over."

Is that why she's doing this? She's afraid to lose me so she just let me go?

"Payton," I whisper, hearing the ache in my own damn voice, but none of it's for me. It's for her and the desperation in her battered blues, her fear staring back at me. "I might not be able to dictate the world around us." I swallow, trying to make her understand. "But I have control over my own actions, and while I might have lost sight of some of my goals lately, I'm figuring it out now, but you're still priority number one. So hear me when I repeat myself. I am not going *anywhere*. I'm here either way, because I love that little boy with every part of me. Maybe more than I love you, and I do, Payton." She buries her face in her hands, but I keep on. "I love you." I reach for her. "I fucking *love you*, Pretty

343

Little, but I don't know what to do anymore. I want you. Hell, I'll take a tiny piece if you'll give it to me."

"Stop."

"I'm dead serious. I can't compete with a ghost, so I won't," I promise. "He can keep your heart for all eternity. Just let me hold you for all of mine."

Payton breaks into a sob but quickly turns it into a growl. She tears away from me with an angry shove that has me stumbling.

"Don't you get it?" she screams, her hands burying themselves in her hair. "You're not competing!" she wails, then collapses, forcing me to catch her just before her knees hit the ground.

Big blue eyes meet mine, and her palm presses to her stomach as if speaking the words is causing her physical pain.

"You're not competing," she seethes, tears rolling rapidly down her beautiful face. "There is *no* competition, Mason. There's no competition, and *that* is the problem."

CHAPTER 34
PAYTON

Before, May

His callused hands wrap around my torso, tugging me closer, and I *go with a smile. All I can think is I want to stay here forever, wrapped in his warmth, in the strength of his arms and the heat of his body, wrapped with mine.*

But I know it won't last.

Soon, I'll wake, and he'll leave me like he always does.

"Deaton?" I whisper, flipping to face him, but the room is too dark. And he never whispers back…

A touch so featherlight it sends tingles through my body, creating a trail of warmth along its path. They start at my shoulder, continuing down my arm at the slowest, most tender of paces. I wait for the feeling to return, for his touch to trail back up and start over again, but it never comes.

With an effort I don't want to think too much about, I force my eyes to open, startled in the best way by the contentment in the ones staring back at me.

"It's a little after seven," Mason finally whispers. "Noah will be here to pick you guys up soon."

Scooting a little closer, I clasp his hand in mine.

His gaze moves between my eyes, the smile that curves his lips sending a sliver of pain through my chest. Not because it's tense or forced but the opposite. It's real, raw. It's promising and accepting, and because of this, it's a bit startling.

My thoughts must show, because Mason's eyes soften, and he reaches up, running his hand through the tangle of my hair, gently tucking it behind my ear.

"Pretty Little, there's nothing to be sad about."

"You're being so good about this."

"I only had hope before, wishing one day you could really be mine, but now I know you will be. Maybe not tomorrow or the next, but one day."

Trying not to cry, I press my lips to his wrist just as his phone chimes behind him.

"That's him." He rolls over, picking up the phone and frowning at the screen. "He's on his way from Ari's dorm."

I push up, accepting the sweater he passes me, and tug it over my body, slipping into a pair of sweats. "I should have gotten up sooner so Deaton doesn't have to get in his car seat right after waking."

"He's been up for a little over an hour now."

My head snaps up, and Mason shrugs.

"I wanted to play with him for a bit before you had to go."

My insides melt, and I nod. "How much did he eat?"

"Little over half the big jar, but I didn't give him a bottle yet. Figured maybe that would help him fall asleep again on the drive."

"That's perfect."

Mason turns away. "I'll…um…get him buckled in his seat and take the playpen down to the porch."

"'K," I whisper, and with every step, I remind myself this is right. I need to do this.

As I move through the motions of the morning, I do my best not to think. I focus on my toothbrush and the taste of the mint toothpaste. I note the bristles of the hairbrush with each swipe through the crazy curls my braids left behind. I count the seconds it takes me to slip my socks and shoes on, and when I walk into the living space, Mason is on his butt in front of the car seat playing peekaboo, and the sadness I was expecting doesn't come. Instead, gratitude is what winds through me.

346

Silently, we make our way outside. Only once we're alone on the porch, the rest of the house still asleep this early on a Sunday morning, does Mason allow me to take the car seat from his hand.

I don't want him to walk us to the car. It will feel too final.

"You can still change your mind, you know. I won't be upset."

"Oh no?" He tries to tease.

I shake my head. "You're a handsome man in college."

"Don't forget the quarterback part," he whispers.

A low chuckle leaves me, and we stare at each other for a long, heavy moment.

"You'll text me when you get home?" he asks, and I hate the hesitance in his tone, but I understand it.

"I will."

"And I'll see you when I come to Oceanside next week?"

"Of course," I breathe.

Finally, Mason sighs. When he steps forward, his right hand gently brushes along Deaton's curls while his left cups my neck, drawing my forehead to his.

"I love you, Pretty Little."

All the air whooshes from my lungs.

"I will wait forever for just the *chance* you'll love me back."

Mason pulls away, turning before I can look up into his big brown eyes, and I'm stuck, standing there on the porch as I watch the man I never saw coming go.

I can't move.

I can hardly breathe.

I stumble slightly, lowering the car seat to the ground and thrusting my hand out to catch myself on the wall.

My lungs burn, my throat is clogged, and I desperately seek the air they refuse, but it doesn't come.

A hand presses to my back, and I jolt.

"Close your eyes," Noah says calmly. "Close your eyes, and count to ten. Come on."

My chin wobbles, and my body shakes, but I do as he says, and

347

the fog clears when I get to eight for the second time. Opening my eyes, I look into Noah's.

There's an understanding there, a softness as he nods, grabs my elbow, and lifts the car seat from the ground. "You don't want to stand here like this. If I know what he's thinking and how he's feeling right now, he's only seconds from coming back out this door. And if not him, someone else will."

"He told me he loves me."

Noah smiles softly, gently urging me to move. "I heard. That's how I know we don't have a lot of time. I don't know what's going on, but I do know you have to decide if you want to wait for him to come back or if you want to be gone when he does."

I don't want to be gone when he does.

I have to be.

I allow Noah to lead me to the curb, and we climb inside.

Just before we take the right turn off the street, my eyes flick to the mirror, and sure enough, there he is, standing at the edge of the driveway.

When the car turns, tearing him from my sight, it's like a crack in the earth's surface, a thundering boom that jolts deep in my chest, and I suddenly regret everything I said last night. I want to take it all back.

That's what he does to me, though. He makes me forget everything I've lost, because with him in my life, I've gained so much more.

Why would I ask for time?

I don't need time.

No, that's not right. I do need it, but I need more of it with him, not without. "I think we should go back." I turn toward Noah.

Noah looks over at me, a sorrowful expression on his face, as if he knows what I'm going through. He understands the overwhelming emotions that come with love and loss and every-thing else both bring. He lost everything, too, hit rock bottom before he found a way to start the climb back up.

Noah pulls to the curb, speaking softly. "We have a little wiggle room, so long as we're on the road in the next half hour."

"That's perfect. I need...just five more minutes."

Just five more minutes.

That would only make you want five more.

My entire body locks tight, my vision blurring as a weight like I've never known falls over me.

My mind reels as I search for the memory those words live in, but it's not a memory, at least not a real one.

They're from my dream.

My dream of Deaton.

I grip the door handle, my knees bouncing.

Oh my god, oh my god, oh my god.

Deep brown eyes and soft dark hair.

Strong hands and callused fingers.

I close my eyes and concentrate.

And there it is.

There *he* is.

Mason's handsome face, right there across from me. Beside me. Above me.

My body starts to shake, months' worth of dreams assaulting me, one after another.

"You should have seen the sunset..."

"I did."

"He is so going to be one of those beach boys when he grows up."

"I look forward to seeing that."

"He's you, Payton, and maybe he'll be a bit of me one day, too."

"Why are you so far?"

"I'm right here, baby."

A choked cry escapes, and I slap my hand over my mouth.

It's him.

It's...Mason.

He's been the man in my dreams, not Deaton.

But for how long? When did I lose him?

Tears fall in steady streams, rolling down my cheeks in quick succession as a cold, hard hate creeps through my veins.

How could I?

"Payton?" A soft hand brushes my arm, and I jump, remembering where I am.

With panic in my eyes and guilt so goddamn heavy I might pass out, I meet Noah's gaze.

"What do you need from me?" he gently asks, a knowing look in his eye.

"Drive," I manage to choke out. "Please, drive."

Noah says not a word, but the vehicle shifts into motion, and my mind spins with each turn of the wheels.

I don't know how I missed it.

I should have known, should have seen it coming, but I didn't.

I was blindsided, now smacked into reality with the hardest, rawest of truths I ignored but can no longer deny. It's a reality so painful, I'd swear my heart was literally bleeding if I didn't know any better.

The love I hold for the boy who is no longer here...is but a spark to the flame of the man who is.

And that's the ugly truth right there. That's where the fear takes root.

The death of Deaton left a hole in my heart, but that hole has been filled.

It overflows now, liquid warmth pouring through my every vein and covering me in a blanket of belonging I've never experienced before.

It's completely and utterly terrifying in an entirely new way.

Because what happens if that blanket is ripped from my back and I'm left exposed and colder than ever?

What happens to my innocent baby boy if I fall to my knees, and this time I can't get back up, because that is exactly what will happen. There isn't a doubt in my mind. If faced with the loss of

Mason Johnson, I will shatter into a million tiny pieces, never to be put back together again.

Losing him would be my undoing, the final blow to my already battered being.

He put me back together, but if he was gone, no one could repair the damage that would cause.

He's everything I didn't know I needed and more than I ever thought I'd have, so again…

What happens to me, to my little boy, if the cold cruel world were to take him from me?

If he himself decided to go?

I can't allow myself to find out.

I have to protect myself, and there's only one way to do that.

Mason's beautiful face slips to the forefront of my mind, and I sob silently.

I have to break my promise.

CHAPTER 35
PAYTON

Now, November

I run. My feet pound against the pavement, and I've never been more appreciative of the expensive stroller my brother splurged on. Tears fog my vision, and my calves burn, but I keep running until my legs begin to shake, veering toward the grass when they do.

I drop onto all fours, Deaton still fast asleep in the carrier, and let my head hang. Guilt and regret weigh me down as if a bag of boulders has been released on me.

Guilt for all the things I feel and all the things I don't.

Regret for all the things I've done and all the things I *haven't* done.

It's a confusing, twisted state of mind I can't get out of. I feel like I'm in a lose-lose situation, every answer as right as it is wrong. It's frustrating, but most of all, it's downright draining.

I'm exhausted battling against the girl in the mirror, and sometimes I forget why. Why am I doing this to myself?

Not just yourself…

The damn tears threaten to come rolling back, but I push against the overwhelming sense of failure trying to take control, searching for a bit of the steel I built around myself before my world fell apart.

When I lived with my mom, I promised myself I would never allow this to happen to me.

No one would get in my head, and I would be stronger than she wanted me to be. Stronger than she was. I thought I accomplished that by running away from home, if you can even call it that.

I ran, and then my entire world fell apart.

That pressure on my shoulders seeps lower, coiling around my ribs and compressing.

I squeeze my eyes closed, inhaling through my nose and out my mouth. I count to ten like Noah taught me. Slowly, the pounding at my temples and the pressure in my lungs eases.

Laughter catches my attention, and I look over.

A group of six or seven students sit on a large blanket, textbooks and laptops strung all around them with an ice chest in the middle.

They smile and study...because this is their lives. Their school.

"What am I doing here?" I whisper, shaking my head as I force myself to stand. "I don't belong here." Wrapping my hands around the handle of the stroller, I begin the long walk back to the other side of campus.

An hour and a half later, I'm standing inside the studio apartment I was assigned thanks to the contract with Embers Elite. With shaky hands, I pull my phone from the little compartment on the stroller and dial the only person who will understand.

He answers on the first ring, and I close my eyes.

"Chase," I whisper. "I need you."

———————

There's a knock on the door not fifteen minutes later, and the moment Chase meets my gaze, his face falls.

He steps in, wrapping me in a hug, and the stupid waterworks come rushing back. My arms close around him, but it's only a moment before he pulls back, a frown on his face as he stares over my shoulder before slowly bringing his green eyes to mine.

"Payton..." He shakes his head. "You can't run from this."

353

"I have to. I have to get out of here."

"But you're on a new contract."

"I haven't signed, and I'm not going to." The mere thought is devastating, the opportunity I never saw coming. It was almost as if the bumpy path had finally smoothed out, as if fate finally found its point of connection and wove it all together.

But fate isn't real.

Taking his hand, I beg him to understand. "You said if I ever needed an escape, you'd be there." I plead, "I need you right now. I need that escape, Chase."

His eyes move between mine, and he swallows, a pained expression tightening his features. He looks to the floor with a nod. "I know what you need," he says, a sad smile on his face as he reaches back, clasping my suitcase in one hand and the folded stroller in the other. "Come on, Princess Payton. Let's go."

My shoulders fall in relief, and the feeling doubles when we're finally pulling out onto the main road.

I close my eyes, doing all I can not to think, pretending every bit of distance isn't tearing at that invisible link to the man I'm leaving behind. Again.

A few minutes later, the car rolls to a stop, but it's not until the engine is killed that I open my eyes. Confused, I look forward to find we're parked behind a random car, and when I glance his way, I realize where we are.

The football house.

Mason's house.

My face falls, and I grip my seat belt for dear life. "Chase, what are we doing?"

His smile is solemn, and he shakes his head. "You can't go, Payton."

"I have to."

"You can't. If it were just you, I...I don't know, maybe I would take you back, but it's not. You can't do this to him, and I don't believe you really want to."

A knot forms in my throat, but I manage to rasp around it, "I need to leave."

"And he needs you," he whispers, reaching out to take my hand. "Please, Payton."

My features grow taut, and I let him, admitting, "I'm scared."

"I know, but so is he. I've never seen him like this. He loves you, both of you. You have to know this."

I clench my teeth to keep them from chattering and close my eyes.

Screaming has them flying right open.

Both our heads yank to the left just in time to see a girl with blond hair run down the steps of the porch, Alister right behind her, shouting at the top of his lungs.

Tears stream down her cheeks, and the door flies open again, Mason and Brady rushing out.

Alister whips around, his posture stiff with rage, and the girl starts to cry harder.

Chase and I look at each other, jumping out at the same time and taking a few steps up the sidewalk in time to hear Mason say, "I don't know what happened here, but you need to break it up or take it somewhere else."

"You wanna know what happened?" Alister rushes forward, screaming, "You fucked my girlfriend and got her pregnant!"

The air whooshes from my lungs on a gasp, and dark brown eyes snap over, locking on to mine.

MASON

"Why the fuck are you here? You came to see him? To throw this shit in my face even more?"

I hear the fucker screaming with my door closed. Brady and I look at each other, then shoot to our feet, our textbooks falling to the floor with a thud, and we hustle down the stairs.

"So much for cramming for that exam uninterrupted," I grumble. "This fucking dude, I swear."

Brady chuckles behind me. "How much do you love this whole 'captain keeps them in check' role, bro?"

I flip him off over my shoulder, the heaviness of the day too fucking much.

I don't have time to deal with this asshole's shit anymore today. He already pushed me once and got the best of me in front of Payton.

And then she ran from me.

She told me there was no competition, and then she ran away.

A deep ache takes root in my chest, but I push it aside, coming around the corner with a hard expression.

"Drama stays outside!" I snap.

Two heads whip my way, and a small frown builds when I get a look at the girl.

"Allana?"

Her eyes go wide with panic, face wet with tears as she looks from Alister to me and back.

"Are you okay?" I step toward her. "He didn't hurt you, did he?"

She opens her mouth at the same time that Alister's mocking laugh fills the space. "This is fucking hilarious coming from you!"

"I can't do this," she squeaks, running out the door.

Alister shoves me on his way by, and the screaming continues.

"Don't run, Allana! Face it! Make him face it. This is bullshit, and you two deserve what comes of this! He already has a kid, you know that?"

She cries harder.

"Fuck's this all about?" Brady frowns.

Sighing, I shake my head, and the two of us follow them to the front.

"I don't know what happened here, but you need to break it up or take it somewhere else."

"You wanna know what happened?" Alister growls, tearing at his hair as he spins, glare pointed my way. "You fucked my girlfriend and got her pregnant!"

Alarm slams into me, and as if the universe hasn't tortured me enough lately, my eyes lift, locking on to a pair of watery blues.

Payton.

Her face falls right before me, and I take a step toward her, but then Alister is *right there*.

He cocks his fist back, and all I have time to do is prepare for the blow. My head whips back with force, but I keep my feet, head snapping right back and frown heavy. There's warm liquid at the corner of my lip, but I don't brush it away.

I look to Allana, and Alister screams.

"You two are fucking sick!" His eyes come to mine. "Does your girl know you have another kid? That she and the kid you have together don't mean shit to you because—"

My fist is cocked back, but before I can throw my punch, Chase's fist whooshes past my face, slamming right into the side of Alister's jaw.

He stumbles, and Chase takes advantage of that, shoving him to the ground. "Shut the fuck up! You don't know shit about shit." Chase looks to Allana with a frown. "I'm sorry, but you need to start talking."

Instantly, the girl crumples, burying her face in her hands.

My shoulders fall, and for a moment, fear sparks low in my gut.

Is this real?

Is it even possible?

My eyes find Payton's, her hands pressed firmly against her chest.

"Allana..." Brady encourages, though there's an unmistakable demand to his tone.

"I lied," Allana cries, and relief flows through me.

I look at Payton, and she offers a tight smile, but her eyes fall to the ground. I frown, but my attention moves back to the shit show in front of me.

"I lied," Allana repeats, regret heavy in her features as she faces Alister. "You said you accepted your offer to Berkeley, so I had to say something to keep you away so you wouldn't find out. And then you showed up here."

"To surprise you!" he screams. "I picked this fucking school, where I'm second fucking string, gave up my chance to start, *for you!*"

My brows shoot up, and I meet Brady's eyes. Damn. That's... rough.

"I didn't ask you to!" she wails.

"No, you just pretended we were good and started fucking your way through your freshman year!"

"Okay." Chase lifts his hands, looking between the two. "Allana, you should go."

"And you can't come back here," I add. "At least not unless he asks you to."

I meet Alister's gaze a moment, and he winces, looking away, but when his eyes move for the door, widening, mine follow.

Cameron of all people steps out, her hair a mess and eyes half-open as if she just woke up from a nap.

She frowns at all of us, her attention settling on Brady. "What's going on?"

Alister takes a step toward her. "Cameron—"

"Alister's been fucking with Mason all season 'cause his ex-girlfriend lied and said Mason was her kid's dad."

Shock, then confusion pulls at her features, and she looks at Alister. "That's why you've been asking about Mason..." She trails off.

Wait, what?

"You said you wanted to learn how to juggle fatherhood and football. You used me." She shakes her head.

My brows shoot up.

Alister takes a step toward her.

"You really want to back the fuck up," Brady tells him, calm as ever, but I can see the strain in his muscles.

Alister stares at her with a torn expression, but Cameron shuffles a step back, taking the shelter Brady offers when he puts himself between them.

Quietly, Allana gets up and leaves, and I take a second to process all this shit.

It all makes sense now.

Why Alister always pushed it with me. Why he freaked out and acted a fool when he saw me talking to Allana that day. Why he used Payton to mess with me and the comments he made. I almost feel bad for the guy. Giving up an offer for a starting position can't be easy, but he did that. He gave it up because he lived in the love he felt.

My eyes move to Payton's, and my ribs constrict.

She knows I'd give anything for her, doesn't she?

I'd leave all this, sweep sand for a living if it meant I got to go home to her at the end of every night.

Wait. I frown, looking at Chase.

He gives a rueful smile, stepping in closer so as not to air my laundry to everyone. "She wanted me to take her home." But instead, he brought her to me.

I swallow, battling against my own thoughts.

She wants to leave in an attempt to escape us, but she can't. No matter what she does and no matter where she goes, she won't be able to run far enough.

She'll see that.

I know she will.

I face my friend. "Take her."

His face falls. "Mase, no. You're falling apart, man. If she leaves…" He shakes his head.

"Take her, my man," I rasp. "I can't leave. Two of my professors are letting me make up some work, and I have a test to retake. I have to get it done, so just…take her. Whatever she needs, be that. Do that."

He glares, studying me, but after a moment, his features settle, and he looks her way, the two of us watching as she climbs back inside his truck.

"She loves you, doesn't she?" he asks.

"Completely." I sigh, looking at him. "Take her. She knows what she needs to do."

He's unsure but nods and starts walking off.

"And, Chase?"

He glances over his shoulder.

"Ice that thing, will you?"

Chase chuckles, looking down at his knuckles. He shrugs, a grin pulling at his lips. "Couldn't have my quarterback getting injured."

I nod. He nods.

And I watch them drive away, hoping to hell letting her go today isn't something I'll regret tomorrow, but if I know her like I think I do, this is far from the end.

I'd even argue it's the opposite.

But only time will tell.

CHAPTER 36
PAYTON

Now, November

The night my son was born, I dreamed of the boy I created him with. We were so happy, holding our newborn baby boy and imagining all the times ahead. We talked about which of us he'd be most like and who we thought he'd resemble as the years went by. We went over everything for hours, and when I woke, it was with a sense of peace that maybe not all was lost.

Deaton might be gone, but he was still there in my dreams, and in my dreams, I could hold on to him. I could tell him about his little boy and how magnificent he was. I could share all I wanted to share, and he would be right there, eager to listen.

In my dreams, he could live on forever.

And then Mason came into the picture, my picture. Somewhere along the way, we went from strangers to friends to more. Guilt wanted me to hold on to the past, but my subconscious was already looking toward the future.

The moment I fell for Mason, the fragile figments of my imagination finally shattered, the pieces carried away by the winter wind, scattering the metaphorical ashes of the boy who taught me how to love. The boy who showed me so much of it, the black hole I felt I lived in finally shone a little brighter.

He was my light, and when I realized what had happened in his wake, I felt like I covered him in darkness. Dirtied his memory by daring to endanger it because the truth was hard to face, because the truth is…

If Deaton was the light, then Mason is the sun.

He's a life-changing constant, a forever presence of warmth and growth.

And how could I possibly survive without the center of my personal solar system?

The simple answer: I couldn't.

The minute I left Mason standing in the grass, the look of utter devastation drawn across his face, I knew what I needed to do, the possibility of what Alister had been led to believe having shocked some sense into me. It shouldn't have taken the thought of Mason with another woman to do so, but here we are.

I realize now that while I was so busy trying to protect myself from the possibility of losing Mason, something I know I would never survive, I was the one making it a reality.

The world didn't take him from me.

I took him from myself, breaking us both, and that's a weight I'll have to carry.

I let fear drive me forward, and in turn, I shoved him back when I should have held on, allowing him to hold me up the way he'd been asking to.

No more, Mase.

It took me two days to work things out, to get ahold of Sarah and Ian, Nate's parents, to help with Deaton and another to convince them not to tell my dad I was en route. He means well, but that's a whole other issue I just don't have the energy or headspace to unpack right now. I guess I'm a little less forgiving of how he let my mother keep me away now that I have a child of my own.

You don't walk away. You walk through the damn fire to get to your baby.

But again, that relationship isn't something I have the energy to think about. My childhood already played a big enough role in the headspace I live in. The last thing I want is to take a step backward when I've finally found the strength to hit the incline.

Maybe if he didn't leave me after loving me, I wouldn't be so afraid of it happening to my son.

Then again, maybe not.

Maybe leaving is human nature or simply a stage of life.

Plain and simple? People leave.

They love you and they leave you, with or without their own consent.

Deaton didn't choose to leave me...but he also *did*.

He left California that day before we could talk, because he didn't want to deal with his parents' wrath had he not. I understand that. It just so happened I chose the opposite.

I ran from my mother, and I refused to go back.

He didn't, and then he died.

I don't know what that means, and maybe it means nothing at all, but it's the ugly truth behind the ache. I knew he wasn't *leaving* me, but if I said I don't sometimes blame him for everything, I'd be lying. And it took me a very long time to realize this. It's not fair, especially since I'm the reason he came to California in the first place. It's just what is.

I was just as mad as I was sad, and I hated that. Guilt was—no, guilt *is* like a second skin in my life, and I don't want to wear it anymore. I want to break free and just...be.

But breaking free means breaking open all the boxes and facing what I've fought against.

The real versus the fake.

The then versus the now.

If there's one thing I've realized in the last few weeks, it's that I'm not helping my son by holding back.

I'm hurting us both.

I'm hurting all of us, and I don't want to hurt anymore.

I thought pushing Mason away was an act of self-preservation, a way of protecting myself from further loss, but in reality, I caused more unnecessary damage. The worst part is my actions didn't only affect me but Mason as well, a fact I'll forever be forced to face.

I could have cost him his dream because I was too afraid to face the fact that he had become the man in mine.

No more hiding, Payton. No more holding back.

Taking one last steady breath, I push the door open.

I step from the car, each rise and fall of my foot heavier than the last until there are no more to take.

The first thing I see when I lift my eyes is his name, carved into the stone. The second is the small picture placed beneath it. It's our little boy, smiling wide with dimples identical to his dad's. The tears come hard and fast, and I fall to my knees, burying my face in my hands.

"I'm so sorry, Deaton," I cry. "I'm sorry you're gone and that I haven't come. I'm sorry I took off in the first place, and I'm sorry you died not knowing if our baby was going to be raised by strangers or by his mom. I'm sorry for being part of the reason you were on the road that day at all and…damn it." I swallow, taking a moment to gather myself. "I don't have anything good to say," I admit in a whisper. "All I can think about are all the things I need to apologize for. Unfortunately, the list feels never-ending, and most of it I'm not so sure you'll want to hear, but I…think I have to tell you anyway."

I look to the sky, his headstone far too agonizing to address.

"I stopped talking to you after I stopped dreaming about you. I didn't know what to say. How could I whisper words I wanted you to hear when another man's face replaced yours in my mind? But I did try to get you back, I promise. I looked at photos and read old letters and messages. I replayed so many days, and I did it for weeks, right before I went to sleep, and still…my dreams would come, and the new set of brown eyes stared back at me. I didn't know how to stop it, and I thought maybe if I quit him, he would go away and you would come back."

I press my fingers to my mouth, pinching the skin there. "But there was no quitting him, and it only got worse after that. It didn't take long for me to realize why. I…" I squeeze my eyes closed, unable to face this head-on but forcing the words from my lips. "I'd already lost you, Deaton, but I hadn't lost him yet. He was still here, and I was hanging on with all I had. That meant the place I thought I saved just for you became his, and I didn't even know it was happening until it already had. I was sick with guilt and scared to death because I knew there was *no way* I could go through that again." *Not with him.*

"So I kept reaching for you, holding on to your memory in fear not only of losing it but of losing myself if my world fell apart all over again. I hardly made it through after you died, Deaton, and even though things have changed, you have to know how much I missed you."

Gasping, I look up, pressing my palms to his name and dropping my head against it.

"I can't believe your body is under here. It's so crazy you're really gone. Like gone, gone. Forever." My shoulders shake, my sobs uncontrollable. "I don't want you to hate me. Please don't hate me. I didn't mean to fall in love with him. I didn't mean to let you go."

Curling in a ball, I lie before his headstone, one hand pressed to the day he left me and the other clutching the photo of the little guy he gave me before he went.

The tears don't stop, the guilt doesn't lessen, but the pain… it slowly fades.

We're together, even if we're worlds apart.

"Payton."

My lips twitch, his voice one of my favorite sounds to hear.

"Payton, look at me."

Slowly, my eyes open, and I smile instantly.

"Hi." He smiles back.

"Hi."

"It's been a while."

I nod, reaching out, and a sob breaks free when I can feel him. The smoothness of his cheeks, the softness of his hands when they lock around mine. "You're here."

"I'm wherever you need me to be."

"But you weren't," I argue. "Deaton, you were gone, and I needed you."

"No," he whispers softly. "You needed him."

An avalanche of emotion falls over me, burying me in grief. "I'm so sorry," I say.

Deaton smiles, that easy, gentle smile he was known for, and then he shocks me when he says, "I'm not."

"Deaton..." My heart stops, his name but a stuttered breath.

"My son, our son, deserves someone else to love him like you do, and if it can't be me, it has to be him."

"How can you be okay with that?"

"Payton," he murmurs, holding my gaze with his steady, unwavering one. "No one will love that little boy more than us, and Mason? He is part of us now."

"If that's true, that means your little boy will grow up and call someone else daddy."

"Not someone else." Deaton's thumb grazes along my cheek. "Him."

"That's not fair to you."

He takes the picture in my hand, lifting it between us. He doesn't speak until my eyes fall to meet my baby boy's. "I helped make him. He helped bring him into this world." My gaze comes back to his. "That seems pretty equal to me."

I break down again, sobbing and falling into him, wishing I could feel the warmth of his arms around me.

"Don't cry," he whispers. "I'm okay here. In your memory. Just think of me sometimes, and I'll never be gone."

"Don't go."

"It's time to wake up now. He's scared. And he needs you."

His support is unwavering, and finally, I nod.

"Goodbye, Payton…"

My eyes flick open, and I gasp, pushing my torso off the grass.

I look to the headstone, to the photo of Deaton on the grass beside me, and then something calls my eyes to the curb, just in time to see Chase's truck rolling to a stop.

I push onto my knees in confusion, but the door opens a moment later, and Mason steps out.

I collapse all over again, a complete and total wreck, but something drags me to my feet. It's strong and unfamiliar. It carries me across the grass, and it doesn't stop until I'm falling forward.

Mason catches me with open arms, twining them so tight around me, I know this is it. That there's no escaping, no running, no pushing.

The cables have connected, the metal has melted, the fractured pieces fusing together and shaping anew.

"Shh," he soothes. "It's okay, Pretty Little. You're okay. This is my fault."

I try to shake my head, but I'm pressed too tight against him.

"I didn't mean to push you or guilt you into coming here. I should have left you to come here when you were ready." He pulls me impossibly tighter. "I just keep fucking up, and I need to sit back—"

"I love you."

Mason's body turns to stone.

Ever so slowly, he lifts his head, and when our eyes lock, it's like the world tilts on its axis. The mountains shift, and the skies open up, and when the sun does quite literally break through the November clouds, as if only shining on us, the barest hint of wind pressing at my back, pushing me to him, I know it's right.

That Deaton is here with us, telling me it's okay. That this is okay.

"Baby..." His mouth moves as if to speak the words, but no actual sound comes out as he waits, as though wondering if he conjured them up in his head.

So I say them again, louder, my every focus on him and him alone.

"I love you, Mason. More than I knew I was capable of. More than I knew was possible. And more than I was ready for, but I'm...I'm ready now."

Mason shakes against me, his hands coming up and gripping my face, holding my eyes on his.

"I'm yours, Mason."

"Mine?" he dares in a broken whisper. "You're standing here, in this place of all places, and telling me that you're mine?"

I nod.

"You understand what that means, don't you?" His eyes are piercing. "If you're mine, he's mine, too."

My lips quiver, and I nod again.

"Payton." He shakes, swallowing hard as moisture builds in his brown eyes. "I need to know you understand what that means. I need to know even if you change your mind one day, and I'll do *everything* in my power to make sure you won't, but *if* you do...I need to know he'll still be mine. I can't lose him, Payton. I will not lose that little boy."

"I understand." My voice trembles with the truth. "He's just as much yours as he is mine."

Mason clenches his jaw, giving a jerky nod. "He is. He's mine, too."

I cry, wrapping my arms around his neck, and Mason buries his face in mine.

I don't know how long we stand there, but when a car door opens, we pull apart, just in time to watch as Chase lifts Deaton from his car seat.

My hand shoots to my mouth to hold the sob in, and Mason takes my other, giving me a gentle squeeze.

368

"We picked him up from Aunt Sarah on the way here," he whispers. "I hope that's okay."

I nod, gaze glued on Deaton. His tiny shoes hit the grass, and like the pro he's quickly become, he breaks into a wobbly run. Relief and resignation have my throat clogging as he marches this way, not stopping until his arms are locking around Mason's leg.

A scratchy chuckle escapes Mason, and he bends, lifting Deaton into his arms, and when Mason comes to his full height, both my boys look at me.

With a deep breath, I step closer, smiling at my son. "Hey, little man. There's someone I want you to meet."

Mason's eyes are soft as they peer down at me. "You don't have to do so much in one day, you know. We can come back another time."

"I know," I whisper. "But I want to."

The pride that stares back at me is enough to drive me forward. Together, the three of us pile around the small space dedicated to Deaton Vermont, the boy who left us too soon but blessed our lives before his was taken. We sit in silence, words not needed.

A little while later, Deaton pushes to his feet, and I watch as he walks over to the headstone, having no clue what it is. Still, when his little palm reaches out to touch it, something has him stretching out his other one until his fingers are pressed to Mason's shoulder.

With one hand on the headstone, the other on Mason, my little boy brings his eyes to mine. He smiles, that big, toothy grin I live for, and suddenly, the pressure that's lived in my chest, the guilt that held me down for the better part of a year…it disappears.

Vanishes.

All that's left is clarity.

It's like suddenly the world makes sense, like I've evolved in the span of a blink.

I know now life won't always be easy, and obstacles will always place themselves in our way, but we can work through them.

We can overcome anything if we can get past this, so long as we do it together.

When I look up, I find Mason staring, and he pulls his phone from his pocket with an uneasy expression. "Can I show you something?" he whispers.

I nod, and he pulls up an old social media profile picture of Deaton.

A frown builds along my brow, but I wait, watching as he tugs Deaton into his lap and places the phone in front of his face.

"Hey, big guy," he whispers. "Who is that?"

Deaton just slaps the screen a few times, and Mason looks up with a sheepish smile, then back down, bouncing him on his knee as he points at the screen again. "Who is that, Little D?"

Deaton smiles, and then he says, "Da, da, da, da."

My mouth falls open, a choppy laugh escaping. "Wha…" I trail off.

Deaton looks up, starting right at Mason, one finger stuck inside his mouth as he grins around it. "Da, da, da."

Mason's head snaps up in panic. "He's not calling me that. I just taught him the word and—"

"He is." I cut him off, and Mason swallows, eyes moving between mine. "He knows, Mase. He knows who you are to him."

"Baby." His jaw clenches tight.

"Deaton is his father." My eyes cloud with tears. "But you're the only dad he's ever known."

Mason reaches out, tethering our hands together. "We'll make sure he knows him, too."

I nod, because I know we will.

We'll figure out everything.

As a family.

Me, Mase, and our son.

CHAPTER 37
PAYTON

Now, November

We left the cemetery just before dark, and while Sarah had origi-nally asked if I'd come back for dinner, I had to call and let her down. The day was too heavy, and I just want to be with my boys. Chase ended up taking Sarah's offer to sleep in Nate's old room, but Mason booked us a room at the little hotel a couple of blocks away.

It's a little after nine now, and we're just stepping into the hotel room, Deaton in my arms and the playpen in Mason's.

He makes quick work of setting it up, laying the last blanket across the bottom as I approach, and I gently lay Deaton down.

He twists instantly, curling up into a little ball, and Mason eases his favorite blanket over him.

Smiling, I turn toward my bag, but Mason's palm presses to my hip.

He pushes until I'm facing him completely, and then he shuffles closer, forcing me backward, and he doesn't stop until my back hits the wall, his fingers locking tight against my skin.

My mouth opens, but he shakes his head.

"No," he whispers, his tone husky, his focus on my mouth, so I snap it closed, and his twitches in the corner. "That's right, Pretty Little," he rasps, his thumb stretching under my chin and tipping my neck up and to the side. "I'm calling all the shots tonight." He dips forward, and I shiver when he runs his nose up my neck. "I've waited so fucking long to have you in my hands." His palm slides along my ribs, past my hips until he's squeezing my ass in his strong hand. He groans, and my chest inflates with a sharp inhale. "And I'll be damned if I don't take time now that you are." His teeth meet my jaw, and I grip his shoulders. "I'm gonna fix you a bubble bath, baby." His head lifts, and he kisses me hard on the lips, hissing as he tears away, his forehead pressing to mine. "And you're not getting out until you've come at least twice."

He shoves off the wall, disappearing around the corner, and I'm left a panting, melting mess.

I drop my head against the wall, my body coming to life at his words, graphic images flashing through my mind and making me shake with anticipation.

"*Payton.*"

I jump, my smile breaking free as I follow after him, stepping around the corner and watching as he takes special care, testing the water of the giant, egg-shaped tub. It's a double spout, so it begins to fill quickly. Mason tears open a small package and dumps the contents into the steamy water. Instantly, hints of lavender fill the air, and then he squeezes some body wash in, and I watch as bubbles start to rise to the water's surface.

He steps back, looking at it for a long moment before spinning to face me. "It's not perfect, but it will do for tonight."

"It's more than enough," I whisper.

"It's not." He comes closer, his fingers grasping the hem of my sweater. "I'll be better prepared next time."

"I love that there's a next time."

"Mmm," he moans in agreement, lifting my shirt over my head in one swift move. His eyes hit mine, and he presses into me. "Tonight, I'm going to love you," he promises. "Tomorrow, I'm going to ruin you, and the day after that?" His voice drops ten octaves, and he tugs my lower lip between his teeth. "Baby,

372

the day after that…I'm going to punish you a little." He bites a bit harder, making me gasp, and then he's swooping in on my chest, licking across the sweep of my breast as he reaches behind, undoing the clasp on the first try. "How does that sound, my sweet girl?"

"Yes." It's all I can say, but he needs no other words.

Mason slides my bra down my arms, and I tremble when his fingertips purposefully apply pressure on their descent.

I start to shake, and he pulls back, his eyes finding mine before lowering to my exposed breast for the first time. He sucks a sharp breath through his teeth, and my pulse jumps as he lowers to one knee, those dark, decadent eyes on me as he brings his mouth to my nipple.

I keep my eyes on his, unable to break the spell he has me under, and when his tongue lashes along my nipple, I cry out.

His pupils blow wide, and he groans, quickly moving to the other side and pulling back, watching in satisfaction as my nipples turn to sharp beads. "So fucking perfect," he rasps, palms gliding lower.

He skims them along my soft stomach, and I wait for the self-conscious part of me to kick in, but it never comes.

My body isn't what it was before my pregnancy. It's thicker now, softer, but he doesn't seem to care. Quite the opposite in fact.

He worships my curves, kissing my flesh and biting at my skin as his fingers slip into the waistband of my leggings. His heated eyes find mine, and ever so slowly, he tugs them down, tearing them off my body until I'm standing bare before him.

Seeing him in front of me, on his knees with a fire in his eyes, is almost too much.

It's too much yet nowhere near enough, as, like him, I've waited for this, too.

Reaching out, I run my hand through his dark hair, and his eyes drift closed for a moment, his chest rumbling.

When he opens them again, he holds my gaze hostage, then snaps his down, lasering in on the most sensitive part of me.

His teeth sink into his lower lip, and his chest heaves. His right hand glides up my outer thigh, his left swiftly sliding to the inner part of my legs, and I hold my breath as his textured palms skate higher.

A shiver runs through me, and I tug his hair, making him moan, but my own follows a moment later when his pointer finger slides between my legs, right through my heat.

"Such a pretty pussy," he murmurs. "And so wet for me."

I'm a shaking mess, and slowly, his eyes lift to mine, now nearly black in color.

His fingers shift, and then he's at my entrance. He drives up, sliding inside me, and I gasp, pushing down onto his hand, begging for more. Deeper.

Mason shakes his head, a devilish smirk on his face as he slowly pulls his finger out of me.

I whine in protest, words no longer humanly possible, and he chuckles, all dark and dirty-like.

"Oh, baby girl. Did you think it would be that easy?" he whispers, raising to his feet and taking my breasts in his hands, kneading them gently as he flicks his tongue along my lips. "I said you would come at least twice, but you'll come when I let you."

"Jesus." I squeeze my eyes closed.

His mouth.

What an epic fucking surprise.

"Get in the bath now, baby."

My eyes open, and I watch as he strips to his briefs, shaking in anticipation of what's underneath, but he just climbs over the tub, lowering into the water, a clear sign he meant what he said. This is all about me, and he's making sure of it…even if I wish he wouldn't.

My disappointment must show, because Mason lies back in the steamy water, his hands running seductively down his chest until he's gripping himself over his briefs. "Come here, Payton. You know the deal."

A quake shakes my spine, and I nod. "Twice and then…"

"And then," he rumbles, closing his eyes a moment as he strokes himself. "Hurry, baby. I'm so fucking hard for you."

I step up to the tub, and Mason raises his free arm, so I slip my hand into his, easing into the water. He spins me, lowering me so my head can lie on his chest.

He grinds up into me, and I moan, pressing back. "Feel that, Pretty Little? Feel how hard my cock is?"

"Yes."

"It's all for you."

"Yes."

His fingers glide along my arms, lifting and wrapping them around his neck from behind. His teeth sink into my forearm, and then his hands are sliding down my stomach. "I'm going to fuck you with my fingers, Pretty Little. First one, then another, and if you're good, I'll stretch you with a third."

My toes curl, and I clamp my teeth closed, heated desperation filling my every pore. "Mase. Please."

"Please what?"

"Please."

"Say it. Tell me what you want me to do to you. Tell me what you need."

"I…" My chest flames. "I want to come."

He growls in my ear, and then his finger is pushing into me, his other hand tugging at my nipple.

My hips buck instantly, my body eager for anything he'll give it.

A second fingers pushes in, and I cry out, shaking when he takes my hands and places them over my own breasts.

"Play, baby," he murmurs, and then his other hand joins the first between my legs.

His fingers pump rhythmically slow and perfectly in sync with the way he rubs my clit. Before I know what I'm doing, my palms are squeezing my own breasts.

I squeeze hard, and then my knuckles glide along my nipples. I moan, so I try something else, twisting them, gently at first, but when the sensation mixed with Mason's work between my legs sends sparks of heat down my spine, I do it harder, tugging, and my body quakes.

"Did my girl find something new she likes?" He kisses my neck.

"Y-yes."

"Do you want to come now?"

"Please."

"Okay, baby." He shifts. Another finger presses into me, and at the same time, he pinches my clit, hard, and heat erupts, bursting and spilling through me.

"Mason," I moan, my body thrashing in the water.

His name from my lips has him groaning into my ear. He bites down, and a second wave crashes through me.

He lets me ride it out, his breathing heavy in my ear, a tempting, torturous sound I want more of. It's raspy and thick, heady. He's sure to leave his lips right there, pressing against my pulse, and when he sucks, I squirm some more.

He's so hard beneath me, and if I move just right...

Mason's arm locks around my stomach, holding me still. "I don't think so, baby. I told you. I'm in charge right now, and right now I say it's all about you."

"But it would be for me."

"No."

"I want you, Mase," I beg.

He hums in satisfaction, sitting up higher in the water and taking me with him. He curls over me, shifting and taking my shin in his hands. His lips take mine in a slow, methodical movement that has my every muscle going limp in his arms. It's like a slow dance of tongues, and I reach for more when he gently tugs away.

"You'll have me, but I need this first. Can you give me what I need, baby?"

God, his voice drips with sex, and my thighs are clenching all over again.

His deep chuckle tells me he knows, and then he's squirting soap into his hands, gently messaging my shoulders, his rough fingers drawing across my collarbone and down to my breasts. He teases my nipples, softly and then roughly, before abandoning them altogether.

Mason washes every part of me he can reach, kneading my scalp and rinsing us with a new wave of steaming water.

I'm a moaning mess at his mercy, and he seems to be living for every second of it, relishing the fact that he's making me feel so good. "You're really good at this."

"This is just the pregame warm-up."

A low laugh leaves me, his cocky response just as hot as his dirty whispers. "So are we warming up for the kickoff?"

"Nah." He shifts, crawling out from behind me so his big body is now hovering *over* me. "We're headed for the Super Bowl, baby, and watch me bring it home."

He slides backward, his biceps bulging as he grips the edge of the tub near my head, his gaze dropping to my chest.

I lift it higher for him, my eyes locked on his as he skates his lips across my wet flesh. His teeth come out to play again, scraping along my nipples, and he smirks up at me as they stand to attention, begging for more.

"You're blushing, baby," he rasps, one hand leaving the tub to grip my hip with a tender squeeze.

"You love that, don't you?"

"You bet your ass I do." He kisses my stomach. "I wonder how many shades of pink I can get your skin to turn." Mason lifts my lower half from the water, sitting back on his knees, and if I was blushing before, I'm a tomato now.

A shivering freaking tomato.

I'm exposed like never before, and while it's a little unnerving, it's exciting in a whole new way.

His hand travels to the apex of my thighs, but a slight pinch forms at the edges of his gaze, his awareness and connection to my mind unmatched, only confirmed when he whispers, "May I?"

I don't have to ask what he means, so I give him something better than a yes, something I know he'll love. I soak in some of the bravery his presence provides and stretch back a little more, tipping my hips a little higher. "You'd be the first."

Before my eyes, his entire demeanor shifts.

His gaze grows tender, the weight of his hand featherlight. His thighs shake beneath my ass, and when his shoulders lower an inch, I smile up at him.

"First," he breathes, his gaze moving over my face before falling between my legs. His thumb comes up, sliding along my clit, and I buck into it. Slowly, his lips curve, and the light of a moment ago is smothered. "I get one of your firsts."

"You have a lot of my firsts, and you don't even know it."

Mason groans, his torso bending as he lowers himself into position. "We are making a list later, but right now...I'm going to taste you, and you're going to come in my mouth."

He gives no other warning than that, swooping down and swiping his tongue between my folds, up and over my clit, and then he takes it into his mouth.

My entire body comes alive as he sucks my clit between his lips, his tongue doing wild things on the inside, and my thighs are vibrating. A ball of heat forms in my belly. It's so hot even my eyes burn, and it only grows, and with each spiral, it winds my nerves tighter.

Mason slides a finger inside, curling up into me, and then his teeth are teasing my clit. He bites, and I gasp. He licks, and I shake.

And when he closes his mouth over me again, I shatter.

My cries are loud and wanton, my body trembling, exploding,

and it doesn't stop. He keeps sucking, and I keep writhing, and before I know it, my thighs are clamped around his head, squeezing, my fingers tearing at his hair, and he growls against me, begging for more.

It goes on forever, and only when I'm nothing but a bag of bones, unable to keep my head above water, does Mason release me.

A satisfied smirk tilts his glossy lips, and he climbs from the tub, lifting me into his arms.

He towels me off, brushes my hair, and then he tucks me into the hotel bed, climbing in beside me. "Sleep, baby. I can promise you, you're going to need it."

I'm out within seconds.

MASON

I sigh, leaning on my elbow and smiling at my two favorite people, sitting on the edge of the creek that runs through the back of my aunt and uncle's property. It's too cold to get in this time of year, but that doesn't stop Deaton from doing his damnedest to try.

We've been in Alrick for two days now, and Payton was finally ready to step out of the room, not that I was complaining about being locked away with her. There's nothing I want more than uninterrupted time with her and Deaton. God knows I've missed too much already, but there's something about watching them with my family that's just as pleasing.

"That's got to be a record."

I look over to find Chase smirking from where he's lying beside me. "What?"

"You've sighed, like, ten times in the last ten minutes."

Chuckling, I push up onto my ass, hanging my elbows over

my knees. "Guess I'm feeling pretty sappy." I swallow, admitting, "I was starting to worry I'd never get here."

"You worried for nothing, my man," he says softly. "There was no way she could walk away, even if she wanted to. It's so obvious, I don't know how the others didn't pick up on it a long time ago."

My lips twitch with a smile, and I look back toward the water, to my little family, but Chase's words repeat in my mind, and I look his way. "When did you know?"

"When I showed up at her place that night and you were already there." He looks away. "I had no idea why she was so upset. I assumed she was having a bad day and needed someone, and I could relate, so I ran home after practice, got some things together, and headed out. When I first saw you, I thought she asked you to come, too, and you just beat me there. I was like, okay, cool, and I didn't feel so bad about it taking me so long to get there, and then you took off." He shakes his head, sitting up and mimicking my position. "I was confused as hell, but she was crying, so I left it alone. Later, I learned she didn't call you at all, and that was right about when she told me it was the one-year mark since Deaton passed. The second she said it, I was like, fuck. I wanted to be there for her, but after all we went through last year, man…" Chase sighs, looking me dead in the eye. "I love you. You're my brother, and I just couldn't, so I took off. It wasn't until I was halfway home that I realized I was making another fucking mistake. I knew you better than that. And pissed off at my presence, angry that she called me, and confused about why, none of that mattered—you'd have still wanted me to stay so she wasn't alone." He looks away. "I swear, it seems to be one fuckup after another for me nowadays. Starting to think that's all I am."

"You're not, man, and you figured it out." He meets my eyes again, guilt in his own. "You were there for her when she wouldn't let me be, and even though I was a dick about it—"

"Even though you reminded me what your right hook felt like." He forces a smirk.

A chuckle leaves me, and I nod. "Even with that, you had her back." Gratitude overwhelms me, a knot forming in my throat, and I look away. "That right there, that's why you're my brother."

His hand lands on my shoulder, squeezing, and I blow out a long exhale.

"I can't believe I almost fucked up my eligibility and put my scholarship a risk. I'd never forgive myself if I let you guys down like that." I swallow. "Or her. Them."

Chase nods, not making excuses but saying, "Yeah, well, at least you got your head out of your ass before it was too late."

I chuckle, and this time when his hand reaches out, he gives a little shove, and my ass flops over. Spinning, I come at him, and we wrestle around the way we have for years, but I've got one up on him now.

"Someone's got some new moves," he notices with a laugh, flipping me and coming down, but I hook him under his knee and around the neck.

"This is a cradle, my boy. Big D's signature move."

He laughs, tapping out, and as we flop onto our backs, a blond sheet of curls falls over my face, and a perfect little man throws himself down on my chest.

I grunt, laughing as I lift him into the air. Bringing him down, I kiss his cheek and look up at my girl. "Time to go home?"

She smiles softly at the two of us, and I don't miss the little blush crawling past the neckline of her sweater. "Yeah, time to go home."

We say goodbye to my aunt and uncle, climb in the vehicle, and then we're off.

CHAPTER 38
PAYTON

As we take the exit toward campus, Mason lifts my hand for what must be the fiftieth time in the last few hours, pressing his lips to my knuckles. I roll my head along the seat, staring at him as I've done most of the trip, and he chuckles, meeting my eyes for a moment before facing forward again.

We drove all day, and I'm exhausted, but I don't dare fall asleep. I don't want to waste a minute of my time with him. It's clear he feels the same, and while he couldn't sleep if he wanted as the driver, he makes sure to touch me every few minutes with both his eyes and his hands.

Thankfully, when I had my moment a few days ago, I didn't call my job, so my room is still mine to come back to at the staff building at Avix U.

My lips tip up as I run my fingers over the small lotus flower Mason gave me, remembering what he said but also what I read when I looked it up for myself the night he left. Mason and I, we are resilient and strong, and we did grow from a place of darkness, finding our own light. I like to think maybe Deaton had a part in this, that maybe his death wasn't in vain but a blessing, offering the promise of new beginnings, just like he did in my dream.

I close my eyes for a moment, then roll my head along the seat to look at the man beside me. "Hey, Mase."

"Yeah, baby?" he asks, his voice thick with exhaustion as he pulls into the parking lot of my building.

He looks over a few times, but I wait until the car is still, the engine shut off.

"I have something to tell you."

He leans forward, taking my chin in his hands and sliding his lips across mine in a perfect tease. "And I want to hear it, but it's late. Let's go inside and get our little man in a real bed."

"'K." I give in instantly, and I don't realize my eyes have closed until I hear his door open.

He takes Deaton from his seat, and we leave everything but the diaper bag in the car.

Inside, Mason gently lays him down on the bed, and Deaton hardly stirs as Mason changes him, leaving him in nothing but a diaper and socks.

I drop onto the mattress, watching as Mason strips his shirt over his head, followed by his jeans. Silently, he climbs into bed, and my heart melts when he reaches down, lifting Deaton and placing him in the center.

He closes his eyes, his arm gently tucking Deaton into his chest.

Moisture pricks my eyes, and I kick my shoes off, climbing in beside them.

Mason's eyes pop open for a split second, but they close just as quickly.

I'm not sure I've ever wished I had my camera on me more than I do in this moment.

Mason falls asleep fast, a ghost of a smile on his lips, and I'm not far behind.

Warm palms travel up my sides, curving along my shoulders and gliding back down my arms until long, thick fingers are curling into mine. My smile is slow, eyes peeling open to find his hovering an inch above my own, a wolfish gleam within them as my arms are lifted and pinned above my head, pressed firmly into the plush pillow beneath me.

"Deaton's in his bed now, baby," he rasps, his voice thick with sleep and dirty promises. "Remember what I said to you?"

"Say it again," I whisper, sighing when his deep chuckle washes over my skin.

He shakes his head, dipping and kissing across my collarbone. "That's not how this part works. Here, you do what I say, and I reward you for it."

"That sounds like a really good plan."

I feel his smile, and my own threatens to break free, but then he sucks, hard, on my neck, and I'm moaning beneath him.

"Open your legs, baby. Open your legs and let me in."

My knees fall to the side with zero protest, and he doesn't hesitate, settling between them.

I gasp, locking my legs against his naked hips, feeling his heated flesh against my skin for the first time. I don't remember him taking his boxers off, but he must have, and thank fuck for that.

He's bare and bulging, pressing right where I want him—no, where I *need* him.

"I'm ready for you, Pretty Little. Sheathed and fucking aching." He tugs my tank down so my breasts are spilling out, bends to suck my nipple into his mouth, releasing with a resounding pop. "Is my girl ready for me, too?"

I squirm, shifting my hips, and the tip presses inside.

Mason groans, lowering his bottom half and pressing me into the mattress. I wish he'd crush me with it. "Behave, baby. You'll have me when I say you can and not a second sooner."

He kisses me then, claiming my mouth with a raw intensity I've never felt, and a low whine leaves me.

"So damn responsive. So greedy for my cock."

I moan in response, chasing his kiss and reveling in the way he makes me feel alive. My body has never known such need.

Mason's hand dives between my legs, fingers finding their way inside me without pause, and my eyes roll back. "Yeah," he breathes. "You're ready for me. So fucking ready."

Ripples of anticipation rage through me, and my head presses into the pillow, my eyes locking on his.

"You have no idea how many times I've been right here in my dreams." He hooks my left leg, drawing it higher. "In my mind, I've licked you everywhere," he whispers, rubbing along my clit and making me squirm. "Had you everywhere, on every surface in every room." He reaches between us, lining himself up at my entrance, his eyes finding mine.

"Mase…"

"I've come on your every curve, and still, every single time, you beg for more." A ghost of pressure is all he gives me, and I'm whining now. "You gonna beg for more, baby?"

His hips slide forward, the head of his dick pressing inside me. My lips part on a gasp, and his eyes flare, roaming across my features so as not to miss a thing. He gives me another inch, and I whimper, my nails digging into his arms.

"Yeah, my greedy girl will beg, won't she?"

I nod feverishly, grasping at his shoulders and locking my ankles behind his back.

I've never been so hot, so full, and he's not even halfway in. I squeeze my eyes closed. "Please, Mase." My walls are stretched around him so deliciously, I'm driven to taste him, my tongue sneaking out and licking across his lips. "Please."

Mason bites on it, and pleasure explodes in my belly, my core already pulsing, clenching and unclenching around him, and finally, he shoves inside.

His eyes snap shut, a pained expression covering his face, and he moans, long and loud, inspiring my own. "Baby *girl*." He groans, slowly sliding in and out, sending waves of delirium through me. "I want to memorize your every moan, learn all the little things you like, and discover new ones."

"I want that."

"I know you do." He thrusts in harder, deeper, and my body jolts beneath him. "You want me to fuck you every way there is to fuck, and then you want to invent new ones. Ain't that right?"

"God, yes."

"Mmm." He sits back on his knees, my ass in his hands as he shoves in and out, in and out. His eyes are locked on my face, my breasts bouncing between us as he stares down at me with pure hunger. His hands are everywhere, touching me with such an enticing possessiveness, it makes me want to claim him right back. I want to own him. Ruin him.

"Harder, Mase."

He growls, slides his arms around my back with such gentle care, but when he hauls me to him, my chest slapping against his naked one, it's so rough, almost violently delicious, that my climax is already cresting. I cry out, clenching around him, but he fixes me with a glare, clamping onto my hips and forcing me to still.

"Don't you dare," he whispers his warning. "We come together."

"But—"

"No buts." He sweeps his legs out, and our pelvises meet, shoving him so impossibly deep my head falls back, my body quaking.

With a gentle yet firm grip, he tangles his hand in my hair, lifting my gaze to his.

His mouth comes down on mine with a crushing kiss, his hips thrusting up as I grind down, and a thunderstorm of ecstasy cracks through me.

His kiss is raw and urgent. It's drugging and demanding and soul-shattering.

"I'm going to come now, baby," he rasps, sucking my tongue into his mouth.

He thrusts once, twice, and my hips work over him frantically, my arms locked around his neck, his around my back.

And when he jerks inside me, I cry out into his neck, sucking on the salty skin there and melting at the shiver that runs through him.

We hold on to each other tightly, hips rolling in slow motion, until the feeling is gone completely, and only then does he collapse backward, taking me with him.

He grins, panting with his eyes closed, and I do the same.

A few minutes go by, and he starts laughing, pushing my sweaty hair from my head, so I lift it and look up at him, a sated smile on my face.

"You look good and fucked," he rasps.

"I am."

"Perfect."

I squeal when suddenly, he has me flipped on my back and he's climbing on top of me again.

He hits me with his big megawatt Mason smile and says, "Time for round two."

We make it all the way to round four before I jump and run from the bed, stumbling my way into the shower on wobbly legs with a delicious soreness that's sure to last for days.

Mason hops in with me but keeps his hands to himself, a sated expression written across his face. I climb out first, throwing our dirty blankets off the bed and piling on some new ones. I've just lain back down, the morning light shining through the room, when Mason comes back in, Deaton smiling in his arms.

"There's your mama." He kisses his cheek, the both of them climbing into bed. Mason smiles as Deaton curls up in my arms, playing with my hair. "I could get used to this," he says softly, reaching over and running his hand over Deaton's tangly curls.

"Waking me between my legs?"

Mason smirks, but there's no mistaking the tenderness of his gaze. "That, too, of course, but not what I meant, Pretty Little. You know that, though."

"I do," I whisper. "And you *should* get used to it."

Confusion draws a line between his brows, and he opens his legs for Deaton to climb between.

"The university is expanding the *Avix Inquirer*. They negotiated a two-year contract with Embers Elite for a full-time, paid position." My heart beats wildly as I gaze into his eyes. "They offered it to me."

Mason stares, his brown eyes boring into mine as he wraps his left arm around Deaton, keeping him close to his chest. "What are you saying to me right now?"

"I'm saying I'm staying instead of preparing to say goodbye. Get used to saying good morning, because we'll be here as long as you are."

Mason swallows, reaching with his free hand and taking mine.

"And after that?" he whispers.

"Where you are is where we want to be." I give his line back to him with a smile.

A harsh exhale pushes past his lips as he slides them along my knuckles.

"No matter what?" His hold on Deaton's back tightens as he tugs me closer, wrapping us in his warm embrace. "Promise me, baby."

Reaching up, my palm covers his on Deaton's back, the other sliding along his jaw and drawing his face to mine. "Tell him, baby boy." I peek at Deaton with a smile. "No matter what. No matter where. With your daddy is where we want to be." I meet Mason's eyes, moisture building in his dark lashes and matching my own. "We promise. *I* promise. I love you, Mason, and I'm never going to run from that again."

"Sorry to break it to you, baby, but I wouldn't let you if you tried."

"Promise?"

Mason chuckles, but there's a slight sniffle in there, too, he tries to hide, and when he presses his mouth to mine, it's with more than just a promise.

It's a life debt, a blood pact. It's a pledge of allegiance from him to me.

From him to *us*, the fractured family he made whole when he didn't have to.

He chose to.

And me?

I choose him.

Forever. Always.

No matter what.

READ ON FOR A SNEAK PEEK AT THE NEXT BOOK IN THE BOYS OF AVIX SERIES

"Have you seen Cameron?" I hear him before I see him and clench my eyes closed.

Damn it. I don't want to deal with him right now.

Leaning over the sink, I peek out the small window facing the front yard, and sure enough, there he is, Alister freaking Howl, the latest male on my shit list, with Ari and Paige standing in front of him.

I grin when my girls cross their arms. Ari's looking away, ignoring him completely, while Paige is too damn poised to be that direct about it. But she does bring a smile to my face when she hits his ass with the best glare she can muster.

"Honestly? Needs work, girl," I muse, hopping up a bit to put a knee on the countertop, where I can damn near press my ear to the glass to eavesdrop.

"I haven't." Paige smiles then, and it's too wide—and purposefully so—as she flutters her lashes his way, going the only route she knows when it comes to confrontation: being sweet as fucking pie. "But if I do, I'll let her know you're looking for her."

Yeah, she will.

She will so I can hide from his ass like I've been hiding for the last few weeks.

Cameron and controversy? We don't mix.

We pivot.

"Give it a rest already, Alister the Asshole," I mutter, eyes accidentally taking him in from head to toe, drawing a pout to my face. "But why do you have to be so hot?"

"I was born that way."

I squeal, lose my balance, and my ass falls right into the sink. One cheek gets stabbed by the stem of a spatula, sending me jumping forward.

Brady Lancaster catches me on the edge of the sink, his head falling back with laughter. When he faces forward again, his glossy eyes meet mine. "Cammie, baby."

"Big guy." I raise a brow. "Having fun?"

"Am now."

I scoff, then remember what I was doing and swiftly spin my torso, only to find the driveway now empty. I press my lips together, unsure if I'm happy or annoyed.

"Let me guess." He cuts a quick glance outside and back. "That little fucker showed up uninvited again?"

"I mean, he is on the football team, and this is technically a barbecue for the football players, but yes. Yes, he did." I sigh, letting my body fall against his big-ass one, and stick my lip out. "I can't shake him, Brady. I've tried, and he just…won't let me."

Brady's eyes search mine with a question I can't read, and I'm not sure it's the one he asks. "Do you really want him to? Let you shake him, I mean."

"Yes." My answer is fast. Maybe too fast, and when that brow of his lifts, I groan, covering my face and burying it in his chest. "No. I mean, I don't know," I mumble against him.

God, I'm so pathetic. Alister literally used me, and he only stopped because he got caught. He knew my best friend was his new team captain's twin, and he used that to his advantage. Used *me*.

Opening my eyes, I meet Brady's. "Am I having one of those dumb girl moments?"

"No. He's just a dipshit." Brady's eyes snap over my head, narrowing, and his lips flatten. "But you need to decide what you want to do, because he's about to walk through the door in five, four—what do you want?"

Panic curls in my belly and I tense up. "I don't know."

Brady's eyes go to the opening door, then back to mine. "Okay, then what do you need?"

"Time." I swallow.

"Time." He sets his can down on the counter, standing to his full, massive height.

"Time to figure it all out, I guess."

Brady nods, slow and several times, his eyes never leaving mine. "I can help you out with that."

The door closes, and in my periphery, I see a streak of color headed right this way.

"How?" I rush, my heart rate spiking.

Brady pushes closer—not that there was much room to go. I'm literally sitting at the edge of the counter, his body still positioned between my legs from when he caught me. Still, he manages it, and when his knuckle presses against my throat, dragging upward until he's hooked me by the chin, my head tips, my long hair tickling my lower back.

Suddenly, his eyes fall, and if I didn't know any better, I'd say they landed on my mouth.

"Brady?" We're running out of time.

He swallows, and a small frown builds across my brow.

"Trust me?" he whispers.

"Always."

I get no warning. No explanation. No period to process.

The unthinkable, the utterly unexpected happens, and it happens fast.

Heavy, demanding lips drop to mine, and they don't waste a second, coaxing them open with a swift flick of the tongue.

And what a hussy my mouth is, opening wide without a word's protest. Suddenly, my hands are around a thick, strong neck, and palms so massive they reach from belt to bra lock around me.

393

Our tongues tangle, my fingers jealous of the action and seeking the tips of his hair to do the same thing, but I never make it past his nape.

He's shoved from the side, but he's massive and pure muscle. He doesn't budge an inch.

He simply lifts his head and my eyes lock on his face, shock setting in at the sight of his swollen lips when he says, "Do you mind?"

Oh my God, those are Brady's lips. Those are Brady's lips because this is Brady before me, and they're swollen from my kiss.

Our kiss.

"What the hell is going on?" This comes from Alister, and the question might be for me, but I've got no words. Only thoughts.

Holy shit is the loudest one.

"What's going on is you interrupted us." Brady glares, his hands still sealed to my sides. "Now if you don't mind" —*good God almighty, I kissed Brady Lancaster*—"I'd like to get back to kissing my girlfriend."

I can't believe that just—

Wait.

What?

Surprise! Cameron's story is next...but who does she fall for in the end? I can't wait for you to find out!

ABOUT THE AUTHOR

Meagan Brandy is a *USA Today* and *Wall Street Journal* bestselling author of new adult and sports romance books. Born and raised in California, she is a married mother of three crazy boys who keep her bouncing from one sports field to another, depending on the season, and she wouldn't have it any other way. Coffee is her best friend, and words are her sanity.

Website: meaganbrandy.com
Facebook: meaganbrandyauthor
Facebook group: facebook.com/groups/130865934291300/
Instagram: @meaganbrandyauthor
TikTok: @meaganbrandyauthor
Merch: teepublic.com/user/meaganbrandy